It was like one of those ridiculous legends.

She had died in exactly the same way as her predecessor, Dermot's first wife. It was too neat. There was a touch of unreality about it.

He said that Dorabella had gone for a swim. She had evidently made a habit of taking a swim in the early morning. The time of year was hardly the best, but she had said she found the coldness invigorating.

It could not be true. She had never been enthusiastic about swimming. She had swum at school with the rest of us, but no physical exercise had ever greatly appealed to her.

There was something wrong somewhere. . . .

THE
GOSSAMER
CORD

Philippa Carr

FAWCETT GOLD MEDAL • NEW YORK

A Fawcett Gold Medal Book
Published by Ballantine Books
Copyright © 1992 by Philippa Carr

All rights reserved under International and Pan-American Copyright Conventions. Published in the United States by Ballantine Books, a division of Random House, Inc., New York.

Library of Congress Catalog Card Number: 91-33438

ISBN 0-449-14875-0

This edition published by arrangement with G. P. Putnam's Sons

Manufactured in the United States of America

First Ballantine Books Edition: May 1995

10 9 8 7 6 5 4 3 2 1

Contents

Incident in the Forest

⚛️

When I look back I can see that it all began one morning at breakfast in our home at Caddington Hall when my mother said casually, looking up from the letter which she was reading: "Edward has asked that German boy to stay with them for a holiday in England."

"I expect he will bring him over to see us," replied my father.

I was always interested in what Edward was doing. I thought he was such a romantic person because of his origins. My mother had been at school in Belgium when the war broke out, and she had had to leave that country in a hurry because of the advancing German armies. Edward's parents had been killed by a bomb when it fell on their house which was close by the school, and the dying mother had extracted a promise from my mother that she would take the child with her to England; and this had been done.

Edward was always full of gratitude to my mother—understandably so, for what could he have hoped for from an invading army or fleeing refugees with themselves to care for and who might not have had much time to spare for a helpless baby.

He lived usually with my maternal grandparents at Marchlands, their estate in Essex, or in the London family home in Westminster. My grandfather had been a Member of Parliament—a tradition in the Greenham family—and now my uncle Charles had taken over the seat.

Edward was about twenty-two years of age at this time; he was going to be a lawyer, and he was, of course, just like any other member of the family.

1

My young brother, Robert, was saying that he expected Edward would pay a return visit to his friend in Germany.

"I wish I could go," he said. "It must be wonderful. They have Beer Gardens and they are always fighting duels. They don't think much of men until they have a scar received in a duel, and it has to be on the face so that everyone can see it."

My mother smiled at him indulgently. "I can't believe that is so, darling," she said.

"I know it is because I heard it somewhere."

"You shouldn't believe all you hear," said my sister Dorabella.

Robert grimaced and retorted: "And you ... you're such a know-all."

"Now," put in my mother, "don't let's quarrel about it. I hope we shall see Edward and this ... er ..." She looked at the letter. "... Kurt," she went on. "Kurt Brandt."

"It sounds rather German," commented Robert.

"What a surprise!" mocked Dorabella.

It was the summer holidays and a typical morning and the family was all together for breakfast.

I can picture that morning clearly now that I know how important it was.

My father, Sir Robert Denver, sat at the head of the table. He was a wonderful man and I loved him dearly. He was different from any man I had ever known. There was not a trace of arrogance about him. On the other hand, he was rather self-effacing. My mother used to chide him about it; but she loved him for it all the same. He was gentle, kind, and I think, best of all, utterly to be relied on.

He had inherited the title on the death of his father not long before. My grandfather and he had been very much alike— entirely lovable—and it had been a great blow to us all when my grandfather died.

My grandmother Belinda lived with us. We always called her Grandmother Belinda to distinguish her from Grandmother Lucie. She did not come to breakfast, but took hers in her room. She was quite different from my grandfather and father. Autocratic in the extreme, she demanded attention and took a mild yet cynical interest in family affairs, while being completely absorbed in herself; but at the same time she managed to be very fascinating. She was beautiful, still with magnificent black hair which had miraculously—or perhaps cleverly—not lost its color, and deep blue eyes which invariably seemed amused and a trifle mischievous. Dorabella and my brother were a little in awe of her; and I know I was.

So on this occasion there were only Dorabella, my brother, myself, and our parents.

Dorabella and I were twins and between us there was that special bond which is often there with such people. We were not identical, although there was a close physical resemblance. The differences had been brought about by our characters, because my mother said that when we were babies, it was difficult to tell us apart. But now that we were sixteen—or should be in October—the resemblance had faded.

Dorabella was more frivolous than I; she was impulsive, whereas I was inclined to pause for thought before I took action. She had an air of fragility, whereas I was sturdy; there was a certain helplessness about her which seemed to be attractive to the opposite sex. Men were always at her side, wanting to carry something for her or look after her in some way, whereas I was left to care for myself.

Dorabella relied on me. When we were very young and first went to school, she would be disturbed if we did not sit together. She liked to sidle up to me lovingly while she copied my sums. And later, when we went away to school, we were closer than ever. There was no doubt that there was a deep affinity between us.

Immediately after the war had ended, my father had come back from France; that was in 1918. He and my mother were married and in the October of the following year Dorabella and I were born.

At the time my mother had been fascinated by the opera. It must have been exciting when they came to London after four years of restrictions and privations and constant fear for their loved ones, and used my grandparents' house in Westminster as their home. During that time they wanted to relish all that they had missed. My mother had always loved the opera; it became a passion of hers during this time, and she had the romantic notion of naming us after characters in two of their favorites. So I became Violetta from *La Traviata* and my sister, Dorabella from *Così fan tutte*.

My grandmother had once laughingly said that she would have protested at Turandot.

Our brother, who was born about three years after us, had to be Robert, because there was always a Robert in the family, which did make it a little difficult at times to know which one was being referred to. But tradition had to be obeyed.

True to our expectations, Edward came to visit us, bringing Kurt Brandt with him.

It was a lovely summer's day in mid-August when they arrived. We were all waiting for him and when we heard the car come into the courtyard my mother, with Dorabella, Robert, and myself, ran down to greet him.

Edward leaped out of the car and I saw his eyes go to my mother. They embraced. I guessed that when he met her after an absence he thought of how she had brought him out of danger when he was a helpless baby. It had made a special bond between them, and I believe my mother thought of him as one of her children.

A young man of about Edward's age got out of the car and came toward us.

"This is Kurt . . . Kurt Brandt," said Edward. "I have told him about you all."

He looked slight beside Edward and very dark because Edward was so tall and fair. He stood very straight before my mother, clicked his heels, took her hand, and kissed it. Then he turned to Dorabella and me and did the same. He shook Robert's hand, which rather disappointed my brother who would have liked the clicking of heels, if not the hand kissing.

My mother said how delighted she was to see Edward and his friend and she led them into the house, for which Kurt Brandt expressed his admiration in good but accented English. The house was very ancient and dated back to the fifteenth century, and people were often impressed by it when they first saw it—so there was nothing unusual about that.

My father joined us for luncheon. Usually he was busy on the estate, but this was a special occasion and my mother had asked him to make an effort to be there.

Kurt Brandt told us that his home was in Bavaria. There was an old schloss which had been in the family for years.

"Not so big . . . not so grand as this house," he said modestly. "Schloss sounds grand, but there are many such in Germany. Castles ... but very small. Ours is an inn now—and has been for some years. Then there were bad times ... the war ... and after ... it was not easy ..."

I thought of my father, who had been decorated for bravery during that war, and remembered that he would have been fighting against Kurt's father. But it was all over now.

"Tell us about the forest," said my mother.

How glowingly he spoke of his homeland! I could see how much he loved it. We listened entranced and, seen through his eyes, the forest seemed an enchanted place. He told us how, during the autumn, the mists arose suddenly—bluish mists which shrouded the pine trees suddenly without warning so that even those who were familiar with the place could lose their way. About the necks of the cows which belonged to the few farms scattered on the wooded slopes were bells which tinkled as the cows moved, and so the sound gave their owners an idea of where they were.

He was a fascinating talker, and Edward sat back smiling because his guest was a success. It was an excellent beginning, not that the rest was disappointing.

Edward was eager to show him something of our country and, as one of his passions at the moment was his new motorcar, he insisted on driving us somewhere each day.

We went to Portsmouth so that Kurt might see Admiral Nelson's battleship; we explored far beyond our neighborhood; then Kurt must see the New Forest, where William the Conqueror had hunted; and after that to Stonehenge, which was of an even earlier period.

We would return each day and chatter over dinner of what we had seen.

During that time we had come to know Kurt very well. We used to sit for a long time over dinner because the talk was too interesting to be cut short. If the weather was hot, we ate out of doors. We had a courtyard shut in by red brick walls with creeper climbing over them and a pear tree in one corner. It was an ideal place for an alfresco meal.

I think Kurt enjoyed that visit as much as we did. He told us a great deal about the difficulties of life in his country after the war. There had been great struggles. The inn had had to be closed for a time and it was not very long since it had been reopened.

"Visitors come now," he said. "They did not come during the bad years immediately after the war."

"It is the people who have no say in making wars who suffer most from the consequences of them," commented my father.

We were solemn for a while and then were laughing again.

We made Kurt tell us more about the forest, his home, and his family.

He had a brother Helmut and a sister Gretchen. They helped his parents manage the inn.

"Helmut will have the inn in due course," he added. "For he is my elder brother."

"And you will be with him?" asked my mother.

"I think perhaps it may be necessary."

No more was said on the subject. My mother probably thought it would be prying to ask too many questions.

It was the last night. Dorabella, Robert, and I would be going back to school in two days' time. Dorabella and I were in our last year.

We were in the garden and there was that air of sadness among us as there can be when something which has been enjoyable is coming to an end.

"Alas," Kurt said at length. "Tomorrow I must say goodbye. It has been delightful. Sir Robert and Lady Denver, how can I thank you?"

"Please don't," said my mother. "It has been an enormous pleasure for us to have you here. I should thank Edward for bringing you."

"And you will come to the Böhmerwald one day?"

"Oh, yes please," cried Dorabella.

"I'll come," said Robert. "The trouble is there is this beastly school."

"There will be holidays," Edward reminded him.

"I wish you could come back with me," said Kurt. "This is the best time of the year."

"I'd like to see that blue mist," said Dorabella.

"And the cows with bells," added Robert.

"It would be wonderful," I added.

"Next year ... you must come ... all of you."

"We shall look forward to it all through the year, shan't we, Violetta?" said Dorabella.

Kurt looked at me and said: "She speaks for you both?"

"She usually does," I said. "And on this occasion ... certainly."

"Then it shall be," said Kurt. He lifted his glass. "To next year in the Böhmerwald."

It was an exciting year for Dorabella and me because it was our last at boarding school. We should be seventeen in the coming October and that was certainly something to set us thinking, so that we forgot about our proposed visit to Germany until at mid-term. Edward was at Caddington and one of the first things he said was that Kurt hadn't forgotten that we had promised to visit him in the summer. Then, of course, we remembered and it seemed an excellent idea.

We said goodbye to our friends at school, and looked round the tennis courts and the assembly hall for the last time without too many regrets; after all, we had become adults and ahead of us was the prospect of going to Germany.

Robert had been invited to spend the holidays with a friend in Devon, so that disposed of him. This was a relief to my mother who had felt that it would be quite enough for Edward to look after us without having to watch over a high-spirited boy.

My parents drove us down to the coast, and in due course we embarked on the Channel steamer and arrived at the port of Ostend. Dorabella and I were in a state of excitement during the long train journey through Belgium and Germany. Edward, who had done it before, pointed out places of interest as we passed along. We wanted to miss nothing. It grew dark and we slept then, but fitfully, waking now and then to be aware of the movement of the train.

When we finally reached Munich, we were to stay a night, as the train to the small town of Regenshaven would not leave until the next day.

"Then," the knowledgeable Edward informed us, "we have another long journey, but not, of course, like the one we have just experienced. We should get to Regenshaven before dark and there Kurt will be waiting to take us to the schloss."

"I can't wait to get there," said Dorabella.

"That is something you will have to do," Edward retorted. "So don't say you can't."

"I mean, I'm just longing to be there."

"I know," he replied soothingly. "So are we all."

It was exciting arriving in the great city. We were taken to the hotel where two rooms had been reserved for us—Dorabella and I sharing.

"Perhaps you would like a rest first," suggested Edward.

We looked at him in amazement. Rest! When we had come to Munich—a town which had been but printed letters on a map until now!

"All right," he said. "We'll have a look round. Just a quick one . . . because I shall be hungry and looking for sustenance."

The middle-aged woman at the desk was very affable. She smiled benignly on us and said in deeply accented English that she hoped we should enjoy our stay in Munich.

Edward, who spoke some German and liked to make use of it, told her that we were leaving the next day for Regenshaven.

"Ah," she cried. "In the forest. That is good . . ." She pronounced it "goot." "Wunderbar . . . wunderbar. You have friends there?"

"Yes, someone I knew at college."

"That is goot . . . goot . . . this friendship. But you must see something of München . . . only a little, alas . . . but the goot things. First it is the Cathedral . . . the Frauenkirche . . . then the Peterskirche . . ."

We asked directions, which she gave, smiling benevolently while we thanked her.

It was certainly a fine city and very busy. There were several museums, I noticed, but there was no time to explore them. Edward said we had the afternoon and referred once more to that necessary sustenance.

Everywhere we were met with friendliness. It was fun to ask the way and receive instructions, and in high spirits we returned to the hotel for lunch.

The dining room was full and there was only one table available; this was for six and we were given that.

Hot soup was put before us and, while we were consuming it, the waiter appeared with two young men. He asked our pardon. Edward was concentrating hard to understand him and, with the help of a little miming, we discovered that the young men wanted a meal; there was no place for them, so should we mind if they shared our table? So it was amicably arranged that they should sit with us.

They were tall and blond and we prepared ourselves to enjoy their company and they ours, it seemed. They were interested when they heard we came from England.

They lived on the outskirts of Munich, which was a very big city—they added proudly, in Germany second only to Berlin.

We looked suitably impressed.

They were in the town on business. Things were different now. They had changed since the Führer came to power.

We listened attentively. There were questions I wanted to ask, but it was a little difficult because of the language problem, though they spoke some English and, with Edward's German, we could reach some understanding.

"We like the English," they told us.

"We have found the people here very helpful to us," Edward said.

"But of course."

I put in: "And we like all we have seen."

Dorabella was a little silent. She was hurt, I thought, because they did not pay her the attention she was accustomed to receiving from young men. These two seemed to me too earnest for frivolity.

"It is good that you come here," said one of the young men whose name we discovered was Franz. The other was Ludwig.

"It is good that you see we are now a prosperous people."

We waited for him to go on.

"We have suffered much. After the war ... there was a harsh treaty. Oh, we suffered. But no more. We shall be great again."

"But you are," said Dorabella, giving one of her most appealing smiles.

Both young men then regarded her with interest. "You have seen this?"

"Oh, yes," said Dorabella.

"And you will go home and tell your people Germany is great again?"

Dorabella said: "Oh, yes." Although I knew she had no intention of doing so and certainly no one would have been interested if she had.

"We are proud," said Ludwig, "because it was here in Munich that our Führer made his great attempt to lead our nation."

"What year was that?" asked Edward.

"1923," answered Franz. "It was the Putsch in the beer cellar."

"Beer cellar!" cried Dorabella. "Can we go to a beer cellar?"

Neither of the young men seemed to hear that. They were staring silently ahead, their faces flushed with zeal.

"It failed and he went to prison," said Franz.

"But that time was not wasted," added his friend. "For out of it came *Mein Kampf*."

"And then when Hindenburg died he became Chancellor. And then Dictator ... and everything was different," said the other.

"Oh, good," murmured Dorabella. "That must have been nice." There was a touch of asperity in her voice. She was a little bored by these too earnest young men. However, there was a very friendly atmosphere at the table and the food was good.

We felt distinctly refreshed and spent a pleasant afternoon exploring the Peterskirche—one of the oldest churches I had ever seen. After that we sat outside a restaurant, drank coffee, and ate some delicious cakes. It was interesting to watch the people strolling by. Edward said we must not stay out too long. We had to think of the journey tomorrow, for we should have to rise early.

We went back to our hotel. Franz and Ludwig were no longer there. We dined and returned to our rooms where Dorabella and I talked of the day's events until we dropped off to sleep.

We were greatly looking forward to arriving in Regenshaven.

As we stepped from the train, I felt I was in an enchanted land. We had traveled through mountainous country of pine-covered slopes with waterfalls and little rivulets which glittered in the sunshine. We had seen the occasional little village with tall brick buildings and cobbled streets, which reminded me of illustrations in *Grimm's Fairy Tales* from my childhood.

Kurt was waiting to greet us, which he did with such joy, and made us all feel like honored guests.

"How glad I am that you have come!" he said. "Ach, but it is a long journey and so good of you to make it to see us."

"We thought it was worth it," replied Edward lightly. "Kurt. It *is* good to see you."

"And the young ladies are here . . . Violetta . . . Dorabella."

"We are here," cried Dorabella. "You don't think we should have let Edward come without us, surely?"

"They are all eager to meet you. My family . . . I mean," said Kurt. "Come. We will waste no time. They are impatient. Is this the luggage?"

Kurt took our bags and we went out of the station and settled into his waiting car. Then we drove through the pine-scented air.

"It is beautiful!" I cried. "Everything I thought it would be."

And so it was. We were soon in the forest.

"The schloss is five miles from the station," Kurt told us.

We looked about us eagerly and soon came to a small town, with its church and old belltower, its cobbled streets, and the square in which were the post office and a few shops. The small houses had clearly stood there for hundreds of years. One almost expected the Pied Piper to appear.

The schloss was about a quarter of a mile out of the town, which I discovered was called Waldenburg. The road to it was slightly uphill. I gasped when I saw the schloss. In the afternoon light it was like another illustration from the fairy-tale books.

It was a castle, yes, but a miniature one. There was a circular turret at each end and it was built of pale gray stone. I thought of a princess at one of the turret windows letting down her long fair hair to enable her lover to climb up to her. I could hear Dorabella's voice: "It's silly. He would have pulled it all out, and think how it would hurt!" But I was more romantically minded than she was, and I thought it was an example of true love to suffer for the joy of receiving one's lover in the turret.

I would have reminded her of this but there was no time,

for standing at the door of this fascinating edifice was a group of people.

Kurt shouted in German: "We're here," and they all clapped their hands.

We got out of the car and were introduced to them. Edward they knew already, and greeted him with great pleasure. And Kurt presented them to us with that dignity with which I was beginning to become accustomed. There were his parents, his grandfather and grandmother, his brother Helmut and his sister Gretchen. Standing to one side were the servants—a man, two women, and a girl who, I guessed, would be much the same age as Dorabella and me.

When the first formal introductions had been made, the welcome was very warm.

We were shown to our rooms. Dorabella and I shared, which we were delighted to do. We stood at the window looking out on the forest where a faint mist was beginning to settle, giving the scene a mysterious aspect and, just for a moment, I felt a certain apprehension which made me shiver. That mist once again reminded me of the forest in the Grimm books, where evil was so often lurking.

It was gone in a moment, for Dorabella hugged me suddenly—a habit she had when excited.

"It is wonderful!" she cried. "I know it's going to be fun. What did you think of Helmut?"

"I am afraid it is too soon for me to have made an assessment. He seemed very pleasant."

Dorabella laughed at me. "You are such a pompous old darling, dear sister. I'm glad all that side of us went to you."

She often said that she and I were one person, really, and the vices and virtues which fell to the lot of most people at birth had been divided between us.

However, on that occasion she did manage to disperse that mild feeling of uneasiness.

I remember our first meal in the schloss inn. I recall going down the narrow spiral staircase to the dining room where we dined with the family, apart from the guests who were staying at the inn; and we had our meal after they had had theirs.

It was a small dining room which looked out—as so many of the rooms did—on the forest. There were rugs on the wooden floor, and two stuffed heads of deer protruded from the walls on either side of the open fireplace.

We discovered that long ago—before the unification of Germany, when the country had consisted of a number of small states—the schloss had been the hunting lodge of some baron, and the animals' heads must have been put there then. One looked somewhat ferocious, the other scornfully resentful. They seemed to intrude into the peaceful atmosphere of the room. There were pictures, too, of the Brandt family which I later learned had been painted before the disastrous years of 1914 to 1918.

It was a merry party. The language represented little problem. Dorabella and I had learned a smattering from our school lessons which was of some small help to us. Kurt and Edward were fairly good; and Kurt's parents seemed to have acquired a little English, possibly through visitors to the schloss; and Helmut and Gretchen had some English, too. So the language problems which cropped up now and then only added to the merriment.

It was a very pleasant evening.

Dorabella and I discussed it when we were alone in our room.

"It's going to be fun," said Dorabella. "Helmut is rather disappointing, though."

"You mean he has not responded to the allure of Miss Dorabella Denver?"

"He's a bit stodgy," she said. "I can't bear these intense people. Like those men in the hotel. Helmut doesn't laugh much."

"Perhaps he doesn't see anything to laugh about, or it may be that he doesn't feel it necessary to let everyone know what he is feeling."

"Tomorrow," she went on, "we shall explore. It's going to be interesting."

"I'm sure it will be ... different from anything we have done before."

I went to the window and looked out. The mist had thickened. I could just see the outline of the nearest trees.

"It looks exciting like that," I said.

Dorabella came to stand beside me.

I went on: "Weird almost. Do you think so?"

"It just looks like mist to me."

I found it difficult to turn away, and suddenly I saw a figure emerge from the schloss.

Dorabella whispered: "It's the maid."

"Else," I murmured. "Yes, that's her name. I wonder where she's going. It must be nearly eleven."

Then we saw a man step out of the shadows. We could not see him clearly, but he was obviously not one of those whom we had seen in the schloss. He was tall and very fair. Else was caught up in his arms and for a few moments they clung together.

Dorabella was giggling beside me.

"He's her lover," she said.

We watched them as, hand in hand, they slipped into one of the outhouses, which in the days of the baron may have been stables.

We left the window. Dorabella got into her little bed and I got into mine.

We did not sleep well that night, which was to be expected; and when I did dream it was of a fairy-tale kind of blue mist which turned into shapes of strange people, and the branches of the trees became long arms that stretched out to catch me.

During the days which followed, we settled into the life of the schloss. I learned from Kurt's mother that the inn was by no means full. They had at the moment only six people staying, and they considered that fairly good. Times had been bad, but they were in some respects getting better as the country became more prosperous.

"It had a long way to come after the war," said Kurt. "Now there are more visitors because people come from abroad . . . from England, America, and other parts of the world. But we have the Beer Garden and when the weather is not good customers come inside. We have the big room with the bar . . . it is from this that we make our living."

"We are grateful for this," went on Kurt's mother.

She was a woman of great energy, and I was impressed by her devotion to her family. In fact, what struck me immediately was this attitude among them all. It was almost as though there was an element of fear in their feeling toward each other. It puzzled me.

The grandfather was rather feeble and spent most of his time in his room reading the Scriptures. He would sit in his chair with a little black cap on his head and his lips would move as he said the words to himself.

The grandmother would be in her chair, knitting most of the time. Among other things she made jerseys for the whole family. She told me that winters in the forest could be harsh.

"We are so high," she said. "Well above the sea . . . and the clouds come down and surround us."

She would croon to herself and Kurt told us that she lived in the past and seemed to be there more often than in the present.

His parents were constantly working. The father was often in the forest. I had seen him felling trees, and logs were brought into the schloss from time to time on a long carriage-like contraption used for that purpose.

There was a great deal to do in the schloss, and I guessed they could not afford much help.

Helmut, that very serious young man, continued to be a disappointment to Dorabella. He showed no more interest in her than in Edward or me, though he was meticulously polite and considerate to us all, but equally so, and clearly he was unaware of Dorabella's special charms—and that did not endear him to her.

Gretchen was a charming girl—dark-haired, dark-eyed like the rest of the family—and I noticed that Edward's eyes were often on her. I mentioned this to Dorabella; she shrugged her shoulders; she was not really interested in the romances of others.

In a few days I felt we had been at the schloss for weeks. Kurt had driven us round so that we could see something of the countryside. Sometimes we descended to the lower slopes and walked among the spruce, silver fir, and beech; then we would make our way up to where the firs grew in abundance.

We walked a great deal which meant much climbing, but it was the best way of seeing the country. It was delightful to visit the small hamlets. They were different from those at home and most seemed to have that Grimm-like quality. I always felt that there was something a little frightening about them. I was reminded of children lost among the trees and finding a gingerbread house or giants lurking in the undergrowth.

I think these feelings were engendered by something I did not understand at the time. It was there in the schloss.

What was it? Beneath all the bonhomie, the laughter, the merriment of the Beer Garden . . . and often in the bar where people came in from the villages around, sitting at tables drinking, often singing songs with beautifully haunting tunes, usually extolling the Fatherland.

If I mentioned this to Edward and Dorabella I felt they would have laughed at me. They would say wasn't I always fancying something? I told myself they were right. It was the forest atmosphere which moved me in some way.

Dorabella and I quite often went out alone. We had taken to walking into the town and we found it particularly enjoyable to sit outside one of the coffee shops, drink our coffee, and partake in one of the fancy pastries which were really delicious. The waiter now knew us as "The English Young Ladies," and he would chat a little to us when he served us. We used our boarding-school German with him which he seemed to like. Then we would watch the people walking by; and after an hour or so of this pleasant occupation, we would stroll back to the schloss.

It was the beginning of our second week. It was a lovely day, slightly less warm than it had been, with the faintest touch of autumn in the air.

As we sat there, a young man strolled past. He was tall and fair, with a marked jaunty air, so different from the rather earnest people we met so often. He had a very pleasant face and, as he went past, he glanced at us. It was not exactly a stare, but he certainly did not look away immediately. I was aware of Dorabella's interest.

He went on into the town.

Dorabella said: "He looked different somehow."

"I think he is a visitor . . . I mean, not a local."

"I thought for a moment he was going to stop."

"Why on earth did you think that?"

"He might have thought we were someone he knew."

"I am sure he thought nothing of the sort. In any case, he's gone now."

"A pity. He was quite good-looking."

"Would you like another pastry?"

"No, I don't think so. Violetta, do you realize we shall soon be going home?"

"We've another week."

"By the way the time flies, we shall soon be there."

"It has been fun, hasn't it?"

"H'm," she said. She was alert suddenly.

She was facing the street and I had my back to it. Her face creased into smiles.

"What is it?" I demanded.

"Don't look round. He's coming back."

"Who?"

"That man."

"You mean ... ?"

"The one who just went by."

She appeared to become very interested in her coffee cup. And then I saw him, for he had seated himself at a table close by.

"Yes," went on Dorabella, as though there had been no interruption. "It won't be long now. I expect the parents will be thinking that two weeks away from their beloved daughters is long enough."

As she talked it was clear to me that her attention was on that other table.

Then suddenly the man rose and came toward us.

"Forgive me," he said. "I couldn't help hearing you were speaking English. It's such a pleasure to meet one's fellow countrymen in foreign lands, don't you think?"

"Oh, yes, I do," said Dorabella.

"May I join you? One can't shout across the tables. Are you on holiday?"

"Yes," I said. "Are you?"

He nodded. "Walking," he said.

"Alone?" asked Dorabella.

"I had a friend who was with me. He had to go back. I hesitated whether to go with him, but it was only for another week, so I thought I would stick it out."

"Have you walked far?"

"Miles."

"And you have just arrived in this place?" asked Dorabella.

"Three days ago. I thought I saw you before . . . having coffee here."

The waiter had approached and the young man ordered coffee, suggesting that we have another with him. Dorabella agreed at once.

"This is a fascinating place," I said. "And walking, you see the best of it."

"That's true," he agreed. "Have you walked much?"

"A little."

"Are you staying in this town?"

"No," Dorabella told him. "In a little schloss about a quarter of a mile away . . . not exactly a hotel, but a sort of inn." She waved her hand in the direction of the schloss.

"I know it. Charming surroundings. How long have you been here?"

"We are going at the end of the week. Then we shall have been here about fourteen days."

The coffee had arrived and the waiter smiled benignly to see us chatting together.

"It is so good to be able to talk in English," said the young man. "My German is somewhat inadequate."

"And so is ours," said Dorabella. "But we have someone with us who is quite good."

"A friend?"

"Well, a friend of the family. He is like a brother . . . only not really."

He waited for us to explain, but as neither of us went any further there was a brief silence. Then Dorabella said: "We are visiting a friend, really. He came to England and suggested we come here for a visit. That's how it was."

"I'm very glad you did. It's comforting to meet someone English . . . although I'm not exactly English."

"Oh?" we both said in surprise.

"Cornish," he said with a grimace.

"But . . ."

"A little quibble. The Tamar divides us and we always maintain that we are a race apart from those people on the other side of it."

"Like the Scottish and the Welsh," I said.

"Celtic pride," he replied. "We think we are as good as . . .

no, better than . . . those Anglo-Saxons . . . as we call you foreigners."

"Oh dear," said Dorabella in mock dismay. "And I was
thinking what fun it was to meet someone of our own race."

He looked at her earnestly. "It is," he said. "It has made this
a most interesting day for me."

"Tell us about Cornwall," I said. "Do you live near the
sea?"

"Sometimes it seems too near . . . almost in it, in fact."

"That must be fascinating."

"I love the old place. Where is your home?"

"Hampshire."

"Some distance from Cornwall."

"Are you looking forward to going home?" asked
Dorabella.

"Not at this moment."

"Shall you be walking tomorrow?"

"I let each day take care of itself."

I could see that Dorabella was enjoying this encounter. Her
eyes were shining; she looked very attractive and I noticed
how his gaze kept straying to her. It did not surprise me. I had
seen it so many times before.

She was telling him, in her animated fashion, about
Caddington, and he responded with some details of his home
in Cornwall.

He told us his name was Dermot Tregarland. "An old Cornish name," he pointed out. "We seem to be either Tre, Pol,
or Pen. It is like a label. 'Where e'er you hear Tre, Pol, and
Pen, you'll always know 'tis Cornishmen.' It's an old saying
I heard somewhere and it is true."

And so the talk went on until I said—although I was aware
of Dorabella's displeasure—that it was time we returned to the
schloss.

We said goodbye and started back.

Dorabella said angrily: "Why did you want to leave as
abruptly as that?"

"Look at the time! They would be wondering where we
were. Don't forget we were about to leave when he came up."

"What did it matter?" There was a pause and she added:
"He didn't say anything about seeing us again."

"Why should he?"

"I thought he might."

"Oh, Dorabella," I said. "It was a chance encounter. 'Ships that pass in the night.' It was only because he heard that we were speaking English that he stopped."

"Was that all, do you think?" She was smiling now . . . secretly.

The next day the weather had changed and there was a definite touch of autumn in the air. Kurt and Edward had planned an excursion to one of the mountain villages, and it had naturally been taken for granted that we would accompany them.

However, Dorabella decided that she must do some shopping in the town. I understood, of course. She wanted to go into Waldenburg and sit outside the coffee shop in the hope that the young man of yesterday would pass by again.

And, of course, I wanted to be with Dorabella. I must, because she could not very well go alone.

We watched Edward and Kurt go off, spent an idle morning, and after lunch went into the town.

We did a little shopping for souvenirs and in due course arrived at the coffee shop. The waiter gave us his welcoming smile and we sat down—Dorabella in a state of expectation, I amused and a little cynical, wondering what she thought would be the outcome of this chance encounter.

We talked desultorily while Dorabella was watchful. She had placed herself looking on the street, the way he had come before, and as time passed she was becoming more and more despondent.

A horse and trap went by, and then some riders—two young girls with an instructor; then a van drew up and a young man stepped out. He was delivering something to the coffee shop.

As I watched him carrying in a large box, I thought there was something familiar about him. He disappeared into the shop, and after a while came out carrying a sheaf of papers. The waiter was with him and they chatted for a while.

Then I recognized the young man.

I said: "Oh, look! Do you see who that is? It is Else's young man."

Dorabella's thoughts were elsewhere. She looked at me impatiently.

"What?" she said.

"That young man who is delivering something. He's Else's young man. You remember. We saw him from our window. He's her lover. We saw them embracing the other night."

"Oh, yes . . . I remember." Dorabella was not interested in that particular young man.

He was standing by the van now. He called out in German, which I could understand: "Tomorrow night, then. See you there."

"They must be friends," I said. "He and the waiter . . . they are meeting tomorrow night."

"What of it?" said Dorabella petulantly.

"Well . . . nothing. Just that I was interested, that's all."

Dorabella continued to glance disconsolately along the street.

I said: "Well, we can't sit here all the afternoon."

She agreed reluctantly.

But I knew that she was bitterly disappointed and, as I often did, I understood exactly how she was feeling.

We walked slowly down the incline which led to the schloss. There was a faint chill in the air and a mistiness in the atmosphere.

"I don't want to go in yet," she said. "I'd like to walk awhile."

"All right. Let's do that, but not for long."

"In the forest," she said.

We left the road and walked through the trees. I wanted to comfort her, as I had always done when she was disappointed. I was reminded of the time when she had lost one of her teddy bear's bootbutton eyes and another time when the face of her favorite doll had been smashed to pieces. I had been the only one who could console her on such occasions. I understood her better than any.

Now I wanted to bring her out of that despondency. It was absurd, I wanted to point out. How could seeing someone with whom she had exchanged only a few words be of such importance to her? It was ridiculous. But that was Dorabella. She felt intensely . . . for the moment. Her emotions did not really go very deep and might not be long in passing, but while they were there they took complete possession of her.

We never went deep into the forest. We had been warned

about that. The road which led from the town to the schloss
had been cut through it and on either side the tall pines rose
to the sky. The trees grew less densely on the edges of the forest. Kurt had taken us deeper into it, but he had warned us always to keep close to the road so that if we could not see it
we were aware of it.

So we continued to walk on the fringe.

We sat down on a log. I tried to talk of other things but
Dorabella was absentminded. I knew this mood. Fortunately it
would not last long. Her moods never did. She had been a little disappointed by the lack of admiring young men during
this holiday. Helmut was too concerned with the running of
the schloss to have given her the attention she looked for; and
I gathered he was not good looking enough to appeal to her.
The Cornishman Dermot Tregarland had been just right. He
had appeared by magic right near the end of the holiday and
that seemed to be the end of him. Poor Dorabella!

I said it was getting chilly and we should return to the
schloss.

She agreed and we started to walk back the way we had
come and then . . . suddenly, I began to be alarmed. We had not
noticed how thick the mist had become. We should have remembered that it could come down quickly. We had been told
often enough. Not that we could really say this was so sudden.
It had been hanging about all day. And now . . . here it was and
nothing looked the same.

"Come on," I said. "Let's get out of this quickly."

But it was not easy. I had thought to see the road, but all
I could discern were the trunks of nearby trees, their branches
swathed in mist.

I took Dorabella's arm.

"It's what they warned us about," I said. "How silly of us."

She was silent.

I went on: "We can't be far from the road. We must find it.
I am sure this is the way."

But was it? Wherever I looked, I could see very little. The
mist was everywhere. I began to feel very alarmed. But I did
not want Dorabella to see how much. The instinct to protect
Dorabella was with me as strong as it used to be in our childhood.

She turned to me as she always did, and I was gratified to see that she still had that childlike confidence in me.

I felt very tender toward her.

"We'll soon be out of this," I said. "We shouldn't have come into the forest, of course, after what they have told us."

She nodded. I grasped her hand firmly and said: "Come on."

We walked on. It might have been for ten minutes, but it seemed like an hour. I was beginning to get very uneasy. The forest had taken on that Grimm-like quality. The trunks of the trees seemed to form themselves into grotesque faces which leered at me. The bracken caught at our ankles like tentacles trying to hold us back.

I glanced at Dorabella. She did not have these fancies.

I had a terrible fear that instead of going out of the forest we were getting deeper and deeper in. As the thought struck me I drew up sharply.

"What is it?" asked Dorabella.

I said: "I am wondering if we should wait here . . . until the mist lifts."

"What! Here! That could be all night."

She was right. But how could we know whether we were getting deeper and deeper into the forest? What idiots we had been to come in the first place! It was not as though we had not seen that there was mist in the air.

I felt exasperated—more so because I was becoming more and more alarmed.

And this had all come about because of that young man in the town. If I had not been so concerned about Dorabella's disappointment I should have insisted that it was foolish to walk into the forest on such a day. Everything that had happened was because of that young man. We might have been safe with Kurt and Edward.

Then I thought of the consternation there would be at the schloss when we did not return. So what should we do? Stay where we were and wait? Or go on and perhaps deeper into the forest?

Despair settled on me—and then I thought I heard someone not so very far off.

I shouted: "Help! Is anyone there?"

We stood in silence, listening.

To our great relief there was a reply. And in English.

"Yes . . . where are you?"

I was aware first of Dorabella's face. It was bright with excitement. She recognized the voice, as I had. It was that of Dermot Tregarland.

"We're lost," I shouted.

"I'll find you. Go on calling."

Both Dorabella and I called: "Here! Here!"

"I'm getting nearer . . ." came the response.

Now he seemed very close and we shouted at the tops of our voices: "Here . . . here."

With what joy we saw him looming out of the mist.

"Oh," cried Dorabella. "How wonderful! We were quite scared."

He was grinning. "I was hoping to find you," he said. "I saw you turn into the forest."

"Where were you?"

"I came for coffee. I hoped you'd be there. The waiter told me you had just gone. Then I saw you down the road. I watched you go into the forest and I hurried down to catch up with you. If I couldn't, I decided I would have a beer in the schloss and await your return."

Dorabella was overcome with delight and wonder. It had all turned out right after all.

Dermot Tregarland took charge.

"This devilish mist!" he said. "It is a shocker, don't you agree? One doesn't know which way to turn. We'd better get out of here fast. It could get worse as night comes on. I know the way I came and I'm fairly good at finding my way around. There was a gnarled old tree I passed . . . struck by lightning, I imagine . . . I guess when we find that we'll be on the right road. There is a small one growing nearby. So . . . Excelsior!"

Dorabella giggled. The nightmare had turned into a thrilling adventure because our perfect, gentle knight had arrived to rescue us. This alone would make the holiday worthwhile and, to tell the truth, before, for Dorabella, it had been a trifle disappointing.

He was indeed all he had implied. He led us with the minimum of difficulty to the stricken tree. He shouted with triumph.

"We're on the way." Then he found the small tree to which he had referred. And there we were on the road.

Dorabella flung her arms round me and, looking over my shoulder at him, cried: "You're wonderful."

"I think we need something to warm us up," he said. "What about a glass of wine—or are you tempted by their really excellent beer?"

Frau Brandt was at the door of the schloss looking anxiously along the road.

She said: "The mist had come up rather quickly, as it often does at this time of the year. I was beginning to think it was time you were back."

Dorabella explained that we were lost in the forest and Mr. Tregarland had brought us out.

"Ach!" cried Frau Brandt, and broke into a stream of German which, we realized, expressed relief. She went on about the ease with which people could be lost in the forest and had to remain there until the mist cleared.

She hustled us into the schloss. It was not weather for loitering in the Beer Garden. What refreshments would we like?

We said we would like a glass of wine . . . a sort of aperitif. So wine was brought and we sat together—Dorabella in a state of extreme contentment. I thought to myself, I believe she is falling in love with this young man, or perhaps trying to convince herself that she is. And he? He was charming, and it was clearly Dorabella who had his attention. She was the sort of girl who changed in the society of men. If she were depressed, this could be completely dispersed by masculine appreciation. She sparkled; she was at her most enchanting best. I suppose there were occasions when I might have felt a little jealous, but I did not now. For one thing, I took her superior feminine charms for granted; and so far I had never felt any desire for the attention of those men who attracted her.

I liked this young man. He was certainly charming, but that was all. Dorabella was inclined to let her emotions flow too easily. I was always afraid that she would—as she had once or twice in the past—have to face some disappointment.

Dermot lifted his glass and said: "To our safe return from the dangers of the forest."

Dorabella touched her glass with his and they smiled at each other.

"How lucky for us that you saw us," said Dorabella.

"It was more due to design than luck," he assured her. "I was so sorry to have missed you. I was so certain that I would find you sitting there sipping your coffee. I was so grateful to the waiter for telling me you had only just left. Then I dashed off and saw you turning into the forest. It occurred to me that it might be misty there. Indeed, it did seem to be getting worse every moment."

"So you came to rescue us," said Dorabella. "It was truly marvelous, the way you brought us out."

They smiled at each other again.

"The English have to stick together when on alien soil ... even if some of them are only Cornish."

Dorabella laughed at everything he said, as though she found it the height of wit. I would tell her when we were alone that she must not be so blatantly adoring.

Then we started to talk about ourselves. We told him who Edward was and how our mother had brought him out of France at the beginning of the war.

He was very interested. "And Edward is the good big brother to you."

"Oh, yes," I said. "He is wonderful to us, always feels he has to look after us."

"He does not forbid you to wander in the misty forest?"

"He will be furious with us for having done so," said Dorabella. "But he has gone off for the day with his friend Kurt—the son of the Brandts. They have known each other for some little time. That is why we are here."

He said he hoped to meet Edward.

He told us something about his house in Cornwall. It had been in the Tregarland family for hundreds of years. In fact it was called "Tregarland's." It was built of gray stone; it faced the sea and received the full blast of the southwest gales. But it had stood up to them for centuries and it seemed would continue doing so. It had towers at either end and its gardens sloped right down to a beach which belonged to the house but there was a "right of way" through it; otherwise people walking along the shore would have to climb the cliff and go round the house and descend again if they wished to continue along the beach.

"Not many people come that way. In the summer there might be a few visitors, but that is usually all."

"Do you have any family?" I asked.

"My father is an invalid. My mother died when I was very young. That is really all the family. There is Gordon Lewyth—he is like a member of the family. He looks after the estate. He's a wonderful manager. Then there is his mother who runs the house. She isn't exactly a housekeeper. She's a distant connection of the family, I believe . . . all rather vague. She came to us when my mother died and has run the house ever since. That must be about twenty-three years ago. It has worked out very well."

"And there you are with your father your only family, really," said Dorabella.

"Yes, but as I say, Gordon Lewyth and his mother are really like family."

"It sounds interesting," said Dorabella.

"And what do you do?" I asked.

"There is a Tregarland estate. Farms and so on. They are let out to tenant farmers and we have an interest in them. Then there is the home farm. I help in the management, although Gordon is more involved than I am. There's a lot to do on an estate, you know."

"It's rather like Caddington," I said. "We know something about the managing of estates, don't we, Dorabella?"

"Oh, yes. Our father is always busy and our brother will take over one day, I suppose. That sort of thing goes on in families like ours."

"That's so. I think it would be a good idea if I stayed here for a meal tonight. Then I can grope my way back to my hotel through the mist later on."

So we talked and eventually Edward and Kurt returned. When they heard about our adventure in the forest Edward looked very severe and reprimanded us for not being more careful. Hadn't we been warned often enough about the mist in the forest?

It was a merry party when we had dinner that night. Dermot was invited to share the meal in the private dining room with the family and everyone seemed to treat him as a hero because he had brought us out of the forest.

Edward was particularly grateful. He told us more than once

that he had promised our mother to look after us. How could
he have known that we should have been so foolhardy as to
get ourselves lost? It was not even that the mist had come up
suddenly. Dorabella begged him not to go on and on. She herself was delighted that she had gone into the forest. Otherwise
how could Dermot Tregarland have shown them how gallant
and clever he was by rescuing us?

Hans Brandt told some stories about people who had been
lost in the forest.

"There are so many legends about these parts. Some people
are sure the trolls are still around and they come out of their
hiding places under cover of the mist."

We sat, warm and content, in the comfort of the schloss and
the merry company.

We lingered over the table while Dermot told stories of his
native Cornwall which could match those of Hans Brandt. We
laughed a great deal at the simplicity of folk and the amazing
stories which could be handed down from generation to generation.

We could hear the sounds from the bar lounge where people
were still drinking, as was their custom. There was no one in
the Beer Garden on this night on account of the mist.

It had been a wonderful evening—a pleasant finale to the
holiday, for in a few days we should be returning home. I
watched Dorabella. She was looking so happy and I felt a
twinge of anxiety. She scarcely knew this young man. Then I
reminded myself that this was not the first incident of this
kind. There had been a friend of our grandfather Greenham
. . . some Member of Parliament who had been staying at
Marchlands briefly. She had been very taken with him. But
that had been about two years ago. He had turned out to be a
devoted husband and father of children. She had quickly recovered from that. Then there had been a man at school who
had come for a term to teach music. He had been another. It
was all right. This was just Dorabella's enthusiasm of the moment. On those other occasions she had been a schoolgirl, of
course. Now she was grown up.

If Dermot Tregarland was not married, if she saw him again
. . . this might just turn out to be not like one of those incidents. He lived some way from us. Perhaps in a few weeks he

would become just another of those passing encounters . . . he would just be a part of the holiday in the Böhmerwald.

However, we parted on very friendly terms that night, and I knew Dorabella had a somewhat restless night.

Edward had made arrangements to go on another jaunt with Kurt the next day and, as we had behaved so foolishly, he refused to leave us behind on this occasion.

A party should be made up which included Dorabella, myself, and Gretchen.

Gretchen was delighted to come with us. I fancied that she was attracted by Edward, as he was by her; but she did not show her feelings—in fact neither of them did—as blatantly as Dorabella showed hers.

Dorabella herself was inclined to be sulky; she would have preferred to go into Waldenburg, and drink coffee so that Dermot could have joined us, but Edward was adamant and so we went off with the party.

It was a pleasant day; the weather had changed again; the skies were blue and we were back in summer. Kurt knew the forest well; there were several roads cut through it and he wanted to show us some of the charming little villages.

I enjoyed it very much; the small hamlets were very attractive with their mellowed brick houses, their cobbled streets, their old churches, and their general air of orderliness.

The people were very friendly. We had lunch in an old inn, with the sign of a mermaid outside—*Die Lorelei* it was called, and we recalled the poem we had learned at school and Gretchen recited it for us. She had a sweet, tremulous voice, and Edward led the applause.

We were taken down to see the ancient wine cellars and were told that at one time the inn had been part of a monastery, and the cellars were those in which the monks had once made their wine.

It was all very pleasant, but Dorabella was impatient to return, because in the evening Dermot Tregarland would be joining us at the schloss for dinner.

I shall never forget that night and the disaster which was all the more horrific because it was so sudden. It was as though the faces of benign friends suddenly changed into those of monsters before one's eyes, leaving us quite bewildered because we were so unprepared.

When we returned from our day's sightseeing, Dorabella and I changed in our room, Dorabella putting on the best of the dresses she had brought with her. She was in high spirits. She was certain now that the end of the holiday would not be the end of her friendship with Dermot Tregarland.

She chattered while we dressed and said how much she would like to see that place of his. It sounded fun and it was not really so very far away. She was going to suggest to our mother that we ask Dermot to Caddington.

He had arrived before we went down. We were going to eat in the inn that night. The family would be busy and would not dine until much later. Kurt and Gretchen would join us.

It was a pleasant meal, with lots of merry chatter, and afterwards we went into the inn parlor, where there were more people than usual. But we managed to get a table to ourselves.

It must have been about nine o'clock when a party of young men came in. It occurred to me at once that I had seen one of them before. I remembered immediately. He was Else's young man, the one whom I had seen delivering a parcel at the coffee shop.

He looked different. He was wearing some sort of uniform, as were his friends. On his right sleeve was an armlet. I wondered if he had come to see Else.

They sat at a table and Else served them with beer. They joked with her and the young man laid a proprietorial hand on her arm. The group laughed loudly. They said something to Else, who nodded in the direction of the dining room. The young man began to sing one of the songs I had often heard. It was something about the Fatherland. Quite a number joined in. Then Helmut came into the parlor accompanied by his father.

That was the signal.

Else's young man, who was obviously the leader, stood up suddenly and shouted something about Jews.

Pandemonium began. Someone hurled a tankard at the wall. Others did the same. One threw his at Helmut. It very narrowly missed him.

Dermot put his arm round Dorabella and she hid her face

against him. Edward took my arm and pulled me to my feet and at the same time seized Gretchen.

He said: "They are going to start a riot. We'd better get out of here."

Gretchen whispered: "Helmut . . ."

Kurt had gone to his brother's side. He was very pale. The two of them stood side by side facing Else's young man. The rest of the people in the room remained in their seats with looks of amazed horror on their faces.

Else's young man had leaped up to stand on one of the tables. He began haranguing the people. I heard the name of Führer mentioned several times. He was shouting and I wished I could understand what he was saying, but I did realize that he was inciting them to join with him in his fury, which was directed against the schloss and its inmates.

Dermot said quietly: "We'd better get out of this."

At that moment one of the tables was overturned and the air was filled with the sound of breaking glass.

Helmut said to Edward: "Get the girls out of here. Take Gretchen. This is no quarrel of yours."

I felt sickened by the look of hopeless despair I saw on Helmut's face. I did not know then what this was all about except that the young man and his friends seemed to be intent on destroying the place.

It was all so sudden . . . so inexplicable. Edward was dragging me with Gretchen toward the door. Dermot held Dorabella. One of the young men was watching us but he made no attempt to stop us. I had the idea that they were aware that we were foreigners and he was glad to see us go. In the room beyond the inn parlor Frau Brandt was standing, her hands across her breast and a look of abject terror on her face. I thought I had never seen such fear before. She was shaking.

I put an arm around her.

"They're here . . ." she murmured. "At last . . . they are here . . ."

"Who . . . are they?" I asked.

"They are intent on destroying us."

"You know them?"

"We are not the first. But how did they guess? We have never . . ."

We could hear the noises from beyond. They were destroying the inn parlor.

Frau Brandt sat down and covered her face with her hands. Gretchen went to her and knelt beside her. "Mutter . . ." she whispered, trembling.

Frau Brandt stroked her daughter's hair.

"It has come," she said. "It is here. I had hoped . . ."

I felt sick with horror.

Dermot said: "There must be something we can do. Shouldn't we get in touch with the police?"

Gretchen said: "It would be no use. These people . . . it is what they do now. We are not the first. We did not think they would bother with us. We are so small . . . we are far from the town. We always believed they would not bother with us . . . until now. We are Jewish. It is something which it is good to hide these days."

"We should go out and give a hand," said Edward. "Clear them off."

"Yes," agreed Dermot. "Come on."

Gretchen clung to Edward. "No . . . no," she said. "You must not interfere with them. They will break up the room and go away."

"Kurt . . . Helmut . . . your father . . . they are there."

Gretchen still clung to Edward's arm.

Dermot said: "I'm going out there. You ladies stay here."

"I'll come with you," said Edward.

I could not understand then what it meant. I just listened in horror. I could hear them singing one of the songs which I was beginning to know by heart.

Then suddenly there was quiet.

Edward was out there, I thought. In danger, perhaps. What I had seen of those young men had led me to believe they were intent on destruction.

Because Edward was there I had to know what was happening. I opened the door cautiously. It was a strange sight which met my eyes. The room was in chaos. There were upturned tables and broken glass everywhere. The young men were all standing very still at attention; they were singing, their hands raised as though in a salute.

The customers remained seated, nervously fingering their glasses; they were mute, dazed. Not one of them, I was aware, had attempted to stop the upheaval which had been started by Else's young man and his half dozen friends. They had allowed these thugs to break up the place. The singing stopped. Else's young man came forward to where Helmut was standing in the midst of the ravages of the room. He stood before him and then deliberately spat into his face and said: "Jew."

When he turned away, Helmut's hands were clenched. Kurt caught hold of him. I thought at first Helmut was going to strike the young man.

The young man was looking straight at me. He stared for a moment. Then he clicked his heels and bowed. He turned away, collected his followers and they filed out of the schloss. I heard the sound of the starting up of car engines and then they drove away.

All the customers were slinking away in relief and, I fancied, with an expression of guilt. We stood in the room then, assessing the damage. There was broken glass everywhere. Several tables had been overturned and some chairs were in pieces.

But it was not the damage which was responsible for the oppressive gloom. It was what it indicated. There was so much I had to learn, but I knew this was not an isolated disaster. It was an evil portent.

I heard Frau Brandt whisper in agonized tones: "What are we going to do? What will become of us all?"

I think that was what was in all their minds.

It was late when Dermot went back to his hotel in the town. He said he would come back tomorrow early and help with the clearing up. He could not understand why the Brandts did not call in the police. It was a pure case of unprovoked vandalism.

They did not want to speak of it that night. They were too shocked to do so. Frau Brandt's attitude told me more than anyone else's. I sensed in it a certain resignation, an acceptance of something that was inevitable.

It was late when Dorabella and I retired to our bedroom. We were both subdued.

She said that Dermot had been marvelous. He had looked after her so carefully. But I did not want to talk of Dermot. My thoughts were with the Brandts.

We did not sleep much that night. I doubt anyone in the schloss did.

The few guests who were staying had breakfast in the public dining room as Edward, Dorabella, and I did.

Afterwards we went into the damaged room where Kurt and the rest of the family were attempting to restore some order. Edward rolled up his sleeves and worked energetically.

Dorabella and I did what we could. The main difficulty was the broken glass which seemed to have embedded itself in everything.

During the morning Dermot arrived to help. He was very angry. He said it was shameful. He had talked to the people at his hotel and they had said it was happening all over Germany. The Führer wanted a pure race in Germany and that did not include Jews.

It had never occurred to me that the Brandts were Jewish. There had never been any reason to mention it. Edward said he may have heard it and thought no more about it. Kurt was his friend and his race would make no difference to that.

That morning we learned what was happening in Germany.

We had worked for several hours and cleaned most of the debris; we had taken away the broken chairs, set up all the upturned tables, washed a great deal of the stains from the walls which had been made by the tankards of beer which had been thrown against them; and in the dim light the room did not look much different from what it had before the debacle had begun.

We were all tired and sat down together. Gloom hung over us as thick as the forest mist.

It was no use ignoring it, and I am sure we found a slight relief in talking of it.

Kurt said: "It had to happen sooner or later. I am only sorry that it was during your visit. I am ashamed that you should have seen it. It is a blight on our nation. But you must not go away and think: 'This is the Germans.' It fills many of us with sorrow. It is an ulcerous growth . . . a cancer. It fills us with shame and, yes, fear. From one day to the next we do not know what our fate will be."

"It is monstrous," cried Dermot. "How can people let it happen? These thugs—they are nothing more—come with their songs and slogans . . . and dare do that! And they get away with it. I think one of the most shameful aspects of the case is that it was allowed to happen and nothing was done about it."

"It has been so for some time," said Hans. "These people are members of the Hitler Youth of the Nazi Party. When Adolf Hitler became Chancellor in 1933 he put Baldur von Schirach in charge of the youth of the country. German boys of ten were registered for what they call Racial Purity and known as the Deutsche Jungvolk. They are investigated to make sure they have no 'alien' blood, and if not, they are eligible at the age of thirteen to join the Hitler Youth Movement, the Hitler Jugend. At the age of eighteen they graduate from this and become members of the Nazi Party."

"Whose aim it is to go round the country breaking up people's homes!" cried Dermot indignantly.

"They are what are called Aryans, it seems."

"It's monstrous," said Edward. "This can't go on."

"It has been going on for some time," said Kurt, "and it grows worse."

"Do you mean to say," cried Edward, "that you live in fear that this sort of thing may happen at any minute?"

"I have lived with that fear for some time now."

"And the people stand by and allow it!"

"They can do nothing else. The Führer has done so much for the country. We were in a dreadful state. Our currency was worthless ... our people in desperation. We are not a race to sit down quietly and accept such a fate. We do something about it. We were defeated in the war and for that we had to suffer poverty and humiliation. Then this man came. He did much good. It is unfortunate for us that he hates our race. I sometimes believe that he wants to exterminate us completely."

"That's impossible," said Dermot. "And this can't go on. It's ridiculous. And all these people who were there did nothing to stop it!"

"They were wise. No one can stand against the Nazis. They are in control."

"It seems incredible that people could be allowed to behave so."

"It is difficult for you to understand. But this is Germany."

"Do you mean," said Edward, "that tonight they may come along and do the same thing again?"

"I do not think they will do that. We are not important enough. We are only small people. They will go somewhere else. They have warned us . . . that is all. They want us to go away. But we have lived here all our lives . . . our forefathers were here before us. That means nothing to them. They do not like our race."

Every one of us wished we knew how to comfort them.

But there was no comfort we could offer.

We were all subdued. I had no desire to go out again. The fairy-tale villages had lost their charm for me. They had a beautiful exterior behind which evil lurked. I just wanted to get away, to go home, where everything would be normal. I looked back over those enjoyable days before I had seen that spectacle of destruction, but I could not forget the expression in the eyes of Else's lover. How could a young man like that behave as he had? He had no pity for the innocent people he had attacked. I could have understood if there had been a quarrel and he had lost his temper, but it had all been done in cold blood. It was a senseless, calculated attack on people because they were of a different race from his own.

I told Edward that the leader of the band was Else's friend. I explained what I had seen.

"I wonder if she knew he was going to do what he did," I said.

"Perhaps," replied Edward. "It explains things. She must have discovered that the family was Jewish. There is the old man in his black cap reading the Scriptures. He might have betrayed the fact."

Edward was thoughtful. He told me later that he had passed on the information to Kurt who had said that it was very likely. They lived among spies. If Else had betrayed them, there was nothing they could do about it. To dismiss her would mean great trouble. Of that they could be sure.

Edward could not bring himself to let the matter rest. He had enough German to speak to Else and he could not resist doing so.

He told me about the conversation afterwards. He had said

to her: "Was that a friend of yours who created all that damage last night?"

"I could see from her expression that she was quite truculent," he went on. "She said defiantly: 'Yes. It was.' I answered: 'And what did you think of what happened here last night?' She replied: 'It was for Germany and the Führer. We want an Aryan Germany. It is the Führer's orders. We don't want Jews here.' I reminded her: 'But those are the people you work for.' 'I should be employed by Aryans,' she answered. 'Why do you work here, then?' I asked. 'It is a job and my friend lives in the town nearby,' she answered.

"It was just hopeless," went on Edward. "I could not get through to her. She graciously made it clear that she had nothing against me. I wasn't German, which was why I could not understand what it meant to Germany to have a pure race."

"Oh, Edward," I said. "It is so horrible. What if Kurt ... his parents ... Helmut and Gretchen ... ?"

Edward looked worried. "I have been talking to Kurt. They should get out."

"How can they?"

"I don't know. But they should consider it."

"We shall be going soon," I said. "It will be worrying to leave them ... knowing what we do ... having seen what we have seen."

Edward looked deeply concerned. I thought then that he was perhaps more involved with Gretchen than I had realized.

I was certain of this when he said: "Gretchen is only a little older than you and Dorabella. Imagine what it must be like for her."

"And Kurt and Helmut. I think they are ashamed in a way. They would rather it had happened when we were not here."

"I suppose that is natural. And when you think that sort of thing is going on all over the country, it is something to be ashamed of. Violetta, how can we go away and leave them here?"

"What else can we do?"

"Well, it was Gretchen I was thinking of in particular. We could take her back with us."

"Take her back!"

"We could say it was a holiday or something. She could

stay with you. I am sure your mother would understand when we explained to her. She always understands."

"I see," I said.

"She is only a girl. How could we leave her here? With that likely to happen at any moment . . . ?"

"You are very fond of her," I said.

He nodded.

I smiled. "Well, you know my mother. She always comes to the rescue of people in distress."

"As I have good reason to know. You and Dorabella could ask her back to stay with us for a while. That would be the best way of doing it."

"And then you come and stay with us while she is there," I said. "Edward, I understand perfectly."

"It will be for you to suggest it," he said. "I could hardly do so. And frankly, Violetta, the idea of leaving her here . . ."

"I understand," I said. "I'll suggest it."

"And I'll speak to Kurt on the quiet. He will see that it is the best thing. I couldn't leave her here after what I saw last night."

I told Dorabella what I proposed to do. She was amused.

"Poor Edward," she said. "He really is smitten."

"She's a beautiful girl."

"Do you think he wants to marry her?"

"I should think it very likely. He is very much in love."

"How gorgeous! One wouldn't expect it of old Edward."

"Most people do things sometimes which one would not expect them to."

"Old wiseacre!" she muttered affectionately.

She was in a good mood. Last night had been horrifying but it had brought her closer to Dermot Tregarland. I guessed she was thinking of a double wedding. Herself and Dermot; Edward and Gretchen. I knew her so well I could often read her thoughts.

I lost no time in suggesting to Gretchen that she should come to stay with us. She opened her eyes wide in astonishment.

I said: "It would be good for you to get away for a while, and you'd be interested to see England."

Her pleasure showed in her face; then I saw the apprehension and I knew that she was thinking that though she might escape unpleasantness, there would be the perpetual anxiety for her family.

I felt a great affection for her in that moment. I think she cared for Edward, and the idea of going with him back to his country away from the ominous shadow which had fallen on her life seemed wonderful to her. If only they could all go . . .

But that was not possible.

Poor Gretchen! She was undecided.

It would be her family who would make up her mind for her; and they did.

Kurt was overcome with gratitude; so were Helmut and the parents; and it was decided that when we left we would take her with us for a holiday.

It was our last day. We were to leave the following morning. Kurt would drive us to the station and in due course the long journey to the coast would begin. We seemed almost like different people from those who had arrived here. I felt I should never be the same again. Whenever I saw anything beautiful I should look for the canker lurking beneath.

I went to say goodbye to the grandparents of whom we had seen very little during our stay, as they kept mainly to their own rooms.

Grossvater was reading the Scriptures and smiled at me rather vaguely. I told him that I should be leaving soon and he smiled on me benignly and gave me his blessing.

Then I went to Grossmutter who was seated in her rocking chair, her knitting in her hand. She was less vague and gave me a warm smile.

"It is good of you to come," she said. I was amazed that she could speak English; and during my stay here I had improved on my school German to some extent so that conversation was possible.

"Grossvater and I, we are the old ones. We stay here in our rooms . . . like two pieces of furniture which are no longer much use."

I protested at this.

"Oh, yes," she said. "Two pieces of furniture without use but which must not be thrown away." She laid a hand on my arm. "They tell me that Gretchen is going back with you."

"Yes, we thought it a good idea."

"What you saw down there ..." She put her face closer to mine. "It told you much ... ?"

"It was a shock."

She nodded. "You now know ..."

"It was so unexpected ... so pointless."

She shook her head. "It has always been," she said somberly. "I was told it would be different here ... and it was so ... for a long time. You see, I do not belong to this country. I am a Brandt only by marriage. When I was eight years old I came here from Russia."

"So you are Russian by birth?"

She nodded. "There it was the same. They called it the pogrom. We never knew when it would happen. Then we would be up ... leaving much behind ... and off we went. So it is to me not new ... though a long time ago."

"This cruel persecution. It seems so senseless to me."

"It is a hatred of our race."

"But why?"

"Ask the Lord. Only He will know. But it has always been. My family thought that coming here would be different. But you see, it has followed us here. We come to Germany ... we leave all behind. I was young. I do not remember clearly. It was a long journey. I remember we had a wheelbarrow. We brought what we could. We were so weary. We slept anywhere we could find a place. Some people were kind to us. I do not know how long it went on. When you are young you forget so much. There are gaps in the memory. One forgets what one does not want to remember."

"Does it upset you to recall it?"

She shook her head. "It helps," she said. "What happened then ... what happens now. There is a pattern to life. That was the beginning ... and now it seems I return to it at the end."

"I am so sorry."

"It is life. We settled in Germany. We think, this is the good country. It seemed so. Those who worked hard were rewarded. My father became a tailor. He was very good. He worked hard. We were poor for a long time ... but then he has his own shop. Then he has two shops ... and three. I had brothers. We all worked together. Then one day, when I was in the shop, a handsome man comes in. My father is to make a suit for him. We met and fell in love. It was the Grossvater."

"And you were happy then?"

"Very happy. I came to the schloss. I have been here ever since. At first it was wonderful and then the war comes. Then not so good. Disaster and defeat. We were not rich any more. But we kept on at the schloss and things grew better. We are becoming prosperous again . . . and then . . ."

"This started," I said. "But to you it was not entirely unexpected."

She shook her head. "I was waiting for it. It has happened to others. My son thought we were too remote . . . not important enough. We have never made much show that we are Jewish. Someone must have told."

I knew who that was. Else had informed her lover.

I did not mention this as the girl was still with them and I guessed it would disturb Grossmutter.

"I want you to know how happy I am that you are taking Gretchen with you. She is a dear girl . . . a good girl. They are pleased . . . my son and his wife . . . that the good Edward feels love for her. He will take care of her."

"I wish we could take you all."

She laughed. "You are a good girl. I knew that when I first saw you. Your sister . . . your twin, eh? . . . she is very attractive . . . but light-hearted. You are a good, kind girl. It is a great weight from our minds that Gretchen goes with you."

"I am so glad that she is coming."

"And the young man . . . he is a good young man. Earnest . . . reliable . . . I hope much that all will go as we hope. It is the old pattern. It is with us through the ages. It is our heritage . . . and who are we to question it? My dear child, I shall think of you and be so grateful that you came to us. You will see what is happening here and you can tell your people at home."

I bent and kissed her wrinkled cheek and she put out a hand and touched mine.

"May the blessing of the Lord God go with you," she said.

When I came down, Frau Brandt said to me: "Grossmutter has been talking to you?"

"Yes," I said. "It was very moving."

"Her childhood in Russia?"

"Yes," I answered.

"Poor Grossmutter. She is sad about all this. She thought

she had done with that when she left her homeland all those years ago. Now here it is again. We have been through some hard years and now that we seem to be coming to some prosperity again ... this comes. Well, I want you to know how grateful we are to you for taking Gretchen back with you."

"She is worried about leaving you."

"Yes, poor Gretchen. But she wants to go ... if she stayed she could not be happy to say goodbye to Edward."

"I know."

Her eyes shone with hope. "And now we are happy for her ... and so grateful to you all. I worry about her more than Kurt and Helmut. The boys can take better care of themselves. We shall be thinking of you."

"And we shall be thinking of you."

"Yes, I know. This has not been just a holiday ... a brief stay with friends, has it? What happened the other night has been significant. I do not want Gretchen to grieve for us. Our people have been persecuted throughout the ages. It has made us strong. We have suffered in the past and we shall in the future. But we shall survive. We always have."

She took me into her arms and we embraced.

She was right. What had happened—deeply shocking as it was—had brought us all together.

Soon after that we said our final farewells and left.

We crossed the Channel that night. The sea was calm and we sat on deck, huddled in rugs, for the night air was chilly.

The stars were brilliant against a dark blue velvet sky. There were not many people on deck. The majority of the passengers had decided to stay below. Not far from me sat Gretchen and Edward, their chairs close. I saw that they were holding hands. And then there was Dorabella and Dermot Tregarland. To her delight, Dermot had traveled with us.

So much had happened during that brief holiday. Love was much in evidence. I thought the course of four people's lives had been changed—five if I considered my own, for what touched Dorabella must be of importance to me, too. Romance and love were charming, and on this occasion they had blossomed among much which was ugly.

I felt apart. Looking up at the stars, I was aware of the enormity of the universe. I felt alone and rather sad, shut out in a way. Edward and Gretchen ... Dorabella and Dermot ...

I wondered if this was significant and whether love was destined to pass me by.

The Cornish Adventure

We parted from Dermot in London. He went to Paddington to get his train to Cornwall, and Dorabella, Edward, Gretchen, and I caught the first train to Hampshire.

From London I telephoned home to ask them to meet us and to take the opportunity to explain that Gretchen would be with us.

I spoke to my father. I was glad he answered, for he always accepted what we did as a matter of course. My mother might have been inclined to want explanations.

"We're home, Daddy," I said.

"Wonderful." I could never hear his voice after an absence without emotion. "What time is your train, darling?"

I told him.

"Daddy," I went on, "we've got someone with us. It's Kurt's sister. We want her to stay for a while. Tell you all about it when we meet."

"That's fine," he said. "I'll tell your mother. Can't wait to see you. It seems a long time."

I was smiling when I put down the telephone. I was thinking of all we had to tell them.

Gretchen said rather apprehensively: "Did you tell them I was with you?"

"I did."

"And ... er ... do they mind? What did your mother say?"

"It was my father. He just said, 'That's fine.' They're used to our bringing people home from school, aren't they, Dorabella?"

"Oh, yes," she said. "Without notice, too. They never minded."

She was looking a little bereft because she had had to part with Dermot, although they had made arrangements to see each other very soon. He was going to be asked to visit us. I knew it would not be long before the invitation would be issued. My parents would be very eager to see him.

They were both at the station to greet us. Dorabella and I flung ourselves at them, and we all hugged each other as though we had been apart for months. There were tears in my mother's eyes.

"I'm so glad you're home," she said. "And you are looking well." She glanced at Dorabella. Her perceptive eyes had recognized that something had happened.

I said: "There are lots and lots of things to tell you."

"Well," said my father, "let's get the luggage in and then we'll hear all about it."

"And this is Gretchen . . . Kurt's sister."

"Hello, Gretchen," said my mother. "How nice of you to visit us."

She kissed Edward and he gave her that special look which meant he needed her help. She was excited. She loved to be involved in family affairs and, of course, Edward was one of the family in her eyes.

It was always wonderful to come home. It had been like this coming home from school. There was always so much we had to tell them.

It was comforting to see Caddington again. Everything seemed so right there. There was nothing ugly lurking in the dark corners of our home.

Dorabella was soon telling them about the most marvelous man we had ever met. "He must be asked here, Mummy. You'll love him."

My mother was all eagerness to hear. Dorabella prattled on.

"He lives in Cornwall. He is Cornish, actually. Dermot Tregarland. Isn't it a lovely name? He's very amusing, isn't he, Violetta? We liked him very much."

"What was he doing in Germany?" asked my mother.

"Walking."

"You met him at the schloss."

"Well, not exactly. He was staying in the town."

"I look forward to learning all about him. And he is coming here, you say?"

"You'll love him," repeated Dorabella.

"When is he coming?"

"I thought we'd work that out with you."

"I'm glad of that," said my mother with light-hearted irony. Then she turned to Gretchen and said how glad she was that her family had let her come to stay with us.

Gretchen replied that it was indeed good of her to allow her to do so.

My mother did not say that she had been given no choice in the matter, but I saw the amused smile on her lips.

She had once mentioned the fact to my father that we rarely consulted her about the people we brought home and it was the custom for her to be presented with them at a moment's notice. To this he had replied in his indulgent way: "Well, darling, it is their home, you know."

When we arrived at the house, Gretchen expressed the usual admiration of its antiquity. Robert came dashing out. He was back from Devon and would, to his chagrin, soon be going back to school. He was introduced to Gretchen.

"Kurt's sister," he said. "Where's Kurt? Why didn't you bring him back?"

"How was Devon?" I asked.

"Brilliant," he said. "But I'd rather have been in Germany. It must have been fun."

And so we had arrived home.

No sooner was I in my room than my parents came to see me. I had expected them. They would want to know more about this young man whom Dorabella seemed to be so involved with.

I gave them a brief account of what had happened, how we had met Dermot, how he had rescued us when we might have been lost in the forest, and I went on to the attack on the schloss and the reason why we had brought Gretchen with us.

They were astounded and deeply shocked.

"Poor Edward," said my mother. "He seems to be fond of the girl."

"It is all rather sudden," said my father.

"Well, these things happen," put in my mother. "Of course, Edward has visited them before and she is Kurt's sister.

Sooner or later he would be thinking of marriage. But what of Dorabella's affair? She is very young."

"We are the same age," I reminded her.

"Yes . . . but she always seems younger. And . . . she is very impressionable."

"It will probably blow over," suggested my father.

"Violetta, how does it seem to you?" asked my mother. "You've seen her go through these stages before."

"I think this is rather more than usual."

"Really! And what do you think of the young man?"

"He's very pleasant . . . very charming. He was extremely good at getting us out of the forest."

They wanted a more detailed account of that adventure.

"It seems a very dangerous place," said my mother, frowning.

"It seemed idyllic until all that happened. Then it became horrible. But it is what is happening all over Germany."

I could see their minds were on Dorabella.

"We'll ask the young man here as soon as possible," said my mother. "Then we'll see what we think of him."

"Perhaps Dorabella has already made up her mind that she is going to marry him," suggested my father.

"She has been known to change her mind . . ."

At that moment Dorabella herself came bursting in.

"I knew I'd find you here. Learning all about it, of course, from *sensible* Violetta. Well, what has she been telling you?"

"About the adventurous time you had in Germany," said my father.

"Oh, it was wonderful . . . until all that put an end to it. Dermot was marvelous, wasn't he, Violetta? The way he got us out of that place . . . and then he rescued us in the forest, you know."

"He was the perfect knight," I said.

"Actually, he is really rather marvelous. Wait until you two see him."

"I suggest we do not wait too long before we do," said my mother. "We'll invite him very soon."

Dorabella hugged her.

"You will love him. You really will. I have never met anyone quite like him. He's the nearest thing to Daddy you can have."

My father was greatly touched, but I could see my mother was wondering whether this was just another of Dorabella's transient enthusiasms.

Edward took Gretchen to see my grandparents. Their house was as much home to him as ours was, for my mother had only been about sixteen when she took him home and her mother had really brought him up.

A few weeks after our return Dermot Tregarland visited us. People sometimes seem different against another background and I wondered whether Dermot would. But no, he was the same exuberant, charming person at Caddington as he had been in the Böhmerwald.

He was interested in the house, which he naturally compared with his own home. There were many similarities, he told us. He wanted us all to pay a visit to Cornwall soon.

By this time it was mid-September and Dermot stayed with us for two weeks and, I think, during that time my parents decided that he would be a suitable match for their daughter.

He met people in the neighborhood—the doctor and his family, the rector and his—and although there was as yet no announcement of an engagement, it was taken for granted that he was Dorabella's fiancé.

Dorabella was at the height of excitement. She was radiant and her happiness enhanced her beauty.

In contrast to her exuberance, I felt faintly depressed. I was lusterless beside her. I came to the conclusion that I did not want change. I wanted us to be schoolgirls again. Perhaps I was a little resentful that she needed me less. Someone else had moved closer to her. Dorabella was in love. I was dearly loved by my family, but it was not the same.

Perhaps I felt envious. Always before, when people noticed her and made much of her, I accepted the fact that I lacked her charm, and I had been pleased that she was so popular. I might be becoming a little tired of being the sensible one . . . the one who was expected to take responsibility . . . the one who must be there when needed to help Dorabella.

It had been my role to look after her, and although sometimes I may have complained, I did not want that changed.

I often thought back to that moment when Else's young

man had suddenly stood up and begun the riot. I thought that after that nothing would ever be the same again.

That was nonsense. This would have come in any case. It had had nothing to do with the riot. Dorabella would have met Dermot—and even if she had not met him, it would have been someone else one day.

But now, because of what had happened, I was aware of evil as I had never been previously. I could not accept life as I had done previously.

It was arranged that we should pay a visit to Dermot's house. My mother decided that we would not wait until Christmas, much to my brother's disgust. He declared that beastly school was going to spoil things for him yet again.

It was October when we left for Cornwall—my parents, Dorabella, and I. We spent a night in London in what had been my grandparents' home in Westminster and which was now the home of my uncle Charles. My grandparents were at Marchlands most of the time but came up to London on this occasion to see us. Edward and Gretchen were staying at Marchlands. I wondered whether Gretchen compared Epping Forest with the Böhmerwald.

"What a nice girl Gretchen is," said my grandmother. "Don't you think so, Lucinda?"

My mother said she did. My uncle Charles and his wife, Sylvia, were very interested in the political situation and as a Member of Parliament, my uncle knew a great deal more about world affairs than we did. He muttered something about not liking the noises that fellow Hitler was making.

We were all too excited at the prospect of the Cornish visit to pay much attention to that, and the next day we left for Paddington and the West Country.

It was a long journey across the country through Wiltshire, with its prehistoric sites, to red-soiled Devon where the train ran along the coast; and then across the Tamar and we were in Cornwall. Very soon after that we arrived at our destination.

Dermot was waiting for us on the platform.

He and Dorabella greeted each other with rapture; then he welcomed the rest of us. His car was in the station yard.

He summoned a porter who touched his cap, and he was told to bring the luggage to the car.

"Yes, Mr. Tregarland, sir," he said in a Cornish accent. "You be leaving that to me, sir."

The luggage was put into the boot of the car and we drove away.

"It is so good to have you here," said Dermot.

My father was seated beside him in the front, my mother with Dorabella and me at the back.

"It's good to be here," said my father. He sniffed appreciatively. "Wonderful air," he said.

"Best in the world, we do say, sir," said Dermot in a fair imitation of the porter's accent. "You know how people are. Theirs is always best. They delude themselves into believing it."

"It is not a bad idea," said my mother. "It makes for contentment."

"I can't wait to see the house," said Dorabella.

"That is something you will have to do, my dear," said my mother. "But not for long. How long, Dermot?"

"It will be for some twenty minutes," he told her.

"Everything seems to grow so well here," said my father.

"We get lots of rain and very little frost to kill things off. We're a cosy little corner of the island, in fact. Though our gales can be terrific . . . very wild. There is something about the place which reminds me of the Böhmerwald, though it is very different. They have their trolls . . . and Thor, Odin, and the rest, but I can tell you we have our little gang of supernatural beings who have to be placated at times. Piskies . . . knackers . . . and specially those who have 'the powers,' as we call them. They can do the most frightful things to you merely by looking at you."

"You are making us tremble," said my mother lightly.

"Don't worry. Ignore them and they will do the same to you. It is only those who go looking for them who get the unpleasant surprises."

"It sounds fascinating," said Dorabella.

Dermot took his eyes from the road to smile at her.

We went through a village with stark gray stone cottages and a plain rather dour-looking building which I took to be a church.

The trees almost met across the road, making a roof for us to pass under; there was lush foliage growing everywhere; and the luxuriant beauty of the country made up for a lack of architectural elegance.

Then I saw the sea and black rocks about which the waves broke rhythmically, sending up white spray into the air.

"Not far now," said Dermot. "Down there . . ." He indicated with his head, ". . . is the little town. A fishing village, really—not much more; the river divides it into two, West and East Poldown, joined by an ancient bridge which was built five centuries ago. There are a church and a square . . . and the quay, of course, and there you'll see the fishermen mending their nets or bringing in the catch while their boats are bobbing up and down in the water. We don't have to go down into the town now. Actually, it's only about half a mile from the house. We can see it from the windows."

We were going uphill and came to a high road. And there, ahead of us, was the house itself.

It looked impressive, perched as it was on the edge of the cliff. It was not unlike Caddington and must have been built around the same time. I thought, Dorabella will be going from one ancient house to another.

"It's wonderful," said Dorabella. "Dermot, you didn't tell me how beautiful it was."

"I'm glad you like it," he replied. "When I saw your home I thought it was very fine indeed, and I wondered what you would think of this."

We were all murmuring our appreciation. I did not say that I thought it had about it an air of menace. I dismissed the thought. It was due to that jaundiced view I was beginning to take of everything since what I had seen at the schloss. Also, it was taking me yet another step away from Dorabella.

There was a drive up to the gate house; we passed under this and were in a courtyard.

"Here we are," said Dermot. "Come along in. Someone will take care of the bags. Oh, there you are, Jack."

A man came forward. He touched his cap to us.

"Take the luggage, Jack. Tess will show you where it goes."

"Aye, sir," said the man.

We went into a stone-floored hall with a high-vaulted ceiling. As we did so, our footsteps rang out on the floor and I noticed the customary array of weapons on the walls very similar to ours at Caddington, to signify that the family had done its duty to the defense of its country, I had always supposed. There was a similarity about hundreds of such houses all over England.

A woman was coming down the staircase at the end of the hall. She was dressed in a pale blue cotton gown with white collar and cuffs. I knew who this was before Dermot introduced us, because he had already described the household to us.

She would be Matilda Lewyth, who had looked after the house since Dermot's mother had died and he was about five years old. She was, in fact, the housekeeper, but not known as such because she was a distant connection of the family. I gathered that she had fallen on hard times when, as a widow, she had come here with her son, Gordon, to manage the household for Dermot's father. She had stayed and looked after it to everyone's satisfaction and had been doing so over the last twenty years. We all knew who Matilda Lewyth was.

She welcomed us now as our hostess.

"We are so pleased that you have come," she said. "Dermot has told us all about you. And this is Miss Denver . . ."

"Dorabella," said Dorabella. "And I know you are Mrs. Lewyth."

"And Sir Robert and Lady Denver," she said, turning to my parents. "And . . ."

"Violetta," I introduced myself.

"Violetta . . . Dorabella . . . what pretty names!"

We explained about the operas and there was gentle laughter.

"What a romantic idea! We are so glad you came all this way to see us," said Mrs. Lewyth. "You will meet Dermot's father at dinner. He suffers . . . from gout . . . and is very often confined to his room. But he is very eager to meet you. We have to be careful with him. He is more than a little infirm. Then there is my son, Gordon. He has grown up here and is deeply concerned in estate business. He runs the place . . . practically." She sent a deprecating smile in Dermot's direction. "He and Dermot between them," she added quickly.

She turned to Dorabella. "But I suppose Dermot has told you a great deal about the family."

"Oh, yes," said Dorabella. "He has talked about you all."

"And now, you must be tired. It's a long journey. Would you like to rest before dinner?"

"Oh, no," cried Dorabella. "I'm far too excited for that."

Mrs. Lewyth smiled indulgently and looked at my parents.

"We are not really tired," said my mother. "We're just longing to meet everybody."

"Well then, I'll have you shown to your rooms and then you can wash . . . unpack, perhaps, and then come down and have a chat and a drink before dinner." She looked at her watch. "I'll have dinner put forward a little, but I'll make sure there's time for a chat beforehand."

We were taken to our rooms. The house was so large that there was plenty of accommodation and Dorabella and I had a room side by side.

I stood in the center of mine and surveyed it. My suitcase was already there. It was a large room with a high ceiling; the windows were leaded and the curtains of heavy dark blue velvet. It was not overfurnished; there was a four-poster bed, a heavy ornate wardrobe, a chest on which stood two highly polished candlesticks, a dressing table with a swing-back mirror, two easy chairs and two smaller ones, and a table with a wash-hand basin and ewer. There was not a great deal of light from the leaded windows and it seemed full of shadows; and because one could not but be aware of its antiquity, one could not help wondering how many people had slept here . . . and what tragedies . . . and perhaps comedies . . . had occurred within the seclusion of these walls. I was in a foolish and fanciful mood, and I could trace it all back to that horrific experience in the schloss. I told myself I must get that out of my mind.

I unpacked my case, washed, put on a dark red dress, and sat before the swing-back mirror to comb my hair. The mirror was about two hundred years old, I guessed, and the glass was slightly mottled. It seemed to distort my face so that the features which looked back at me did not appear entirely to be my own.

What was the matter with me? I was looking for evil everywhere, I admonished myself. I must forget that scene. But I could not get out of my mind the memory of Else's lover in that moment when he had risen from his seat and set the riot in motion. There had been what I could only call the look of a predatory animal on his face . . . mindlessness, unreasoning hatred . . . in love with cruelty . . . cold and pitiless.

Matilda Lewyth seemed to be a kindly woman; the house was wonderful . . . ancient, yes, but so was Caddington, my own home. I did not feel that overpowering aura of the past there; yet it had its histories, its legendary specters as such houses will have, but it was dominated by my loving parents who had completely suppressed such echoes from the past.

I could not shake off this ridiculous feeling even though I reminded myself continually that it was all due to that unfortunate incident at the schloss.

There was a tap on my door and, without waiting for me to answer, Dorabella came in.

She had put on a blue dress and looked very beautiful.

"Oh, Vee," she cried, using the shortened version of my name. "Isn't it exciting!"

I could only agree that it was.

A maid came to take us down. She was Myrtle, she told us. She was black-eyed, black-haired with a rather Spanish look. She told us her sister, Tess, worked at the house, too. She spoke with a pronounced Cornish accent, which had a certain melody to it, but was not always easy to understand.

If we wanted anything, either she or Tess would bring it.

"All you do have to do is say, Miss," we were told.

We thanked her. I noticed her lively eyes examining Dorabella intently while I received only a cursory glance.

We were taken down some stairs along a corridor and down another set of stairs.

"This be the punch room," said Myrtle. "This be where Mrs. Lewyth 'ull be waiting for 'ee."

She opened a door and we went in.

Matilda Lewyth rose and came toward us. I noticed a man sitting in an armchair and guessed him to be Dermot's father. He seemed rather old. Dermot must have been born late in his life as was sometimes the case. One of his legs was bandaged.

Dermot came forward smiling.

"Do come in," said Mrs. Lewyth. "James . . ." She turned to the man in the chair. "These are the young ladies."

We approached the chair. I thought he must be in his sixties. He had rather penetrating eyes, very lively, very shrewd, and

I had a feeling that he was regarding us somewhat mischievously, for his chin moved a little, as though he were finding it difficult to suppress secret laughter.

Dermot had come to stand between us. He put an arm through mine as he did with Dorabella.

"Father," he said. "This is Violetta and this is Dorabella."

The old man's eyes were on Dorabella . . . assessing her . . . rather boldly, I thought . . . appreciatively?

"My dears," he said in a very musical voice, "you must forgive my not rising. This accursed gout. It is devilishly incapacitating at times."

"It is so kind of you to invite us here," said Dorabella. "We are really very excited to be here."

His eyes were turned on me.

"Twin sisters," he said. "That is interesting. You must tell me about yourselves . . . sometime . . ."

Matilda Lewyth came forward.

"Please sit down and tell me what you would like to drink. Dorabella, you sit there near Mr. Tregarland. Violetta . . . you here."

My parents arrived then.

"I am glad you sent that nice maid to bring us down," said my mother. "We should have been lost otherwise."

I watched the introductions and Mr. Tregarland's interest in my parents.

When we were all seated we were given our drinks, and the conversation was of that conventional nature which is often employed when people meet for the first time. The differences between Hampshire and Cornwall were discussed, the journey, the state of the government, and all the time I was wondering what old Mr. Tregarland and Mrs. Lewyth were really thinking about us; and whether they were as eager to welcome Dorabella into the family as they seemed to imply.

Then Gordon Lewyth arrived.

I knew who he was, of course, because Dermot had explained the family to us and had referred more than once to Gordon Lewyth; but I was unprepared for such a man.

He was dark-haired and tall—being well over six feet—which gave him a commanding appearance. He was also broad-shouldered, which accentuated that certain effect of power.

Matilda Lewyth rose and cried: "Gordon . . . my dear." She went to him and he kissed her lightly on the cheek. "Our visitors," she added.

He shook hands with my father and then my mother.

"These are the twins—Violetta and Dorabella," said Matilda Lewyth.

His handshake was firm and strong.

"We are pleased to see you," he said. I wondered if it was a little like the royal "we." Was he a little arrogant? I wondered. I thought he might be. There was a nonchalance about him, which might have been deliberate, as though he were telling us that although he said he was pleased, that was merely for the sake of convention and he was quite indifferent to our presence.

"Dinner is about to be served," said Matilda, and I had an idea that we had been waiting for his arrival.

"Then let us go straight in," he said.

I noticed that his attention was on Dorabella. She seemed a little flustered, but pleased, and aware of his attention. I imagined he was not assessing her charms so much as wondering what such an acquisition to the family would mean.

We went into the dining room. Dorabella was seated between Dermot and his father. Next to me was Gordon Lewyth and on the other side of him my mother.

I noticed his strong hands. He emanated strength, and I wondered what his position was here. It was true that Matilda Lewyth was treated like a member of the family, but I guessed they might be poor relations. Perhaps a deep consciousness of this fact might account for his determination to assert his importance. It was almost imperceptible, it was true, but it was there.

And what was his real position in the household? The son of the housekeeper! Yet he seemed to be managing the estate . . . with Dermot. If one had not known that, one would think that he was the master of the house.

He talked to my mother and then, dutifully, turned to me. He asked about Caddington and the estate there.

I said: "I suppose there is a similarity about all estates."

He replied that this was possibly so. But in different parts of the country there must be different ways of going about things. There were hazards . . . and blessings . . . of certain climates, for instance, and it was amazing how they could vary throughout the country.

"We have a rainfall which in some ways can be very provoking and in others a blessing. Then there are the strong winds at times along the coast."

"The estate is very large, I suppose."

"Not compared with some. Perhaps in this part of the world it would be called large. It extends inland. Being near the sea has its handicaps."

"Are you very isolated?"

"Not really. Poldown, the little fishing village—a town in miniature—is not very far away."

"You can see it from the windows, I believe."

"That's true."

"I'm looking forward to visiting it."

"I doubt you will find much of interest there. I suppose you visit London frequently?"

"Well ... occasionally. My uncle has a house in Westminster. When we go to Town we stay there usually. But we are in the country, mainly. My sister and I have only recently left school, so we have been away from home for a lot of the last few years."

"I see. Well, you asked if we are isolated and the answer is no. The estate fans out, you understand. Perhaps when it gets inland it might be a little isolated. You could ride some way without meeting anyone. There is an estate which adjoins ours, Jermyn's."

"I see."

"We're not good friends with them. The families never liked each other. It's some quarrel which goes back for generations. I am not quite sure what it was all about. It was long before my time. However, the Tregarlands and the Jermyns don't mix."

"A sort of Capulet and Montague affair?"

"It might be that."

"That sort of thing is usually the result of something which doesn't really matter at all. Then the daughter of one house marries the son of the other and all is happy ever after."

"I have a vague idea that in this case it may have started something like that. So there would have to be a different sequel."

I laughed.

"So we shall not meet the Jermyns," I said.

"I can assure you that they will not be invited here." He looked at me intently. "So you and your sister are twins," he said.

"Yes."

"There is a slight resemblance."

"I think it is quite a strong one, and you say slight."

He said: "Yes, I repeat, slight."

I immediately thought: He means I am not as attractive as Dorabella and that he probably finds me rather dull.

I became intent on my food and he turned to my mother.

There was little conversation which I recalled after that, and when the meal was over we went back to the punch room where coffee was served; and after an hour or so Matilda Lewyth whispered to my mother that we must be tired after our journey and she was sure we should like to retire early.

My mother said that was a good idea, so the party broke up and we went to our rooms.

There was a fire in mine, yet the eeriness I had sensed on my arrival had increased. I went to the curtains and drew them back. There was enough moon to show a path of light across the water. I could hear the faint murmuring of the sea as it broke against the rocks below.

I turned back to the room. I would leave the curtains open. If I did not, I should feel shut in.

I waited for the door to open, for I guessed Dorabella would come in. I was right.

She looked beautiful in her blue silk nightdress and negligee, with her hair hanging about her shoulders.

She stood leaning against the door, smiling.

"You don't have to look surprised," she said. "You knew I'd come. What do you think of all this?"

"Interesting."

"It's more than that. It's fascinating . . . meeting them all."

"It must be for you, if you are going to be part of it . . . mistress of this place. Just think of it."

"It's a bit like Caddington, isn't it? Except for the sea . . . we don't have that."

"Nor the people. What of them?"

"I say . . . what do you think of *him*?"

"As there were several members of the male sex, which one do you mean?"

"Gordon Lewyth, of course."

"I don't know him well enough to say."

"You are maddening. You are so precise about everything. I mean what was your impression?"

"I think he wants everyone to know he is not merely the son of the housekeeper."

"Well, Matilda Lewyth could hardly be called a housekeeper."

"I don't know enough about them yet. It's all rather unusual."

"Oh, it's perfectly clear. She came here when Dermot's mother died. It was a sort of favor. They were members of the family ... poor relations, I imagine. I think she is very nice, don't you? As for him ... Gordon, I mean ... well, I think he's interesting. And ..." She giggled. "I think he's rather pleased ... about me."

"You're not thinking of transferring your favors, are you?"

"Don't be an idiot!"

"When you are married you will have to settle down, you know."

"What's all this about? I merely said I thought he was rather pleased ... and interested."

"I suppose anyone would be interested in someone who was going to join their family."

She looked at me in exasperation, and I felt vaguely perturbed. She had fallen in love with Dermot at great speed. I wondered whether she could fall out of love as quickly. This was absurd. She had always been susceptible to admiration—and she would naturally assume that Gordon Lewyth's interest was admiration.

She said: "I think the father liked me, too. He told me it would be a pleasure to have a pretty young girl about the place."

"So you have made a good impression on your future in-laws."

"I think so. Dermot wants to get married in the spring. Do you think that would be a good idea?"

"It seems rather soon. Has it occurred to you that this time last year you did not know him?"

"What's that got to do with it?"

"Something, I should imagine. After all, you want to know quite a lot about people with whom you propose to spend the rest of your life."

"Dermot and I know a good deal about each other."

"And he still wants to marry you?" I retorted in mock surprise.

"Don't tease! I think we are going to have an exciting time here. I was dreading it in a way. I did not think it would be like this. They have welcomed me so wonderfully . . . Matilda . . . and . . . Dermot's father."

"And Gordon Lewyth," I said.

She frowned slightly. "I'm not altogether sure about him. He is not easy to know. I think he is very interested, but . . ."

I laughed at her. I said: "If Dermot's father approves, that's all that matters really. And as for Matilda . . . she likes you. I suppose she will continue to run the house and frankly, I can't see you wanting to do that. I'm sure she can't, either, and that will surely please her."

She laughed.

"It is wonderful. I am sure about this, Vee . . . I really am. Particularly now I've seen it all."

"Well, then, everything should be all right. So . . . should we say goodnight."

"Goodnight, Twinnie."

I smiled. It was the name she used for me when she was in some quandary from which she wanted me to extricate her. Now it was meant to be a reminder of the closeness between us, but I did wonder if she was quite as contented—and as certain—as she wanted me to believe.

When she had gone I undressed and got into bed.

I lay for a long time listening to the gentle swishing of the waves below and wondering what the future would be. She would marry and come here and we should be apart for the first time in our lives.

The days were full of interest. Dermot and Dorabella were together a great deal and he liked to take her riding, or they would go off in the car. He seemed very proud of her and he wanted to introduce her to some of the tenants and people in the neighborhood. She was enjoying it all immensely. My mother was very interested in the running of the house and my father in the estate, and consequently he had formed a friendship with Gordon, which was natural as they shared an enthusiasm.

That left myself who was interested in them all as people but shared no special enthusiasms with any of them.

My mother, of course, always drew me into whatever she was doing, and when Matilda Lewyth said she was eager to show her the house, she insisted that I would be interested to accompany them on a tour of it.

My father had gone off with Gordon to see some new contraption which was being put into one of the barns on the home farm, and Dorabella was with Dermot—so there were just the three of us.

Matilda was very knowledgeable about the house and she showed a great love for it. My mother said afterwards that she seemed to care about it more than James Tregarland did, or Dermot, for that matter, who would one day own it.

"I find these old places quite fascinating," said Matilda. "It is amazing how they have stood up to attacks in the wars, and then there are the hazards of the weather. Mind you, *they* have taken their toll. After the gales there is usually something wrong . . . roofs of the farm buildings and so on . . . fences blown down . . . and all that."

"How far off is the home farm?" asked my mother.

"About half a mile. It's close to Jermyn Priory . . . that's the Jermyns' place."

"The enemy," I said.

She laughed. "Oh, you've heard then."

My mother wanted to know what we were talking about.

"There's a feud between the two families," Matilda explained. "It's been going on for years. We're not sure what it's about. The details are lost in the past, but somehow it remains."

"And they live nearby?"

"The estates border on each other."

"That's very close."

"Not really. Jermyns is vast . . . bigger than this, and we are by no means small. We rarely see them."

"And if you do," I said, "I suppose you behave as though you don't."

"We might give a nod of recognition, but no more. I never heard what it was all about. It goes back far into the past."

"You'd think it would be forgotten."

"We Cornish keep these things going. We stick to the old ways and traditions. You English are inclined to let such things slide away. We don't."

"You mean you bear grudges?" I asked.

My mother looked at me sharply. I was noted for speaking my mind.

"Well," said Matilda, "I suppose that sort of thing becomes a habit."

"I wonder what it was all about," said my mother.

Matilda lifted her shoulders and the matter was dropped as we examined the house.

"The main building is Elizabethan," said Matilda. "But the west wing was added after the Restoration and the east after that . . . so it is a bit of a hotchpotch of periods."

"Which makes it more interesting," I said, and my mother agreed.

We first went to the great hall, which was one of the oldest parts of the house. It must have looked much the same when it was built. On its stone walls hung weapons from the past, perhaps to warn any intruders that this was a warlike family accustomed to defending itself. There was a long table.

"Cromwellian," said Matilda, "and the chairs date from the reign of Charles II. The family were fiercely Royalist so that they had a bad time during the Protectorate, but all was well with the return of the King."

Leading from the hall was the chapel. It was small with an altar, pulpit, and a row of pews. There was an atmosphere of chill in the place. I looked up at the waggon roof with its stone corbels, and then at the carved angels who appeared to be supporting the pulpit. I could imagine the family's gathering here in times of tribulation—and rejoicing, too. A great deal would have happened in this chapel.

"It is not used a great deal now," said Matilda. "James—Dermot's father—says that when he was young there were prayers every morning and all the servants had to attend. He laughs and says he always declared that when he came into possession people should be left to look after their own souls without any help from the Tregarlands. James can be a little ir-reverent at times." She was smiling indulgently.

We mounted the main staircase and were in the long gallery. Here were pictures of Tregarlands, which must have been painted over the last three hundred years. I recognized James Tregarland. I could detect that mischievous look in his eyes which I had noticed at our first meeting.

Matilda stood looking at him rather sadly.

"He has always lived very well," she said. "He was one to enjoy life. He married late in life. She was quite young . . . his wife, I mean. She was delicate, though. She died when Dermot was very young."

"And he didn't marry again."

She gazed at the picture. I could not understand the expression in her eyes.

She shook her head firmly. "It would have been the best thing," she said. "The right thing . . ."

"Well," said my mother. "It has all worked out very well. You look after them beautifully."

"I do my best. If we take this staircase we come to the upper rooms."

There were several bedrooms—one in which Charles I slept during the Civil War.

It was an interesting morning.

Our visit, which was to be of a week's duration, was nearly over. During the day a strong wind blew up and by the evening it had become a gale.

We had heard them speak of the ferocity of the gales and during the morning my mother and I had gone into Poldown.

It was a charming place with the small river cutting the little town in half, so there were East and West Poldown.

In the harbor the fishing boats were tethered; they were bobbing up and down because of the rising wind. *The Saucy Jane, The Mary Ann, The Beatrice,* and *Wonder Girl.*

"Why," I asked my mother, "are boats feminine?"

"Not all," she answered. "Look. There's *The Jolly Roger.*"

Seated on the stones the fishermen were mending their nets; overhead the gulls screeched, swooped, and rose again; the wind caught at our skirts and pulled at our hair.

Although we had been here such a short time, some of the

inhabitants of Poldown seemed to know us. I had heard us referred to as "They folk up to Tregarland's." We walked through what was a sort of high street with shops on either side in which were displayed souvenirs ... shells, ashtrays with "Poldown" printed on them, crockery, glassware, and little figures of strange creatures which I understood were piskies. There were buckets, spades, nets, and swimming gear. A smell of baking bread and cooking pervaded the air. We saw Cornish pasties and cakes for sale. It was a busy little place.

We bought a few things for the sheer pleasure of hearing the people speak.

"How be enjoying Poldown?" we were asked.

We told them very much.

"Ah, it be grand up there in the big house, certain sure. There be a real gale working up. I wouldn't want to be out on the sea as it'll be tonight ... not for a farm, I wouldn't. Old Nick himself 'ull be out there, looking for them as 'ull keep his fires going."

We listened and thought it was all very quaint. Then we walked back to the house. It was hard going uphill against the wind which was blowing in from the south-west, and we were quite breathless when we reached the house.

Matilda said: "I'm glad you're back. It's no day to be out. I was afraid you might be blown off the cliff."

That night we heard the full force of the gale. I looked down from my window on a sea which had become a seething torrent. The waves rose high and flung themselves against the house with such fury that I felt it might be battered to pieces. I could not believe that this raging fury was the same sea which a few days before had been so calm and pellucid ... reflecting an azure blue sky. It was possessed of a maniacal anger and seemed intent on destruction.

I could not sleep. I lay listening to it and it was not until the dawn came that it started to abate.

The first thing I noticed when I awoke was that the wind had dropped. I went to the window. There were still frothy white horses riding the waves and I saw debris on the shore—broken pieces of wood and seaweed.

I dressed and went into Dorabella's room.

"What a night!" she said. "I thought it was going to blow the house away."

"We've now experienced one of the gales which they are always talking about."

"It's all right now, though. Dermot is going to take me into Plymouth today . . . for a special reason." She looked a little arch.

"Ah," I said. "The ring. Is that it?"

"How did you guess?"

"You know I always guess your thoughts. I detect that acquisitive look."

"Our engagement ring! Isn't it wonderful?"

"Yes," I said. "Life can be wonderful."

"What will you do?"

"I'd rather like to go for a ride this afternoon."

"With whom?"

"I rather fancy my own company."

"Do you really mean that?"

"Yes. I would like to take dear old Starlight. That's her name, isn't it?"

"You mean the chestnut mare?"

"Yes. I like her and I don't think she is averse to me."

"I daresay no one will object."

I did not think they would, either.

We breakfasted at odd times so that we could have it at our convenience to fit in with our plans.

My mother and I went down to the town in the morning. We saw that some of the fishing boats had broken their moorings and had drifted out to sea.

"These October gales can be something cruel," Miss Polgenny, who ran the wool shop, told us. "We had warnings enough, I will say. Sometimes there be none. That can be terrible, I can tell 'ee. Why, Tommy Yeo was lost out there . . . him and his brother Billy. 'Twas said that they did meet parson on the way to the boats. Everyone do know that to see a parson before you sail be unlucky."

My mother and I exchanged a glance. We should take a long time to learn all that must be done to escape the forces of evil.

My mother was buying some wool and Miss Polgenny gave her attention to that.

" 'Twas three ply then, was it? And what a pretty color. You be going to enjoy work on that."

She put the wool into a bag. I leaned forward to take it and in doing so dropped my glove. I stooped and picked it up.

"Oh," said Miss Polgenny, looking at me with horror. " 'Ee shouldn't 'a done that. That means a disappointment before the end of the day."

"What should I have done?" I asked.

"You should 'a left it there, me dear—and let someone else pick it up."

"What sort of disappointment?" I asked.

" 'Twill be someone you'll meet and maybe 'twere better you didn't. Now, if someone had picked it up for 'ee . . . that would have meant it would be someone it would be good for 'ee to meet."

"Can we go back and do it again?"

"Oh, no, me dear. The die be cast. 'Tis done and there be no going back."

My mother and I were laughing as we came out of the shop.

I said: "They must be constantly on their guard for fear of upsetting those influences which decide their fate."

"Do you think they really take it seriously?"

"Deadly so."

We went back to the house and lunched with Matilda alone. Dermot and Dorabella had gone to Plymouth and would be lunching there, and my father had gone off with Gordon to look at some damage which had been done to one of the gates on the home farm.

"What shall you do this afternoon?" asked my mother, and I told her I should either take a walk or a ride.

"Don't bother about coming with me. I'm quite happy to go alone."

"Well, we'll meet later on."

I decided to ride. I enjoyed ambling along through the narrow winding lane with little danger of getting lost because once one found the sea one knew where one was.

I went to the stables. One of the grooms came out at once.

"You be wanting Starlight, Miss?" he asked.

"Yes, please. I thought I'd take her for a short ride."

"She'll like that. Get on well with 'er, do 'ee, Miss? Her's a good little creature, that 'un."

"Yes. I like her very much."

"I'll get her ready for 'ee if you give me a minute."

He said a few words on the topic which was on everybody's lips: the gale.

"It be hoped we don't have another just yet. They'm got a habit of coming in twos and threes. Started late this year."

We chatted for a while and then I was ready to leave.

The air was fresh. I could smell the sea. The wind was coming in—not exactly gentle but exhilarating.

I turned away from the sea. I decided to explore a little inland today.

I rode along thoughtfully. I was thinking of Dorabella and could not help wondering how she would settle into life here. She was ecstatically happy just now and would be until the wedding. And then? I wondered.

I liked Dermot, but against the background of his home, it seemed that there was something lightweight about him. In Germany he had been so self-sufficient. The manner in which he had brought us out of the forest had given him a knightly and masterful image in our eyes. I kept seeing him in contrast to Gordon Lewyth, who was so absorbed in the estate that he could only be mildly interested in visitors—except my father, who could talk with him on his own subject.

It was strange how people could change when seen against a different background. I tried to brush off feelings of uneasiness which had come to me since I had arrived in this place.

I had mounted a slight incline and come to a winding path. I had not been this way before.

The rain which had accompanied last night's gale had made the countryside glisteningly fresh. It was a pleasure to inhale the scents of the trees and shrubs mingling with that of the damp earth.

It was quiet apart from the soughing of the light wind in the trees making a soft moaning sound.

I pulled up and looked round.

I was thinking: Two more days and we shall be going home. When I was away from all this I should see it more clearly. I would talk to my parents and I would discover what they felt about the situation. One thing was certain: They could not share my feelings, for they would have shown them if they had; and they seemed quite contented.

There was a fork at the end of the road. I pulled up, wondering whether to take the right or left turn.

I decided on the right.

I rode on, still thinking of Dorabella. She really knew so little of them. His family showed no objections, but I was uneasy. What was it? My overactive imagination? My sense of melodrama? Was it because I was going to lose my sister . . . well, not exactly lose her, but our lives would no longer be close as they had been until now? The parting would be exciting to her. But what of me?

It was selfish in a way. Was that why I was trying to convince myself that it might not be right for her?

I had come to an open space bordered by trees. There was nothing growing there. Commonland, I supposed.

Starlight threw back her head. She was tired of ambling. She wanted movement. Almost before I could indicate that I agreed with her, she had broken into a canter and we started across the field. I was not sure how it happened. One never is on such occasions. Time itself seemed to slow down. I did see the tree . . . but not until it was too late. It seemed to sway before my eyes and then it was lying right across my path.

Starlight pulled up sharply and I felt myself thrown sideways. Fortunately she immediately stood perfectly still. I slipped rather inelegantly out of the saddle and fell to the ground. I could sense the tension in the mare, but she was well trained. If she had galloped off at that time I should have been badly injured, for my foot was caught in the stirrup. Hastily I dislodged it and just at that moment I heard the sound of hoofbeats.

As I scrambled to my feet I saw a rider coming toward me. He pulled up sharply, slipped out of the saddle, and gazed at me in horrified surprise.

Then he cried: "Are you all right?"

"I think so."

"Any pain anywhere?"

"I don't think so. I just slid down."

He looked at me anxiously for a moment. "Seems all right. Nothing broken . . ."

"Oh, no. It wasn't violent enough for that. My horse was standing still when I fell."

He laid a hand on Starlight and said: "She did well. Didn't you see the tree?"

"It fell just as we came up."

"That gale," he said, and added: "Look, she's cast a shoe."

"Oh, dear. What, er . . . ?"

"You can't go far like that."

I looked at him blankly.

"The smithy is close by," he said. "He'd shoe her for you. It's the only thing to do."

I looked perplexed, and he went on: "You're new here?"

"Yes."

"I thought so. Staying nearby, are you?"

"Yes. At Tregarland's."

"Oh." He looked amused, and regarded me thoughtfully. "There's only one thing to do. If you are feeling up to it, I'll take you along to the smithy. It's fortunate for you that you didn't take a toss. She must have pulled up with some precision."

He turned to Starlight.

"You're a good old lady, you are. Full marks." The mare seemed to understand. She nuzzled her nose in his hand and he patted her again.

"She'll be all right," he went on. "We'll get her to the smithy. Let's see if you are all right, too." He looked at me steadily. "Sure there's no pain anywhere?"

"No, none. I'm a little shaken, I suppose."

"That's natural."

"You're very kind."

"I'm responsible in a way. That tree's on my land."

"Your . . . land . . . ?"

He smiled ruefully. "Actually, you're trespassing."

"Oh . . . I'm sorry. Then you must be . . ."

"Jowan Jermyn. You look taken aback."

"I . . . had heard your land adjoined Tregarland's. I am so sorry."

"I apologize on behalf of my tree. Now, are you sure you're all right? If so, let's go. The sooner that mare gets a new shoe the better."

I took stock of him as we walked along. He was as tall as Gordon Lewyth, but he lacked Gordon's massive frame, and was rather slender. He had regular features, merry blue-gray eyes and an easy-going, pleasant expression. I thought: So this is the enemy? How fortunate that he does not extend his venom to Tregarland guests.

I was still shaken by my fall and this following on immediately made me feel a little light-headed.

As we walked across the field, he said: "Something will have to be done at once about that tree. Others on the estate may be in a similar state. Very dangerous. The gales here are a menace."

"I imagine so. Something happened on the Tregarland farm. A roof or a fence or something."

"Not only theirs, I imagine. How are you feeling now?"

"All right, thank you."

"You're shaken up a bit, I expect. You need a stiff brandy; there's an inn close to the blacksmith's shop . . . appropriately called Smithy's. We'll look in there and get that brandy."

"I can't tell you how grateful I am to you. I should have been completely bewildered if you hadn't come along." Then I found myself laughing.

"It is amusing?" he said.

"Yes. This morning, in the town, I dropped my glove and, because I picked it up myself, I was told I should meet a stranger whom it would be better for me not to. It seems like a reversal of the prophecy."

"Well, if that tree hadn't fallen, we shouldn't have met in the field. So you could say it was right in a way."

"I think we should have passed each other somewhere near and you would have told me that I was trespassing. So you could say in another way that she was right."

"I am sure I should have been too polite to mention it. Ah, here is the smithy. I told you it wasn't far."

He took Starlight from me and led her into the blacksmith's shop. The blacksmith was a ruddy-faced man with black hair and bright black eyes.

"Jake," said my companion, "here's a job for you. The mare's cast a shoe."

"That be so," said Jake. "How did it 'appen, then?"

"In Three Acres. One of the trees came down suddenly in front of the horse and rider."

"That dratted gale."

"That dratted gale indeed!"

" 'Twon't be the only one, mark my words."

"I mark them well, Jake, and endorse them. But how soon can you shoe the lady's mare?"

"Could start on 'un right away, sir."

The blacksmith was looking at me intently.

"You be from Tregarland's, b'ain't 'ee, Miss?"

Jowan Jermyn gave me an amused look. "Jake is the fount of all knowledge," he said lightly. "The blacksmith's shop is one of the news centers of the neighborhood."

"Mr. Jermyn do mean I likes a bit of gossip," Jake explained to me with a wink.

"That is a slight understatement," commented Jowan. "But he is the best blacksmith in the Duchy. That's so, is it not, Jake?"

"If you do say so, sir, I wouldn't be the one to contradict 'ee."

"Now, if you will get on with the job, I am going to take the young lady into Smithy's and give her a good strong tonic. She's had a bit of a shock, you know."

"I'd guess that, sir."

I saw his chin wag and I knew it was with amusement. This would be a nice little piece of gossip. The enemy of Tregarland's looking after Tregarland's guest.

Now that I was beginning to recover from the shock, I was enjoying this adventure.

It occurred to me that this was the sort of thing that happened to Dorabella. If she had been with me, I believed those friendly glances would have shone in her direction rather than in mine.

The Smithy was warm and inviting. A fire was burning in the big open fireplace around which badges and ornaments had been attached. They glistened in the glow from the fire. There was no one else in the inn parlor.

"Sit down," said my companion. Then he went to the door and called: "Tom, Tom, where are you?"

Then, as a woman appeared: "Ah, Mrs. Brodie, here you are. Jake's shoeing this lady's mare. She cast a shoe and there was a bit of a spill."

"Oh, my patience me!" She was large and round, had rosy cheeks and little sparkling dark eyes which studied me with great interest. "Not hurt, I hope, Miss . . . ?"

"No, thank you very much."

"Fortunately," went on Jowan. "But she needs a brandy. We'll both have one, please, Mrs. Brodie."

"I'll get 'un right away, sir." She smiled at me. "It'll do you the world of good."

I sat back in the armchair and smiled at my companion.

"This is extremely good of you," I said.

"You have already mentioned that. Let me tell you that I am only too pleased to be of use."

I went on: "It is good of you . . . particularly in view of . . . the feud."

He laughed. I noticed his strong white teeth as he did so.

"That!" he said. "That's only between the families, you know."

"I was just thinking how glad I was that it did not extend to the guests."

"My dear Miss . . . I am sorry, I don't know your name."

"It's Denver."

"My dear Miss Denver, even if you possessed the accursed name of Tregarland, I could never desert you in distress."

Mrs. Brodie appeared with two glasses.

He said: "Perhaps we should have something to eat."

Mrs. Brodie stood there, smiling from one of us to the other.

"There are those wonderful brandy cakes. Mrs. Brodie is the champion cook in Cornwall. Is that not so, Mrs. Brodie?"

Mrs. Brodie's answer was the same as the blacksmith's.

"If you do say so, sir."

I thought: He knows how to treat these people. And I was sure that, in the feud, he would have them on his side. Gordon Lewyth's dour manner would not have the same appeal; the old man might have been different at one time, but he would not go around now; and Dermot . . . I was unsure of Dermot.

"The lady should eat something with her brandy, shouldn't she, Mrs. Brodie?"

"Certain sure, sir."

"Then brandy cakes it is." He smiled at me. "You'll like them."

The cakes were brought. They looked delicious. I took a sip of the brandy. It was warming and comforting, and the shaken feeling was fast disappearing. The cosy room, the firelight on the brasses, the excitement of meeting the man who was concerned in the Tregarland feud ... it was all amusing and exciting and just what I needed in my present mood.

"I must confess, Miss Denver, that I know who you are," he was saying. "You are going to marry Dermot Tregarland."

"You are wrong. That is my sister—my twin sister."

"Oh, I see. I am not as knowledgeable as I thought. I was wondering where the prospective bridegroom was and why he was not accompanying his fiancée on her ride."

"My parents are here," I said, "and naturally I came too. It is just a brief visit."

"Your twin sister," he mused.

"The news service was not as good as you thought," I said.

"I shall complain," he replied with a grin. "Well, that is interesting. Your parents and you with your sister ... inspecting the terrain ... and the family."

"It is not exactly like that."

"That's putting it bluntly. Please forgive me. Naturally your parents want to see whom your sister is proposing to marry."

"I daresay his family would want to inspect us."

"Very likely. And how was this? Amicable? Did all meet with approval? Forgive me again. You see, I should never have been invited to meet your family because ..."

"Because of the feud."

"That is why I consider myself extremely fortunate to have met you in this most unexpected way."

"My parents will be full of gratitude to you when they hear what you have done for me."

"It was a great pleasure. Do have another of these cakes of Mrs. Brodie's. They really are good, aren't they?"

I agreed that they were.

"And are you really feeling better now?"

I assured him I was.

"I am so glad of that." He looked as though he meant it sincerely. I thought: There is something very pleasant about him. What a pity he is not on speaking terms with the Tregarlands. I should have liked to bring my parents to thank him. I suppose that would not be possible in the circumstances.

"This feud," I said. "How long has it been going on?"

"About a hundred years."

"Surely now ... ?"

He lifted his shoulders.

"It passed on through generations. We're rather like that in these parts. We don't let go of the past easily."

"If it were something good, something worth remembering, I could understand it. But in a case like this . . ."

"Well, we have never had anything to do with each other, so we don't miss anything. It is just there."

"How did it start? Nobody seems to be sure at Tregarland's."

"Nobody? I daresay old Mr. Tregarland remembers. Whom did you ask?"

"I haven't really asked anyone. I thought it might not be ethical to do so. Mrs. Lewyth did not seem to know."

"Well, she isn't one of the family, is she? Or is she?"

"She is a great friend of them all."

"And looks after the place. And the son . . . well, he *is* Tregarlands . . . as far as the estate is concerned."

"He seems to be very involved in that."

"Far more so than the son of the house."

"So Mr. Lewyth really runs it."

"That's common knowledge. The son does not seem to have much feeling for the place. He gets away when he can."

"We met him in Germany," I said.

"He's always been away a good deal. You can't run an estate like that by not being there. So, you haven't had a very long acquaintance with him?"

"No. There was just this meeting. We were visiting friends and he was on holiday. He and my sister . . ."

"Fell in love at first sight."

I was amazed at myself for talking to him so frankly; I supposed it was because I was really in a very grateful mood after what had happened, and there was something about him which inspired confidences. I forgot that I had met him only a short time before.

I said: "Tell me about the feud."

"Oh . . . now, let me see. It was a love affair, you know. It is amazing how many of life's problems start that way. One of my ancestors . . . now what was her name? I have heard it. Arabella? No, Araminta. That was it. She was very beautiful, as behoves the heroine of such a story; and as a matter of fact, there is a portrait of her in the house—and she was. The story goes that a match had been arranged for her with a gentleman whom the family considered to be highly eligible. Araminta did not agree. He was thirty years older than she was and he was very rich. I imagine it was this last which put him into such high favor with the family, for apparently finances were low at the time. The estate was not as it should be, and the gentleman's money was needed to prop it up. This he was prepared to do in return for the hand of seventeen-year-old Araminta."

"Poor girl!" I said.

"Poor girl, indeed. But a common enough story. Certainly nowadays there is more freedom of choice. But in those days the will of Papa was the law. However, the son of Tregarland was young and handsome. His name was Dermot."

"Oh, the same . . ."

"These names run in families. Tregarland's is spattered with Dermots. I am by no means the first Jowan in mine."

"The way the story is going, I guess that Dermot and Araminta fell in love."

"You are absolutely right. How could it have been otherwise? At that time there was no feud between the families. I gather that the finances at Tregarland were in no more healthy a state than those of Jermyn; in any case poor Araminta's future had been decided. She was to marry her wealthy admirer, restore the crumbling family mansion, forgo true love, and learn to live happily ever after with the husband of her father's choice."

"Which she did not. It is really very sad."

"Indeed, it is. Dermot Tregarland was not a man to stand aside and let his love be whisked from him. He made plans. He was going to elope. There was treachery somewhere and the news leaked out. It might have been through the servants. They are like detectives in our houses, especially so in those days where there were many more of them. However, it became known to the Jermyns that their daughter was planning to elope with her Tregarland lover who was to creep into the grounds by night when she would slip out to meet him. It was easy to lock her in her room, but they set a trap for him. There was a fearsome contraption which they used to set in the woods to warn off poachers. It was called a man-trap. Well, the outcome was that when Dermot came for his bride he was caught in the trap."

"Did it kill him?"

"Unfortunately for him, no. It was not meant to kill. His leg was so mangled that he could never use it again."

"What a terrible story! I am not surprised that the Tregarland family hated yours."

"It *was* terrible. But that was not the end. Araminta, broken-hearted, locked in her room, was unable to get out while her lover lay in agony on the trap until in the morning one of the servants found him."

"Surely they were punished for doing such a cruel thing!"

"They had a good defense. There was a robbery in the neighborhood. They were protecting their property. Man-traps were not unknown. It was reckoned that those who were caught in them had no right to be in that spot."

"And what happened to the lovers?"

"Dermot Tregarland was an embittered cripple for the rest of his life."

"And Araminta ... did she marry the rich suitor?"

"The preparations for the wedding went on. Everyone thought the marriage would take place. There were to be great festivities ... a grand ball ..."

"And what about the Tregarlands? Did they retaliate? They had not wanted the match, but ..."

"What could the lovers do? Dermot was lying in his bed knowing that he would never walk without crutches again. He was in no state to stage a romantic rescue. Araminta took matters into her own hands. The night before the wedding, she went down to the sea. She walked into it and never came back."

"What a terrible story! So she killed herself, and her lover was maimed for the rest of his life."

"Pretty strong stuff, you see. In a way it makes you understand the feud."

"But all those years ago! Do you feel this hatred? After all, Araminta was one of your family."

"Well, the Tregarlands were wronged more than we were. We were, after all, the instigators. It was my great-great (I am not sure how many greats) grandfather who set the trap which gave Dermot Tregarland the scars for the rest of his life. They have more reason to hate us than we have to hate them. Araminta died by her own hand because of the cruelty of her own family. Over the years which followed the tragedy, they provoked us wherever possible. Anger flared up between us. Throughout his life, Dermot could not forget that we had not only robbed him of his love but maimed him for ever."

"It's a sad story, but I am glad I know. It was about a hundred years ago, you say. It is rather a long time for something to fester like that. None of the people concerned in it are living now."

"That Dermot would have been about twenty years old when it happened to him, and he lived until he was sixty—nearly forty years of smoldering resentment. It takes a long time to eradicate. The story was handed down. The family would be taught to hate those wicked Jermyns. They would be told not to go near our land. We were the ogres ... it was awkward, our being neighbors."

"I understand it more now. I am glad you told me."

"Oh. It is something best forgotten."

"Yes, I agree. After all, those of you who are living now are not to blame and, when you think of the terrible things that have happened in the past, there must be many similar stories."

He smiled. "Yes. It should be forgotten. This is a rather depressing story, isn't it? Are you feeling better now?"

"Much."

"That's good."

"I wonder how Jake is getting on."

"He will do a good job."

"It must be rather strange, living in a place like this and never speaking to those whose lands are closest to yours."

"Oh, the feud again! It can have its awkward moments. When people invite guests, if the Jermyns are included the Tregarlands won't be and vice versa. We are like strangers to each other. But people come down here more and more nowadays. During the holiday season there are many strange faces around. There is no problem, really."

"I think it is a shame nevertheless."

"No doubt."

"You do not bear any rancor?"

"Why should I? We were the ones who inflicted the damage, though the Tregarlands were as much against the match as we were. The Jermyn fortunes were at the time in decline with those of the Tregarlands. They did not want the marriage any more than we did. So both of the young people would have been forbidden to marry their choice. The course of true love never did run smooth, you know."

He was anxious to introduce a light note into the conversation and the story of the star-crossed lovers had brought a touch of gloom. I could not help thinking of how that poor girl must have felt when she walked into the sea; and there was the young man who was crippled for life. Hers was perhaps the easier fate.

He asked about my home and we talked of Caddington and my parents, of Dorabella and how she and I had left school only that summer.

A great deal had happened since then.

There was something about him which led me into talking more than I normally would have done to a stranger, and soon I was telling him about what had happened in the schloss.

He looked grave and said he had heard of the youth movement which was growing very strong in Germany. He was not sure of their new leader, though he had heard that he had done a lot of good for the country.

"You will not wish to go there again for a while," he said. "But when your sister marries, I daresay you will be visiting here."

"I imagine we shall. We have been together all our lives . . . as twins are."

"Of course."

"So I can be confident that we shall meet again."

"It seems possible. Which reminds me—they will be wondering what has happened to me. Do you think the horse will be ready now?"

"We'll see. I imagine it is possible."

We rose. Mrs. Brodie gave me a pleasant smile and I guessed it would not be long before others knew that the guest from Tregarland's had been in her inn parlor with Jowan Jermyn.

In the smithy's the smell of burning hoof filled the air and Starlight was standing patiently while Jake put the finishing touches to her shoe.

"There," he said. "She'll do a treat . . . a real treat. That be better, eh, old girl?"

I was wondering about paying.

Jake guessed my thoughts.

"That be all right, Miss. I'll put it to Tregarland's. 'Tain't the first time I've done this for Starlight."

As we rode away, I told Jowan Jermyn again how grateful I was to him.

"I cannot think what I should have done if you had not come along when you did, Mr. Jermyn."

"I am known quite often as J.J. It's the name you see, Jowan Jermyn. Alliteration's artful aid. Not so artful on this occasion. Perhaps a little clumsy."

"Not in the least."

"Oh, you are determined to be tactful. At school, they became impatient with the two Js and dropped one of them. Jay. I am not sure that I like it. Jay! What is it! A bird. The dictionary says it is also a foolish person. A person who acts recklessly. One who crosses the road recklessly and is liable to be run over is a jay walker. You see, I am rather hoping that, apart from that artful bird, I am not very aptly named."

"What's in a name? What of Violetta?"

"What of it?"

"It happens to be mine."

"It's charming."

"From the opera, of course. And my sister is Dorabella."

"The twin. Also charming. I can't speak for Dorabella, but you do not really bear a resemblance to La Traviata."

We rode through the field.

"Keep clear of the trees," he went on. "In case another should fall. I'll have them inspected as soon as possible. There may well be others. I expect to be getting a list of damages on the farms, etc."

We had passed through the fields and come to one of the winding lanes. When we reached the end of it we came to a wider thoroughfare.

He pulled up. "This marks the boundary between Tregarland and Jermyn land. We don't trespass. Do you know where you are now?"

"Yes, I think so."

"Go straight along . . . you'll soon see the sea. So I will say goodbye, or perhaps *au revoir*, because, if you come down to see your sister, we shall meet again. In secret, perhaps, because your sister will be a Tregarland. Would you agree to such subterfuge?"

"I think I might."

He bowed his head and lifted his hat. "Then, Miss Violetta, *au revoir.*"

I started to thank him again but he cut me short.

"It has been a great pleasure for me," he said.

"For me, too," I told him.

He turned his horse with an air of reluctance, and, smiling, I did the same, and rode back to Tregarland's.

There was consternation when I arrived. Where had I been? My mother was anxious. She had expected me back before this.

I told her briefly what had happened.

"Lost her shoe! Good Heavens, you might have had a bad fall!"

"She's a wonderful horse. Mr. Jermyn said so."

"Mr. Jermyn?"

Then it was necessary to tell her everything. Matilda Lewyth arrived and heard what had happened.

"He was very good," I explained. "In fact he was particularly kind and helpful."

"Did he know you came from Tregarland's?"

"Oh, yes. I told him I was staying here. He knew something about Dorabella. He says there is a good news service and the blacksmith's is one of the headquarters of it. After falling off . . . but not badly, because Starlight was stationary . . . it was rather fun and quite amusing."

"Well, I am glad it turned out like that," said my mother. "It might have been so different."

Dorabella returned from Plymouth with a beautiful diamond ring which delighted her. She showed it round with great pleasure and that night, as she was officially engaged, champagne was brought up from the cellars and my afternoon's adventure slipped into insignificance.

Dorabella did come to my room afterwards. She was extremely happy and kept glancing with delight at her engagement ring. She was only vaguely interested in my adventure.

"This Jermyn man sounds interesting," she said.

"Oh, he was. I was fortunate that he came along when he

did." I told her about the origin of the feud and that did hold her attention for a little while.

"Walked into the sea!" she said. "It's rather romantic in a way ..."

"Romantic! It's tragic."

"But not as bad as what happened to the man. Fancy living for the rest of his life like that. And his name was Dermot."

"It's a family name evidently."

"It is all very exciting, anyway. I am glad you had a little adventure, too."

"This will be a visit we shall always remember," I said, thinking of sitting in Smithy's, drinking brandy.

"For ever," echoed Dorabella, gazing rapturously at her diamond ring.

A few days later we left Cornwall.

It had been decided, after a good deal of discussion, that the marriage should take place at Christmas.

The First Wife

❦

We returned to weeks of feverish preparations. My mother had a few qualms of uneasiness. She thought it was too soon and they should have waited a little longer.

"Why?" demanded Dorabella. "Why should we wait? What's the point? And being so far apart it isn't easy to see each other."

My mother said: "The spring would have been a good time. Or, say, May . . . or June . . ."

"Why? Why?" demanded Dorabella.

My mother looked at her and smiled. "Well, as you both seem so sure . . ."

"Of course we are sure."

My mother left it at that, but when we were alone she talked to me, as she often did. She had always discussed a problem with me rather than with Dorabella.

She began: "I wish they had agreed to wait awhile."

"Dorabella never wants to wait for anything."

"I know. She is so impulsive. She doesn't always see things clearly, she doesn't look at all the possibilities."

"But you liked the family in Cornwall. You got on very well with Matilda Lewyth."

"Yes. And, of course, she is in charge. I can't see any conflict between her and Dorabella over that."

"Dorabella certainly wouldn't want to take on the management of the household."

"No, indeed not. But . . ."

"They were charming to us," I went on. "And they seemed to like Dorabella. There was no objection, as there sometimes is in such cases."

"I don't know. It is just that it all seems too quick. I should have liked a little time to get . . . to get to know more . . ."

"Well, we were there for a week. It wasn't exactly a conventional household. But perhaps most households are not."

"What do you mean?"

"Well, on the surface they seem conventional sometimes and then you discover all sorts of things are going on under the veneer, if you know what I mean. There is the housekeeper who isn't really a housekeeper; there's her son who runs the place; and there is Dermot who doesn't seem to take much interest in it. And the father just sits there. He reminds me of a puppet master holding the strings."

"Did he really seem like that to you?"

"It was just a thought that occurred to me. And then there was the feud."

My mother laughed. "It was amusing that you met one of the enemy. I wonder what they thought of that? They didn't give much sign . . ."

"No. That's what I mean. I had a feeling that something was going on underneath."

"That's your imagination."

"Well, there is something about that part of the world. Superstitions and such like. All those things you mustn't do, like meeting parsons on the way to the boats, and dropping gloves which have to be picked up by someone else."

"Your stranger turned out to be a blessing. If you ask me, it's time they dropped their silly old quarrels about something which happened a hundred years ago. And Dorabella is going into all that. I wonder how she will fit in?"

"Well, she is in love with Dermot."

My mother nodded, but she was frowning.

"Don't worry," I said. "She always falls on her feet."

"She's going to miss you."

"And I her."

"That's the disadvantage of being twins. That closeness is wonderful at times, and then comes the inevitable separation."

"But she is not going to the other end of the world," I cried. "And I shall go and stay there and she will come here often, I am sure."

"I suppose Dermot will be able to."

"Of course. He's got Gordon Lewyth to look after the estate."

She frowned again. I was surprised, for I had thought she had been pleased by what she found in Cornwall; but, like myself, she had a faint stirring of disquiet that all might not be as it seemed.

Christmas was close—a very special Christmas, dominated by the wedding which was to take place. The church had been beautifully decorated; Dermot was to arrive a few days before, and there would be rehearsals in the church. I was to be the Maid of Honor, and Uncle Charles's small daughter was a bridesmaid, his little boy a page—our brother being too old for the role and overcome with horror at the thought of it.

Dorabella's dress was hanging up in the wardrobe; she looked at it a hundred times a day and wondered whether it was too long, too short, and whether the skirt needed an extra flounce of lace. There was another question: Should she wear the wreath of orange blossom round her head? My mother was anxious that she should because she had worn it at her wedding.

"Is it a little old-fashioned?" Dorabella asked again and again.

"What if it is?" I asked. "What does it matter?"

"What does it matter! This is my wedding!"

"It looks beautiful and Mummy wants you to. It will bring back memories of her wedding."

"But this is *my* wedding."

"Nobody is going to forget that. You wouldn't let them."

"You'll have to wear that orange blossom at *your* wedding."

"Mine? If there ever is one."

"Of course there'll be one. Once I'm out of the way, you'll have a chance."

We laughed together and I was reminded of how lonely I was going to be without her.

Dermot arrived at the beginning of the week. He was exuberant and Dorabella was wildly happy at the sight of him.

My mother and I watched his arrival from one of the windows. We looked down on him and Dorabella clinging together.

We smiled at each other.

"It will be all right," said my mother. "He's a good boy."

Then we went down to greet him.

There was much laughter at dinner that night. Dermot was clearly very happy—and so was Dorabella.

All would be well.

The next days sped by. Guests arrived. The house was full and the bustle of preparation at its height. The day after Boxing Day the bridal pair would leave for their honeymoon. Dorabella could talk of little else. They were together most of the time. I went riding with them once or twice, but I felt a little redundant and when I declined to accompany them they made no protest, but if they were relieved they hid the fact carefully.

On Christmas Eve I happened to go into the kitchen. Mrs. Mills, the cook, was at the table stirring something. She was talking to one of the maids when I came in and I heard her remark:

"Well, say what you will, I don't reckon it's right. They should have made some other arrangement. It never was right and never will be. I mean to say ..."

"What isn't right, Mrs. Mills?" I asked.

She looked embarrassed and shrugged her shoulders.

"Oh, nothing really, Miss Violetta. I've had so much work to do these last days that I don't know whether I'm standing on my head or my heels."

"Perhaps we could get Amy Terrett in from the village to give you a hand."

"Amy Terrett! No thank you. I'd be telling her what to do half the time instead of getting on with it. Quicker to do it myself."

"Well, I am sure my mother would be happy to get her if it would help."

"Don't you say nothing of this to her ladyship. I'm not complaining about the work. This is a wedding, and weddings only come now and then, and if I'm not capable of handling them I don't know who is."

"But there is something. You said it wasn't right."

"You was always like that, Miss Violetta, wasn't you? Right from a baby. Wouldn't let nothing go. Why this, why that, and on and on till you got an answer. Now, Miss Dorabella, she's different. Unless it was something about her, of course."

"Is this something about Dorabella?" I asked.

"It's all one of them mountains out of molehills, you might say." She looked at the kitchen maid and lifted her shoulders. "You won't rest till you get it out of me, will you? All I was saying was that Mr. Dermot Tregarland ought not to be here."

"Why not?"

"Because he's the bridegroom, that's why."

"Well, he has to be here. We can't have a wedding without him."

"That's true enough. But he should have stayed somewhere else . . . at a hotel or something."

"There's plenty of room here."

"It ain't right for bride and groom to sleep under the same roof on the day before their wedding. It's unlucky."

"Oh, Mrs. Mills, I never heard such nonsense. He's been here before and we've visited his family. We were all under the same roof then. Nobody thought anything about it."

"This is the night before the wedding."

"I don't understand."

"Well, it's only yesterday you were a little 'un, Miss Violetta. There you were, sitting at my table and popping raisins in your mouth when you thought I wasn't looking. And there was Dorabella with you. There's things you have to learn. I can only tell you it's unlucky for bride and groom to spend the night before the wedding under the same roof."

I laughed. "Well, they'll be married soon and it won't matter about their being under the same roof."

"I didn't say it would. I'm only telling you what I've always heard. But I wouldn't like Miss Dorabella to know."

"Don't worry. She wouldn't care if she did."

"That's a fact. She never saw anything she didn't want to."

There was a glass jar of raisins on the table. I leaned forward, took one, and, smiling at Mrs. Mills, I put it into my mouth.

"You're cheeky, you are," said Mrs. Mills.

And I went out of the kitchen and remembered later that I had not told her there was an extra person for dinner.

* * *

It was Christmas Eve. The Yule log had been brought in. In the kitchen they were baking mince pies and preparing the mulled wine for the carol singers when they came. Hampers were being sent to the people in the cottages. Caddington always kept up the traditions and customs of the past.

My uncle Charles with his family were with us, accompanied by Grandmother Lucie. The house was full.

Grandmothers Lucie and Belinda were closeted together, talking about old times. Their lives had been very much entwined—often dramatically—and there was a certain relationship between them, rather like that which had existed with my mother and my aunt Annabelinda who had died violently and mysteriously many years before. We did not talk about that. Grandmother Belinda did not like us to, and my mother was always reticent about her, too.

Christmas was a time for stirring memories, and I suspected that when Lucie and Belinda were together there was a great deal of talk of those early days.

Edward arrived with Gretchen. They were now engaged to be married.

I often thought what a significant time that had been in Germany. There would not have been these preparations for this wedding now but for that. Edward and Gretchen? Well, he had met her before, but I could not help feeling that the incidents we had seen in the Böhmerwald had precipitated them into a binding relationship. It had certainly made Edward see that he could not leave her in Germany.

There was much merriment at the dinner table that night. We pulled crackers and produced our paper hats and read our mottoes while we laughed at the useless little articles we found in them—hearts of mock-gold and silver, keyrings, tin whistles, and so on.

My father sat at the head of the table. He was very happy. He loved to have the family around him and he, at least, I was sure, had no qualms about the coming marriage, except perhaps to hope that Dermot would become more interested in the estate which would be his . . . as dedicated as Gordon Lewyth was to ensure its prosperity.

But that might be my imagination again. His daughter was marrying into a family in Cornwall whose position was similar to his own. And I supposed that was something most fathers would want for their daughters. It was really all very satisfactory.

When we rose from the table the carol singers arrived. I heard them in the courtyard. We all went out to greet them as we had every Christmas I remembered. We sang with them, "Hark! the Herald Angels Sing," "Once in Royal David's City," all the carols which we knew so well. The singers came into the hall where Mrs. Mills was waiting with the mince pies and mulled wine.

"Merry Christmas, Merry Christmas . . ." The words echoed round the hall.

"Long life and happiness to Miss Dorabella."

Dorabella, flushed, excited, beamed on them all. Dermot was beside her and everyone said what a beautiful bride she would make to stand beside such a handsome bridegroom.

At last the singers had departed and my mother said: "Now it is time for bed, I should say. We have a big day tomorrow."

We retired to our rooms. I undressed and got into bed. I felt a certain sadness. This was the end of an era. Tomorrow she would be not so much my twin sister as Dermot's wife.

I was not entirely surprised when she came to me. She stood by the bed. In her blue nightdress with dressing gown to match, her hair about her shoulders, she looked very young and in some ways vulnerable.

"Hello, Vee," she said.

"Hello," I replied.

"It's cold out here." She took off her dressing gown and let it fall to the floor, then she leaped in beside me.

We laughed.

"You all right?" I asked.

Her arms were tight about me. "H'm," she murmured.

"You don't sound sure. You're not going to call the whole thing off, are you?"

She laughed. "You're joking!"

"Nothing would surprise me with you."

"No. I'm wildly, ecstatically happy."

"Are you?"

"Well . . ."

"A little scared?"

"Perhaps."

"They say marriage is a big undertaking."

"Dermot will be all right. I can look after him."

"You usually can, as you say, look after people."

"As I have looked after you all these years?"

"Now it is you who are joking. As I remember, I did most of the looking after."

"Yes, you have, dear sister. That's true. And what I want is for you to go on doing it."

"What! From miles away?"

"That's what I don't like about this ... being miles away. It won't be the same, will it?"

"Of course not! Talk sense. How could it be? You won't be Miss Dorabella Denver any more. You'll be Mrs. Dermot Tregarland."

"I know."

"Dorabella? Seriously, you are not having second thoughts, are you? It is rather late."

"Oh, no. It's just that I wish you were coming with me."

"What! To Venice? A honeymoon à trois! I wonder what Dermot would think about that?"

"I didn't mean that. I meant afterwards. I wish you were coming to Cornwall."

"I shall come for a visit."

"You will, won't you? Often ..."

"And you will come here."

"Yes, there is that. But ... I'd like you to be there all the time."

"No, you wouldn't. You're a big girl now. You don't need your alter ego there beside you all the time."

"That's just it. I do. I have been feeling this for some time. We are like one person. When you think of all that time before we were born ... when most children are alone ... we were there ... growing together. We're part of each other. There is something between us, something other people can't understand."

"I understand perfectly."

"Of course you do. You are part of it. You were always there. Do you remember that frightful Miss Dobbs at school? She was always trying to separate us. 'You must stand on your own feet, Dorabella.' Do you remember?"

"Of course I remember."

"I hated her because she wouldn't let us sit together."

"And you could not do your sums."

"Which you were clever at, of course."

"You would have been all right if you had tried. Miss Dobbs was right. You should have stood on your own feet."

"Why should I, when I had yours to stand on? And you know, you liked me to. You were always pleased when I couldn't do those ghastly old lessons without you. You would click your tongue . . . just like Miss Dobbs. 'You are really hopeless, Dorabella.' I can hear your voice now and see the smile of satisfaction on your face while I copied your sums. You were an old swot. You liked to score over me, you liked it when I couldn't do without you."

We were laughing together. It was true. I had always wanted her to lean on me. She might charm them, but I could win admiration with my superior scholarship. At least I had that!

Then we began: "Do you remember . . . ?" And we rocked with laughter. There was so much to remember.

I heard the clock in the tower chime midnight.

I said: "Listen. This is your wedding day."

"Yes," she said and held me tightly.

"Fancy you, a married woman!"

"It will be wonderful, won't it?" She spoke lightly but I fancied she was asking for reassurance.

"I know what's the matter with you," I said. "It's something they call prewedding nerves."

"Is that what it is?"

"I'm sure of it."

"I . . . I'm not frightened of Dermot. It's just that it's the end of the way it used to be . . . with us."

"I shall still be here and you're not miles away, just in a different part of England. There are trains. I only have to get on one, or you will, and we are together."

"That's what I keep telling myself. Vee?"

She waited for a while and I said: "What?"

"Promise me this . . . if I wanted you . . . suddenly . . . you'd come. You won't think that, just because I'm married, there's any difference between us. You'll always be with me, won't you, 'till death do us part' . . . ?"

I was going to give some flippant answer, saying that that was what she should say tomorrow and she had muddled the occasions, but I sensed the urgency in her, so I repeated, "I'll be there ... whenever you want me ... 'until death do us part.' "

She kissed me and I released her. She got out of bed, put on her dressing gown, and stood smiling at me.

"And so to bed," she said. "Busy day tomorrow."

I lay for some time after she had gone, thinking about her, and I could not dispel the faint feeling of uneasiness.

Everything went according to plan. Dorabella and Dermot were married; the beautifully decorated church was filled not only with friends and relations but the servants from the house and the people from the village.

Dorabella came up the aisle on my father's arm and went down it on Dermot's. Everyone was saying how beautiful and radiantly happy she looked, and that it was a wonderful wedding.

There was merrymaking throughout the day; messages of congratulation; people calling; and the reception in the great hall which was scarcely big enough to accommodate them all.

None of Dermot's family was present. His father had a bad cold and Matilda Lewyth could not leave him; Gordon knew that we would understand that he could not leave the estate at such a time when most of the staff would be thinking of Christmas and being with their families.

This was commented on by Mrs. Mills in the kitchen and no doubt she thought it was not a good omen, especially as the bridegroom had slept under the same roof as the bride the night before the wedding.

However, no one else seemed to have any qualms. The bride and groom were so obviously in love, and I could detect none of that apprehension I had sensed in Dorabella when she had come into my bed on the previous night.

All would be well, I told myself. I should visit them often. It would be fun. I might meet that interesting man Jowan Jermyn again. That would be amusing.

All would be well.

We drank the champagne. My father made a speech. Dermot responded and it was all according to tradition.

The day after Boxing Day the married pair left for Venice.

Then I realized how lonely I felt without her. She had been right about the bond between us. It was as strong as ever. I had liked her to lean on me. I had truly reveled in her copying my sums.

I knew my life was going to be different without her close by. I felt an emptiness ... a deep loneliness.

Dorabella and Dermot had returned from their three weeks in Italy. She had written to say she had had a wonderful time. She wrote often and her letters indicated that she was happy at Tregarland's.

The weather had been rather severe. We had had snow and my mother caught a cold. She was rarely ill and when she was I had always taken on the task of looking after her. But for this I might have gone to Cornwall for a visit.

My mother said: "Dorabella will probably be better settling in on her own. It is all new to her and she may be hankering after her old home for a while. Let her get used to it and we'll go down in the spring."

Hearing that my mother was not well, Edward came to see us, and it was then we heard about his coming wedding, which was to be in March.

"It will make things easier," he said. "We always intended to, but Gretchen feels she should visit her family and, quite frankly, I don't like her going over. If we were married, she would be English ... and that will make a difference."

"They haven't had any more of ... that sort of thing?" I asked.

He shook his head. "But that man is still around, and I don't like it."

"I understand that," said my mother.

When he had gone my mother expressed a certain fear to me.

"There is no doubt that he cares deeply for Gretchen, and she is a nice girl, but I wonder if he is marrying her out of pity."

"Well, what is wrong with that?" I asked.

"It just is not enough."

"He was very interested in her because of that business in the schloss."

"Oh, I expect it is all right. I always looked upon Edward as my baby."

"I know. I hope you'll feel well enough to go to his wedding."

"I've made up my mind that I'm going."

She did, though the cold was still hanging around. The Greenham grandparents arranged this one. I wondered what Mrs. Mills would have said about its taking place from the bridegroom's home, which I imagined was stepping aside from convention. But, of course, in this case the bride's home was in Germany, so perhaps the fates would have made a concession on that account. It was not like Dermot . . . who could have stayed in a hotel.

I told my mother what I was thinking and we laughed together over it.

It was a charming wedding. Gretchen looked delightful and happy, although she suffered some anxiety over her family, but at least no trouble at the schloss had been reported.

During the honeymoon she and Edward would see her family, and later she did tell me that they were very happy about the marriage.

My parents and I with Grandmother Belinda traveled back to Caddington; I saw immediately how fatigued my mother was and that her cold had worsened, so I said she must go to bed and I would have supper with her there.

She declared she was much better and over our food we talked of Edward.

She said: "It was so moving to see him there, a grown man, actually getting married. When first I saw him he was a baby in a perambulator in the Plantains' cottage garden."

"Who were the Plantains?"

"They were his foster parents," she told me. "He was to be brought up by them because Madame Plantain had just lost her own baby. It had been stillborn. She had been heartbroken . . . until Edward was brought to her."

"What happened to Edward's parents?"

She said: "I suppose you will have to know one day. I remember his great-grandfather's saying, 'There is a time for silence,' and it was then. But now . . . it is a long time ago."

"Do you mean Jean Pascal Bourdon, Grandmother Belinda's father? The one who left Edward that house in France?"

She was silent for a moment. Then she said: "This is for

you only. Don't tell anyone, not Dorabella particularly. She could never keep a secret. Jean Pascal Bourdon was Edward's great-grandfather. He arranged it all. He was a very sophisticated aristocrat. He knew how to manage things. You see, it all came about when Annabelinda, Grandmother Belinda's daughter, your father's sister . . ."

"Aunt Annabelinda . . . the one who died in that old house?"

"It's a complicated story. But Annabelinda, when she was at school with me, fell in love with a young man. He was German. Edward was the result. Annabelinda was only a schoolgirl. We were in Belgium. Jean Pascal arranged it all and for Madame Plantain to take the child in place of her own. She lived near the school. I met her and saw the baby, though I did not know at first that he was Annabelinda's. I found out by chance and they had to let me into the secret. Then the war came; the cottage was bombed, the Plantains were killed, and I came along and found the baby in his perambulator in the garden. I brought him home. But the fact of his birth was hushed up."

"Does Edward know?"

"Yes, he does. I told him only recently. I talked it over with your father and Grandmother Belinda. For some time I could not decide what to do for the best. Jean Pascal had been so certain that he should not be told. Edward does not know everything, not exactly who his father was. But he knows he was German and that his mother was Annabelinda. So he knows that he is one of us, and I think that pleases him very much. He belongs to the family, and we thought he should not be kept in the dark any longer. People have a right to know who their parents are."

"I expect he will tell Gretchen."

"I daresay. I am glad that he married her."

"But you thought it might have been out of pity."

"I believe it will be all right, though. It is like a pattern, you see. He is half German and he is attracted by a German girl. Don't you think it is significant that they should be attracted by each other?"

"It seems so. And by Kurt, too, when they met at college. They were drawn together, I suppose, and they became great friends. It could well be something to do with their being of the same nationality, even though they did not know it. And then, of course . . . Gretchen."

"I am sure they will be very happy. I am glad that he has married her and taken her away from that . . . unpleasantness."

Dorabella married. Edward married. There is change all about us. For so long everything went on as it always had . . . and now . . . change.

I had heard from Dorabella now and then. She had a rather unexpected trait; she liked writing letters, and, of course, most of what she wrote would come my way. So far they had been short—an indication that everything was going well. I believed she was not missing me as much as I was her. I had replied and told her about our mother's health and what was happening at Caddington. I explained that the reason I had not been to see her was because of our mother's persistent cold and, as she would want to accompany me to Cornwall, I did not feel it would be wise to come.

They were ordinary letters. Then one came which was different. Because it was a long letter, I took it to my bedroom so that I might enjoy it without interruptions.

"Dear Vee," she had written.

"How are you? I wish you were here. It would be lovely to talk, and there is no one to whom I can talk as I can to you."

I felt a quiver of alarm at that. It must mean that all was not going well. Why could she not talk to her husband?

This is a strange place. It is not like home. It makes you feel there is something in the air. The sea makes strange noises at night. I don't think I shall ever get used to it. Matilda is very good. She manages everything. I never interfere with that. I am not interested and I would not want to face that old dragon of a cook every morning to discuss the meals. These servants are not *cosy* like ours. I suppose that's because ours have known us for years.

Vee, I don't know how to describe this to you. But . . . this house . . . I can't get used to it. It was all right when you were all here. It felt different then, like home, with you and the parents . . . and all that. You made it feel . . . normal. It's different now. I feel people are watching me.

They aren't really. It's just a feeling I have. The eyes in the people in the portrait gallery . . . they follow me, stare at me, and it seems as if they change when I'm looking at them. They are laughing at me, sneering . . . some of them look as if they are warning me.

This is silly, of course. I think it is because I don't fit.

Dermot is wonderful. He is very kind and gentle, all that I thought he was in the beginning. It's the others I don't understand . . . I mean the old man and Gordon. The old man seems amused by something . . . by me, I think. Gordon, well, he's alert in a way. The old man is always telling me how pretty I am and how he likes to see me there. He likes me to sit close to him and keeps patting my hand. It's welcoming in a way and yet somehow it seems as though he is laughing at me. But not only me, at the others as well. As for Gordon, he's working most of the time. He doesn't say very much, but I get the impression that he would rather I wasn't here.

Matilda is kind. I believe she knows how I am feeling. She said to me the other day: "You are finding it hard to fit in, aren't you, Dorabella?" I hesitated. It seemed rather rude to agree, but it's the truth.

She said: "It's strange no doubt. It must be so different from your home."

I told her the house was not so different. We lived in an old house and there is a similarity about old houses. No, it wasn't the house.

"It must be the people," she said.

I assured her it was not. Everyone had been kind to me.

"Of course they have," she said. "It is your family now, your home. I think you miss your sister. You were always together, I suppose."

I told her yes, we had been, and she said she understood absolutely and it would all come right. I try to keep feeling that it will, but it isn't the same, Vee.

I think I have been trying to work up to this. It shocked me very much when I heard. Don't tell the parents yet, not until I say you may. I don't know what they'll think. I know it will be that we ought to have heard of it before. I don't know whether it would have

made any difference. I don't think it would. I should still
have wanted to marry Dermot.

The fact is, Vee, Dermot was married before!

I paused. Married before! That was what was upsetting her.
Why hadn't he said so? Now I understood all this about the
portraits watching her. I guessed she was very shaken.

Yes, he was married before. She died. It was two years
before we met. He confessed it to me one night. I can tell
you it was a shock. He said, why should it be? It didn't
make any difference to *us*. He was young and impetuous
and had rushed into it. It was different from what had
happened to us. There had never been anyone like me, he
said. It was rather strange, really. There was that story
about the feud ... do you remember? That man Jermyn
told you. I haven't seen anything of him, by the way. I
heard someone say in one of the shops that he was
abroad somewhere. Well, Dermot's wife was drowned.
She went out to swim and there were cross-currents or
something ... and she ought not to have gone. Her body
was washed up some days later, on the beach right in
front of the house. It was odd, after what happened to that
girl in the feud. She drowned herself of her own accord.
It revived it all. Dermot said it was all very distressing.
He didn't want to think about it. He just wanted to forget, which was why he couldn't bear to bring it up. I suppose the sea being so near made it easy for the Jermyn
girl. And then, of course, Dermot's wife ... her name
was Annette. It's rather pretty and feminine.

I was ever so shocked when I heard. "Why didn't you
tell me before?" I kept asking Dermot. He said he
thought it might have made a difference. Well, it would
have in a way. He always seemed so young and carefree.
He didn't seem like a man who had had a wife who had
died like that.

He said it was a bad time. There was an inquest. The
verdict was, of course, death by drowning. He said the
sea was safe enough most of the time, but you have to
watch for winds and cross-currents.

That really is what I wanted to tell you. It has made a

difference. I wanted you to know first, but somehow I really didn't want to think about it . . . so I kept putting off writing.

If you were here, I could talk to you. That would be easier. When one is writing it seems more serious, more important. If I could only *talk* to you, it would be so different.

So, don't tell the parents . . . yet. I wonder what they'll say? I'm just telling you at the moment. Everyone here knows about it, of course. There's always gossip. The servants are watching all the time. As I said, they are suspicious of me. I am not one of them. I heard one of them refer to me as "Mr. Dermot's foreign lady." I did mention this to Matilda and she laughed and said, "Everyone's a foreigner from the other side of the Tamar." So you see how it is.

I had to let you know this. Oh, how I wish you were here!

Your twin sister,
Dorabella

The letter disturbed me. Had she been in a certain mood when she wrote it? How much did it portray her real feelings? I knew her well. She could change her mind from one moment to another.

But whatever her mood, the fact remained that Dermot had been married before—and it was certainly strange that he had not mentioned it.

I think we should have seen him rather differently if we had known. He had seemed so light-hearted, so young. Had he been afraid of losing Dorabella? Why otherwise should he want to keep his first marriage a secret?

I should have liked to talk it over with my mother, but Dorabella had expressly said: "Don't tell the parents yet." And I must respect this confidence.

So I did not tell her that I had received the letter; she would have expected to read it if I had, for we shared Dorabella's letters.

I hated the subterfuge, but I decided that I must wait for Dorabella's permission before I divulged this secret.

I thought a great deal about Dorabella after that time and

wondered whether I ought to go down to see her. I was still anxious about my mother. She was not really ill, but I liked to make sure that she did not go out in cold winds or rain which she might do without me to restrain her. Her cold still hung on and I felt torn between them.

And then came the next letter.

This was change indeed. This was Dorabella exultant ... and yet a little fearful.

My dear Vee,

What do you think? I am going to have a baby. I am so excited. Can you believe it? *Me* ... a mother!

I have been to the doctor and it is confirmed. I would not have told you until it was. Dermot is thrilled. So is Matilda ... and the old man, too. And as for Gordon, even he seems quite interested.

I'm a bit scared, just a little, of course. It is rather an ordeal, you know. It has happened rather soon, but there's a long time to go yet.

Just fancy! You'll be Auntie Vee. It sounds a bit fierce to me. I think Auntie Violetta sounds much softer. Names are important. I'll have to get the right one for him/her.

Isn't it marvelous? I'm writing to the parents. I wonder who'll get their letter first, you or them. If you get yours first, tell them right away. Mummy will be Grandmamma and Daddy Grandpa. What nice ones they'll make!

Lots of love from,

Dorabella,

"Mother-to-be"

I had taken the letter to my room to read, wondering whether there would be more revelations about Dermot's first marriage. Revelations there had certainly been, but on a different subject.

Almost before I had had time to read the letter my mother came into my room. She had obviously received hers by the same post.

She was flushed and excited.

"You have heard, too," she cried.

I nodded. She was smiling.

"Dorabella a mother! I can't believe it. I thought it might be some time, of course . . . but not quite yet. How will she manage a baby?"

"People you least expect do turn out to be good mothers. She'll have a nanny, I suppose."

"We'll both go," said my mother. "And now we must tell your father. He will be so thrilled!"

The Cottage on the Cliffs

Before that week was out we were on our way to Cornwall.

Dermot and Dorabella met us at the station. Dorabella looked radiant and beautiful; the prospect of motherhood had changed her in a subtle way: There was a softness about her which made her seem more vulnerable than ever.

She flung herself at us. My mother hugged her and then it was my turn.

"It is wonderful that you have come," she cried.

"With news like this, what did you expect?" asked my mother.

"Everybody's thrilled, aren't they, Dermot?"

Dermot confirmed this and tenderly told her not to get too excited.

My mother smiled fondly at this display of husbandly concern, and we got into the car and drove to the house.

Matilda was waiting to greet us.

"How nice to see you," she said. "Dorabella has been hoping you'd come for ages. Of course, the weather has not been good."

"It's lovely now," said my mother.

"Spring is here."

We went to the rooms which we had had for our last visit.

The old man came down to dinner and Gordon Lewyth was there, too. They both said how pleased they were to see us.

The old man was smiling that strange smile of secret amusement which I had noticed before.

"What do you think of the news?" he asked.

"We are delighted," said my mother.

He nodded, smiling. "We are looking forward to the new arrival, aren't we, Matty . . . Gordon? All of us . . . we can't wait to see the little fellow."

"You seem to be sure it will be a boy," said my mother.

"Of course it will be a boy. Tregarlands always have boys."

He was laughing to himself, as though it were some big joke.

Gordon asked about my father. I think he was disappointed because he had not come with us.

The old man was saying: "Gordon is especially delighted. He is looking forward already to the little one's growing up and helping him with the estate. That is so, is it not, Gordon?"

Gordon's face twisted into a smile.

"You're looking very far ahead, Mr. Tregarland," he said.

"It's always a good idea to look ahead. Well, there is one thing we can be sure of. My grandson will have a good welcome when he arrives."

Again I had that feeling that there was some sort of innuendo intended, and the uneasiness I had felt during my previous visit came back to me.

We had little time to talk to Dorabella alone, but my mother did corner her and asked the question, "When?"

"November," said Dorabella.

I was hoping she would join me for a chat, which she would in due course, but I must be patient, it seemed.

My mother said to me, "November. That's seven months' time. We shall have to be with her then."

"We will. They all seem so delighted about it."

"Families love babies, and this will be the first to be born for years. They won't have had any babies around for a long time. I am going to ask to see the nurseries here. I'll get Matilda to show me. I am sure she will be very helpful. Dorabella is not the most practical person. She'll need looking after."

"It is wonderful that she is so happy."

"I hope she will be all right. Pregnancies can be trying times. What about Nanny Crabtree?"

"What about her?"

"For Dorabella, of course. I could see if she were free."

Nanny Crabtree had played a big part in my youth—and that meant Dorabella's. Plump, with a double chin, what had fascinated us about her from our earliest days had been a large wart on that second chin from which a solitary hair protruded.

We had often speculated about it and wondered why she did not pull it out.

"If she did," I prophesied, "two more would grow in its place."

Nanny Crabtree could be stern in the extreme and tell dire stories of what happened to little girls who did not eat up their rice pudding. They never grew up and remained little all their lives; if they made a face over it, God would be so angry with them and He would make them go through life with their tongues stuck out in a hideous scowl. But when we fell over we would fly to her ample lap to be comforted and have plaster or whatever was necessary from her spacious medicine cupboard; and if we were in some trouble which had been brought on through something not our fault, we were told that we were our Nanny Crabtree's Pet and that was enough for anyone. The mention of her name brought her back clearly to my mind.

"Nanny Crabtree sounds a wonderful idea," I said.

"And," said my mother, "we must make arrangements to be here at the time. And in between now and November it would be nice if one of us was here ... often. I know that is what she would like."

I could not sleep that night. It would be all right, I assured myself. November would soon be here. My mother would make sure everything was all right.

Yet I could not rid myself of that uneasiness which settled on me as soon as I was alone.

I lay listening to the sea breaking on the rocks below. It was like whispering voices.

The three of us spent a lot of time together. After all, it was the reason for our coming.

My mother discussed the practical details and we went into Plymouth and bought clothes for the baby and some for Dorabella when she would become advanced in pregnancy. We lunched at a restaurant near the main shops and talked animatedly as we ate as to what would be needed.

"November may seem a long way off now," said my mother, "but time flies. We must be prepared."

She had already told Dorabella that she was thinking of asking Nanny Crabtree to come.

Dorabella was amused and she and I went into a long "Do you remember?" conversation which resulted in much laughter as we recalled our childhood adventures with that redoubtable Nanny Crabtree.

Our mother listened with amused tolerance and then she said: "Well, you can trust Nanny Crabtree. She was heartbroken when you girls went away to school. I knew she would come back if she were free. Matilda is quite amenable. I discussed the matter with her, so there won't be any difficulty there. I shall write to Nanny Crabtree as soon as we get home."

While we were going round the shops I had an opportunity to ask Dorabella if she had told my mother yet about Dermot's first marriage.

"Yes," she said. "I told her this morning while we were waiting for you to come down."

"What did she say?"

"She was surprised. Not shocked really. She just said, 'Why didn't he tell you?' I said he didn't really want to talk about it, and that we never mention it now. Dermot said he had been afraid to tell me in case it made some difference. He thought it might change my feelings for him, and I might not want to marry him. That's what I told her."

"She doesn't think very much of it then?"

"Not all that much. She understands why he didn't want to tell."

"That's all right, then."

"I don't think about it now. When I wrote to you it was fresh in my mind and then it seemed . . . important. Matilda has referred to it once or twice and she said she's glad to see Dermot's happy now."

Later that day my mother came to my room, and I knew at once that she wanted to talk about Dermot's first marriage.

"I was astounded when she told me," she said. "You knew, of course. She said she had told you and bound you to secrecy. Well, it's over, isn't it . . . odd, he didn't say he was a widower."

"Perhaps he thought that sounded too mature. I think when they met in Germany he was very attracted to her and he wanted to be young and carefree, as she was, certainly not like a man who had been married."

"People get these notions. He's absolutely devoted to her. I was a little anxious because it was so rushed, but being here and seeing them together makes me feel better about it. I wish they weren't so far away. Matilda is very efficient, and I think she is quite fond of Dorabella. She's relieved that there is no interference with the running of the house which she might have got from some. So that side of it is all very amicable. I am not worried, really. We'll keep an eye on Dorabella and, if I can get Nanny Crabtree in residence, that will be fine. Thank goodness we have a little time to get all this worked out."

I was naturally hoping to see Jowan Jermyn again. I could remember every detail of that meeting with him from the time I was cautiously getting up from my fall to the moment we parted at the boundary of the two estates.

Starlight was still available and I had ridden her once or twice. I usually rode alone. It was early days yet, but Dermot was anxious that Dorabella should not ride. My mother was often in Matilda's company, discussing nursery preparations; Dorabella would now and then feel tired and want to rest. So I found that it was not difficult for me to slip away on my own.

I went to the stables. The groom, whose name I had discovered was Tom Smart, said: "Good morning, Miss. I reckon you be looking for Starlight."

He remembered that I had ridden the mare when she cast a shoe and I had had to take her to the blacksmith.

"She be in right good order this day, Miss," he told me. "None of they there shoes coming off this time."

"I hope not."

"She remembers you well. That's for certain sure. Her be pricking up her ears. Let her have a bit of a nuzzle and you'll see."

I followed his advice and it was clear that Starlight did remember me.

"I'll have her saddled in a tick," said Tom.

"Thank you."

" 'Tis a nice day for a ride," he said as he waved me off.

It *was* a nice day for a ride. April, I had discovered, was a beautiful month in Cornwall. Spring comes a little earlier there than to the rest of the country; there were wild flowers in the hedgerows; the trees did not thrive near the coast but inland they were magnificent; the heavy rainfall made for luscious growth. Some trees, however, were battered by the force of gales which had twisted them into odd shapes, which a few quirks of the imagination could transform into something from Dante's Inferno. A strange country, I thought. Sometimes it was warm and cosy, at others forbidding.

The screeching of the ever-present gulls sounded almost malignant, a warning mingling with the murmur of the sea.

I suppose I was being fanciful again. It was because I could not feel perfectly at ease at Tregarland's.

I turned toward the Jermyn land. I would have no excuse for trespassing this time, yet I had an urge to retrace my footsteps and recall that incident in every detail.

It was foolish of me, but there was no one around so I took the turning which I had taken before and found my way to the field.

There was the spot where the tree had fallen. I rode up to it and inspected the gap where it had been. I looked at it for some moments, thinking of that fall and how I had extricated my foot from the stirrup as Jowan Jermyn had arrived.

I rode across the field, trying to remember which way we had walked to the blacksmith's place. Once there, my trespassing would be at an end, because that would not be Jermyn land.

I was on a path which I had seen before. I came to a clearing and pulled up sharply. A group of men were standing together. There was a cottage close to a hedge and they were looking at something there. I would have turned and gone back, but one of the men had started to come toward me. I saw at once that it was Jowan Jermyn.

I felt overcome with embarrassment. I was caught trespassing again.

He called: "Hello there."

He came toward me.

"Why!" he said. "It's Miss . . . er . . . Denver."

I was surprised and rather pleased that he had remembered my name,

"I'm sorry," I said. "I'm trespassing again."

"No, no. Friends are always welcome."

"Thank you. I was trying to find that Smithy Inn. Am I near it?"

"Very close. Give me a moment and I'll join you."

He went over to the men while I waited. He very soon returned.

"We're doing some repairs to that cottage," he said. "It's becoming derelict. It hasn't been occupied for some time. Now, you are looking for Smithy's ... not the blacksmith's but the inn. No more lost shoes, I hope?"

"Oh, no. I thought I should find it more easily. I am very sorry to have trespassed again."

"I'm glad you did. I was getting a little bored with that cottage. They can manage very well without me. What have you been doing since I last saw you?"

"We had a wedding, you know."

"Of course. We all knew about that. And Dermot Tregarland returned with his fair bride. We are kept well informed, you know."

"Well, apart from the wedding, I have done very little. My mother has not been very well this winter and I have been helping to look after her."

"I hope she has now recovered?"

"She wasn't really ill. And thanks, she is quite well now. As a matter of fact, she is here in Cornwall with me."

"Good. Look. Here we are. Now you are here, you must try a glass of their very special cider."

"That sounds rather a good idea."

"I assure you it is. Let's take the mare to the stables. She'll be all right there."

We did so. I thought she must have been there before because the man in charge seemed to know her. Everyone here seemed to know everyone else.

The inn looked just as it had last time I had seen it—the fireplace with the glistening brasses, the cosy atmosphere. Mrs. Brodie came out to serve us. She recognized me immediately.

"Well, Miss, so you be back with us then? That be nice. Come back to see your sister, 'ave 'ee?"

I was amazed at her memory and told her so.

"That be part of the business, Miss. We do remember our customers."

"I told her she must try some of your excellent cider," said Jowan Jermyn.

"That be nice of 'ee, sir."

"The best in Cornwall," he added.

"And who am I to say nay to that? I'll get two tankards right away. That right?"

"Absolutely."

He smiled at me when she had gone. "She's a dear old soul," he said. "She has a mind like the Records Office. She knows what happens to every one of us from the time we were born."

"Isn't that rather uncomfortable?"

"It has its drawbacks, naturally, unless, of course, you are living a blameless life. That isn't much use to Mrs. Brodie. She likes a bit of excitement. But there are advantages. A visit to the inn and you can come out knowing more about your neighbors than you did when you went in."

"I think I would prefer anonymity."

"Does that mean . . . ?" He raised his eyebrows. "But, no, I am impertinent."

"Not in the least," I retorted. "I merely mean that I should not like to have my actions put on record. I suppose she will tell people that I, coming from Tregarland's, took a tankard of cider with the enemy across the boundary."

"Undoubtedly."

"Which cannot be of great interest to anyone."

"I disagree. But it does depend on what news is going around at the time. The system has to be kept going and any scrap of news is better than no news at all. Besides, you have forgotten the feud."

"But I am not really involved. I am not one of the enemy."

"That," he said, "is a nice thought."

Mrs. Brodie appeared with the tankards.

When she had gone, he said: "How long shall you be here?"

"It isn't decided yet, but it won't be a long visit. Though my mother and I will be here for the birth . . . and before that, I daresay."

"Oh, the baby."

"My sister is going to have one. But I expect your excellent news service has told you that already?"

"It has indeed. I am very interested and delighted that you will be a frequent visitor."

"My sister likes to have her family around."

"Naturally."

"And as she and I are twins . . ."

"Of course. Well, let us hope it all goes well."

"But of course it will," I replied with conviction.

"Of course. The cider is good, isn't it?"

"Very."

"The West Country is famous for it, you know—Devon and Cornwall."

"So I have heard."

"You did tell me last time we met that you had left school last summer. Shall you stay at home or take up some career?"

"Because of my sister's sudden marriage, I have not thought of anything but that. Until the baby is born I think we shall be quite preoccupied with that."

"And you will be here often, so that we shall be neighbors. I am sure they are very happy at Tregarland's about the child."

"Oh, yes, they are."

"It will be a comfort . . . after what happened."

"You must be referring to Dermot's first wife. I think he is very happy now. That other is all in the past."

"Oh, yes."

"I suppose people round here know all about his first marriage."

He lifted his shoulders as though to imply what did I expect.

"Did you know her?"

"Not personally. I had seen her around. She lived with her mother in one of the cottages right on the cliff looking down on West Poldown. One saw her around quite a bit. She worked at the Sailor's Rest."

"The Sailor's Rest? Isn't that the inn on the west side overlooking the river mouth?"

"That's it." He grinned at me. "Something of a mésalliance, I fear."

"I didn't know that."

"Shock waves ran round the place when they married. I can't imagine old Mr. Tregarland was very pleased with the choice of his son and heir. People liked her. Annette, she was ... Annette Pardell. Mrs. Pardell still lives in ... er ... Cliff Cottage, I think it is called. She never got over it. She's a widow and Annette was her only child. You didn't know this?"

"No, not the details. Dorabella told me that Dermot had been married before and that his first wife had died. She had drowned when bathing."

"Annette was a great one for the sea. They say she was in it every day during the summer. A big, strong girl, the last you'd think to go that way. She'd been swimming since she was a child. They came down here from the North of England—Yorkshire, I think. I gathered Mrs. Pardell had some sort of pension, enough to get by. She rented Cliff Cottage and has been there ever since she came to Cornwall. Annette was a fine-looking girl. Mrs. Pardell had plans for her and was not too pleased when she landed up in the bar. She was an excellent barmaid, bright and saucy. You know the sort. She got on well with the men customers, and the women liked her, too. There was talk when she married the son of the big house, as you can imagine—and then she died like that."

"Was Dermot very upset?"

He was silent for a while.

"I don't know," he said at length. "But I don't think it had been very good at the house. You know how it is. Annette did not really fit in. And there was the baby ..."

"What baby?"

"Oh ... she was going to have a baby. That was why she shouldn't have gone swimming. She was not in a fit state to do so. It was foolish of her. There was no one about apparently. It was early morning. She'd always liked a swim first thing in the morning. The temptation must have been too strong for her. Of course, in her condition, she should have known better. She went down to that beach below the Tregarland gardens and went in from there. Her body was washed up a week or so later. There was mystery for a few days, but her bathrobe and slippers were there on the beach to indicate what had happened."

"What a terrible tragedy! And the baby ..."

"I reckon they are overjoyed now that there is another little one on the way."

"Oh, yes. They are thrilled, of course."

"I understand that. And I am delighted because it means that you will be down here often, and you and I can have a little rendezvous. You can't invite me to Tregarland. I am wondering whether I can ask you to my place. This is the first time that stupid feud has been a nuisance."

"Tell me about yourself," I said.

He lifted his shoulders. "What do you want to know?"

"You love your estate. I believe Jermyn Priory has been in your family for years."

"Yes. It was a priory in the fourteenth century. In the sixteenth it was destroyed with countless others and later the house was built using some of the stone from the desecrated priory. My family came here at that time and we have been here ever since. My father was a younger son, and I did not inherit the place until two years ago. I have an excellent manager. We get on well together and he lives in a house close to the Priory. He has an efficient wife who has taken upon herself to see that I lack nothing. I have a good housekeeper and am surrounded by excellent people, so I am well cosseted. There! You couldn't get better than that from Mrs. Brodie."

"You seem to be well satisfied with life."

"Up to a point. I often go to London and now and then travel on the Continent. I should like to see more of my neighbors, but it is surprising how this stupid feud gets in the way. It's ridiculous after all these years. But there it is."

"Perhaps if you made a few advances . . . ?"

"I did try once and was refused. The Tregarlands are not very sociable, you know. The old man is a bit of an enigma and he is the head of it. He lives rather like a recluse now, but he had quite a reputation in the past. He was once a very merry gentleman—very fond of the ladies—traveling around, living riotously. Dances, card parties, and then suddenly he became ill. It was the gout, I believe, which incapacitated him somewhat. He married in his forties, but he didn't really settle down then until the gout grew worse. His wife died a few years after Dermot was born, and then Mrs. Lewyth and her little boy came to live there. She looks after him very well, I believe. There's a rumour that she is a distant relation—a poor one—but no one seems quite certain of that."

"I am not sure, either."

"Well, he has become much more sober since then. Enforced, of course. But all that was years ago."

He looked at my empty tankard.

"Would you like another?" he asked.

"No, thanks."

"I see you are a wise young woman. It is rather potent."

"Yes, it certainly is."

"You'll get used to it in time." He smiled at me. "As we can't invite each other to our houses, we shall have to have a meeting place. Not too often here." He raised his eyebrows. "For obvious reasons, we do not want to figure too often in the news bulletins. We will go somewhere else. There are some interesting places around here."

"I daresay I shall be going home soon."

"We must meet before you do and make arrangements for your next descent upon us."

I felt very pleased that he had suggested this, and we arranged to meet two days later in the field where I had fallen and we would go out to the Horned Stag, which was a little way out on the moor.

We parted at the boundary and I rode back to Tregarland's exhilarated by the encounter, but I could not stop thinking of Annette who was to have had Dermot's child and had, one morning, foolishly gone swimming in the sea.

Next morning I could not resist going along to have a look at Cliff Cottage. There it was, as Jowan Jermyn had described it, set on the west cliff, looking down on the town. It was very neat, with white net curtains at the windows and a front garden which was clearly very well tended.

I lingered and a woman came out of the cottage. I had a notion that she had seen me through the lace curtains.

She did not speak; she had a somewhat dour expression— one might say bellicose almost, as though she were warning me to keep away.

"Good morning," I said pleasantly.

She nodded acknowledgment of the greeting and somehow managed to imply that, as far as she was concerned, that was the end of the encounter.

I was disappointed. I had hoped she would be like so many of the people hereabouts, eager for a little chat.

I said: "I was admiring your garden."

I had hit on the right note, for her expression softened ever so slightly. I had guessed she was devoted to her garden. I pressed home my advantage.

"How do you manage to get these lovely things to grow here? It must be difficult, for you would get the full force of the wind, I imagine."

"Aye," she said grudgingly. "The wind's a problem."

"It must be hard work, and, of course, you have to choose what will thrive."

"You a gardener?" she asked. Her voice was quite different from the soft Cornish accent which I had been hearing all around me. I remembered that Jowan Jermyn had said she came from the North.

"Not an expert one," I said, falsely lying by implication, for I was no gardener at all. "But it is a fascinating hobby."

"You're right. Gets a hold of you."

"Those firs . . . they are . . . ?"

"Lawson's cypress. Make a good hedge. The rate they grow, too!" She was definitely relenting. "They came through the post in an envelope . . . just a little packet, a bunch of sprigs. Now look at them."

"Miraculous," I said, gazing rapturously at them.

"They grow stubby . . . not tall, then they stand up to the wind. That's something you have to think about in this place."

I knew that it would be fatal to try to take the subject away from the garden.

She volunteered: "Climate here is soft and damp. Plants here are four weeks in advance of those in the North."

"Is that so? What healthy-looking plants those are. What are they?"

She looked shocked because I did not know something so commonplace.

"Hydrangeas, of course. Grow like wildfire here because of the damp. This is going to be a good year for the roses."

"Is it?"

She nodded sagely. "I know the signs."

"You have some lovely ones."

"Some varieties, yes. I'd like to get my hands on a good Christmas rose."

"Can't you . . . er . . . get your hands on one?"

"There's one variety I want. 'Ee, it's gradely, that one. I've only ever seen one in these parts. In the big house garden." Her face hardened perceptibly. "Up at Tregarland's. They've got just the one I'd like. They can grow it, and they're as exposed as I am. Can't get one anywhere. I've tried. I reckon it's a hybrid. It's a special sort. Like a Christmas rose yet different . . . in a way. Not quite, you see. I've never seen one just like it."

"Wouldn't they give you a cutting or something?"

I was afraid I was betraying my ignorance of horticulture and that she would sense there was some ulterior motive behind all this.

"I wouldn't ask them. I wouldn't have aught to do with them."

"Oh, that's a pity."

I had blundered.

She said: "Well, I've got work to do."

She nodded curtly. It was dismissal.

I had imagined a cosy chat, being invited into the house, perhaps a glass of homemade cider or elderberry wine. Far from it! I should find it very difficult to get any information out of her.

I wanted so much to talk to her, to hear about the daughter who had worked as a barmaid at the Sailor's Rest, who had married the heir of Tregarland's, who had met an untimely death. But there would be nothing of that from Mrs. Pardell.

Disappointed, I retraced my steps.

I wished I could talk to her. She would be down to earth; there would be no flights of fancy, only solid facts. I believed I could have had a clear picture from her.

But why did I want it? It was all in the past. Yet what I had learned had made me think differently. People were not always what they seemed. Dermot himself . . . the charming, rather debonair young man on a walking tour in the German forest had given no hint of the tragedy in his life which could not have left him unscathed. How different he would have seemed—to me at any rate—if I had known that he had had a wife who had been drowned not long before her baby would have been born. Then there was the old man who had led a riotous life and nowadays was more or less a recluse with a keen and, I was sure, mischievous delight in what was going on around him. Matilda, of course, was easy to know. Her son Gordon puzzled me a little. He was so aloof, so wrapped up in the estate toward which Dermot seemed almost indifferent.

On the way back to Tregarland's an idea came to me.

I really did want to see more of Mrs. Pardell, and I should have no excuse for calling again. I could not just hang over the fence and gaze at the garden. And if I did, it would not be long before she would discover my ignorance. And then I imagined that shrewd Northern lady would soon suspect other motives—particularly when she discovered I was a guest at Tregarland's and the sister of Dermot's second wife. How much did she know? The Cornish were suspicious of foreigners and she would undoubtedly be dubbed one.

I decided to act on the idea which had come to me. It might misfire, but there was no reason why I should not give it a trial.

When I returned to the house, I went to the garden which sloped down to the sea and the private beach—that beach where Dermot's first wife had gone to bathe on that fateful morning. I stood for a moment, letting the faintly scented air gently caress me. It was beautiful here, but I kept thinking of Annette's coming down the slope. She would walk slowly, being heavily pregnant. How could she have done that? She must have known what a risk she was taking. I was lost in thought until I reminded myself why I was here.

I saw one of the gardeners at work some little way off, and I went to him.

I knew his name was Jack, so I said: "Hello, Jack."

He touched his cap and leaned on his spade.

"Nice day, Miss," he said.

"The gardens are looking beautiful."

He looked pleased.

"They'll be a real treat in a week or so. Let's hope us don't get no more of them there winds."

"They are the garden's biggest enemy, I suppose."

He scratched his head. "There be others, but you can't get away from them there winds. And here . . . well!" He lifted his shoulders in a helpless gesture.

"You've got that plant," I began. "Is it some sort of Christmas rose?"

"Oh . . . I do know what you mean. It be a Christmas rose

... with a difference like. It's not one that you come across every day of your life."

"Could you show it to me? I'd like to see it."

I followed him up the slope a little way.

"It be over 'ere, Miss. There. Beauty, ain't she?"

"Jack, can you take cuttings of these things?"

"Well, Miss, course you can. Trouble is they don't always take root. This 'un ... well ... 'er likes it here. Perhaps her fancies a bit of breeze now and then, and there's the salt in the air. You'll get some as flourishes by the sea and there's others can't abide it."

"I met someone who was asking about that rose. Is it possible to take a cutting that I could give her?"

"Well, Miss, I don't see why not."

"Would you do that for me?"

"Course I would, Miss. Don't guarantee it'll take."

"She's a good gardener and would try very hard."

"Someone round here then?"

"Someone I got into conversation with. She mentioned the rose, you see ..."

"Oh, aye. Right you are, Miss. When would you want it?"

"Tomorrow?"

"You come to me, Miss, and I'll do it then."

"Oh, thank you, Jack. She'll be delighted."

"I just hope it takes, that's all."

I smiled. I did not care greatly whether it "took" or not. I was obsessed at the moment about having a talk with the mother of Dermot's first wife.

The following morning I took the cutting to Cliff Cottage. The transformation was amazing. She stared at it and a smile of pleasure crossed her face. I could not believe that she often looked like that. It changed her completely.

"You got it then?" she said.

"It was no problem. I just asked the gardener. I think he was pleased that someone had admired it."

"I can't tell you ..." She took it from me almost reverently, and started to walk into the house. I followed her.

"He said it might not take."

"I know that. It happens now and then."

"If it doesn't, you must let me know and I will get you another."

We were in a hall, shining with polish, and then went into an equally immaculate kitchen. I knew I was being bold and perhaps brazen, but I had not made this effort for nothing, and she would have to be polite to me since I had brought her such a prize.

I do believe she was truly grateful.

She said: "It was good of you."

She was doing something to the cutting. She stood it in a glass of water and turned to me.

"Perhaps you'd like a cup of coffee ... or some tea?"

I said I should like a cup of coffee.

"I'll put you in the sitting room while I make it."

"Thank you."

I was seated there. It was just what I had expected. I could smell the furniture polish. The wooden floor, with its rugs, looked slightly dangerous. I was careful not to slip.

Almost immediately I saw the photograph in a silver frame on a small table. The girl was plump and as unlike Mrs. Pardell as any girl could be. She was smiling and there was a hint of mischief in the smile. She had a retroussé nose and a wide smile. Her blouse was low-cut, revealing the beginnings of an ample bosom.

Annette, I thought. And what had Mrs. Pardell's reaction been to her daughter's working as a barmaid at the Sailor's Rest? It was an incongruous occupation for the daughter of such a woman.

She came in with two cups of coffee on a tray, and the words "That is your daughter, I suppose?" came to my lips, but I restrained myself in time from uttering them. I must act with care, or I should never be invited here again.

"This is kind of you," I said instead.

"Least I could do."

She made it sound as though it were a necessary payment for my efforts; and I knew that I must be very cautious.

My eyes kept straying to the picture of the girl, and it occurred to me that, as she must be aware of my interest, it would seem odd if I said nothing.

"What an attractive girl!" I said.

"Think so?" Her lips tightened.

"Is she your daughter?"

She nodded. "Was. She's gone now . . . she died."

"Oh, I am sorry."

She was cautious. I sensed that, cutting or no cutting, she would have no prying.

I changed the subject.

"You come from the North, I believe?"

"Yes. Came here with my husband. He got a bad chest at his work and, as was right and proper, they gave him a sum of money. Well, we came here. Climate was better for him, they said."

"And you like it here?"

"Some ways do, some ways don't."

"Well," I said philosophically, "that's life, isn't it?"

"It's good growing grounds."

So, I thought, we are back to the garden. I must be very careful not to reveal my ignorance and a certain lack of enthusiasm for the subject.

I said: "This coffee is good. It is so kind of you."

She frowned. I could see she was thinking, Southern claptrap . . . saying what they don't mean. The coffee's all right and after all, as I had procured the cutting, she naturally had to make a show of hospitality. That was all it was . . . so why pretend?

She said: "In the North you know where you are. Here, well, there's a lot of soft talk. Blah-blah, I call it. Me dear this and me dear that, and when you turn your back they're tearing you to pieces."

"People are more forthright in the North, I am sure. So you live alone?"

"Yes, now."

I was on dangerous ground again. If I were not careful, I should not be asked again.

Gratitude for the cutting, however, lingered on, and I did want to hear her account of her daughter's death.

She said suddenly: "You on holiday here?"

"Yes . . . at Tregarland's."

"Yes. I know. You got the cutting from the gardens there."

She was holding her head high and nodding a little. Her lips were tightly drawn together.

I said: "You probably know it is my sister who has married into the family."

She nodded. It was not a good recommendation: the sister of the wife who had taken the place of her daughter.

I said hastily: "I shall not be there long. My mother and I are going home in a few days."

She nodded again. I think that made her feel a little more kindly toward me.

I realized she was not going to share any confidences with me. I was wasting my time. But I was not going to give up yet.

I said, putting the cup down close to Annette's picture: "Well, thank you. That was very nice. I do hope the cutting takes."

"We'll have to see about that."

"I wonder . . . if you'd mind . . . ?"

She looked at me intently and I went on boldly: "I wonder, on my next visit, if I might call so that you could show me how it thrived?"

Her face changed. The gardener was a different woman from the bereaved mother.

"Of course, you must come. I'll be glad to show you. And I'll tell you this: It's going to be happy in my garden. You'll see. When you next come, it will be settled in a treat."

I came out of Cliff Cottage smiling.

Not exactly a successful enterprise, but it was not completely closed.

I started on my way down to the little town, thinking of Mrs. Pardell and wondering if I should ever succeed in getting her to talk to me as I wanted her to. It was a challenge, and I could not help feeling proud of myself for thinking of such an astute move in taking the cutting. She was forthright in the extreme. She would pride herself on calling a spade a spade. She would not tolerate deception, as she would call the diplomatic but not quite sincere methods of the Southerners in making life comfortable with a few white lies. I knew her type well. For her the bare truth must stand, however disagreeable.

There was a slight breeze bringing with it the smell of seaweed. The path along the cliff was uneven. One went downhill and then up again. Tom Smart, the groom, had said: " 'Tis a bony road along they cliff paths," and I knew what he meant. In places the path was narrow—not safe for children—and in parts there was a direct drop to the sea. Farther along, I knew, there was a section where the path was particularly narrow and the drop exceptionally steep. A fence had been erected there since, Matilda had told me, one day an elderly man had slipped on an icy surface and plunged over the cliff to his death.

I stood still for a moment to fill my lungs with the invigorating air.

Few people used this part of the cliff. It was very rugged and particularly beautiful. I supposed I should get to know it very well in time, for Dorabella and I would never tolerate being apart for long, and I supposed I should be here often.

I watched a greedy gull snatch a titbit from the mouth of another. He swooped triumphantly while the victim screeched in anger.

Then I heard footsteps coming along the path. I started to move and came to the narrow spot with the fence. It certainly did not look very strong. Above the path rose the cliff face and below it the steep drop to the sea.

"Violetta," said a voice. I swung round. Gordon Lewyth was coming toward me.

"Oh," I said. "It's you."

"I saw you coming out of Cliff Cottage."

"Did you? I didn't see you."

"Visiting Mrs. Pardell?"

"Oh, yes."

"How did you manage that? She is not known for her hospitality."

"No," I replied. "But she is a very keen gardener, too."

"A common interest? So you are a keen gardener, too?"

"Well, not exactly."

He was standing very near to me. I did not know what to think of him. I never had. He was a very secret person, and I felt it would be very hard to understand what was in his mind. His height, his broadness, seemed to dwarf me so that I felt a certain vulnerability. I had the sudden feeling that he could be very ruthless, and I seemed very much alone and unprotected.

I heard myself explaining: "I looked at her garden when I was passing, and she came out and talked and told me about some plant she had seen in the gardens at Tregarland's, and I got a cutting for her from Jack. I took it to her and she asked me in for a cup of coffee."

"That was a great concession. She is not very friendly with us at the house."

"I have heard of the connection."

He nodded. "And did you have an interesting chat?"

"Well, no . . . it was about gardens, of which I know very little."

"Oh," he said, and put his hand on the fence. "People don't use this road very much," he went on.

"There are lots of ups and downs," I said.

"There is the higher road above . . ." He nodded upwards. "But it is a long way round. Wet weather, frost, could be a hazard on this road."

He seemed to be watching me intently, and again I felt a twinge of uneasiness.

"The fence is not very strong," he said, gripping it and shaking it a little. "If someone fell against it . . . Well, it wouldn't stand up to much, would it? It should be repaired. They don't move very fast about that sort of thing in these parts."

I wondered why we were standing here, but he seemed to be barring my way. I felt a sudden relief when I heard a footstep. Someone was coming along the path.

I moved forward and he could only walk beside me. I was glad when we had passed the fence, and it was comforting to hear the voices of people coming along behind us. They were visitors to the place, most likely, as Gordon did not know them.

We walked in single file when the path narrowed and then again we were side by side.

He told me he had business in the town and talked a little about the place.

"The river mouth makes a nice little harbor," he said. "The town owes its prosperity to that. The fishing is good here. And how is your father?"

I said he was well.

"I hope he will come with you next time."

"I don't know. He is always so busy on the estate."

"I can understand that."

We were descending rapidly and he held out a hand to steady me when the ground grew rougher. Then he apologized for the gesture.

He was a strange man. I could not help feeling that he was someone quite different from the person he appeared to be. I was not sure whether I was repulsed or drawn to him.

He said suddenly: "Do you propose to call on Mrs. Pardell again?"

"We are not really on visiting terms. In due course I might be allowed to see if the plant is flourishing. That is all."

A slight smile touched his lips.

"If you go," he said, "be careful on that path. The way round the top road is much longer and you'd have a steep descent to reach the cottage."

"Thanks. I think I'll risk the path. But I shall have to wait until the plant has taken root, or whatever it has to do."

He smiled. "You certainly don't sound like the dedicated gardener."

"No, I am not."

He was looking at me with a quizzical expression. I knew he was asking himself how I had managed to insinuate myself into Cliff Cottage. It must seem like a very calculated operation to him, and he must be wondering why I should take so much trouble merely to talk to Mrs. Pardell.

He said: "I shall have to leave you here." He looked at his watch. "I have to meet someone in five minutes."

"Goodbye," I said.

As I walked back, I thought it seemed rather a strange encounter, but I had spoken to him more during it than I had all the time I had known him.

That afternoon I met Jowan Jermyn in the field at the spot where the tree had fallen.

It was clear that he was delighted to see me.

Dorabella had been feeling very tired and was resting, otherwise it would not have been easy to get away. I had been out all the morning.

I did not tell her about my adventure with Mrs. Pardell. I was not sure how she felt about that first marriage of Dermot's, and I did not want to upset her in the slightest way.

She did not protest when I went off. I think she was content because my mother and I were there and if she wanted us, one of us would be at hand.

She would be amused when I told her about my meeting with Jowan Jermyn, for she was already taking an interest in him and was intrigued by the manner in which we had met.

He had been waiting for me.

"Right on time," he said. "I do like punctual ladies."

"I am always punctual, unless, of course, something unforeseen happens to prevent it. We were brought up to believe that it was the height of rudeness not to be. My mother used to say that to be late implied that you were not very eager to come."

"What an excellent doctrine! And your sister . . . she is the same?"

"Well . . ."

He laughed. "And how is she?"

"A little tired, I think. My mother will be there if she wants company."

"That is nice. Now, away to the moors and the Horned Stag."

"It sounds rather ferocious."

"Wait till you see the creaking sign over the door—a venomous beast—enough to drive customers away rather than entice them in. But it is a cosy spot and there isn't another inn for some miles."

I was fascinated by the moor. There was something rather eerie about it. I could see no sign of human habitation. Here and there great boulders stood out among the grass and away in the distance was a ring of stones which looked like figures.

"The moor!" announced Jowan. "What do you think of it?"

"Strange. Uncanny in a way."

"You're not the first to think of that."

"Those stones . . . one could think they were people."

He brought his horse close to mine.

"At certain times of the year," he said in a tone of mock awe, "they say they come to life, and woe betide anyone who sets eyes on them."

"What?" I cried.

He laughed. "You look scared. Don't worry. They won't come alive for you. They did once—so they tell me—for poor old Samuel Starky. That was fifty years ago. Poor Samuel, he came into the Horned Stag crying, 'They'm all alive. The

Stones have come to life! Death and destruction is to come to Bandermoor!' That's the name of the little village which I'll show you later. ' 'Twill be destroyed this night.' You see, the grocer's wife had run off with the postman, and the grocer had taken a woman into his house. Sodom and Gomorrah had come to Bandermoor, and the Stones had come to life to wreak vengeance."

"And what happened to Bandermoor?"

"Oh, it went on in its peaceful way and the Stones remained. Oddly enough, people still think there is something supernatural about them. Well, this is the Horned Stag. Take note of the animal. Isn't he fearsome?"

"I think it is because the paint round his eyes has become a little blurred."

"What a practical young lady you are! Practical and punctual. I like it. Come along."

We first took our horses to the stables and then went in. The inn parlor was almost a replica of that of the Smithy. Tankards of cider were brought to us.

"I believe you are getting quite a taste for the stuff," he said.

"It's certainly very pleasant."

"Tell me," he said, "when shall you be leaving us?"

"The day after tomorrow."

He grimaced. "So soon? But you will be here again?"

"I should think so."

"Your sister is quite well?"

"I think everything is going according to plan."

On a sudden impulse I told him I had met Mrs. Pardell.

He was surprised.

"Really? She has not a reputation for making friends easily."

"I would not aspire to friendship."

I told him about the cutting.

He was amused. "What a devious plan!" he said. "I can see you are a mistress of diplomacy. Why were you so eager to meet her?"

"I have to admit that I am by nature curious."

"Curious, practical, and punctual," he murmured. "The last two are virtues. I am not sure about the first. Why were you so curious to meet the lady from the North?"

"Naturally because of her daughter. I was taken aback when my sister told me there had been a previous marriage, but I did not know who the first wife was until you told me."

"And then you wanted to know more about her?"

"It was a natural feeling, wasn't it?"

"Indeed, yes. I daresay your sister would want to know."

"I don't think she cares very much. She never liked anything that might be ... uncomfortable. She likes everything to go smoothly, and if they don't, push them out of the way where they can be forgotten."

"But you are not like that?"

"No. I want to know everything, no matter what it is."

"I understand perfectly. But what did you think you would get from the lady?"

"I thought I might hear something about the girl ... Annette. What she was like, how it all happened."

"I doubt you got much from Mrs. Pardell."

"Nothing at all."

"Too bad after such a clever plot with the plant. But congratulations on a piece of imaginative strategy. Pity it was wasted."

"Not entirely. I am to go again next visit to see whether the thing has flourished."

"Clever! I'm overcome with admiration. What profit do you hope to get from all this?"

"The more you know of people, the more you understand them."

"Are you anxious about your sister?" he asked searchingly.

I hesitated. Was I? I had always been a sort of watchdog for us both. I remembered our first day at school—her hand tightly clasping mine, myself trying not to show her the trepidation I felt; seated together at the little desk. Dorabella close to me, reassured because I was there, the strong one; and she did not know that I was only pretending, as much for her sake as my own.

I was certainly uneasy about her. I could not rid myself of the feeling that there was something not quite right at Tregarland's. It was a strange notion, but there seemed to be something slightly unreal about the people there.

I could not explain this to Jowan Jermyn. I had been too frank already. What had possessed me to tell him of my little subterfuge in getting a footing into Cliff Cottage by means of the cutting?

The fact was that I felt at ease with him. I laughed at his way of taking everything lightly and finding it amusing. I realized that what I felt about the Tregarland household was all speculation. They had all been kind to us and very welcoming to Dorabella. My mother seemed satisfied. I was inclined to let my imagination run on, to conjure up drama where it did not exist.

He was watching me intently and asked if I were worried about my sister.

"Well," I said. "It has all happened rather quickly. This time last year we did not know of the Tregarlands' existence ... and then to find one's sister married and about to have a baby in a place quite a few miles from home."

"I understand. You feel there is much to know and your sister's husband's first wife is part of it."

"Yes, I suppose that is what I feel."

"It's just a straightforward story. The heir of Tregarland married the barmaid; she was about to have a child, and there was a tragedy. That's all."

"Do you mean that he married her because she was going to have a child?"

"I believe that was so. It was the verdict of the news agency, at least."

"I see. As you say, it is not an unusual story."

"The family wouldn't have been very pleased, of course." He shrugged his shoulders. "But these things happen in the best regulated families. It is all in the past. I gather they are delighted with this marriage."

"Have your sources told you this?"

"Certainly. And they are rarely mistaken."

He started to tell me of some of the legends of the place; of the celebrations on the moor on Midsummer's Eve; the bonfires hailing the dawn; Hallow E'en when the witches thrived.

"And Cornish witches into the bargain are far more malevolent than other people's witches."

He also told me of the Furry Dance which heralded in the spring, when people danced through the streets of the towns.

I was absorbed and disappointed when it was time to go.

"You'll be back," were his parting words, when we said

goodbye at the boundary. "I shall hear, of course, when you return, and we shall meet in the field, the scene of our first encounter. Is that a promise?"

"It is," I said.

And I intended to keep it.

Rescue on the Rocks

❧

Two days later, my mother and I traveled back home. My mother sat back in the carriage with a look of satisfaction on her face.

"Everything seems to be going well," she said. "I can't wait till November. If only we could get Nanny Crabtree there I think everything could be just perfect. Dermot is such a nice young man. I liked him more and more." She frowned. "Gordon is somewhat . . ."

I waited while she paused, searching for the word she needed to describe him.

"Overpowering," she said at length. "Although he says very little, he does behave as though *he* is the son of the house. Well, I suppose we shall be going down again soon. I think Dorabella would have liked you to stay."

"Well, I daresay I shall be making the journey back there very soon," I said.

When I was back at Caddington I saw things differently. My mother was right. Everything was going well.

I thought often of Jowan Jermyn. It would be amusing to see him again. I rather liked the fact that we had to meet . . . well, not exactly secretly . . . but to take certain precautions not to be seen too frequently at the same place.

I wondered if Mrs. Brodie had reported that we had called in twice at Smithy's. It was very probable. It had been tactful of him to suggest the meeting at the Horned Stag.

My father was delighted to see us. He said that he wished Dorabella could come home for a while.

My mother said: "She is at her own home now, and you

could hardly expect her to leave her husband. And her husband has an estate to look after."

"Gordon does that very well," replied my father. "I don't think Dermot would be missed all that much."

It was as near as he could get to a criticism and very unusual with him. It showed how much he wanted to see his daughter.

I missed her, too, but I was sure it would not be long before I went to Cornwall again. I wanted to be with her. Moreover, it was exciting, and a little mysterious in a way, which appealed to my penchant for intrigue. I could not rid myself of the idea that there was something strange about the household, and I felt it would be very interesting to discover what it was. And then, of course, there would be meetings with Jowan Jermyn.

My mother was overjoyed to hear from Nanny Crabtree. She would be free at the beginning of September and would take a short holiday to stay with her cousin in Northamptonshire. She would be ready to go to Cornwall at the beginning of October which would give her a few weeks to settle in before the baby arrived.

We heard from Edward that he and Gretchen would like to come and see us and perhaps stay a couple of weeks. They had a friend who would like to see Cornwall. Should we mind very much if they brought him with them?

"I am sure you will like Richard," he said. "He is a lawyer and has been a great help to me."

My mother was always delighted to see Edward and wrote back enthusiastically of her pleasure at the proposed visit.

Edward was now attached to a law firm in London. He and Gretchen were living in the Greenham family house in Westminster at the time but were looking for a house of their own. Edward wrote to my mother regularly so that she could keep in touch with everything he was doing. Although she was only about fifteen years older than he was, he looked upon her as a mother, which was not really surprising, as she was the one who had brought him out of Belgium when the Germans had been invading that country.

They arrived in the early afternoon. Gretchen looked very happy; so did Edward. We were introduced to the friend, Richard Dorrington, a tall, pleasant-looking young man who thanked my mother profusely for asking him.

I could see immediately that she liked him. She told him that Edward's friends were always welcome.

It was an interesting visit. My father quite obviously liked Richard Dorrington, too—but then he liked most people—yet I did sense a rather special feeling for this young man.

Edward said he was going to show Richard some of the local sights, for Richard, who had lived most of his life in London, did not know this part of the country at all.

Over the first meal Edward talked about the places he had in mind.

"You'd like to see some of these spots again, wouldn't you, Violetta?" said my mother.

I agreed that I would.

"Robert will be very cross when he hears you've been here," said my mother to Richard. "Robert is my young son. He's always annoyed because he is at school when we have visitors here. Well, the four of you must go together. You must take Richard to that old Chidam place for lunch. It is really rather fun. Ye Olde Reste House, pretending to date back to the days of Henry VIII when it was actually built about ten years ago. Ye olde Tudor beams—put in all of ten years ago! I expect they have a ghost. Anne Boleyn will appear one day."

"I don't think she ever went near the place," said Edward.

"That's of no account. They'll find a way of fitting her in with ye olde Tudor beams. It is really quite amusing with the waitresses in Tudor costumes, complete with lipstick and permanently waved hair."

"It sounds amusing," said Richard.

"It is . . . just for once. You will take him, Edward?"

Then we talked about Edward's househunting in London.

"I'd like to be near Chambers," said Edward.

"Richard has a fine place in Kensington," added Gretchen.

"I think," said Edward smiling at her, "we shall have to go for something less grand."

"Our place has been in the family for some years," said Richard. "My grandfather bought it. Then it went to my father and now to me."

"In a quiet square," added Gretchen.

"One of those big family houses, built round a garden

square for exclusive use of the residents who surround it," explained Edward.

"There are some lovely houses in those squares," said my mother.

"You need a family to fill them," put in Gretchen.

"I have my widowed mother and sister Mary Grace living with me," said Richard. "It has always been home to us."

"Then you have old Mrs. what's-her-name to keep everything in order," said Edward.

"That's the housekeeper," Richard explained to us. "Yes, she is one of the old faithful kind. She makes everything run smoothly."

"I know the type," said my mother.

My father liked to hear what people thought of the political situation. He always felt that people from London would know more of what was going on than we did in the country.

"What do you think of the new Prime Minister?" asked Richard Dorrington.

"It's early days yet. He's only been in office just over a month. He did some good work in the past, and it was time Baldwin went, I suppose. Though he did very well over the Abdication. He probably needed a rest after that, hence his resignation. I would say that Neville Chamberlain has not had long enough to be judged."

"I don't like the situation on the Continent."

Edward said: "It is certainly thought-provoking."

"Mussolini is being closely watched," went on Richard. "Europe is very uneasy about him, but they all stood by when he invaded Abyssinia. They were horrified, shocked, and disapproving, but they did just nothing. If the countries had stood together then, if they had imposed sanctions, he would have had to withdraw in a few weeks. But they stood by, saying how disgraceful it was, while he snapped his fingers at them and went on. I was in Rome this time last year . . . no, a little earlier. It was May. It was in the Piazza Venezia; the crowd was great. I heard there were about 400,000 gathered there, and I could well believe that. Mussolini came out and announced to us all that after fourteen years of fascist rule Italy had an empire."

"What sort of a man is he?" asked my father.

"Powerful, charismatic in the extreme, with a hypnotic quality. One sensed he had them all in his power. I think these forceful dictators must arouse a certain uneasiness in the minds of many people. They are too powerful, and their people do not seem to question their actions. They can't, I suppose. They dare not. He is modeling himself on his ally, Adolf Hitler."

I saw the change in Gretchen. She lowered her eyes, and I was taken back to those terrible moments in the inn parlor at the schloss.

"What about the Rome-Berlin Axis?" asked my father.

Richard Dorrington smiled grimly. "It means Germany and Italy are allies. I think Mussolini longs to be a Hitler."

Edward glanced at Gretchen and said: "Well, we shall have to wait and see. I want to tell you about the places I plan for us to visit."

The next day we went off in the car—the four of us together. It was most enjoyable. A few days later there was a picnic in the nearby woods. My mother and father came with us and it was a very jolly party. My mother was overjoyed by Edward's visit. I would often see her looking at him reminiscently, and I knew she was thinking of the helpless little baby whose life she had saved. Of course, my grandmother had undertaken the main responsibility of bringing him up, but he would always remember that but for my mother, he would not be one of us now.

There was something else. I detected a certain speculation in her eyes. I knew her well and could read her thoughts. She liked Richard; she was constantly talking of him to Edward. She wanted to know all about him. I thought, she is looking out for a suitable husband for her daughter. Dorabella is safely settled, now she thinks it is my turn.

I rather wished the thought had not struck me. It had an effect on my feelings for Richard, and I fancied I was a little more aloof than I might have been. Why did mothers always want to get their daughters married? They wanted to see them settled, and because they remembered them as babies, they thought they needed someone to look after them, I supposed.

I wanted to assure her that I was quite capable of looking after myself. And she must not, as so many mothers do, set out to find a husband for me.

The days were passing, and very pleasant they were. My father enjoyed discussing the state of affairs in Europe and was speculating with Edward and Richard whether Chamberlain would do well, and whether it was a pity that Baldwin had seen fit to resign at this time.

The visit was coming to an end. We were into July and that evening at dinner Richard said, looking at my mother, for he knew she would be the one to make the decision: "You must come to London. There is so much to do there. Everything won't be so crowded at this time. Why not?"

"You must come as soon as we get our house," began Edward, when Richard interposed:

"You must stay with us. Mary Grace loves having visitors. So does my mother. It would cheer her up a good deal."

"Richard's place is not very far from Kensington Gardens, and then there is the High Street with all the shops," Edward added.

"Well, we should very much like to," said my mother.

She came to my room that night when the household had retired.

"What do you think about this visit to London?" she asked.

"Well, perhaps sometime."

"It sounds fun. I'd like to see that house and meet his people. Mary Grace sounds very charming."

"Oh, yes . . ."

"I like Richard, don't you?"

"Yes. Edward and he seem good friends, and I think he and Gretchen are happy."

"I think so, too. It is a pity her people are so far away. I think we ought to pay that visit and we shouldn't leave it too long, either."

I smiled at her. I could read her thoughts so easily.

I did have a chance of a quiet talk with Gretchen. Although she was happy, and obviously cared deeply for Edward, I often saw anxiety in her eyes.

It was the day before they were due to leave when I found myself alone with her.

I said: "Gretchen, is everything all right?"

"You mean . . . my family . . . ?"

"Yes."

She did not speak for a while. Then she said: "They have not been molested. But I believe it is no better . . . perhaps getting worse."

"You mean what we saw happen . . . is still going on?"

"Yes," she said. "And more often. I wish . . ."

"What a pity they can't get out."

"It is difficult. I talk about it with Edward. I wish they could come to England. But it is not easy."

"I can see that. They would have to leave the schloss, their home, everything."

She said: "Some are getting out. Friends of ours have gone. They are in America. And some in Canada, South Africa, and other places."

"If you and Edward get a house . . . perhaps . . ."

She shook her head. "My father would not go. Nor would Kurt. If they were rich, perhaps, as some have done."

"It may all blow over . . ."

She lifted her shoulders. "There is such hatred for our race. My family is not important enough to attract much notice, fortunately. It is the rich they attack first. But in time . . ."

I laid my hand on hers. "I am glad you are here."

"I am the fortunate one. My family rejoice in my good fortune. But I suffer for them."

"Dear Gretchen, I hope it all comes right soon."

"One can hope," she said, but I saw the hopelessness in her face.

My mother talked again of the proposed visit to London.

"It will be fun to go househunting for Edward," she said.

The visitors left with the assurance that we should all meet again soon.

The next day I had a letter from Dorabella.

Dear Vee,

You said you were coming down. It will be August soon and ages since you've been. I am really huge now and looking forward to Nanny Crabtree's arrival. There'll be the usual talk. She'll go on about what a "caution" I always was . . . the naughty one . . . not like good Miss Violetta. Such a good girl *she* was. I can't get about much. I'm just stuck here. I have to lie down and rest. It's boring and not very comfortable. I mustn't do this and I mustn't do that.

This is an S.O.S. Come please *soon* . . .

While I was reading the letter my mother came into the room.

"About this trip to London," she began.

I waved the letter in my hand.

"From Dorabella?" she asked.

"Yes," I replied. "I must go to Dorabella first."

It was exciting to be traveling down to Cornwall. This time I was alone, as my mother could not leave just then.

Dorabella would be satisfied if one of us went, we had decided.

Dermot came to the station to meet me. He greeted me warmly.

"Dorabella is so delighted that you are coming," he said. "And so are we all."

"I am glad to be here. How is she?"

"The doctor says she is fine. She gets a little restless. She was always one for dashing around."

"I know she doesn't like this enforced inactivity."

"Indeed. She does not like it at all."

"It will be good to see her again."

"It has been a long time, she says."

"My mother has so many commitments at home, and there is my father who can't always get away from the estate."

"I know. However, here you are and it is good to see you."

I was thinking: And I shall be able to see Jowan Jermyn. It will be time for the plant to have taken root. I can make another attempt to talk to Mrs. Pardell. I was drawn into an atmosphere of intrigue and mystery—which might be of my own creating, it was true—but interesting nevertheless.

Dorabella was waiting for me. She hugged me fiercely.

"You might have come before," she said, scowling and then laughing. "But it's wonderful that you are here now. I know it's a long way to come . . . and there is that nice Richard Somebody our mother mentioned in her letter. *You* might have told me about him."

"So Mummy has been writing to you about him?"

"Of course. And our father thinks highly of him. You know . . . that sort of thing. Well, she wouldn't want my other half to be left on the shelf when I have been so perfectly disposed of."

"What nonsense! I hardly know the man."

"And you liked him?"

"Moderately."

"I know you and your understatements."

"More to be relied on than your wild enthusiasms."

"Well, here I am, a married woman about to replenish the earth. Oh, Vee, thank goodness you've come. It's lovely to have you here. Now I want a detailed account of everything you've been doing."

"First," I replied. "I have to have one from you. Mummy wants to hear all about you—a truthful account."

"My life is full of action. You'll never tell it all in one letter. I lie in bed until they bring my breakfast. I rise, bathe, and amble round the gardens. Lunch and rest. Doctor's orders. I may go down, or have it in my room. Then I sit in the garden perhaps, discuss layettes and nursery furniture with Matilda, see the midwife if it is her day to call. Then dinner and bed. You see, it is a riotous existence."

"Well, it won't be very long now before the great day arrives."

"It approaches inexorably and fills me with both longing and dread."

"It will soon be over and then we shall have the marvelous child."

"You mean I shall."

"We've always shared."

"You'll be a doting aunt."

"I daresay."

"You must see that man again . . . the enemy in the feud."

"Perhaps I shall."

"What do you mean by perhaps you will? I shall insist. You have come down here to amuse me, remember."

"I promise I will."

"Amuse me and see him again?"

"I am determined to do that."

"What? Amuse me? Or see him?"

"Both," I replied.

"Oh, Vee, how wonderful that you have come."

I was with her all that day.

During the next morning the doctor came to see her and said she was a little tired and must rest more.

She scowled but obeyed the rules, and that gave me an opportunity to be alone.

I wondered whether the news of my arrival had reached Jowan Jermyn, and I turned over in my mind whether I should take Starlight to the field and hope to see him there or walk to Cliff Cottage.

Dorabella's talk about Richard Dorrington and Jowan Jermyn had made me feel a little uncomfortable about both men. It was rather disconcerting to contemplate that because one was growing up and unattached, people always wanted to link one with some prospective husband. It made plain friendship difficult.

I decided, however, that I would pay a call on Cliff Cottage. I remembered then that the last time I had been there I had met Gordon Lewyth on the dangerous part of the cliff path on the way back.

I had seen him briefly when I arrived, and I had thought his attitude had seemed a little warmer toward me than previously. During that walk down to the town he had unbent considerably. I was rather glad that we had made some advance—albeit small—in our relationship.

I had been with Dorabella all the morning and after lunch she had her rest. I set out for Cliff Cottage.

I had not told her where I was going. In fact, I was still uncertain as to her reaction to Dermot's first marriage. I think it was one of those subjects which were vaguely unpleasant, to be thrust aside and not spoken of.

It was a warm day, but there was little sunshine. The sea was a dullish gray color, quiet but with a sullen look about it.

The gulls were noisy. When I came down the east cliff into Poldown and walked along the harbor I saw the fishermen there mending their nets. Some people were buying fish that had come in that morning and the gulls were screeching wildly, looking for titbits which, for some reason, could not be sold and were flung back into the river, where they were immediately seized on by the swooping birds.

One or two people recognized me.

"Oh, 'ee be back then?"

"Not much sun about today."

"Nice to see 'ee, Miss. Lady up house well, I hope?"

It was rather pleasant to be remembered.

I thought of what Jowan had said about the news service. I expected they were all well informed.

I crossed the ancient thirteenth-century bridge to the west side and started to climb up the cliff. It was steep and I paused every now and then, not so much to get my breath as to admire the weird formation of the black rocks with the waves gently swirling around them.

I came to Cliff Cottage. It looked as neat as ever. Boldly I opened the wooden gate and went up the short path. There was a porch on which were stone containers in which flowers grew. The front door had frosted glass panels.

I rang the bell and waited.

There was a short pause. I could see her through the glass peering at me. I wondered if she would recognize me. After a few seconds, when I feared I might not be let in, the door opened and Mrs. Pardell stood facing me.

"Oh," she said. "It's you. So you're back, then."

"Yes. How are you?"

"I'm all right, thanks."

"And ... er ... the ..."

Her face was illuminated by a smile. "It took," she said. "It took a treat."

"Oh, I am so relieved."

She looked at me for a moment and I thought her Northern shrewdness would reject my enthusiasm for the gushing insincerity it was. But, like most people with obsessions, she could not believe that they were anything but marvelous in the eyes of all.

"You like to see it?" she asked.

"Oh, I should love to."

"Come on, then."

Proudly she took me to it. I was shown the spot. It was like a shrine. The plant looked bigger than when I had brought it. I thought to myself, Thank you, little plant. It is clever of you. Through you I have gone up in the estimation of this uncommunicative lady.

"It's done wonders," I said.

"I can tell you I've taken a bit of trouble. I saw where it was up at that place, and I reckoned I knew the spot to put it. Gets the sun—but not too much—and there's shelter ..."

"Oh, yes. This sturdy plant here ... protects it in a way."

"That's so."

"I am so glad."

She nodded. "It was thoughtful of you to bring it. I was that pleased . . ."

"I could see how much you wanted it. And why shouldn't you share it? I knew you would appreciate it."

"Well, thank you."

Was that to be all? I wondered. The end of the mission?

I felt deflated.

I said desperately: "If there is anything else you liked, I daresay I could get it for you."

It was the right note. I could see the cupidity in her eyes. I had offered the irresistible.

"That's gradely, that is. There might be one or two."

"Well, you mustn't hesitate to ask."

"I take that as a real kind thought."

I was glowing with confidence.

"Your garden is a picture," I said. "This is the best time of the year, I suppose."

"Spring is better," she said. "Least I think so."

"Yes, spring. We're getting on in the year now." I inhaled the air. "It's gloomy today. It makes one thirsty."

It was a hint and she hesitated for a moment. "Would you like a cup of tea?"

"Oh, that would be wonderful."

So once more I had effected an entrance and I was in the sitting room with the picture of Annette of the saucy smile and ample bosom smiling at me.

Then I thought, go carefully. I was not going to give up now, if I could help it. That offer of more plants had been a good one. It was irresistible to her, and it was becoming something of a passion with me to discover more of Annette, and her mother could surely tell me as much as anybody.

She came in with a tea tray on which were two cups, milk, sugar, and a teapot over which was a cosy of pink and beige wool, obviously homemade.

She was a knitter then. That might be a subject to embark on, but alas one of which I was abysmally ignorant, as I was of gardening.

She poured out the tea.

I said: "This is very pleasant."

She did not comment, but she did not look displeased.

"What an interesting teacosy," I went on.

That was the right approach.

"You have to make these things yourself if you're going to get what you want."

"So you knitted that?"

"It's not knitted. It's crocheted. I do knit a bit, though."

"Are you knitting at the moment?"

"A jersey," she said tersely.

"That sounds interesting."

"Had trouble getting the wool. This place . . ."

"You'd probably get what you want in Plymouth."

"It's a long way to go for a bit of wool."

"You are really very talented," I said rather obsequiously. "Making these things . . . and the garden as well. That's really a show place."

I was going too far. My desire to get onto the subject of her daughter was getting the better of my common sense.

She said: "How is your sister?"

"She is quite well. She gets tired easily."

"Reckon you'll want to be with her when her time comes."

"I shall probably go home before that. It is not until November. But, yes, I shall want to be here then."

She twisted her lips in a slightly mocking way, and, to my surprise, she said: "My girl . . . she was going to have a baby."

Here was triumph indeed. I could scarcely believe I was hearing correctly.

"Yes," I said. "That was a great tragedy."

"Brings it back," she said. "This new wife . . ."

"It would, of course," I said encouragingly.

She looked at me intently. "You want to be careful of her . . . that sister of yours. There was something fishy . . ."

"Oh?" I said, daring to say no more for fear of stopping this much-desired and unexpected turn of the conversation.

"Well," she went on, "after that other one . . ."

"Which other one?"

"People here are full of fancies. It was a long time ago. It was the same time of year. That old story. Have you heard the talk about those two families quarreling, and the girl going into the sea and not coming back?"

"Yes, I have heard of it. And you mean your daughter . . . ?"

"She went swimming. People said there was something that made her go then. They found her body. *She* wouldn't have gone swimming. Hadn't she been told not to?"

I was a little lost but afraid to stop the flow. I said tentatively: "Do you feel there was some connection between your daughter's death and that girl long ago?"

"It was drowning for both of them. Happen that's what got people talking. Two drowned, you see."

"It may be that several people have been drowned off this coast."

"Happen. But then these two were connected with the house. You know what these people here are like? They say some spirit beckoned her into the sea. It's a lot of rot. But that's what they say ... and there were the two of them."

"The girl in the legend killed herself because she was not allowed to marry the man she loved."

"That's the tale. My Annette would never have killed herself. She wanted that baby, she did. How could she have gone swimming of her own accord when she knew it was dangerous for the child? That's what I'd like to know."

"Then how ... ?"

"Who can say? All I know is that I don't believe she would have risked that baby's life. I wasn't pleased about what happened. I never wanted her to do that sort of work. She liked it, though. She'd never been what you'd call a quiet, good girl. There was always men about her. She liked that. She was one to go her own way. Wouldn't listen to advice."

"She was very pretty," I said.

"That's what they all said. Turned her head a bit. I never thought a daughter of mine ..."

She stopped and stared ahead of her. I could imagine the upbringing. There would have been few demonstrations of affection from her mother. I wondered what her father was like. I could imagine him—grim, dour as his wife, working hard, getting his compensation when he was unable to work any more, coming to the Cornish coast which the doctor had said would be better for his health than the harsher climate of the North.

Annette may have looked elsewhere for expressions of affection, for laughter and gaiety. I wondered if she had found what she sought with Dermot.

I could scarcely believe that Mrs. Pardell, who had been so reticent, should now be talking to me thus. I imagined it was because I was the sister of Dermot's second wife, who had replaced her daughter. Perhaps it was something to do with the fact that she was going to have a child. The position was similar. Annette had been going to have a child, too.

It suddenly occurred to me that she might feel it was her duty to warn me in some way. Mrs. Pardell was a woman who would do her duty, however she might wish not to.

She leaned toward me suddenly and said: "I don't believe she went swimming of her own accord that day."

"What?" I said, taken aback.

"She wouldn't have done. I can't tell you how much she wanted that child. It changed her. Mind you, we hadn't been on the best of terms because of what she'd been up to. But she wouldn't have gone. She knew it was putting the child in danger. I don't because she would never have done that . . . and nobody could make me believe it."

"Tell me what happened."

"I expect you know something about it. It gets round. It's the sort of thing people talk about. You know she was working there at the Sailor's Rest. There she was, every night, laughing and joking. They were pleased to have her. She brought the customers in. I used to lie in bed waiting for her to come home every night. I said, 'I'd rather see you cleaning someone's house than doing that sort of job.' It wasn't a lady's job and we'd tried to bring her up right."

"I understand," I said soothingly.

"There's no need for me to tell you. I expect you know already how these people talk. That young man and his new wife has brought it all up again. When he married for the second time everyone was talking about Annette. With her, it was a case of having to get married. I don't think he would have asked her otherwise and she'd still be there at the Sailor's Rest. She might have married that young farmer at Perringarth on the moor. He was mad about her. But there it was. That Dermot Tregarland had to do the right thing by her. He seemed a decent young fellow then, but you can imagine what it was like up at Tregarland's."

She paused for a while before she went on slowly: "You might wonder why I'm telling you all this. It's not like me to talk of it, but I'm thinking of your sister. I think you ought to look out for her."

"Look out for her? In what way?"

"I don't rightly know. It happened to my girl. It was about this time of the year . . ."

"I don't see the connection."

"Well, I just thought . . . you see . . . Annette and me . . . we wasn't on speaking terms for a long time. When I heard she was going to have a baby and no wedding ring, I was flabbergasted. I told her her father would have turned her out. She laughed at that. Annette laughed at everything. She was never a good girl, always wayward, but . . ."

"I think she sounds rather lovable."

Mrs. Pardell nodded her head without speaking. Then she went on: "When she got married and went to the big house, there was a lot of talk. I was in a way proud of her. He must have thought a lot of her, because there was his father up there, and I know he wouldn't have liked it . . . her being a barmaid. She came to see me once or twice. There was one time . . . I knew it would be the last for some time because she wouldn't be able to do that walk till after the baby was born. She had her car and she drove into Poldown, but she'd have to do the climb up the west cliff on foot. I am glad I saw her three days before she died. After all, she wasn't the first one by a long chalk who had had to get wed in a bit of a hurry. She was happy enough. Dermot was a good husband and she could make him go her way. She said to me: 'I can't wait for this baby to come.' She'd talk frankly about it, which I can't say I liked very much. Sort of immodest, but Annette was like that. She said: 'I can't do anything now, Mam. It's no good fretting about that. I can't go swimming.' I said: 'Of course you can't, you silly girl, in your state.' "

She sighed and I, amazed by this flow of confidence, just sat back quietly, fearing that at any moment it might stop.

"She'd always loved the water. I remember when we first went to the seaside. She was about eight years old then. I took her down to the seaside. She held up her hand . . . wonderstruck like . . . and ran right into the sea. After that it was swimming at school. She took to it like a fish. Regular champion she was. Won prizes. I could show you."

"I should like to see them some time."

" 'Well,' she said to me: 'It's awful, Mam. I can't swim. The doctor said no . . . some time back. It could hurt the baby.' 'Well, who'd want to swim in your state?' I said. 'I'd like to, but I wouldn't do a thing to harm this baby. Mam, I've never wanted anything more. I'm going to love that baby like no baby was ever loved before.' That's what she said."

She looked at me, her eyes blazing.

"Are you going to tell me that she went swimming on that early morning?" she demanded.

"But . . . she was in the water . . . the cross-currents . . ."

"Cross-currents, my foot. She could have swum in the roughest sea, that one. But she didn't go in that morning. You're not going to tell me she went in of her own accord."

"Are you suggesting that she was lured in . . . by some spirit . . . of that girl who died long ago?"

"That's what people here said at the time. But I don't hold with all that nonsense."

"Then what do you think happened?"

"I don't know. But you've got a sister up there. She's going to have a baby. They say there's some curse put on Tregarland's by them Jermyns. It's all nonsense, but . . . Well, you look after that sister of yours. You wouldn't want what happened to my girl to happen to her."

She sat back in her chair, looking into her cup where the tea had grown cold. She looked exhausted.

She was like another person. The hard shrewdness was just a veneer. She was a woman mourning a daughter whom she had loved and lost.

I said: "I am sorry . . ."

She looked at me searchingly. "You really mean that, don't you?" she said.

"Yes, I do."

She nodded and we were silent again. I knew it was time for me to go.

I stood up and said: "If you will let me know what cuttings you would like, I am sure there would be no difficulty in getting them."

She gave me a rare smile. I felt glad that she was not regretting her confidences. In fact, I had a notion that she felt better for talking to me.

It was almost as though we were friends.

* * *

When I left the cottage I felt bemused. She had so convinced me that Annette could not have gone swimming of her own accord. When? How? On those wild cliffs one could almost believe there was some foundation in the legends which abounded here.

I walked thoughtfully down the west cliff and into Poldown. I crossed the old bridge to the east side and made my way toward the sea.

On impulse, I decided I would go back right along the shore rather than take the cliff road. I set out, my thoughts still with Annette. I could picture her clearly, for the photograph told me a good deal. She was a girl who loved pleasure, and she was determined to get the most out of life; she was very attractive to the opposite sex and well aware of it. She was impulsive, living in the present; she was everything that her mother had taught her not to be.

A slight breeze was blowing in from the sea. I walked close to the frilly-edged waves and listened to their murmur.

A young couple with a small boy, carrying bucket and spade, came along. Holiday makers, I thought. We exchanged smiles as we passed.

Deep in thought, I went on. I came to a barrier of rock which went out into the sea. I scrambled over it and found that I was in a kind of cove. There was another rock barrier which shut it in. The high cliff protruding over it made it look rather cosy, shut in by the rocks on either side as it was.

I decided to sit down for a while and to go over my conversation with Mrs. Pardell. I settled with my back to the cliff, thinking how strange it was that she had suddenly begun to talk to me. I congratulated myself afresh as to the cleverness of my approach. Perhaps I had caught her at a moment when she felt the need to confide in someone. Poor Mrs. Pardell! How very sad to lose the daughter for whom, in spite of her disapproval, she had cared deeply.

I wondered what life had been like in that cottage when Annette became a barmaid at the Sailor's Rest. I imagined her admirers, Dermot among them. He was perhaps rather susceptible. He had almost immediately fallen in love with Dorabella. It might have been the same with Annette. I could imagine the quick romance, the consequences, and when she knew she was going to have a baby, he was brave enough to fight the family opposition and marry her.

And then . . . she died.

I stared out to sea watching the waves advance and recede. What had Mrs. Pardell said about Dorabella? She had warned me. Did she think that some supernatural being was going to lure Dorabella into the sea? She was a practical woman, priding herself on her down-to-earth approach to life, and her good Northern common sense would not allow her to believe that what had happened was what it seemed. And she had told me this because she had thought I needed to know.

The answer must be that Annette had believed she would be safe swimming because it was something she had always done expertly. It might be that she had been overcome by cramp. That was possible. There must be a simple, logical reason why she was drowned that morning.

It was time to go. I was not sure how long I had been sitting there, so completely absorbed had I been in my thoughts.

I rose and went to the barrier rock. I was about to scramble over when, to my dismay, I realized that while I had been sitting there, the tide had come right in. I had failed to notice that the cove was on much higher ground than the beach on either side of the rocks, and if I stepped over them I should be waist high in water.

I looked about me and saw that the sea had crept well into the cove itself while I had been sitting there. I must have been there for nearly half an hour.

I ran to the other side. The sea was splashing about the rocks. It had come in a considerable distance; and even in the cove now there was only a narrowing strip of dry sand.

I was panic-stricken. What could I do? I could not make my way along the beach. The tide was coming in rapidly. In a short time the cove would fill. I was not a good swimmer.

I looked up at the overhanging cliff. I could not climb that. It was unscalable. There were a few clumps of valerian to cling to, but how strong were they? And in any case they were too few and far between.

What a fool I had been! While I had been complimenting myself on my cleverness in extracting so much from Mrs. Pardell, I had stupidly walked into this trap.

I looked about me in dismay. The implacable sea was creeping in slowly but very surely. For some seconds I stood helpless . . . not knowing what to do. How long, I wondered, before the sea filled the cove? How long could I survive? Could I attempt to scale the cliff? I knew it would be impossible. I was going to be drowned like the lovelorn maiden of the legend and Annette. Could there possibly be some curse . . . ?

I was getting hysterical. I must not do that. I had been foolish and brought this on myself. Oh, why had I made that foolish decision to forsake the cliff path for the beach? I was to blame. This was no mythical revenge.

But what was I to *do*?

The sea was creeping nearer. Soon it would be rushing into the cove. I must do something, but what? I was completely unprepared for such a situation—helpless, ignorant.

Then my heart seemed to stop beating, for I heard a voice.

"Hello . . . there!"

Relief swept over me. It was a voice I knew—that of Gordon Lewyth.

I gazed upwards. He was standing looking down on me from the cliff path.

He put his hands to his mouth and shouted: "What are you doing down there?"

"I seem . . . to be cut off by the tide," I shouted back.

"You can't stay there." There was a moment's silence. Then he cried: "The cove will be flooded in ten minutes."

"What?" I cried.

He was gone.

I was filled with fear. Why had he disappeared? Why didn't he try to help? He had gone and left me to my fate.

Panic rose in me. What did it mean? I remembered how he had followed me when I had paid another visit to Mrs. Pardell. He had watched me come out of her house. I recalled the uncanny feeling I had experienced when he had stood close to me near that fragile fence. He knew I was here and he had gone away and left me.

What could it mean? Why did I have this feeling about Gordon Lewyth? Was it some premonition? I was rambling on in my panic-stricken mind. What did it matter what his motives were now? I was here and he had left me to my fate.

"Violetta!" It was a shout to the right of me. I turned sharply.

He was on the cliff, more than halfway down, holding on to a piece of rock which projected slightly.

The relief was almost unbearable. He had not deserted me.

"Get hold of the rocks on the side there," he shouted. "See if you can scramble up a little."

Panting, I managed to take a few faltering steps upwards. Cautiously he descended a foot or two. He was coming close. He leaned down and stretched out his hand.

"Can you take my hand?" he asked.

I tried and failed.

"I'm coming down a little," he said. "Look out. It's tricky."

Very slowly he descended a few feet. Our fingers almost touched.

"Just a minute," he said. "I have to get a grip here. Now . . ."

He had grasped my hand and I almost cried out with relief.

He said: "You've got to try and edge your way up. There's a ledge along here . . . just a few inches more."

His grasp seemed to be crushing my fingers, but I rejoiced in it.

"Come on. Be careful. Make sure your foot is firm before you lift the other."

I edged toward him.

"Now . . . watch it," he cried.

I was on a level with him.

"Just let me lead," he said. "Hold on to my coat. I need both hands. And for God's sake, don't let go."

Slowly and very cautiously we moved upwards. The rocks were damp with seaspray and slippery.

"Hold tight," he cautioned, and I clung to his coat with all my might.

It seemed a long time before we reached that spot where the rock had formed itself into a ledge which was like a narrow seat. It was just a freak in the formation. The rock must have been broken away there, and on the resulting ledge four or five people could have sat huddled together.

It was not very wide, but we were able to sit on it, not with any great comfort, it was true, but it was a haven of rest for me.

"Now, your hand," he was saying. "Be careful. It's safe to

sit here but watch out all the time. It might have been cut out of the rocks for this purpose. Phew, what a climb!"

I felt my voice tremble. "I don't know how to thank you."

He shrugged his shoulders. "We can't climb up. Look at that rock."

"You climbed down."

"I know. It's tricky. But I know these cliffs well. It's not the first time I've been down here. When I was a boy there was a group of us. We used to dare each other to take risks. You don't know fear when you're young. I must have been ten at the time. I got right down and sat on this ledge."

"I am so grateful to you."

"You wouldn't have stood much chance down there, you know. The tide comes slowly into the cove at first and then with a rush. It's due to the formation of the cove. Are you all right?"

"Yes, thank you."

"It's safe enough but it doesn't allow for wriggling. You must keep alert. The least jerk and you could go hurtling down."

"I realize that."

I noticed that his thick dark hair was damp with spray and exertion.

"I think," he said, "it would be safer if you held my arm."

"Thank you. I'd feel safer, too."

"What a boon this place is! Look down there and see the way you came up."

"I didn't think I should be able to. It looked so hopeless."

"You were lucky to be at that particular spot. There is just one place where it can be possible. I discovered it long ago. Not that it was easy. You could have fallen and that would have been fatal. I had done it once or twice and that stood me in good stead."

We were silent for a while, watching the tide slowly creeping in.

"It's nearly high now," he said. "Then it will start receding. When it has a little, we can pass along the shore. Then we have the job of getting down. It might be easier than coming up, but we shall have to be very careful."

"I understand. I just don't know how to thank you."

"I've lost count of the number of times you've said that."

"I shall be saying it again, and so will my parents and Dorabella when they hear."

"We're not yet safe and dry."

"I feel sure we shall be now."

"That's the spirit. It's no use undertaking things expecting failure. You have been to Mrs. Pardell's again."

"How did you know?"

"I saw you leave."

"Oh . . . you did last time."

"Yes," he said. "I was not far behind you going down into the town. Then I lost sight of you. I had some business to do there which detained me for a time and then, coming along the cliff road, I looked down and saw you."

"It was idiotic of me."

"It was . . . very reckless. Didn't you know the tide was coming in fast? It is especially high just now."

"I never thought of it."

"It is wise to remember such things where the sea is concerned. It can be very dangerous, you know."

"I do know that now. If you hadn't come along then, I could have drowned. What can I say . . . ?"

"We're coming dangerously near to that old theme," he said.

We laughed and it occurred to me that I had not heard him laugh before.

I was wondering about him. He had been so capable, so knowledgeable. He had nobly come to my aid and nothing would convince me that he had not risked his life in doing so. It was not what I would have expected from him.

We sat silently side by side for a few moments. I felt slightly chilled, in spite of the fact that it was a warm day. Perhaps it was emotion which made me want to shiver. After all, I had come close to death.

Death by drowning, I thought, like those others before me.

"We shall have to wait a bit for the tide to recede sufficiently to enable us to get along the beach," he was saying. "Then, the descent. I wouldn't want to risk your life trying to climb up to the cliff road. There'll only be a narrow strip along the beach."

I nodded, glad that he was in charge.

"We'll make it all right. It's the descent that will be tricky. Did you have a rewarding session with Mrs. Pardell?"

I was a little startled. "Rewarding?" I repeated.

"Well, I think you wanted to talk to her, didn't you? The flower was a success, I believe, and she was grateful."

"She was rather pleased."

"And in return?"

"There was no question of reward."

"I think you are rather interested in her."

"Well, perhaps, in view of the family connection. What sort of girl was Annette? You must have known her."

"She was rather ... er ... unsuitable. We were all astonished when Dermot married her."

"In spite of ... ?"

"In spite of the circumstances? Particularly so, as it might not have been his responsibility."

"He must have thought it was."

"I imagine she was persuasive, and Dermot is somewhat impressionable."

"She must have been very worried."

"I daresay. Women usually are in such circumstances. Well, they married and a few months later she was foolish enough to go into the water in spite of her condition, and the fact that she had been warned against doing so."

"People do foolish things sometimes."

He looked at me and I saw the hint of a smile on his lips. He was surprising me very much. Now that I felt safe, I was beginning to find the adventure exhilarating. I refused to think of the climb down to the cove which had to come, for I was certain that, under his direction, it would be safely accomplished.

"Dermot must have cared for her," I said.

"My mother did everything possible to make her comfortable. She was so good to her. She looked after her and helped her in every way."

"And Mr. Tregarland?"

"You mean the old man ... ?"

"He's not really so very old, is he?"

"He must be in his sixties. He married late, in his forties, I think. He has only become infirm during the last few years. His gout cripples him. One never really knows what he is thinking. I once knew a boy who liked putting spiders into a bowl from which they could not escape. He used to watch them for hours seeing what, captured as they were, they would do to each other. He reminds me of that boy, because it is as though he is watching us all in the same way."

"I understand what you mean," I said. "That is exactly how it seems to me. One gets the feeling he is watching everyone . . . in a rather mischievous way."

"He has always been very good to my mother and me. It is many years ago that we came to Tregarland's. I remember the time before that only vaguely. And suddenly we were at Tregarland's . . . and we have been there ever since."

"It is a wonderful old place."

"It is."

"And you are very interested in the estate."

"Yes, but . . ." He did not continue, but stared out to sea. Then he said: "I think the tide is turning now."

"They will be wondering where I am."

"I'm afraid they will. Was your sister expecting you back?"

"I am usually with her when she has had her rest."

"I hope she doesn't get too anxious. Yes. I am sure it is on the turn."

"How long do you think before we can attempt the journey down?"

"I am not quite sure. Some little time yet. I want to make certain that it is safe before we do so. It isn't very comfortable sitting here, I'm afraid."

"I am sure being submerged in the cove would have been far more uncomfortable. If you had not come along . . ."

"Shush," he said.

"I was just going to say what a happy coincidence for me."

We were silent for a while, then I said: "Tell me about your coming to Tregarland's all those years ago."

He paused and I had the impression that he was thinking he had said too much already. He was, I guessed, by nature reticent.

However, he went on: "It's all rather vague to me. We were in a little house near dockland. When we arrived at Tregarland's it was as though some genii had transplanted us to a castle. My mother told me that Mr. Tregarland was a distant connection. I've never found out what that connection was. I think it must be very remote. Anyway, Mr. Tregarland's wife had died. There was a son, slightly younger than I, and she was going to keep house there. She was not to be treated quite like a housekeeper and she could take me with her to be brought up there. It seemed like an excellent arrangement for us at least, and I am sure for Mr. Tregarland. My mother is one of the most capable people I have ever known. Life became luxurious suddenly."

"And has been ever since?"

"Well, people soon get used to comfort, particularly children."

"And you have made the estate your mission in life."

"I have worked hard at it."

"And Dermot?"

"He is inclined to take everything for granted. The place will be his in due course."

"But you will always be there."

He did not answer for a moment. Then he said, as though talking to himself: "A place of one's own could make one very contented. To stand in the fields and say, 'This is mine.' Do you see what I mean?"

"I do."

"I am very interested in Tregarland's. Proud of it, you might say, but . . ."

"My father, who knows a great deal about these things, says you manage it excellently."

He looked pleased.

"He has his own estate."

"Yes, it has been handed down from generation to generation, as I suppose Tregarland's has. I have a brother, Robert, who is being trained to take over one day."

"And Tregarland's will go to Dermot and his sons."

"But Dermot does not feel about it as you do."

"No, but it will be his." There was the faintest trace of bitterness in his voice.

"But you will always be there. How could they manage without you?"

"Oh, Dermot could find a manager."

"And you?"

"I cannot say."

"What you really want is a place of your own."

"Yes, that is what I want."

"Do you think . . . ?"

"I shall ever have it? To use a well-worn phrase, that is in the lap of the gods."

"You told me a little time ago that when something is important to you . . . like climbing the cliff . . . you are determined to do it. That must apply to wanting your own place. So you must not think of failure."

He turned to me and I saw that smile again.

"I tell you this," he said, and his jaw was firm. "I am going to do everything I can to get it."

"I shall wish you luck—although at the same time I can see it would be a bitter blow for Tregarland's."

After that we fell silent and neither of us seemed eager to break it.

I watched the waves. I could see the cove from where I sat. The sea was gradually receding. It would soon be time to do the difficult descent.

The way down was hazardous. It took time and great care. Gordon Lewyth went ahead of me. Sometimes he held my hand, at others he made me cling to his coat.

I was full of thankfulness for his fortuitous appearance and admiration for the manner in which, through his childhood memories of the rocks, he had brought us to safety.

Eventually we stood side by side in the cove. It was wet and soggy and the sea was very close. A great joy swept over me. It was so good to be alive.

We looked at each other and, in those seconds, I thought he was going to kiss me, for he swayed toward me and then moved back.

I said tremulously: "I know I'm supposed not to, but I am going to say thank you. I have rarely felt so grateful to anyone in the whole of my life."

He looked embarrassed.

"Come on," he said. "We shall be very late. We'll have to pick our way carefully across the sand. It will be slippery as the tide has just gone out. Mind the rocks."

"I will," I said, and we walked side by side along the beach.

There was a great deal of fuss when we reached the house. I had been expected back three hours earlier. They were all in the hall—Dorabella, Dermot, Matilda, and the old man. I could not fail to see the excitement in the latter's eyes.

Dorabella came to me and hugged me while she scolded. "Where have you been? We've been frantic."

I explained while Gordon said nothing.

"He was absolutely wonderful," I finished. "I could never have climbed the cliff alone."

I saw Matilda's lips twitch as she regarded her son with pride.

"I am so glad . . . so glad," she said.

"Whatever made you walk along the beach?" demanded Dorabella. She had been really scared and wanted to go on blaming me.

"It was silly, but I didn't think . . ."

"Well, you are back now," said Matilda. "Both of you must be exhausted . . . and chilled."

"I'm hot now actually," I said.

"Nevertheless, I think you need a good strong drink. Brandy, don't you think, Gordon?"

Gordon thought it would be a good idea.

I was briefly reminded of that other occasion when I had taken brandy with Jowan Jermyn in Smithy's.

They all sat round while we drank, and I described exactly what had happened. Gordon had lapsed into his habitual reticent manner while I did the talking. Dorabella sat close to me, and every now and then she would touch my arm as though to reassure herself that I was still there. I found that very endearing.

I repeated how wonderful Gordon had been, how he had so cleverly hauled me up to him, how we had sat on the ledge in the cliffs which he remembered from his childhood days, waiting for the tide to recede before we scrambled down.

"I could never have done it alone," I said. "I did not know which way to turn."

"You could have been drowned," whispered Dorabella.

"I think that is very likely. I have to thank Gordon."

Gordon said: "Oh, you would have clambered up somehow."

"Good old Gordon," said Dermot.

"It was a miracle that he came along in time," said Matilda. "And he is always so calm in any emergency. Most people would have panicked and dashed off to get help and, by the time that came, it could have been too late."

"I was lucky to know the cliffs so well," said Gordon.

"And I was lucky that you saved my life," I added.

"Yes," said Matilda firmly. "It was a wonderful rescue, and I'm proud of you, Gordon."

I caught the old man's eyes. I could not read the expression there. He said: "Well, my dear, we are all happy that we have not lost you. It will be a warning to you. Don't take risks with the sea."

"I shall be very careful in future, I assure you."

Dorabella said: "I feel exhausted by all this. I shall have my meal in bed and Violetta must have hers with me. I want to get used to the idea that she is safe. Otherwise I shall have nightmares."

Dorabella looked very pretty, sitting up in bed with her hair falling about her shoulders.

She demanded to know *everything*, for she was sure there was more than I had told the others.

"Fancy Gordon," she said. "One doesn't see him exactly in the role of gallant knight, does one?"

"He was very practical."

"It's so romantic."

"You should have seen us climbing the cliff. Most inelegant, I am sure, and far from romantic."

"Now, Vee, of course it was romantic. Damsel in distress, gallant young man rides by."

"He was walking."

"It was like Sir Lancelot."

"I did not know he ever rescued anyone from drowning."

"Well, one of them must have done. And what was he like? He must have been different. He's always so aloof ... what did he *say*?"

"We talked a bit."

"What about?"

"Nothing very much really."

"You can't be all that time sitting on a ledge talking about nothing much. Come on, tell me, or I shall be very cross and that is bad for my condition."

"He told me a little about his childhood before he came to Tregarland's and how, when he was a boy, he explored the cliffs, which was a great help to us then, and how he would really like a place of his own."

"A place of his own?"

"Well, he only works here, doesn't he?"

"What does he want a place of his own for? He runs this one."

"It will be Dermot's in due course. A man such as he is, who cares about the land, would naturally want his own place."

"He didn't ... er ... make any approaches?"

"Approaches? Gordon? What do you mean?"

"Well, a man and woman in those circumstances ... barriers come down and all that."

"You are talking about Gordon Lewyth. Your mind runs on one thing. I am not the frail little piece of femininity that all men wish to protect. I am plain, no-nonsense, usually able to look after myself."

"It did not seem like it this afternoon. He does like you, I'm sure. Even if he didn't before, he will after this. People always like those whose life they save. Every time they look at them they are reminded how wonderful they were and how the saved one must be eternally grateful."

I laughed.

"Where were you going anyway?"

"I was coming back to Tregarland's."

"Naturally. But where had you been?"

I hesitated. I did not want to tell her I had been with Mrs. Pardell. I was still not sure how she felt about Annette. Perhaps I would tell her later ... choose my moment. To talk about the death of her predecessor might upset her in her present state.

"Oh, just for a walk," I said.

"And what about this Jermyn man? You haven't seen him yet."

"No."

"Well, you usually do when you come here."

"Perhaps I will."

"Do you know, Vee, you are a dark horse. Grim Gordon risks his life for you. Then there are secret meetings with the family's enemy. That's two of them. I believe you are a *femme fatale*."

"Oh, no. That is your role."

"We are really one. You know that. We are different, of course, but that is because we are one person. I used to think that the foolish side was myself and the sensible side you. But not after this afternoon. Who was silly enough to get caught by the tide? I shall taunt you with that throughout our lives, whenever you put on one of your superior acts. When did I ever do anything so foolish as that?"

"I'll consider it. I am sure I shall be able to come up with something."

She put out her tongue at me and laughed. She was so happy and I knew it was because I was safe and back with her.

She went on: "I am longing to hear more of the enemy."

"You are thinking of that silly old feud. Jowan Jermyn is not an enemy."

"He will have heard by now of your adventure. News travels fast here. We may be something of a backwater, but our communication service is superb. I have discovered that lots of people here are related to each other—many sisters and cousins are working for the various people around. So news is circulated quickly. Most things we do are recorded as soon as they take place. We are all living in glass houses, so that adventure of yours on the cliffs will be headline news, or would be if they had newspapers. Mr. Jermyn will know of it by now and gnashing his teeth because he was not the one to make the gallant rescue."

"What nonsense!"

"Promise me you'll go and see him tomorrow ... when I am having this ridiculous rest of mine ... you go to the meeting place and see if he is there. You must promise me. In my condition I have to be humored."

We were laughing again.

"And when you come back, I want you here with me ... to tell me every detail."

I promised.

The next afternoon, true to my promise to Dorabella, I decided I would go to the field and see if Jowan Jermyn were there. I did not believe Dorabella was right in believing that he would already have heard of my adventure, but he might know that I had been in Cornwall for a few days. In any case, there was no harm in riding to the field. If he were not there, I would just ride around and tell Dorabella that I had kept my promise.

I went to the stables. Jack was not there. A young man was grooming one of the horses. I had seen him before and I knew he was Seth. He was about nineteen or twenty and had large gray eyes which seemed to be looking at something the rest of us could not see. I had heard that there was something strange about Seth. He was "piskymazed," said some. "Something missing in the top story," said others. He was always referred to as Poor Seth, but all admitted that he had a way with horses.

I said: "Good afternoon, Seth."

He nodded in acknowledgment and went to Starlight's stall. He was muttering something to her, patting her as he led her out. I noticed the loving way he touched her and I saw her response. Oh, yes, he had a way with horses.

He started to saddle her. Then suddenly, he looked at me with those strange eyes and said: "Be careful, Miss. What did happen yesterday . . ."

He had a slurred way of speaking, as though his tongue were too big for his mouth, and I had some difficulty in hearing him.

"Master Gordon . . ." he said. "If 'e 'adna been there . . ."

"Oh, yes," I said. "He saved my life. There was no way I could have escaped from the cove if he hadn't come to help me."

" 'Twere 'er again, Miss."

"Her?"

"Her from over Jermyn's."

I looked puzzled.

He went on dealing with Starlight, murmuring to her as he did so.

" 'Tis the curse, Miss. 'Er drowned herself, didn't 'un. 'Twere 'er. She be after folk at Tregarland's. Women . . . 'er wants 'un with her . . . so 'er comes back to get 'un."

This sounded like garbled nonsense to me. He was "piskymazed." Poor boy. But I wanted to know what was in his mind.

"Tell me, Seth," I said. "What do you know about her . . . coming to get them?"

" 'Er drowned, didn't 'er? It was 'cos of Tregarland's. 'Er's doing to them what was done to 'er. There were Mr. Dermot's first wife . . . her from the Sailor's Rest."

"What of her, Seth?"

" 'Er went down to the sea . . . and that baby went with her. That's what her wanted."

"Her?" I repeated.

" 'Er from Jermyn's. 'Er 'ave it in for Tregarland women . . . well, 'er would, wouldn't 'er?"

"But she is dead, Seth. How could it be?"

He looked at me in amazement. " 'Er comes back, don't 'er? I seen 'er."

"You've seen her! But she's dead."

"She come back and 'er got the first Mrs. Tregarland, didn't 'er? 'Er beckoned her into the sea. I seen 'er. Then . . . Miss . . . the sea nearly got you."

"I'm not a Tregarland, Seth."

"Aye . . . but your sister be. That's close enough for 'er."

Poor Seth. He was indeed crazy. But now he had saddled the horse and she was ready for me.

"Thank you, Seth," I said, smiling.

"She be a good 'un," he said. He patted Starlight lovingly. "You be a good 'un," he said in her ear and she rubbed her nose into his hand.

I rode out of the stables, wondering what was going on in Seth's muddled mind.

I made my way to the field. There was no one there and I felt deeply disappointed. I was about to ride away when I hesitated. After all, there had been no fixed arrangement. I looked at my watch. It was about five minutes earlier than last time.

I dismounted and, tethering Starlight to a tree, I sat down, leaning against a hedge. I was still thinking about Seth and how pleasant it would be to talk to Jowan Jermyn when I saw him riding toward me.

He pulled up sharply.

"Oh," I said, "so you came."

"Naturally. I came yesterday and the day before."

"I am sorry. But it wasn't a definite arrangement, was it?"

He shook his head. "Well, now you are here, it's cider time once more. Let's see, it was the Horned Stag last time. This time it shall be the Lion's Head. That's in another fishing village slightly smaller than Poldown, similar and yet different. I think you will like it. May I say how pleased I am to see you."

"And I you."

"That is nice to hear. Would you like to go now?"

I had risen to my feet and he helped me mount Starlight and soon we were riding out of the field.

"Did you have an interesting time in London?"

"Very interesting, thank you. And you . . . here?"

"Much as usual. We go westwards. It's about four miles along the coast. Will that suit you?"

I said it sounded good.

He asked about Dorabella and we talked lightly as we rode along. Often we had to go in single file through narrow lanes so it was not possible to hold much of a conversation.

We climbed fairly high and then descended into the fishing village to the Lion's Head on the sea front.

There were stables where we could leave the horses and we did this and went into the inn parlor.

There was a similarity between these hotels and it would be hard to distinguish one from another. There was the traditional inglenook and the cosy, intimate atmosphere.

We sat down and he ordered cider.

"You'll find little difference in that, either," he said. "I expect it all comes from the same source."

When we were alone he went on: "Congratulations! I heard you have been snatched from the jaws of death."

I laughed. "Dorabella was right . . ."

"In what way?"

"She said you would have heard of it through the local news service."

"But of course. I was told at breakfast this morning by one of the servants. He has a dramatic touch. 'That there Miss what's-her-name, you do know, sir, the new one's sister up at Tregarland's, 'er had a near shave 'er did. Caught in that there cove. You do know how easy that can be, sir, the way that old tide do come in there . . . all of a rush like. And what was 'er doing down there? Didn't know nothing about tides seemingly.' "

His reproduction of the accent was very good. I laughed and he sat back surveying me.

"The reporting is fairly accurate," I said. "I was caught by the tide."

His face was grave now. "It could have been dangerous," he said.

"I know now. I just didn't think of it."

"Very remiss of you."

"Well, it was an experience."

"I believe someone said, 'Experience is the name we give to our mistakes.' "

"It could only have been Oscar Wilde. It's true, of course. But our mistakes do teach us not to repeat our follies."

"Well, then, it was not in vain."

"Gordon Lewyth was wonderful."

"I am sure he was. Quite a feat, I imagine, on that cliff face."

"It was a great good fortune for me that he happened to be passing and saw me."

He looked at me intently and said: "That was his good luck. I wish it had been mine."

"That's very kind of you."

"Poor Lewyth. He's in an invidious position."

"He is devoted to Tregarland's."

"Yes, but the place will never be his. A pity. He's done more for it than anyone. James Tregarland . . ."

"That's old Mr. Tregarland?"

"Yes. He was letting the place run to ruin. He was not meant for the land. He's clever, they say. He used to be something of a wit, I believe. He spent hardly any time here. He was always in London. Something of a gambler. He married late in life . . . a charming lady, by all accounts, but he wasn't the sort to settle down. He just married for the sake of the family—so I've heard. His wife provided the required son, Dermot, and after a year or so, she died. Then the Lewyths came. She was a good-looking woman . . . some vague family connection, it was said, and with her her young son. Things settled down for a while, but James Tregarland was never one for the land. It was lucky that when Gordon grew up he could take over. He saved the place from disaster . . . just in time. Such estates can stand one indifferent generation but no more, so it was like a miracle that Gordon could take over and so efficiently. Though it is all for Dermot's benefit."

"Dermot has the same indifference."

"It seems so. They should thank Heaven for Gordon."

"As I did yesterday. By the way, that boy in the stables. Do you know anything about him?"

He looked puzzled.

"I wondered if he would be an item of news. He seems a little mad. He said such a strange thing to me today just as I was coming out. He had evidently heard what happened on the cliffs yesterday, and he seemed to think that some evil force was at work to harm *me*."

"Harm you?"

"Because of my connection with the Tregarlands . . . sister of the bride."

"Oh? What did he say?"

"Something about the curse. That ancestor of yours who walked into the sea because of her blighted love affair is now taking her revenge on Tregarland women."

"Poor old Seth, was it? He's said to be a little addlepated."

"Piskymazed, I have heard."

"It's the same thing. It means mental confusion. He must have heard about your adventure yesterday and he thought of the first Mrs. Tregarland who was drowned. He connected the two."

"Has he always been like that?"

"Oh, no. Something happened to him when he was about ten. He is the son of one of the grooms. He has a way with horses. There was an incident in the stables one day. A wild horse which broke free. The boy was there. He was knocked down and the horse rode over him. It damaged his head, and he has been strange ever since."

"That would account for it, I suppose."

Then I told him about Mrs. Pardell and how she had talked to me.

"You did well," he said. "She is not usually so forthcoming."

"I was sorry for her. I think she really cared about her daughter."

"She is one of those people who find it difficult to express their feelings. They always miss something, I think, don't you?"

I said I thought they might.

"But I sensed when I was with her that she loved her daughter and grieved for her," I said. "She talked a little about Annette. She seems to have been a very bright person."

"Indeed, yes. She was very suited to her job. There would always be a crowd of admirers round her."

"Dermot among them," I said.

"You know how people talk. They said he was one of several and that she chose the right one to blame for her condition."

"And he accepted it," I said.

"Dermot is a kindly young man. He would do what he thought was right."

"I daresay he was in love with her."

"I don't know. There is certain to be talk about that sort of situation in a place like Poldown. However, it is in the past. Let us drink to the present Mrs. Tregarland, and may she bring forth a healthy son and live happily ever after."

"I'll drink to that."

He smiled at me across the tankards. "I should like to meet her."

"And she would like to meet you."

"You have mentioned me to her?"

"To her, but to no one else, in view of this ridiculous feud. When she is active again, she and I will put our heads together and see what we can do to break it."

He lifted his tankard. "To your success," he said.

I felt happy to be in his company. We rode back together and made arrangements to meet a few days later.

The Promise

❦

I arrived back in Caddington in early September. I was sorry to leave Dorabella. Moreover I was finding myself more and more absorbed in the life of Tregarland's. However, I knew my mother thought I ought not to stay too long.

My mother said: "I know Dorabella loves to have you, but she has a husband now and should be building up her own family life. Besides, it is not fair to you to be tucked away down there all the time. You have a life of your own to lead. You must not allow yourself to become just part of Dorabella's."

I knew what was in her mind, of course. She was planning dinner parties to which she was going to invite eligible young men. I found this a trifle embarrassing. I did not want to be put up for auction, I told her.

"What nonsense!" she replied. "You want to see a bit of life, that's all."

She was delighted when Edward suggested we should go to London.

He wrote: "Richard Dorrington would like you and Violetta, and Sir Robert, if he could come, of course, to spend a week with them in London. You will want to see our house. It is a little topsy-turvy at the moment because we haven't properly settled in. You could stay with us, though, for a time. Mary Grace is going to write to you."

"I suppose they feel they ought to ask us because Richard stayed here," I said.

"It is a nice, friendly gesture," replied my mother. "I'd like to go. I am not sure about your father."

My brother Robert had gone back to school. It was a constant complaint of his that, because of school, he had to miss so many interesting things which the rest of the family could do.

"You'll emerge from it in time," I told him. "It has happened to all of us."

I was rather pleased by the prospect of going to London; and it turned out to be interesting to visit the Dorrington family.

Mrs. Dorrington was charming, and she and my mother got along very well. I liked Mary Grace. She was slightly younger than Richard—a rather quiet, shy girl whose main occupation seemed to be to look after her mother.

The house was large, well staffed, and comfortable. It faced a quiet garden square and was characteristic of many in the area.

Edward's newly acquired house was not very far away—in a row of houses in a tree-lined street. He and Gretchen seemed very happy and contented with each other, though at times I saw shadows in Gretchen's eyes and guessed the reason. She would be thinking of her family in Germany. As far as I could gather, the situation had not changed there.

Richard Dorrington was very eager that we should enjoy our visit. He had arranged trips to the theater, and we usually had supper afterwards in a small restaurant near Leicester Square which was frequented by theatrical people. It was exciting after life in the country.

Richard and Edward were working during the day and my mother and I were able to make full use of the shopping facilities. Our purchases were frequently for the coming baby. Mary Grace was very interested and sometimes accompanied us.

She and I went to an exhibition of miniatures in one of the museums and I realized at once that she was quite knowledgeable about the subject. Her shyness dropped from her and she became enthusiastic and eloquent.

I was pleased to see her interest and listened intently; she went on talking more than she ever had before and revealed to me that she herself painted.

"Only a little," she added, "and not very well. But . . . it is quite absorbing."

I said I should like to see some of her work, and she shrank visibly.

"Oh, it's no good," she said.

"I'd like to see it all the same. Please show me."

She went on: "There are some people one sees and knows immediately that one wants to paint them. There is something about them."

"You mean they are beautiful."

"Well, not necessarily conventionally beautiful. But there is something . . . I should like to paint you."

I was astonished and, I admit, flattered.

I laughed and said: "My twin sister Dorabella would make a very good picture. We are alike in a way but she is different. She is vital and very attractive. I wish you could see her. You'd want to paint her. She is going to have a baby quite soon. Perhaps after it is born you could paint her. I am sure she would be a better subject than I."

Mary Grace said she liked to feel that special urge to paint before she did so. So far no one had sat for her. She saw a face she liked, sketched it from memory, and then worked on it. She made life-size sketches and then got down to the intricate work.

"All right then," I said. "You can do some rough sketches of me."

"Oh, will you let me? Don't tell anyone."

"It is our secret."

The next day I went to her room, and she made the sketches, but she would not show them to me. She did, however, show me some of the work she had done. There were several miniatures in watercolors. I thought they were charming and told her so. She was flushed with pleasure. I had rarely seen her look so pleased.

My mother said: "I am so glad you get on well with Mary Grace. She seems to like your company very much."

"She is a nice girl," I said, "but she is too self-effacing."

"Not like her brother. What she needs is someone to bring her out of herself."

That evening we went to the opera. It was wonderful to be in Covent Garden. The opera was *La Traviata*. Richard had known that it would be performed that evening and he had gone to great trouble to procure the tickets. From the moment the curtain went up on a scene of Fragonard-like elegance and Violetta was greeting her guests, it was pure enchantment.

We had a supper afterwards in a restaurant near the Opera House and we were quite hilarious, and much play was made of my name, which was the same as the heroine's.

"There," said Edward, "the resemblance ends."

My mother said: "People laughed at me when I gave her the name, but I don't regret it one little bit. I think it is beautiful . . . and don't you think it suits her?"

They all agreed that it did.

"And," I said, "Dorabella had the greater burden to bear."

"Dorabella," said Richard. "That's beautiful, too. What a pity she is not with us here tonight."

"I shall give her a detailed account of the evening when we meet," I said.

It was late when we arrived home. It had been a wonderful evening. I was thinking about Dorabella, who would have loved to share in it—and I found myself wondering afresh how she would fit into life in Cornwall.

Next morning my mother said to me: "Wasn't it a wonderful evening? I think Richard is delightful."

"Yes," I said. "He is very thoughtful."

"It was so good of him to plan the opera. He said it was *Traviata* that made him determined to go . . . your being Violetta, of course."

"The similarity ends with the name, as Edward pointed out."

"I should hope so," said my mother. "I should hate to think of you leading that sort of life and fading away before your time."

I laughed and she said: "Do you know what is coming up soon? I'd almost forgotten it with all this excitement about the baby. Your birthday."

"Of course . . . next month. I haven't got Dorabella's present yet."

"Nor I. What would you like?"

"I'll have to think."

"We'll get it while we are in London. We'll go and look tomorrow. But think about it."

"I will."

There was a dinner party that night. The Dorringtons had

invited a lawyer and his wife with their newly married daughter and her husband.

The conversation at dinner was mainly about the situation in Europe. The elderly lawyer said he did not like the way things were going.

"The alliance between the Italian and German dictators is an unholy one, I reckon," he said.

"We should not have stood by while Italy took Abyssinia," said Richard.

"What could we have done?" asked Edward. "Did we want to go to war?"

"If all the states of Europe with America had stood together against it and imposed sanctions, Mussolini could not have gone on."

"Too late now," said the lawyer.

I glanced at Gretchen. She was looking uneasy, as she always did when the politics of Europe were discussed. I wished they would change the subject.

They eventually did, but I think the evening was spoiled for Gretchen.

The next morning Mary Grace said she had something to show me. I went to her room. Laid out on a table was the miniature.

Mary Grace pointed at it and stepped back, looking away as though she could not face my reaction.

I stared at it. It was beautiful. The colors were soft and exquisitely blended. It was my face, but there was something there, something arresting. It was a look in the eyes, as though I were trying to prove something which I could not understand. The mouth was smiling and seemed to belie that expression in the eyes.

I could not believe that she had created such an exquisite piece of work. I turned to her in wonder and she forced herself to look at me.

"You don't ... like it," she stammered.

"I don't know what to say. You are a true artist, Mary Grace. Why have you kept this hidden?"

She looked bemused.

"I think it is wonderful. It really is. Everything on such a small scale and yet ... it's there, isn't it? It is the sort of portrait which makes one pause and wonder what is behind that smile. What is she thinking?"

Did I really look like that? What had I been thinking of when I sat for Mary Grace? That subject, which was always uppermost in my mind? Dorabella and Dermot . . . their marriage . . . Mrs. Pardell who did not believe that her daughter had died as it was said she had . . . that sly old man who was watching us all the time as though we were spiders in a basin from which we could not escape. Those were the thoughts which had dominated my mind as I sat there.

I looked at Mary Grace in wonder. Her talent really did amaze me.

I said severely, trying to introduce a light note, for she looked very emotional: "Mary Grace, you have been hiding your light under a bushel. Have you heard of the Parable of the Talents? You have been given this talent and you have hidden it away. If you have such talent you must surely use it."

"I can't believe . . ."

"You have to believe in yourself. I am going to buy this miniature from you. I am your first client."

"No . . . no . . . I shall give it to you."

"I shall not accept it as a gift, but I very much want it and will have it. Listen. You have solved a problem for me. It is my sister's birthday in October—mine also. I have been wondering what I am going to give her. Now I know. I can't accept a gift from you which I am going to give to someone else. This is a blessing. She does not see me so often now, though we were always together until she married. This will be the ideal birthday present. You and I will go out and buy a beautiful frame for it, and that shall be my birthday gift to her. She will love it. It is beautiful and it will be so unexpected. Oh, Mary Grace, thank you so much. You have made a beautiful picture of me and at the same time solved my problem."

She was staring at me, her lips parted in sheer astonishment.

"My dear Mary Grace," I cried. "You look piskymazed, as they say in Cornwall."

I carried her along on my enthusiasm. She was a most unusual artist. The few I had met had an inflated idea of their own excellence and a word of criticism could make an enemy for life. Mary Grace was modest and genuinely surprised. She was that rare creature—a good artist and a modest one.

I was already imagining Dorabella's face when she saw the miniature. She would surely want one of herself. A commission for Mary Grace, I thought delightedly.

Mary Grace and I announced that we were going shopping that morning. There were certain things we wanted to get. We took the miniature with us and went to a jeweler's shop in the High Street. I had noticed it before because there were several unusual pieces in the window—secondhand, some of them, rare and beautiful.

A bell tinkled over the door as I pushed it open and we went in. An elderly man came toward us to stand behind the counter.

"Good morning, ladies," he said. "What can I do for you?"

"We want a frame—a small frame—to fit this." I laid the miniature on the table.

He looked intently at the miniature and smiled at me.

"Very nice," he said. "An excellent likeness."

I glanced sideways at Mary Grace, who was blushing.

"Have you anything?" I asked.

"It has to be small," he said. "There are not too many of this size around. Small and oval-shaped, of course. Most frames are the more conventional types. A piece of work like that needs something special, doesn't it?"

"Yes, it is going to be a present."

"It's lovely." He was thoughtful. "A pair of silver frames came in the other day. Excuse me a moment. Thomas," he called.

A man appeared. He was considerably younger than the one who was serving us.

"Yes, sir?" he said.

"What about those frames that came in the other day . . . with the Marlon lot."

"Do you mean those small silver ones, sir?"

"Yes. They'd take a picture like this, would they?"

The man came and looked down at the miniature.

"Beautiful," he said, smiling at me. "You'd want something really nice for that."

"Can you put your hands on those frames, Thomas?"

"I reckon so, sir."

The older man turned to us. "They came in only the other day. We haven't had much chance to look at all the stuff that came with them yet. Secondhand, you know. From a sale of one of the stately homes. Been in the family for years, then someone dies and everything's up for sale."

He chatted awhile until Thomas appeared with the frames. They were beautiful.

"They'd be some two hundred years old," we were told. "They knew how to make things in those days. Craftsmen. We could do with more of them nowadays. Well, I reckon we could make that picture fit. Trouble is, they're a pair."

I had an inspiration. "It might be that we should want the other one as well," I said. For if Dorabella wanted a miniature of herself to match mine, the frames should be similar.

"Unfortunately," I said, "I am not quite sure about the other one."

"Well, you could take the one and let me know, eh? I'll put it on one side for a while—say to the end of October? After that I'd let it go. They should go together, of course, but as it fits . . ."

"That would be wonderful," I said. "Could you fit the miniature into the frame for us?"

"I think we could do that," said the old man.

Thomas appeared again and was asked if he could fit the picture into the frame.

"Have to be trimmed a little," he said. "Needs a bit of care, but we can manage it. It's always like that. Pictures rarely fit the frame exactly. Could you call in this afternoon?"

We said we could and agreed on a price and triumphantly came out into the street.

Mary Grace continued to look bewildered.

Later my mother said: "Had a good morning's shopping?"

"Very good," I said, which she might have queried if she had not been so engrossed in her own plans.

I could scarcely wait for the afternoon.

The miniature looked more beautiful than ever in the silver frame. I wanted to show it to them all.

That evening we assembled in the Dorrington drawing room for an aperitif before dinner.

I said to my mother: "I have a most lovely present for Dorabella."

"You must have got it today," she said.

"It was completed today."

"What is it?"

I cut her short. "I want to show you before I explain."

"Well, where is it?"

"Wait," I said. I looked across at Mary Grace, who was talking to Edward and Gretchen. "I'll get it now."

I ran to my room and returned with the miniature wrapped in tissue paper.

I unwrapped it and held it out to my mother.

She took it and stared at it.

"Why!" she cried. "It's lovely."

I said: "Mary Grace came with me to get the frame."

"But ... it is *you*," went on my mother.

"Come on, Mary Grace," I said. "Confess. I have scolded her already for hiding her light under a bushel." I turned to Richard, who was staring at the picture in amazement. "Didn't you realize you had an artist in the family?"

"Mary Grace ..." began Richard.

"I knew she dabbled about with paints," said Mrs. Dorrington.

"You call that dabbling about with paints?" I cried indignantly. "I discovered what she was doing and she did this of me. It is wonderful and Dorabella is going to be so thrilled. I shall take Mary Grace to Tregarland's with me and she will do one of Dorabella. There is the frame for it in the jeweler's shop. She is going to have this for her birthday, and perhaps I shall have one of her for Christmas."

Everyone was talking at once and attention was focused on Mary Grace. She was embarrassed but, I believed, gratified; and I was very happy for her.

Over dinner they went on talking about Mary Grace's work and the wonderful way in which she had caught my likeness.

My mother was particularly pleased. She thought the miniature was the most delightful present. She was envious, she said, for whatever she found would have to take second place to my gift.

Mary Grace herself was talking with some animation and I

believed she was enjoying the company as she never had before.

My mother was saying: "We shall have to go to Cornwall soon. The girls have always celebrated their birthdays together. It was a double celebration, of course. I don't know what Dorabella would say if we were not together on that day. In a few weeks we shall have to be going. Your father will have to make it for this occasion, Violetta, whatever happens. It's a pity you can't come, Edward. It won't be the same without you."

Edward said: "I wish Dorabella had not gone so far away. It would have been nice if Gretchen and I could have looked in on the party."

"I certainly wish she were nearer," agreed my mother.

We left the men over their port and when they finally joined us I found myself sitting with Richard.

He said: "I want to thank you for what you have done for Mary Grace. She is like a different person."

"I didn't give her her talent. It was there all the time."

"Yes, hidden away. You brought it into the light."

"She is really very talented, I believe. I am going to ask her to paint my sister, and I shall show her portrait of me to my friends. I am sure there will be commissions."

"She will be wanting a studio in Chelsea soon."

"Why shouldn't she?"

"Well, it has certainly changed her. Look at her talking over there to Edward. You are a marvel, Violetta."

"Thank you, but *I* did not paint the miniature. All I did was recognize the talent."

"This has been a wonderful visit for us all." He looked at me earnestly. "You have enjoyed it, I hope."

"Immensely. I was wondering if Mary Grace would come to Cornwall and stay at Tregarland's. I am sure when my sister sees my picture she will want Mary Grace to do one of her. We shall be going down for our birthday—mine and Dorabella's—and I shall suggest to my sister that she invites Mary Grace. Do you think she would come?"

"I feel sure you could persuade any member of the Dorrington family to do what you want them to do."

"Do you really? I was not aware that I had such persuasive powers."

I glanced across the room and saw that my mother, who was talking to Mrs. Dorrington, was watching me. There was a smile of deep satisfaction on her face and I felt a twinge of uneasiness.

When we left the Dorringtons we went to stay for a few more days in Edward's house. My mother was often out with Mrs. Dorrington. I did not accompany them and she did not suggest it. I knew she wanted to get my birthday present and it would be a secret.

I spent a good deal of time with Gretchen and we had some talks together.

It was no use pretending that her anxieties did not exist, and I raised the subject of her family.

She said life did not improve. In fact it grew worse. She heard from them now and then and, though they always said that everything was all right, she knew differently. They lived in perpetual fear.

"All the young men are joining the Nazi Party. They march through the town. They are everywhere. It is fortunate that my family are in a rather remote spot, and any day they cannot be sure what will happen."

"Gretchen, do you think they should try to get out?"

"They are not in a position to do that. They would lose everything. Can you tear up your roots? Not when they have been there so long. Edward says we shall go over next summer. But I do not know. There is change everywhere. They do not tell me all, but I know they are afraid. They do not want me to worry. They say all is well. I am so fearful for them."

I was trying to think of that horrifying experience which I knew I should never forget. The terrible blustering indifference to human suffering . . . the sheer terror and hopelessness I had seen in faces that night. It made me despair that human beings could show such careless delight in the sufferings of others. And for what reason? I could have understood anger at some outrageous act, but this senseless persecution because of the hatred of one race for another was beyond my comprehension. What sort of people were they who could behave like this?

I felt sickened with anger and despair every time I thought of what I had seen that night.

"There is something I have to tell you, Violetta," said Gretchen.

"Yes?"

"I am going to have a baby."

I hugged her. I was so happy for her. This, with her love for Edward, could compensate her in some degree for the anxiety she suffered through her family.

My parents and I traveled down to Cornwall for the birthday celebrations. It would only be a brief visit, for my mother and I would come again in November when we should stay until the baby was born. My mother would want to assure herself that everything was in order before she left; it was possible that I would stay on for a while.

We had not yet made plans for Christmas, but it seemed likely that we should spend it in Cornwall as the idea that we should not be with Dorabella was unthinkable, and the baby would be too young to travel at such a time.

Dorabella showed her delight in seeing us and seemed very well. She hugged me and said: "You've no idea how I have missed you. It is just not right . . . our not being together. How can people cast off a habit of a lifetime?"

She spoke with a certain earnestness which was unusual with her; and the thought flashed into my mind that she might be, well, not exactly regretting the choice she had made, but perhaps questioning it. Yet Dermot was devoted and they seemed very affectionate toward each other. Perhaps being pregnant had an effect on her.

She embraced our parents with great fervor and it was really wonderful to be together again.

"It is only another month to go now," said my mother. "Then you will find it has all been so worthwhile."

"And you are only staying a week!"

"Well, we shall be down again in less than a month."

When she saw the miniature she was overcome with delight.

"But it is beautiful!" she cried. "And it is mine. I love it. It will be almost like having you with me. I shall never, never part with it."

She studied it closely. "It *is* clever. It's lovely. Mind you, it flatters you a little."

"Thank you for your sisterly candor," I retorted.

"Well, it does. It is not exactly a raving beauty, but it is interesting . . . like the Mona Lisa."

"Good Heavens!" I cried. "I never cared for that Gioconda smile."

"I don't mean you look like her. You look like yourself. But . . . it's beautiful."

"The compliments grow every minute."

She laughed. "It is so good to have you here, Vee," she said sincerely, and there were tears in her eyes. "I've missed you. You can't know how I've missed you."

"I've missed you, too," I told her.

"It's not right that we should be apart. We've been together right from the beginning of our existence. We ought never to have been separated. We are really part of each other. You ought to marry some nice Cornishman and live here with me. Nothing else will please me. You have a chance. There is that Jermyn man. That would be fun. And the feud and all that. Perhaps Gordon? But I prefer the Jermyn."

"All very funny," I said.

"And you have been gadding about in London, I hear. I am told that Edward's friend Richard is very charming. You went to the opera . . ."

"We all went."

"*Traviata*. Our dear Mama looks just a little cosy about Richard's choice of *Traviata*."

"You would have loved it."

"I would rather have had mine. Perhaps if I had been there, he would have chosen the one with Dorabella in it."

"I am sure he would."

"You don't mean that at all. But what fun it must have been . . . and then getting that lovely miniature painted. I should like one of myself."

"I knew you would. I was going to suggest you have yours done. It can be your Christmas present to me."

I told her about Mary Grace.

"Richard's sister, eh? The plot is thickening. You *are* getting on well with his family."

"I found this frame. Don't you think it is exquisite?"

"Lovely."

"There is another just like it. They are a pair."

"Where?"

"Waiting in the shop. They are holding it until I know whether you'll agree to have your miniature painted."

"But of course I will. She'll come here, will she, this Mary Grace?"

"I thought when the baby was born."

"Not until then?"

"You can't think about that sort of thing while you're waiting for the baby. Besides, it will be better when you are quite normal again."

"I like the idea," she said.

"You can write to Mary Grace. I'll take the letter back with me. You could ask her down for a week or two. She would fit it in. She works very quickly. The whole thing will be completed by Christmas."

"How glad I am to have you here! It makes life exciting!"

"What! You need me when you have an adoring husband and baby whose arrival is imminent? You still need your sister!"

"Always," she said earnestly. "You are not just an ordinary sister. You are a part of me."

Our stay was a brief one. I saw Jowan Jermyn once. I told him then that I should be down again in November and that this was just a birthday celebration. We drank mulled wine in a hotel two or three miles out of Poldown and he said as we parted: "I shall see more of you in November. You won't make it such a short visit then, I presume."

I said I was unsure. I might even stay until after Christmas.

"We haven't decided yet what we shall do," I explained. "My parents would like Dorabella to come home for Christmas, but it will be too soon for the baby to travel."

"You will be here," he said.

Gordon was a little more approachable. The memory of our adventure lingered on. He said how pleased he was that we were here and Dorabella seemed to miss me very much.

"You know what twins can be like," I said.

"Yes. The relationship is very close."

That was all. And then we left and came home.

A week or so later there was a letter from Nanny Crabtree and one for me from Dorabella.

They arrived when we were at breakfast. My mother opened

hers immediately. I liked to take Dorabella's letters to my bed-room that I might be alone when I read them, because she of-ten wrote very frankly, for my eyes only. My mother knew this and would ask later what I had heard from her.

"Wonderful!" she cried, reading her letter. "Nanny Crabtree is already there. Just the same old Nanny Crabtree. She is go-ing to make some changes in the nursery. She says Dorabella is doing well and everything seems to be in order. She's quite satisfied with her condition. She's not sure of the doctor, though. You have to watch these country doctors, she says."

Nanny Crabtree herself came from London and believed that everyone who did not could not be expected to share that certain shrewdness which belonged to those born in the capi-tal.

"She was just the same with us at Caddington," said my mother, with a grimace. "She'll be even more critical with the Cornish. It's even farther from London. I'm so glad she is there. She'll know exactly what's what, and as long as she doesn't alienate the doctor, all should be well. I wonder what Matilda thinks of her? The trouble with people like Nanny Crabtree is that they believe they are right and everyone who disagrees with them is wrong. Actually nine times out of ten she is right."

"I thought you were absolutely certain no one but Nanny Crabtree would do."

"I am, but she can rub people up the wrong way."

"Dorabella wants her."

"Oh, she'll be fine with her darling Dorabella, and the baby couldn't be in better hands, but Nanny Crabtree will have things done her way."

"Perhaps that's no bad thing."

"I'm sure it isn't."

I wanted to get away to read Dorabella's letter, and so I went to my room.

Dear Vee,

  Well, Nanny Crabtree has arrived in all her glory. Dermot went down to the station to collect her and I have an idea that she doesn't approve of him. Who could dis-approve of Dermot? He was meek with her and answered all her questions as well as could be expected from a mere man. She is a little critical of the house. She thinks it's draughty. "What can you expect?" she said. "With all that sea outside." She's changed the nursery round a bit and she makes me rest more. I was always the self-willed one. "Not like that Miss Violetta." You have become a paragon of virtue. It was always like that, wasn't it? The good twin was the absent one.

She goes off every now and then into something we did when we were three . . . or four. Well, she has anecdotes for all ages. The baby is *her* baby. I am allowed a slight proprietorial interest. You wouldn't think Dermot had anything to do with it. Nanny Crabtree's babies are all hers. Poor darling, I hope when he/she arrives, he/she does not find her too overpowering.

Matilda is so patient and goes along with everything she suggests. Dermot quite likes her, although she behaves toward him as though he is one of those half-witted men who wouldn't know one end of a baby from the other. Gordon, she thinks, is a bit of a misery. She doesn't know what to make of the old man, though they rarely meet. I am sure she considers him of no importance whatsoever.

Dear old Nanny Crabtree. I'm glad she is here. She makes me feel . . . comfortable.

What I want most is for you to come. It won't be long now. By the way, tell Mummy I am thinking of names. I have decided to keep up the opera tradition. If it's a boy, it's to be Tristan, if a girl Isolde. Ask her if that will suit her. I don't think she is as fond of Wagner as she is of our two. But it will be particularly appropriate as these are Cornish names . . . and Nanny Crabtree's baby will be half that.

When I told my mother about the suggested names she was amused.

"I like that," she said. "They are both lovely names. I wonder what it will be. Your father doesn't mind much what sex it is as long as they are both all right. Nor do I, for that matter. Perhaps a boy would be nice. They would like that down there, I expect."

She was looking at me wistfully, and I felt that faint, embarrassed irritation when I saw matrimonial plans in her eyes. It might be that she believed I must be very lonely without Dorabella.

There was little thought now of anything but the baby. We went to London to stay with Edward and, of course, saw the Dorringtons.

I had a chance of telling Mary Grace about Dorabella's reception of the miniature and that, just as I had thought, she wanted Mary Grace to do a picture of her.

"I expect you persuaded her," said Mary Grace.

"I can assure you Dorabella makes up her own mind. She thinks you have genius and she can't wait. That is why I wanted to make sure of that other frame. When the baby is born you must come down. You'll find Cornwall quite interesting."

"Do you really mean that?"

"Of course."

"I can't believe it."

"And you will come to Cornwall and do the miniature?"

"I want to . . . more than anything. It has been marvelous."

"We'll get the frame tomorrow and make sure we have the pair."

It was a successful visit. There was the usual excitement of shopping and we went to a theater and to supper with the Dorringtons.

Gretchen seemed a little more serene. She was preoccupied with the coming baby. It was not due until April but already it absorbed her. I was so glad, for it undoubtedly took her thoughts away from the anxieties she felt about her family.

We could not stay long, for, as my mother had said, we had to prepare for our visit to Cornwall.

"I want to be there in good time," she said. "Dorabella will feel happier if we are around. When it is all settled down, I shall have to come back. I can't leave your father too long. He hates to be alone, though he never complains. You might like to stay on a little, and if Mary Grace is going to be there, you would want to be there, too. We shall have to make plans for Christmas. I suppose we shall have to go there. Nanny Crabtree would never allow such a young baby to travel. We seem to be spending our lives on trains these days. I thought the Dorringtons rather hinted that we might spend Christmas with them."

"Oh, we should have to be with Dorabella."

"Of course. But I wish she were not so far away."

And in due coure we were traveling down to Cornwall. It was a dark November day and as the train carried us into the West Country the light was fading. It would be dark by the time we arrived.

Dorabella flung herself at me and clung to me. She was very emotional. The birth was clearly imminent; she was quite unwieldy and, I could detect, a little scared.

Then she clung to my mother, who was very reassuring.

Nanny Crabtree welcomed us with restrained pleasure.

"It's going to be a boy," she said. "I can tell by the way she's carrying it. That Mrs. Lewyth said she thought it would be a girl. 'A girl, my foot,' I said. 'She's carrying a boy if ever I saw a boy being carried.' "

"Well, I hope little Tristan comes punctually."

"Tristan!" snorted Nancy Crabtree. "What a name! What's wrong with a nice Jack or Charlie?"

"Nothing at all," retorted my mother, "except that Dorabella has decided on Tristan."

Nanny Crabtree clicked her tongue. At least she could not have her way over that.

Dorabella showed us the now completed layette and told us what arrangements had been made.

The midwife was coming as soon as Nanny Crabtree gave the call and there would be the doctor, too; and Nanny Crabtree would be on hand to welcome the new arrival.

"Everything is ready," put in Nanny Crabtree. "I've seen to that. Now all we've got to do is wait for the little darling."

That was what she was longing for. Then she would be rid of the midwife and the doctor and herself be in complete command.

Dorabella was a little exhausted and went to bed immediately after dinner. We did not see Dermot or Gordon. Matilda told us that they had both gone to some landowners' conference which was being held in Exeter. They would be away for two nights probably. "Dermot wanted to cancel it when he heard the day you were coming, but Gordon thought they could not easily do that, nor that he should go without

Dermot," Matilda told us. "And the baby is not due for a few more days, so he knew you would understand."

"Of course," said my mother. "He can see us when he gets back."

My mother came to my room for a little chat after we had retired.

"Well," she said. "I think everything is in order."

"It seems so."

"Matilda is very good. I did think Nanny Crabtree might have made some difficulties, but Matilda is the soul of tact and seems to realize what a treasure she is, so long as you don't mind her ways."

"Yes, I think Matilda likes a peaceful life."

"As for the rest of the servants ... well, Nanny Crabtree would be on her own and wouldn't come into contact with them very much. The nursery is her life. That's why the baby couldn't have a better nanny. Well, all we have to do is wait for the day."

"I think Dorabella is getting a little scared."

"Who wouldn't be? It's her first and she isn't sure what she has to face. She'll be all right. She's strong and healthy, and we'll make sure that everything that can be done will be."

"That's a comfort."

"I'm glad you're here. A pity your father couldn't be with us. But he wouldn't be much use in the nursery."

"He'd be a comfort and it's always good to have him around."

My mother nodded and smiled. "That's true," she said. "But there is the estate, and we do seem to be on the move all the time. When the baby has grown a little, she'll be able to come to us and there won't be all these journeys." She yawned. "It's been a tiring day. I'm exhausted. I think it is time I was in bed. You, too."

We said goodnight and she left me.

I was indeed tired. I got into bed and lay for some time listening to the murmur of the sea. Why did I always feel there was something a little uncanny about this place?

I dozed and awoke with a start. I heard the creak of a board and I knew that I was not alone. Someone was in my room.

My heart was beating wildly. I was not yet fully awake. I

had been startled out of some dream which had vaguely filled me with foreboding.

I sat up in bed, peering at the furniture which I could see in the faint starlight.

Dorabella came out of the shadows to stand by my bed.

"I've frightened you," she said. "I did not know you'd be so easily scared."

"Dorabella! What are you doing?"

"I couldn't sleep ... then I had this dream ... it's not the first time. It terrified me."

She was wearing a light dressing gown over her nightdress and her hair was loose about her shoulders.

I said: "You'll get cold."

"I had to come and see you."

"You can't stand there."

"No," she said. She took off her dressing gown, flung it onto a chair, and got into my bed.

There flashed into my memory those days when we had been away from home ... on some holiday ... or visiting people. If she had been put into a different room she always came into mine. She would say, 'I couldn't sleep,' or 'I've had a bad dream.' At home we had slept in the same room ... in two beds fairly close together. As she snuggled close to me, I was reminded of those long-ago days.

"Thank goodness you're here," she said.

"Why? Is there something ... ?"

"Why?" she repeated. "Because I want you here. That's why. I hate it when I can't come in and talk to you whenever I want to. I've got to talk to you now, Vee."

"Well, why not begin? Here I am ... awakened from my slumber."

"I'm sorry if I frightened you. Did you think I was a ghost? Perhaps that Jermyn ghost—the one who walked into the sea. I am worried, Violetta. I really am. This dream was so vivid ... and I've had it before. I think it is a premonition."

"You've just had it, have you?"

"Yes, and a few nights ago. It's just the same every time."

"What happens in the dream?"

"I have the baby ... and die."

"What a foolish notion! Why should you? Thousands have babies safely. You have everything satisfactorily arranged, the best attention. Mummy and I are here with you and you have Nanny Crabtree. She would never let ... that ... happen to you."

"Don't joke! I'm serious about this. It's the baby ..."

"What about the baby?"

"I'm dead, you see, in this dream. I die having him, but he's all right. He's fine. I'm gone and he is still here. Perhaps when you die you can watch people ... you see how they act. That's what I'm doing in this dream ... watching. I see you there and our mother ... and you are so unhappy."

"Really, Dorabella," I said severely. "You are being overdramatic. You are perfectly all right. The doctor said so."

"Doctors don't always know and there are sometimes ... complications."

"You are the last person I should have thought to get morbid ideas. Listen to me. You're going to have a baby ... any time now. It's natural that you're scared. I suppose anyone would be. We all know babies don't arrive in the mouth of the stork or are found under gooseberry bushes and that the process of birth is a painful one. It is happening all over the world, but it is the first time for you and you always hated discomfort of any sort. You are not looking forward to it, naturally, but that's all. Just imagine when you hear little Tristan or Isolde yelling his or her head off. It'll be wonderful. Your own baby. And you'll know it's all over then. Oh, you are lucky, Dorabella."

"You would like to have a baby, would you?"

"All women like to have babies ... or most of them."

"Only the maternal type. I think you are one of those."

"You will be."

"Just suppose ... ?"

"Suppose what?"

"Suppose ... like the dream ... I don't come through."

"I refuse to think of it for a moment."

"Dear, dear Vee, we should never be apart. I don't feel the same without you. I feel half-finished. That's why ... I know you don't like this, but it could happen. People do die and often those least expected to."

"Forget that silly dream. It's what they call prenatal nerves."

"Do they? I expect you have swotted up on the subject of birth."

"I keep my ears open."

"That's because we have always shared everything. I'll tell you what I want, Vee. If I don't come through . . ."

I made an impatient gesture.

"Listen," she commanded. "Just suppose. If I weren't there, I want you to take little Tristan . . . or Isolde. I wouldn't want anyone else. Do you understand?"

"What do I know about babies?"

"As much as I do . . . and I'm having one. You'd have Nanny Crabtree to guide you. But I'd want *you* to have the baby. Mummy would be there, too. She'd have a hand in it. But the baby would want one person to stand out against all others, someone to take the place of its mother. And I would want you to be the one because you are part of me."

"Of course I'd be there . . . but it is all nonsense."

"Yes, perhaps it is. But swear. 'Cut my throat if I ever tell a lie.' "

I laughed at the old childish saying. I could see her so clearly when she wanted me to promise to keep some secret . . . licking her finger: "See my finger's wet"; then drying it: "See my finger's dry. I'll cut my throat," drawing a hand across her throat, "if I ever tell a lie."

"I swear," I said. "But you're soon going to be laughing at all these fancies."

She stretched out contentedly.

"I feel better now," she said. "Whatever happens, it will be all right . . . I mean the baby will be. You know how it is with us. We're like one, Vee. It will always be like that . . . whatever happens. If I died . . ."

"Oh, please, stop talking about death."

She said dreamily: "You've given your promise. We always kept promises, didn't we? You see what I mean, don't you, when I say you are part of me and I am part of you? We've been together right from the beginning. We're bound together. It's there, isn't it? Other people can't see it. It's so fine . . . it's like a cord . . . strong but invisible. I think of it as a gossamer cord that binds us together . . . for always, even if one of us died . . ."

I sighed impatiently.

"All right," she went on. "I won't talk about it any more.

You've promised . . . and whatever happens, that cord is there. Now, you'll stay here, won't you?"

"Well, I'm here for a while."

"I'll tell you what I want you to do. Marry that nice Jermyn man and stay here altogether."

"Certainly, Madam. If that will suit your convenience."

"Fancy! We'd be neighbors. What fun! Though Mummy has her hopes on the London lawyer."

"Really! I wish you would not discuss that sort of thing. It's embarrassing. Particularly when there's nothing in it. I think you were rather wise to get yourself married and so escape these speculations."

"All mothers are the same," she said. "They hate losing their daughters, yet they are not content until they see them married. It is rather perverse of them."

She laughed. Her fears seemed to have disappeared.

I wondered whether there had really been a dream. She loved drama and it was essential to her that she should be at the center of it. She probably liked to contemplate a household in mourning for her, a motherless baby just arrived into the world, a twin sister who was part of her, bound by "a gossamer cord," becoming a surrogate mother. She enjoyed that as long as she could be there to look on at the drama.

It was a long time before she returned to her room. I went back with her and tucked her in. She clung to me for a while.

"Remember," she said. "You've sworn a sacred oath."

Back in my own room I found sleep evasive. In spite of my rejection of her fears, they had conjured up some of my own. Just suppose . . . No, no. I could not entertain such an idea.

She would be all right. She must. Everyone said so. She was young and healthy. Everything must go right.

I lay there, dozing now and then, half dreaming uneasy dreams.

Below the sea seemed to have lost a little of that serene murmur; and had taken on a malevolent whisper.

At last I slept.

A few days later Dorabella's ordeal began.

There was a hushed atmosphere throughout the house. The doctor had come and the midwife was with him. My mother and I sat tense, waiting. Nanny Crabtree was ready to pounce on the baby. The moment she heard the cry of a child, she would be there. But the doctor and the midwife had made it clear that her presence would not be needed until that moment.

I could not stop thinking of Dorabella's coming to my room, and the dream which she had more than once.

My mother was equally nervous. We sat talking of other things—anything but Dorabella—while we waited for news . . . and feared it.

At last we heard the footsteps on the stairs. The doctor was beaming at us.

"It's a boy. You can see her now . . . just for a few minutes. She's very tired."

"She . . . she's all right?" I stammered.

"Right as a trivet," he answered.

We dashed up to her room. There she lay, flushed and triumphant. The midwife was holding the baby—red-faced—a tuft of fair hair on his head, squirming and irritable.

"He's a beauty," said the midwife, as the child opened his mouth in a wail of angry protest.

Dorabella held my hand and that of my mother. My mother was almost in tears of relief and happiness.

Dorabella looked at me.

"I managed it," she said.

"I knew you would."

"What do you think of Tristan?"

"He's wonderful," said my mother. "Only a daughter of mine could produce such a child."

Tragedy on the Beach

❧

When Dorabella had recovered from her ordeal, James Tregarland insisted that the baby's health be drunk in his vintage champagne. Tristan was by this time looking very different from the little old man of ninety whom he had resembled at birth. His skin was a healthy pink, his hair, though sparse, had a golden tinge, and his eyes, which he occasionally opened, were amazingly blue.

Nanny Crabtree held him and was watchful of any who came too near.

Dorabella sat in her chair, looking completely restored to normal. Dermot stood beside her, the proud father; Matilda, with Gordon, smiled happily on us all; and my mother and I sat close to Dorabella.

The old man lifted his glass.

"Welcome to Tristan," he said. "Our grateful thanks to his parents for giving us this blessing."

We all drank to that.

Dermot said how happy he and Dorabella were by this exciting event.

"Well," said James Tregarland, his eyes glistening with that look which I had seen many times. "This is a great occasion. The succession is secure." He was smiling at Matilda. "Don't you agree, Matty?"

Matilda replied with something like faint embarrassment: "Yes, indeed it is."

The old man's chin wagged slightly, as I had seen it do before, and I think he implied some secret amusement. What was amusing him now seemed to concern Matilda. Was it some joke they shared?

Matilda, however, was smiling serenely.

"I am so glad," she said, "that it is all over. It has necessarily been a worrying time."

"And you and Gordon have been as anxious as the rest of us," said the old man. "And now all is well. It's a great weight off our minds. We have our little one."

He was still smiling at Matilda.

"Yes," she said. "Dear little Tristan. It will be wonderful to have a child in the house."

The baby suddenly opened his mouth wide and yawned, which made everyone laugh.

"He seems a little bored with the proceedings," said the old man with a grin.

"He wants his rest," put in Nanny Crabtree. "I'll be getting him down."

She left us, taking Tristan with her.

When she had gone, the old man said: "She'll make sure he's all right, that one."

"She can be a little officious at times," said Matilda. "But I am sure she will be a wonderful nurse."

"She certainly is," said my mother. "That is why I was determined to get her. She looked after my girls and you couldn't have a better watchdog."

"Watchdog," cried the old man. "You think there is going to be an attack on the youngster, do you?"

"I meant a watchdog against the hazards of childhood," explained my mother. "She'll see that he has the best care and is not allowed to take risks. She regards him as hers."

"That's what he needs," said the old man, smiling to himself.

I thought he was very odd, and wondered whether he was slightly deranged. He seemed to be greatly amused by some secret joke.

A few days later my mother said she must go back. She had decided, after consultation with Nanny Crabtree, that the baby would be too young to travel at Christmas so we should spend the festive season at Tregarland's.

Mary Grace was to visit us here shortly. Dorabella was very eager to sit for her portrait and grew really upset when I talked about returning when Mary Grace did; and finally I agreed that I might as well stay until after Christmas.

My mother left and Mary Grace arrived.

She and Dorabella liked each other immediately and Mary Grace started on the picture.

She was welcomed by the family. The old man came down to dinner and was clearly interested in her. She sat next to Gordon at dinner and she and he seemed to get on well together. They had all seen the miniature I had given Dorabella for her birthday and were impressed by Mary Grace's work.

Surprisingly Gordon knew a little about art and they had something to talk about; Mary Grace blossomed and seemed to be a different person from the one I had first met.

I was contented. Life seemed to be running smoothly now. Dorabella's fearful prognostications had proved to be without foundation; Mary Grace was much happier and I could not help feeling a mild self-congratulation on that score, since I had been the one to bring her talent to light. Doing good turns to others gives one such a glow of pleasure. Well, I was contented.

I had not seen Jowan Jermyn since I had come down. In the first days we had been too concerned about the birth to think of anything else; and afterwards there was so much to do with Mary Grace's arrival. I had simply not had the opportunity of going off alone.

But now there were the sittings and that left me a certain amount of free time.

I did not feel I should go to the field in search of him, for it was hardly likely that he would be there. It was some little time since I had arrived in Cornwall and I had made no attempt to see him. I could not expect him to be there every day just on the chance that I might come.

What a ridiculous state of affairs this feud was! If he could have telephoned to Tregarland's it would have been so different.

I would just take a ride. The country was always interesting; and at this time of the year there were no visitors, which gave it an added charm.

I rode inland, skirting the Jermyn estate, past woods and fields which were new to me. Every now and then I caught a glimpse of the coastline. It was beautiful on this day. There was a benign touch about the wind which came in from the sea. It was caressing.

I felt pleased with life. Dorabella was well. She had really frightened me with her talk of dreams and making me swear to look after the child who, she was sure, would be motherless.

That was Dorabella. Always looking for drama.

I loved Tristan already. When I went to the nursery Nanny Crabtree would allow me to hold him and he did not protest.

Nanny Crabtree said: "He likes his aunty Violetta, don't you . . . little pet?"

He cast on her that inscrutable look which gave him the appearance of a sage. Then he turned his blue stare on me.

"I believe he's smiling at me," I said.

"Could be a touch of the wind," said Nanny Crabtree, taking him from me.

He opened his mouth in protest and she handed him back. He settled in my arms and stared at me. That gesture endeared him more than ever to me. He was mine after that.

I was thinking of this as I rode along.

I was not far from the Jermyn estate when I met Jowan. He was riding a big black horse and saw me from a distance and came riding up.

"Hello!" he cried. "Why haven't we met till now?"

"Because our paths have not crossed until this moment."

He gave me a reproachful look.

"I was at the rendezvous."

"Oh, I am sorry. We've had a busy time."

"I know, of course. The news has come through. A boy. Tristan. A good old Cornish name."

"That's what my sister said, and she is keeping in the opera tradition at the same time."

"Splendid. What about a drink at one of our inns?"

"I'd like to, but I haven't time now. My sister will be expecting me back."

He looked disappointed, which gave me a great deal of pleasure.

"I think," he said, "that you and I should break this foolish habit!"

"You mean . . . ?"

"If I cannot call on you, you must come to my place. Then we won't have to meet as if by chance or a sort of haphazard arrangement. I am going to invite you to my home. Will you come?"

I hesitated.

"Oh, please. We are not going to allow ourselves to be governed by this silly story which has been going on all this time. We'll break through it. We'll scandalize the neighborhood. Come to my home. When shall it be?"

I said: "It would be something which we should undertake with some caution, perhaps."

"Why? If we are going to kick through restrictions, shouldn't we do it boldly?"

"I am only a guest here, you know. It is hardly for me to blaze a trail."

"Do you mean you won't come?"

"Suppose I came for tea? I could do that without having to make an announcement to the household. I do not understand Mr. Tregarland Senior. I think he might be amused. I am not sure of my sister's husband, nor Mrs. Lewyth ... who, I believe, takes a great pride in the family."

"And your sister?"

"She would be in full agreement with you. She would think such a visit would be interesting and amusing."

"Well then. Tomorrow afternoon. Three o'clock? Half past two?"

"Half past two," I said. "My sister rests at that time. I shall tell her. Then she will not be worried if I don't get back promptly. She does worry about things like that."

"For instance at the time of the cliff rescue?"

"Yes, that was certainly one time."

"How is she?"

"Very well, but she still gets a little tired."

"And the baby?"

"He's delightful."

"And you've got your old nanny."

"So you have already heard of her."

"She seems to be a person of some standing. But she is not Cornish and that is a black mark against her."

"I can assure you Nanny Crabtree is a match for any."

"That is what I gathered."

"You are so well informed."

"The subject is of particular interest to me."

I felt light-hearted, as always, with him.

His last words were: "Tomorrow. Two thirty. I shall wait your coming with pleasure."

When I arrived back I went straight to Dorabella. She was lying on her bed and when she saw me she cried: "Where have you been? What's happened? You look different."

"What do you mean . . . different?"

"Something exciting has happened. I know what it is. You've seen that Jermyn man."

"Well . . ."

She laughed. "You have . . . then?"

"Yes . . ."

"I always know. He must be fascinating. You ought to bring him here."

"Well, as a matter of fact, I am going to visit him tomorrow."

She was overcome with amusement.

"I can't wait to hear the outcome."

"Oh, it's nothing much."

"Nothing much! Right into the enemy's camp. We won't say anything about it here. You never know how they'd take it."

I wondered if they would care. I had seen very little animosity to the Jermyns here and I knew Jowan felt none toward them. The feud was something which was kept going because the families were too indifferent to change it; it was the people around who liked to create a drama where it did not exist.

The next afternoon when I was setting out for the appointment, I encountered Seth in the stables.

"You be wanting Starlight, Miss?" he asked.

I told him I did. He looked at me strangely. I wondered if he had heard where I was going. He could not have done so yet. So far it was between Jowan and myself. It would be after I had visited his home that the gossip would start.

Seth was trying to say something. He stammered: "Don't 'ee go there, Miss. Don't 'ee go."

I was amazed. I thought, Can he really know where I am going?

" 'Ee don't want to see 'er again, Miss. It might not be . . ."

"Go where, Seth?" I asked.

He pointed toward the sea.

"You mean the beach? No, no, I shan't be going there. I wouldn't dream of taking Starlight down to the beach."

"There's some of them take the horses there. They go along the beach at a gallop."

"I don't plan to do that."

He gave me a sly smile. "Don't want to tempt 'un, Miss."

I really wasn't sure who was to be tempted. I guessed it was the Jermyn ghost who he believed had lured the first Mrs. Tregarland into the sea.

Poor Seth. I was sorry for him. And it was kind of him to be concerned for me.

He patted Starlight's flank lovingly, and I rode out of the stables.

It was another warmish day, ideal for riding. There was scarcely any wind and inland I could see a faint blue mist settling over the trees.

I turned my horse and rode toward the Jermyn estate. This time I should go straight to the house.

I rode along for about half a mile and there was the house. It was not as ancient as Tregarland's but impressive. It was built in that silver gray stone which they call Elvan and with which I had become familiar since my arrival in Cornwall.

I went through a gate into a turfed forecourt and facing me was a heavy iron-studded door. I was wondering whether to dismount when the door opened and Jowan stood there.

"I was waiting for you," he said. "Punctual as usual."

He patted Starlight as he smiled at me. Then he held me to dismount.

"Charlie," he shouted, and a man hurried out.

"Yes, sir."

"Take the lady's horse."

He turned to me and took my arm.

"So this is your home," I said.

"Yes. Do you like it?"

"From what I have seen, it is magnificent."

"I like it," he said. "I'm looking forward to showing it to you."

I stood in the hall and looked around. It was not unlike all such halls. It had a plaster ceiling, the main ribs of which were set on corbels decorated with oak leaves. On one of the walls were the entwined initials J and S.

My eyes rested on it and he said: "Jowan and Sarah. They built the house three hundred years ago, and it was the custom to have such entwined initials. It could become embarrassing if the marriage didn't work out and there was a second wife, and she had to spend her married life with the constant reminder of her predecessor. I can tell you that is not the only spot where you will find those initials."

He pointed out the minstrels' gallery.

"I plan to use that one day for its original purpose, out of respect for old customs. Some of them are worth preserving. Now let me show you the rest of the house and you can tell me what you think of it."

"It is beautiful," I said. "You must be proud of it."

"It has not been long in my possession and I am still a trifle bemused by the fact. But come along. Here are the screens—they lead to the kitchen. That is a part I will leave to your imagination. The servants are there." He grimaced. "It would make their deductions too easy if I introduced you to them. Let us leave them to their own speculations."

"They are going to talk about my being here."

"Let them. But you are not a Tregarland, so perhaps that will modify the betrayal of the past. Now, there are several rooms leading from the hall. This staircase goes to the library and beyond that is the drawing room. That is the old solar. It is the best room in the house. We shall have tea there. It is very light, with semicircular bay windows—of a much later period than the rest of the house. They were put in over a hundred years ago."

I followed him through the house. The west wing was in a dilapidated state.

"It has been much neglected," he told me. "My plan is to restore the place completely."

I could hear the pride in his voice as he pointed out the special features, showed me the restoration work he had already completed, and told me what he planned to do.

He said: "I can't show you everything on one visit. This is just a cursory look round. We can go into it with more detail at some other time if you are interested."

"I am," I said.

"I'm glad because it is something of a passion with me. I

want to make this house what it should be and what it was before it was allowed to deteriorate."

He seemed different from the young man who had sat with me in those inn parlors drinking cider or mulled wine. It occurred to me that people could be very different against their own backgrounds. I felt that I was seeing him as he really was. He was really earnest about the restoration of his own house; previously I thought he could not be serious about anything and that life seemed to him little else but a joke.

In due course we returned to the solar which was filled with pale December sunshine. Tea was brought by a maid who could not hide her curiosity. I guessed that she knew I came from Tregarland's.

I learned more about Jowan Jermyn.

He had owned the house for two years, although he had spent his childhood here. His father was the younger son of that Charles Jermyn on whose death the house had gone to Jowan's father's elder brother, Joseph.

"The house had been neglected for years," he said. "I always had a special feeling for it. We had a place on the north coast, for, when my father married, he went to live in north Cornwall, where I was born. My mother never recovered from my birth and died three years after it. My grandfather had been artistic and was not interested in the material things of life. I came here and was brought up by my grandmother. Uncle Joseph was of a somewhat profligate nature. He was a great gambler and spent a great deal of time in London. He had little feeling for the country. His lack of interest grieved my grandmother. Uncle Joseph was an unsatisfactory Jermyn. He did not marry, although he had several children. He did not want family ties, and so on. He inherited the house in due course. My father, who loved this place, could not bear to be near and it not be his. He knew the way it would go because old houses need constant attention, and when some little deterioration shows it should be dealt with immediately. So I was deposited with my grandmother while he went to New Zealand. I was to join him when he was ready to have me. I did not want to go. I wanted to stay with my grandmother in this house."

"But you came back to it eventually?"

"It worked out unexpectedly. I was eighteen when my father

died. He had left his place in New Zealand to me. I did not want to go abroad; my grandmother did not want me to leave. She was very sad about the house, which was in a dire state by this time. Uncle Joseph was only interested in the revenues which came from the place."

"And you went to New Zealand?"

"Yes. I was there for four years. Then I heard that Uncle Joseph had died prematurely, which was not altogether surprising. He had been drinking too heavily for years. My father was heir to the estate and, since he had died, it fell to me. I sold up everything in New Zealand and came home. I have been here ever since."

"Your grandmother . . . ?"

"You'll meet her. She is in her room most of the time nowadays."

"You mean she is here?"

He nodded. "Where else would she be? She loves the place. It is an interest we share."

"And . . . what about the feud?"

He laughed. "She feels about that as I do . . . as you do. A lot of nonsense."

"That's the sensible view, of course."

"Yes, but in spite of that, it has been going on for a long time."

"It is due to the superstitious people around us. They have kept it going all this time."

"I suppose it supplies a little excitement, something to talk about."

"That's so, and, of course, since the first Mrs. Tregarland died it brought it up again."

"But the families were never friendly. We needed a visitor from 'foreign parts' to set it right."

I laughed. "Do you think the fact that you have invited me here is going to change all that?"

"I think it is the first step."

We talked for a long time and I glanced at my watch.

"I shall have to go," I said, "Dorabella will be anxious to hear about this visit."

He stood up and, taking my hand, helped me to rise. He held it for some time while he smiled at me. I felt deep pleasure.

"Before you go," he said, "you must say hello to my grand-mother."

"I should very much like that."

"Come on, then."

He led me up a staircase, through a gallery to a corridor, and then up more stairs.

He opened the door of a room which was clearly a sitting room and, through an open door, I saw a four-poster bed. Mrs. Charlotte Jermyn was sitting in a chair, a piece of crochet work in her hands. She looked over the top of her spectacles as I came in.

"Grandmother," said Jowan. "I have brought her to show you and to show you to her."

She smiled. "Well, this is nice." She had dropped the crochet into her lap and held out her hand.

"I'm a bit stiff today," she said. "It's my rheumatism. It is worse some days than others. They say this damp climate is not good for it. Well, Miss Denver, it is nice to see you here. Jowan has told me about you."

"I am so pleased to be here and to meet you."

She laughed. "It's time someone put their feet through that nonsense. I guessed Jowan would be the one to do it. And now your sister is up there and you are a frequent visitor."

"I came for the birth of the baby and shall be staying until after Christmas."

"That is good. We always have a real Cornish Christmas here. We call it keeping up the old customs. Tell me about your sister and the new baby."

I told her and we talked awhile.

Jowan watched us in an amused way, pleased, I could see, that we were getting on well together.

I was sorry that I had to leave, but I could imagine Dorabella's impatience, so I said I must go.

"You'll come again," said Mrs. Jermyn. "I shall look forward to seeing you."

It was with reluctance that at last I left.

Dorabella was very impatient to hear what had happened. She was eager to meet Jowan and suggested that he be invited to the house. To dinner? To lunch, perhaps, would be best for a start.

"He sounds fun," she said, looking at me searchingly.

I knew what was in her mind, just as I knew what had been in my mother's concerning Richard Dorrington.

I said: "You should make sure that the family approve. Don't forget, this feud has been going on for a hundred years or more. You come into the family and want to break it up."

"*I* want to break it up! Who fell off her horse and started it up by meeting him secretly, going to his house, meeting his grandmother . . ." She giggled. "All right. I'll suggest it to Dermot."

"I think Dermot's father should be the one to make the decision. After all, he is the head of the household."

"Very well. But I think he'd love it."

"And what about Matilda?"

"Well, I suppose, now *I* am the mistress of the house. Matilda, after all, is only a glorified housekeeper."

"Don't let her hear you say that."

"It is for your ears alone."

The result of this was that Jowan and his grandmother were invited to lunch.

As we had guessed, old Mr. Tregarland had no objection and enjoyed the meeting tremendously, as I am sure Jowan's grandmother did. I think they relished the behavior of the servants and I imagined the news would travel fast. The Jermyns were making friends with the Tregarlands, and it was all due to the second Mrs. Tregarland and her sister!

It was a very pleasant lunch.

The days were passing quickly. Mary Grace had returned to London, taking with her the finished picture of Dorabella which was to be fitted into the frame. My mother would bring it with her when she came for Christmas.

Then Christmas came. My parents joined us and we were all very merry.

There was the ceremony of bringing in the log and what they called the "wassailing," when the head of the family stood by a bowl of spiced wine from which he drank before passing it round so that everyone might have a sip. It seemed a rather unhealthy procedure, but we were told that it had been done since Saxon days and it was considered unlucky not to cling to the old ways.

Carol singers came; they were invited into the hall to partake of wine and cakes. Then there were the guise dances, when the young dressed up in any costumes they could find—the girls mostly as boys and the boys as girls; those who had no costumes just blacked their faces and danced through the lanes and into the courtyard.

Jowan knew a great many more old customs and said some of them went back to pre-Christian days and most people nowadays had forgotten them.

It always meant that when the dancers and the carol singers arrived at the big houses they must be invited in and given food and drink. It was all part of the Christmas spirit.

On Boxing Day we were invited to the Jermyns. It was a buffet supper and there would be dancing. Dermot, Dorabella, and I went. It was amusing and there were people there whom we had never seen before.

There were two whom Jowan had met when he was traveling on the Continent: Hans Fleisch, a young German, and a Frenchman, Jacques Dubois. They were painters who had found inspiration in the wild Cornish coast and were staying at an inn nearby.

They were lively and amusing, and they clearly thought Dorabella charming and paid considerable attention to her, which delighted her.

It was a pleasant evening and confirmed once again that all the nonsense about feuds was at an end.

I was sorry that I should be going home soon, but I had been away for a long time.

My mother said I really must come home. Dorabella was her old self now. She was contented, and she had her own life to lead.

I felt uncertain. I had become more friendly with Jowan Jermyn and was seeing him in a new light; but I could not escape from the feelings of uneasiness which overcame me at Tregarland's.

I remembered our trip to London; the fun we had had and how gratified I had been to discover Mary Grace's talent. It seemed like a different world; and if I enjoyed being with Jowan, I had had a very good time with the Dorringtons.

Perhaps it would be pleasant to return to Caddington for a while. I would leave with my parents.

In the town people seemed to take a special interest in me. They would know, of course, about the changed relationship between the Jermyns and the Tregarlands. I wanted to escape from the gossip. It would be pleasant to go to London where one was a private person and no one had the faintest idea what was happening in one's life.

Seth was very broody at this time. He seemed to be more concerned about the friendship between Jermyns and Tregarlands than anyone—but perhaps he showed it more.

One day I spoke to him about it. When I had gone to the stables he regarded me with melancholy eyes.

"Seth," I said. "Why do you look like that?"

"It won't do no good, Miss. It won't . . ."

"What, Seth?" I asked.

"Meeting with 'em."

"Meeting with whom?"

He waved his hand upwards. "They'm angry. That's what they be. They won't let 'ee forget. 'Twas you, Miss, after all, as started it."

I laughed. "Don't worry about it, Seth. It's of no account."

"It'll be of account to 'ee, that it will. You mark my words."

"Never mind, Seth," I said. "Now . . . I want to take Starlight for a farewell ride."

As the time for our departure grew near, Dorabella became really sad.

She said: "You've been here so long now, it seems as though you are part of the place. It's going to be very lonely when you have gone."

"But you have Dermot and Tristan."

"I'll miss you. It is different with us. We are like one person. We've always been together until now. Why can't you stay?"

"When Dermot married you, he didn't want your family around all the time."

"But *I* want you." Her face was petulantly puckered and I was touched because she looked as she had so many times during our childhood.

She went on: "Isn't it exciting enough here? You want to go to London, don't you? It's more interesting there."

"We have promised to go and stay with Edward and Gretchen. There'll be the baby that is coming and the new house. You know how Mummy feels about that. Edward is like a son to her."

"I don't want you to go."

My mother came in at that moment.

"Have you packed yet?" she asked me. "Why, Dorabella, what's the matter?"

"I don't want you to go."

"Why! We'll be back in the spring. Perhaps you can come to us. I am sure Nanny Crabtree will allow Tristan to travel soon."

Dorabella said nothing more about our traveling, but when we left she clung to me rather desperately.

While we were traveling home in the carriage my mother, who was staring thoughtfully out of the window, said suddenly: "I hope Dorabella hasn't made a mistake."

"What?" said my father, coming sharply out of a half doze.

"She seemed so upset about our going, particularly at losing Violetta."

"Well," said my father, "they have always been together so much. She's all right."

"I wouldn't like to think . . ." mused my mother.

"What?" I asked.

"Oh, nothing. She's all right. She wants Dermot, the baby, and you as well. That's just like Dorabella."

I felt a certain relief to be home. Everything seemed normal. There was quite a different atmosphere from that of Cornwall.

Memories of Mrs. Pardell came back to me—her resentments, her suspicions; then old Mr. Tregarland, whom I could not understand; Gordon Lewyth, who had seemed like a different person when we were on the cliffs together, though he had gradually reverted to the aloof man I had first known; then there was Seth with his vague and inarticulate warnings. He was half crazy, I told myself, but I was vaguely disturbed by him.

One night I dreamed I had been walking along the beach when a figure had risen from the waves and beckoned. I awoke in a fright and was relieved to find that I was in my bedroom in dear, normal, old Caddington, the home of my childhood, where everything was prosaically reasonable.

In February my mother and I went to stay with Edward and Gretchen. The house was looking more lived in now. The new baby was expected in April and my mother said we should be there for the great event. Gretchen could become quite excited discussing the baby, but I knew she was still very anxious about her family.

Of course, we were invited to the Dorringtons. Mary Grace and Mrs. Dorrington were delighted to see us. It was afternoon when we called and Richard was not at home.

"He will be so pleased to hear you have arrived," we were told. "Edward did tell him you were coming. You must come and dine. What about tomorrow night?"

My mother promptly accepted the invitation.

In my room I took out the miniature of Dorabella which I had brought with me. I set it on the table by my bed and remembered my mother's words when she had spoken of her misgivings. I had begun to wonder, too. We must remember that Dorabella often acted and spoke on impulse. She often gave more stress to her utterances than they deserved. She was lonely, she had said. That was because she liked to have us all around; my adventures with Jowan Jermyn provided a certain interest and amusement.

I studied the miniature. Mary Grace had caught Dorabella's personality quite uncannily. Dear Dorabella. I hoped she was going to be happy. I remembered the joy in her face when she had seen my picture. She kept it in her bedroom, she said, but when I was not there she put it away because she did not want to look at it and miss me more. Though, she said, she did take it out at times to talk to it. I would understand her feelings because we always had understood each other.

I wondered whether I should have insisted on staying. But my mother was right, of course. She was sure it would be better for Dorabella to stand on her own feet now that she was married. As for myself, I should be seeing friends and enjoying visits to London. I must not be shut away in a remote part of the country.

"There in Cornwall," she said, "you are not aware of what is happening in the world. They seem so shut away. They are more concerned with ghosts and shadows, superstitions and such things ... remote from what is really going on in the world."

"You mean the speculation about what is going on in Germany?"

"Well, yes."

"I think Gretchen and Edward think about that a great deal."

"Well, they would. Poor girl. She must suffer great anxiety about her parents. It's not good for the baby. Thank God Edward was able to bring her out, at least."

"She is safe now."

"She has a husband to protect her, but that won't stop her worrying about her family. Kurt is such a nice young man. I think he came over to see them just before Christmas."

"It was a pity they could not go there."

"I don't think Edward would want Gretchen to go to Germany just yet."

"Perhaps it will all blow over."

"These things often do."

There was no mistaking Richard Dorrington's pleasure in seeing us. He took my hands and held them firmly.

"I've been wondering when you would come," he said.

"We have been away, of course."

"Yes, in Cornwall. I hope your sister is well. Mary Grace told us a good deal about the place when she came home after that lovely holiday you gave her."

"It was lovely to have her, and Dorabella was very pleased with her picture."

"Dear Mary Grace! You have brought her out, I can tell you. We are all so grateful to you, my mother and I as much as Mary Grace."

"She could really be a great artist."

"She is very diffident. She says miniatures are not much in fashion now."

"She must make them a fashion. She can, with a talent like hers, I am sure."

"You see how good it is for us all to have you back."

Over the dinner table at the Dorringtons it was impossible to keep the subject of Germany out of the conversation.

There were four other guests—a lawyer and his wife and a doctor and his.

As we had come through the streets to the house, we could

not help but see the placards, and the newsboys were shouting: "*Standard, News* . . . Read all about it." "Hitler meets Austrian Chancellor." "Schuschnigg at Berchtesgaden."

"What does it mean?" asked my mother as our taxi took us to the Dorringtons.

Edward said: "I don't know. But I don't like the sound of it."

He took Gretchen's hand and held it for a moment. I wished we had not seen those placards.

As we sat at dinner the doctor said: "It looks as though Hitler is planning to take over Austria."

"He couldn't do that," said Edward.

"We shall see," replied the doctor.

I wished they would stop talking of the situation, but naturally it was a subject which was uppermost in people's minds at this time. The papers were full of it, and many were waiting with great interest to hear the result of the meeting between Hitler and Kurt von Schuschnigg.

The lawyer said: "We should have been firm long ago. Hitler and Mussolini are hand in glove. Dictators, both of them. No one can stop them, not among their own people anyway. It's impossible to curb dictators except by deposing them, and it would be a brave man who tried to shake those two. In my opinion, Hitler is bent on conquest. He wants an empire and he is going to do everything he can to get it. He has got rid of Schacht who has tried to call a halt to the excessive storing up of armaments because it is crippling the economy. Blomberg and Fritsch and others have gone because they were professional soldiers who advised caution."

"And where is it all leading?" asked Richard.

"I think a great deal depends on the outcome of this meeting. Schuschnigg is no weakling. He won't allow Hitler to walk over him."

"We shall know in due course," said Richard.

I managed to catch his eyes and looked toward Gretchen. He understood. As for her, she had turned rather pale and was staring down at her plate.

"Now tell me," went on Richard immediately, "what are you planning to do while you are in London?"

"So much," I replied, "that I am sure we shall not succeed in doing it all."

"There is a remedy," he said. "Stay longer."

While the men lingered over the port, I had a chance to talk to Gretchen in the drawing room.

"You must be very excited about the baby," I said.

"Oh, yes."

I laid my hand on her arm and said gently: "Don't worry, Gretchen."

"I think of them," she said quietly. "Hitler is getting more powerful every day. I don't know what he will do next to our people."

"Have your family been . . . ?"

She shook her head. "Not yet . . . but they must expect . . ."

"They should get out, Gretchen."

"They won't leave. I have written to them. So has Edward. Edward says, 'Come over here. We'll manage somehow.' But they won't. They are so stubborn . . . so proud. It is their home, they say, and they are not going to be driven out of it."

"What are they going to do?"

"They will stay as long as they can."

"How glad I am that you are here!"

"Edward did that. It is wonderful for me, but I think much of my home and family."

"Dear Gretchen, let us hope that some day it will be different. I am so pleased that Edward brought you out, and now there is the baby. My mother is delighted. She wants to be here for the birth. Did you know that?"

She nodded and I was glad to see her smile.

"When the baby comes . . . you will feel better."

She looked at me and smiled rather sadly and I wished there was something I could do to comfort her.

My mother and I spoke of the evening over breakfast next morning.

"I wish that people would not talk all the time about what is happening in Germany," I said.

"It is certainly the topic of the moment and it is, of course, very important."

"I know, but the papers are full of it and it does so much upset Gretchen."

"She can't help wondering what is happening in her old home. I do hope everything is going to be all right."

"She'll be better, perhaps, when she gets the baby. She won't have much time then to think of much else."

She was certainly cheered when we went shopping together. There was a great deal of discussion about prams and cradles.

Edward was delighted that we were there, and when I saw him with Gretchen it occurred to me that there did not appear to be the same unwavering devotion between Dermot and Dorabella. But then Edward and Gretchen were earnest people. Both Dorabella and Dermot were light-hearted and perhaps did not betray the depth of their emotions as Edward and Gretchen did.

Mary Grace and I went to see an exhibition of paintings which was interesting. The lawyer and his wife came and had a drink with us and I showed them Mary Grace's portrait of Dorabella, which I had brought with me. When the lawyer's wife admired it enthusiastically, I suggested she herself would make a good subject.

I was delighted to have secured a commission for Mary Grace.

I had an idea that the lawyer's wife lived a fairly busy social life and I was sure that when the miniature was completed, if she were satisfied with it, she would show it to her friends. I should be surprised if at least one other commission did not come out of it.

Knowing my mother's fondness for the opera, Richard took us all to see *Rigoletto*, which was an evening of sheer enchantment. We had supper afterwards and talked animatedly about the setting and costumes as well as the wonderful music. I laughingly said I might have been Gilda instead of Violetta.

"Violetta is much more charming," said Richard, "and it is better to have a namesake dying gracefully in her bed taking her top notes with ease rather than lying in a sack."

There was a great deal of laughter, but the evening was marred slightly by the news which greeted us when we were on the way back to the house.

Hitler had forced Schuschnigg to sign an agreement before he left Berchtesgaden giving the Austrian Nazis a free hand.

A few days later Richard invited me to dinner. There were to be just the two of us.

It was strange because usually we went in a party. There was a reason, of course, and my mother knew what it meant.

Richard took me to a quiet little restaurant near Leicester Square. We had a table which was fairly secluded and after we had ordered and the food had arrived he said: "It has been wonderful to have you here."

"We have thoroughly enjoyed it."

"My mother was saying that Mary Grace has changed a good deal and it is all due to you."

"Someone would have discovered her talent sooner or later."

"Well, you did it. We are grateful to you, Violetta . . . all of my family are indebted to you."

"I am flattered. But it all came about so naturally. She showed me her work and I saw immediately that it was good. Dorabella was absolutely enchanted with the picture of me."

"We are all so fond of you. It is not only I . . ."

"And we of you all, of course."

He paused for a moment, then he said simply: "As for myself . . . I love you."

"Oh," I stammered. "I . . . er . . ."

"You're not going to say you are surprised and it is all so sudden, are you?"

"Well, we haven't known each other very long."

"Time doesn't count. I know I love you. I want to marry you. How do you feel about that?"

"Well, I know it is supposed to be some sort of joke to say it is so sudden, but it does seem a little so. You see, we really don't know each other very well."

"One can get to know people very well in a short time."

I felt uneasy. A picture of Dorabella and Dermot flashed into my mind. I had let that remark of my mother's upset me. Everything must be all right with them. And what about Richard? I liked him. I found his company pleasant, stimulating. But I was not like Dorabella to rush into commitments with great haste.

"Marriage is such a serious matter," I said. "It is a lifetime together."

"Does that appeal?"

"I just feel bewildered."

"You must know how fond I am of you."

"I knew that you liked me. But this is more than that. We are talking about marriage."

"There is no one else . . . ?"

"Oh, no . . . no."

"You don't seem oversure."

I was seeing Jowan Jermyn in the field when I had fallen, then smiling at me over a tankard of cider, showing me his house.

"Oh, no," I said. "There is no one."

"Then . . . ?"

I looked at him. He was so earnest, a man of honor and integrity, who was devoted to his family, who lived an interesting life. Here in London I felt alive. I liked to be among people, people who were hurrying around on their own business, not watching you all the time, knowing where you came from, what you were doing. I liked Mrs. Dorrington . . . I was fond of Mary Grace . . . and Richard, too.

He was looking a little crestfallen.

"It is too soon, I see," he said. "I just seized on the moment."

"Yes, it is too soon," I agreed. "I was never one to make hasty decisions. I should want to be absolutely sure."

"So you do like me?"

"Very much."

"You like my family?"

"Of course."

"Mary Grace would be so pleased and so would my mother."

"Mine would be, my father, too."

"Then," he said, smiling warmly, "the matter is in abeyance for the time being. Would that be all right?"

"I think it is an excellent idea," I said.

"You are going to get to know me very well while you are in London."

"And you will have to get to know me."

"I know all I want to know already."

"Am I so easy to read?"

"No, but I'm besotted."

I laughed and he went on: "It is not No. It is just, 'I am not sure.' That's it, isn't it?"

"That is it," I said.

"Well, I shall have to be content with that." He held up his glass. "Let's drink to it."

It was a happy evening. I could not help feeling a certain gratification. I suppose it is comforting to be loved, and I had so often been overlooked because Dorabella attracted so much attention.

I liked Richard very much, and I was already beginning to believe that we could have a good life together. There was something real about Richard. I must be comparing him with Jowan Jermyn and in a way with Gordon Lewyth.

Richard was different. I supposed because he belonged to the town. I liked him. I felt I understood him. I thought I could be very fond of him.

But it was too soon. I should get to know him and his family.

When I returned that night my mother came to my room. She could not hide her excitement, and I knew that she was hoping I should announce my engagement.

"Was it a pleasant evening?" she asked.

"Oh, yes."

There was a brief silence.

"Well," she went on.

"Well what?" I asked.

"Did he . . . er . . . ? Did everything go all right? Did he . . . er . . . ask you to marry him?"

"How did you know?"

She laughed. "My dear, it was obvious what was afoot. He is in love with you and has been ever since he saw you. He is such a dear. I am so glad."

"You are going too fast," I said.

"What do you mean? Didn't he ask you?"

"Yes."

"You didn't accept?" She stared at me in horror.

I said: "Are you so anxious to be rid of me?"

She looked deflated and came to me and put her arms around me.

"You know how important your happiness is to me and your father. Richard is such a good man . . . well, so right for you in every way."

"I have not said no," I told her. "But it is too soon yet."

The relief in her face was obvious. She smiled indulgently.

"You were always the cautious one," she said, and I knew she was thinking of Dorabella because of the faint uneasiness which came back into her eyes.

She said: "What is going to happen, then?"

"I've told Richard I like him very much but it is too soon for me to know whether or not I want to marry him."

"Oh, I see," she said. "He'll understand that."

"Yes, he does."

"He's a very understanding person ... with good, sound common sense. Well, he is a lawyer."

She leaned toward me and kissed me.

She stayed awhile and talked and then said goodnight and went to her room, not entirely dissatisfied.

The news was disquieting. The papers were full of it, and everywhere one went it was discussed so that there was no escaping from it.

Schuschnigg had returned to Austria where he had repudiated the agreement which Hitler had forced him to sign, and had announced that there should be a plebiscite as to whether there should be a political and economic union—an Anschluss—with Germany. Hitler's response was to invade Austria.

He had the support of his Italian allies, while Britain and France, amazed by what was taking place, stood by and did nothing to prevent it.

Hitler was cheered by the people when he marched into Austria; there was no opposition to his mighty army, which could have been because Austria had no power to do otherwise.

However, it did show people clearly which way the German dictator was going.

Richard said: "There is no end to his ambitions. I rather think this is the beginning."

He was right. Hitler was turning his eyes to Czechoslovakia.

Then something happened which drove the troubles on the Continent completely from our minds.

My mother and I had been out shopping with Gretchen. We had had a busy morning and returned to the house for lunch.

We were about to sit down at the table when my father arrived.

We could not understand what had happened, and when we saw him we were immediately apprehensive, for he looked quite different from his normal, happy self. He was strained, bewildered, and clearly desperately unhappy.

My mother ran to him and put an arm round him.

"Robert, darling, what is it?" she said.

He opened his mouth to speak, but did not seem to be able to find the words. He was choked with emotion.

"Sit down," said my mother gently. "Now ... tell us what has happened."

"I had to come ... I couldn't tell over the telephone ... I came immediately. She went down to swim ... her clothes were on the beach ... and she had gone ... gone ..."

We were staring at him in horror. He turned from my mother to me and his eyes were full of misery.

He said: "Dorabella ... she is dead."

The Open Window

※

Incoherent with grief, my father found it difficult to talk. It all seemed so unreal. Dorabella, so full of life, so young and beautiful . . . I could not believe that I should not see her again. She was part of my life, part of me. She could not be dead. It was some mistake. I could not believe it. I *would* not believe it.

It was like one of those ridiculous legends.

She went for a swim, they had told him. She had died in exactly the same way as her predecessor, Dermot's first wife. It was too neat. There was a touch of unreality about it.

My father could not tell us very much. I really believe he had been too stunned to take in what was said. All he knew was that she was dead.

Gordon Lewyth had telephoned. He had said he had some terrible news and he did not know how best to break it. Then he said that Dorabella had gone for a swim. She had evidently made a habit of taking a swim in the early morning. The time of the year was hardly the best, but she had said she found the coldness invigorating.

It could not be true. She had never been enthusiastic about swimming. She had swum at school with the rest of us, but no physical exercise had ever greatly appealed to her.

There was something wrong somewhere.

Gordon had had to get into touch with Dermot, who had been away for a few days on one of the other estates. He was prostrate with grief. The entire household was in chaos.

My mother stood still, clenching her hands. Her face was ashen. She was looking at me with a blank expression of misery and disbelief.

Then she was clinging to me, sharing the misery, refusing to believe this terrible thing was true.

"It can't be. It can't be," I insisted. "I don't believe it."

My mother said: "We'll leave at once. We'll go to Cornwall. I want to know what this is all about."

"We've missed the ten o'clock train," said my father. "We'll find out what time the next one goes."

It was late when we arrived in Cornwall. There was, of course, no one to meet us, but we were able to hire a car to take us to the house.

I believe they were not surprised to see us.

"We had to come," said my mother simply to Gordon and Matilda, who were in the hall to greet us.

"This is terrible," said Matilda. "I can't believe it."

"We want to hear exactly what happened," said my father.

Matilda insisted on some food being prepared for us, although none of us felt in the least like eating.

We sat in the drawing room and talked.

Matilda seemed too shocked to say much, and it was Gordon who did most of the talking.

"It was so sudden, so unexpected," he said. "She went down to bathe, presumably before the rest of the household was awake."

"Did anyone see her?" I asked.

"No, but we knew she went. She had mentioned it. She said she had discovered the delights of early morning bathing. We said it was too early in the season because the water doesn't warm up until mid-summer, but she insisted that she liked it as it was. When Dermot was away she did not come down to dinner always. He had gone to the Brenton estate and it was too far to go there and back in one day. She had swum the previous morning. I saw her coming into the house and she said the sea was wonderful first thing in the morning and it really was the best time for a swim. And then ... the next morning ..."

"What happened then?" demanded my mother. "Nobody saw her ... ?"

"No. We didn't see her around much in the mornings. We thought she had breakfasted and gone off to Poldown to shop. When she did not come back for lunch, we grew anxious and then one of the gardeners came in and said her clothes were on the beach ... her bathrobe and her shoes. There was no doubt that they were hers. So ... there is only one explanation. We informed the police. Boats have been out looking for her. A plane flew over. There was no sign of her. She must have been carried right out to sea. Perhaps her body will be washed ashore." He turned away, biting his lip.

"It is so unlike her to go swimming," I said.

Gordon nodded. "Yes, we thought it strange. But she insisted that she liked it. The currents can be very strong there, and ..."

"Didn't anyone tell her?" I asked desperately. My grief was so bitter, so intense, that I wanted to blame someone for this devastating catastrophe.

"It could happen to anyone," said Gordon. "People are bathing all the time ... and now and then ..."

"I can't take it in ..."

"Her clothes were there ... and she was gone."

I could only sit there, limp with misery, clinging to that persistent disbelief. It was the only way I could endure this.

"Poor Dermot," went on Matilda. "He is heartbroken. He blames himself for not being here. He is suffering terribly ... so soon after his marriage ... and he is so proud of the little boy. I can't bear to think of it."

There was nothing anyone could say.

We sat back in blank and hopeless silence.

I went up to the nursery to see Tristan. He was sleeping.

Nanny Crabtree came and embraced me, holding me tightly against her. She kept saying: "This terrible thing ... my Miss Dorabella."

"Nanny, it's not real. It can't be true, can it?"

She shook her head and turned away. She had always been embarrassed about showing emotion.

Her eyes were red-rimmed and she sniffed. She had a habit of sniffing. It usually meant disgust or criticism.

She said: "And what about this motherless mite? I expect Lady Denver will take him."

"Nothing has been arranged."

"Well, it will be, and the sooner the better. We'll get out of this place. I never liked it. There's something creepy about it.

All this talk about quarrels between families, and what's going to happen to you if you do this and that. I never heard such nonsense. Yes, that's the best thing. We'll get my boy to Caddington and back to the old nurseries there."

Her lips trembled momentarily and I knew she was thinking of Dorabella and me there as children.

She went on: "That'll be best and it's the only thing to do. Here?" She looked contemptuously and sniffed again. "That'll be it, and the sooner the better."

I went over and looked down on Tristan.

"He's got a look of you, Miss Violetta," she said. "Well, it's natural like . . . he reminds me more of you than of his mother."

Sleeping as he was, she lifted him up.

"Here, sit down," she said. I did so and she put him on my lap.

A great tenderness swept over me. He looked so vulnerable. I felt a momentary easing of my desperate unhappiness. Here was something left to me of Dorabella.

When I left the nursery I went straight to my mother's room. She was sitting at the window, staring blankly out.

She turned to me and smiled wanly.

I said: "I've been to the nursery."

"Poor Nanny," she said. "She's heartbroken."

"She thinks that we should take Tristan back to Caddington with us."

"That is our intention . . . your father's and mine. We've already talked about it. It's the natural thing."

"Nanny Crabtree doesn't like this place."

"I don't think any of us will want to come here again."

"What about Dermot? Tristan is his son, remember."

"Dermot seems not to know what he wants." Her voice was faintly critical. Like me, she wanted to blame someone. No doubt she was thinking that if he had not been away at the time it would not have happened. Why wasn't he looking after his wife? Why didn't he forbid her to go bathing on the very beach where his first wife had died? Forbid Dorabella? That would be like urging her on. Poor Dermot! He was as desolate as we were and could not bear to do anything but shut himself away with his misery.

My mother was now thinking, If only Dorabella had never met Dermot. If only we had never seen this place! If only she were safe at home with her children around her.

I understood. She wanted to get away from this house ... as Nanny Crabtree did. We had to blame something, if it was only the place.

"I'd like to get away as soon as possible," she was saying.

"You don't think that there has been some mistake? I can't get out of my mind that she is not dead. I know it's fanciful, but she and I ... well, there were times when we were like one person. Often I knew what she was thinking ... and I can't get over this ... well, almost certainty ... that she is ... somewhere ... that she will come back."

"I know, I know ..." said my mother soothingly. "I can't believe it, either. But we have to face it ... and we shall do that better when we get away from this place."

I could not explain to her that, although everything pointed to the fact that Dorabella was dead, I had a feeling that she was somewhere, and I would one day find her. I could not and would not accept the fact that she was dead.

My mother said she would speak to Matilda. She would tell her that we would go away and take Tristan with us.

I was amazed, later, when she told me that Matilda was shocked by the suggestion.

"She looked at me with real dismay," my mother told me. "She said, 'I don't know whether Mr. Tregarland would agree to that. The child is *his* grandson. This is a big estate and when Dermot inherits, Tristan will be his heir. It's a tradition in the family that the heir is brought up here.' I replied that we were not proposing to cut him off from his family. It just seemed more convenient for us to take him to Caddington. After all, we are his grandparents and it would be easier at our place. I could see she was shaken by the idea. She said she would put it to Mr. Tregarland. I said, 'You mean Dermot?' 'Dermot and his father, of course,' she answered. I then remarked that I thought Dermot would know very little about bringing up a baby and that his father would not be very interested. I was sure, also, that she herself had too much to do with running the household to want to take on the care of a young child. 'There is Nanny Crabtree,' she said. 'She would stay, of course.' I was astounded. I thought they would have been only too glad for us to take him."

"Well, what is going to happen?"

"I don't know. She talked as though it were the old man who would make the objections. I can't quite see that somehow. I expect it will be all right."

But it was not. Mr. Tregarland was adamant.

He said: "I appreciate your feelings, and I am sure the boy would be very well looked after with you, but he is a Tregarland. He is my grandson. He will own this place one day. No, no, I thank you for your kindness, but I could not allow the boy to leave his home."

Both my mother and I were dumbfounded.

My father said: "We shall have to accept. His father will insist that he stay."

"I don't think Dermot would insist."

"He will stand with his father, poor chap. He is stunned by this. He has lost his wife. It is natural, I suppose, that he does not want to lose his son as well."

There was a great deal of discussion and at last my mother had to accept the fact that she was not going to be allowed to take Tristan back with her.

As for myself, I was in a quandary.

There had been a time when I had felt I wanted to get away from this place, and now I was realizing that I did not want to go.

I could not rid myself of the notion that Dorabella was alive. I felt certain that one day I should see her again. There was a mistake. I thought of the most wildly impossible solutions. She had drifted out to sea; she had lost her memory; she had been picked up by a ship. She was alive somewhere. Her body had never been found, and I knew that until it was I should believe she was alive. It was ridiculous, of course, but I had to cling to something. She and I had been so close; we were, as she said, like one person; there was that bond between us ... that gossamer cord to which she had once referred. I felt it there now.

I dreamed of her and in that dream she came to my room as she had in reality. She said: "Remember your promise. If I am not there, you will look after my baby. Swear ..."

And I had given my promise. It had been a sacred one. I had to keep it.

I said to my mother: "Dorabella once said a strange thing. She made me swear that I would look after her child if she were not here."

"What?" cried my mother.

"She came to my room one night. She said we had always been like one person and if anything happened to her I was to look after her child. I swore I would. When you go . . . I shall stay here."

"Violetta, listen to me. That sounds noble, but you can't shut yourself away down here. It is not fair to you. Oh, if only they'd be sensible and let me take Tristan!"

But I had decided that, whatever the opposition, I must keep my word to Dorabella.

I had a chance to speak to Dermot. He looked strained and all the gaiety was gone from him. His eyes were bloodshot, and I noticed how his hands trembled. I hardly recognized him as the merry, insouciant young man whom we had met in the Böhmerwald.

He kept saying: "I can't believe it, Violetta. I can't believe it."

"Nor I," I told him.

A wild look came into his eyes. "And, to go that way . . ." he murmured. "What does it mean?"

I shook my head.

"It's the same . . . it's so strange . . . How could they both . . . in the same way?"

"She shouldn't have gone to bathe."

"I knew. I didn't think that could happen. People do bathe in the early morning." He put his hands over his eyes. "She took to it suddenly. For a week or so before. She used to go down to the beach in the early morning. I was surprised, but she was always surprising me. It was what made her so attractive."

"Yes, I know. Some idea would come to her and she would be all enthusiasm and then she'd forget all about it."

He nodded miserably. Poor Dermot. He had really cared deeply for her. I had come to realize that he was rather weak, leaving everything in the hands of Gordon Lewyth, wanting a life devoid of responsibility.

"Dermot," I said. "There is one thing I want to ask you. It is about Tristan."

He gazed at me questioningly, with tears in his eyes, and I went on: "Dorabella once spoke to me very seriously. I think she must have had some premonition that she was not going to live. It was just before his birth and I imagined she thought she was not going to survive. She and I were exceptionally close . . . as twins are sometimes. She asked me if I would look after Tristan if she were not here. We would have taken him back to Caddington with us, but your father does not wish it. But I have given my word to Dorabella and I want to keep it. I *must* keep it. I want to stay here for a while . . . to look after Tristan."

"I am glad," he said. "I feel that is what she would have wanted."

"She did want it. She made me swear I would. Dermot, will it be all right for me to stay until I can work something out? At the moment I feel so muddled and uncertain about everything. But if I may just stay . . ."

"But of course. You will be very welcome."

"If you would tell Matilda and your father that Dorabella particularly wanted me to be with the boy . . ."

"I will speak to my father and Matilda." He looked suddenly resolute. "I know it would be what Dorabella would have wanted. Thank you, Violetta. I am glad you will stay."

My parents left soon after that. They were reluctant to leave me, but everything was so inconclusive. How long did I intend to stay, my mother was wondering. She said I was putting myself into a backwater. She would be thinking that Richard Dorrington could help me to grow away from this terrible grief. At times like this it was better to look ahead to the future.

The baby was too young to miss his mother, and Nanny Crabtree was remaining. She thought in due course the Tregarlands might realize that Tristan would be better off with his maternal grandparents.

When I had said goodbye to them, I felt very melancholy and went to the nursery to see Tristan.

It brought me comfort to hold him in my arms. Nanny

Crabtree stood by watching. We were her children . . . myself as well as Tristan, and she knew what the loss of Dorabella meant to me.

She said: "He knows you. Look at his little face. You and me, Miss Violetta, we'll see that he's all right."

A few days after my parents returned I received a letter from Richard.

> My dearest,
>
> I have been talking to your parents. What a terrible tragedy this is! I have heard that you intend to stay with the child. Your mother has explained to me.
>
> I hope you are thinking about our marriage. It is what I want more than anything on earth. Do write to me. I shall come down to see you there as soon as I can arrange it. Then we can talk of the future.
>
> I am feeling this with you. I have heard from Edward, as well as from your mother, how close you and your sister were, and I know what you must be suffering. I wish I could be with you to show you how deeply I feel for you.
>
> Please write to me. I want to be in constant touch.
>
> All my love to you,
>
> Richard

It was a comforting letter. I was reminded of how kind and understanding he was.

It amazed me that, ever since I had heard that devastating news, I had not given him a thought.

I was surprised when Jowan Jermyn called at the house. One of the maids came to tell me that he was in the hall and had asked to see me. I noticed the look of surprise and excitement on her face.

Surprise, of course, that he had the temerity to call, and excitement at the thought of what a stir this news would create when she released it.

It was true that he had been invited to the house for lunch, but that was some time ago, and since then there would have been plenty of rumors. I had no doubt that Dorabella's death would be attributed to some uncanny connection with the feud.

I went down to the hall, and there he was, standing with his back to the fireplace, his hands clasped behind him.

He came forward and took my hands, holding them firmly in his.

"I am so sorry," he said earnestly.

I found it hard to speak and he went on: "I had to call. Perhaps I should not have done so. But there is no other way of getting in touch with you."

"Thank you for coming," I said.

"I should so like to talk to you," he went on. "I heard you were staying here for a while, although your parents have left."

"That's so," I said. "There is the baby . . ."

"Could you come and have lunch somewhere?"

"Do you mean today?"

"If that is possible. I have a car outside."

I hesitated. My spirits lightened a little at the prospect. I could leave a message for Matilda that I should not be in to lunch today.

As we drove through the country lanes, he said: "I know a quiet place close to the moor. We can talk in comfort there."

"I suppose you know everything that has happened," I said.

"I don't know about everything, but there is no talk hereabouts of anything but this tragedy."

"It seems incredible to me still."

I was staring blankly ahead, seeing her face, laughing at me, scorning me because of some priggish sentiment I had just expressed. I would have given anything to hear her laugh like that again.

He took his hand from the steering wheel and placed it over mine for a moment.

"So," he said, "you have stayed on though your parents have gone."

"Yes. I am helping with the baby."

"Yes, with the nanny whose name is Crabtree."

"She was nanny to my sister and to me. Mother procured her for Tristan."

"Her name is often mentioned."

"You mean by the gossips."

"Oh, yes, she's something of a dragon by all accounts. At least she hasn't much time for the people around here."

"I think she despises most people who weren't born within the sound of Bow Bells."

"Ah, I see."

We were silent for a moment. I sensed that he wished to talk about the tragedy but was not sure what effect it would have on me.

We were seated opposite each other in the small hotel on the edge of the moor, when he regarded me gravely and said: "Do you mind talking about it?"

"It is uppermost in my mind," I confessed.

"Do you think it was all a little strange . . . ?"

"Yes, I do," I replied.

"Do you believe in coincidences?"

"I suppose there are such things."

"Yes, I suppose so, but . . ."

"You mean the *way* she died?"

"Yes. Two in the same way. Doesn't that sound a little odd to you?"

"Yes."

"You know what they are saying here?"

"I can guess."

"That it is the revenge of the Jermyns on the Tregarlands, of course."

"Oh, they can't really believe that."

"They can. They seize on this as a proof that the feud is as firm as ever; and the attempt to break it has not pleased my unfortunate ancestor."

"I suppose it could have come about naturally. Dorabella was not a strong swimmer. Dermot's first wife was, according to her mother. I cannot understand why Dorabella should have suddenly decided she wanted to take an early morning swim. If only I had been here . . . I should never have left. She did not want me to. In fact, she pleaded with me to stay. I said I would come back soon and she would be able to come home to us when the baby was older . . . and this happened when I was not there . . ."

"Do you think if you had been here you would have been able to prevent it?"

"I just have a feeling that it might not have happened then."

He was silent for a while.

"It is odd," he said. "Two of them to die that way. People

here naturally put their own construction on it. Of course, it could have happened quite naturally. My ancestor did not want to live and she walked into the sea, never intending to come back; Annette . . . she could have had a sudden attack of cramp . . . and your sister, well, that could have happened to her, too. It is just an extraordinary coincidence that a man should have two wives who die by drowning at the same spot."

"What are people suggesting?"

"I don't quite know. But . . . I am a little uneasy. I think . . . you should be watchful."

"What do you mean? That you . . . suspect something?"

"I don't know what I feel. I just don't like the thought of your being there . . . in a place where two such events could take place."

I looked at him in surprise. He had always struck me as being a practical man who would scoff at fancy.

"What on earth do you think could happen to *me*?"

"I don't know. I merely think that you are there where extraordinary things happen. That's why . . . I want you to be watchful."

"What am I to watch for?"

"I don't know. That's just it. I have this vague uneasiness, though. If it were anyone else . . . it wouldn't occur to me."

I looked at him questioningly and he returned my gaze steadily.

"I care what happens to you," he said. "Perhaps that is why I am particularly sensitive."

"That is very kind of you," I replied.

He shook his head. "It is something over which I have no control. All this seems too contrived to be natural, and I am uneasy because you are in the midst of it."

"Would you feel better if I went home?"

He smiled at me ruefully. "I was not at all pleased when you stayed away so long. In fact, I was definitely *dis*pleased. I had rather you came back for reasons other than this one."

"How I agree with you on that!"

"Get in touch with me . . . at any time if you need anything. Telephone me. Do you have the number?"

I said I did not and he gave it to me and I put it into my handbag. I felt an uplifting of my spirits such as I had not known since I heard of Dorabella's death. I was so gratified that he was concerned for me.

I told him then that I had promised my sister that I would look after Tristan if she were unable to be there.

"It was very strange," I said, "almost as though she knew she was going to die. She made me swear because she did not want anyone else to look after him. So I am here because they would not allow us to take Tristan back with us."

"That is something I should be grateful for. If they had allowed you to take him, you would probably never have come here again."

"That might well have been. At least, the visits would be rare."

He stretched across the table and took my hand.

"I should have had to come to see you," he said. "You know I would do that, don't you?"

"Well, no. It hadn't occurred to me that you would."

"Well, it does now, I hope."

"Since you tell me."

"Listen," he went on. "I have been thinking a great deal about this. If at any time you need someone to confide in . . . to help . . ."

I tapped my handbag and said: "I have your number. I can get in touch with you at any time . . . and I will."

I met Seth in the stables. When he saw me his face changed and he looked almost furtive.

"I did tell 'ee, Miss, 'twere so."

I knew what he meant. He had warned me of the ghost of the sea and I had shown my disbelief. He was now telling me how wrong I was to be skeptical.

"Poor lady, her be gone . . . her be gone like t'other. Reckon her was beckoned in, this one . . . not like t'other."

His words were thick and slurred and it was not easy to understand what he was saying. I often wondered whether he knew himself; but I supposed there was some reasoning in that muddled head of his.

He leaned his big ungainly body against the walls of the stables.

" 'Ee be wanting Starlight, Miss?" he asked.

I had changed my mind suddenly.

"No, thanks," I said. "I think I'll take a walk."

He nodded and mumbled: "I did tell 'ee, didn't I, Miss? Didn't believe me, did 'ee? Poor lady ... who'd a thought. She was a laughing lady, she were ... just like t'other. They wouldn't listen. They laughed ... but it got 'un in the end."

"Did you see my sister go down to bathe?" I asked.

He shook his head. "Not that 'un," he said.

"Then did you see the first Mrs. Tregarland go down to bathe, Seth?"

A cunning look came into his eyes. "No, no. I didn't see nothing. Ask her ... I didn't see."

"Ask whom, Seth?"

He turned away, shaking his head, and I saw a certain fear in his eyes.

"I didn't see nothing," he went on. "I didn't. Her just went into the sea like. Nothing to do with I."

Poor Seth. He really did not know what he was talking about. He was obsessed by the legend. His eyes were worried, his loose mouth slightly open. He was puzzled, as though trying to understand something, and my question had clearly disturbed him.

He disappeared into one of the stalls and I heard him talking to one of the horses there.

"All right, my beauty. 'Tis old Seth. Don't 'ee worry ... only old Seth."

I came out of the stables. I had an hour or so before I need go back. Nanny Crabtree was busy in the nursery and liked to be free at this time. If, as she said, she could get the lord and master off to sleep, she would have the time to do what had to be done.

I came out into the fresh air. It was invigorating with a light breeze blowing in from the sea with its salty tang and smell of seaweed.

I took the cliff road to Poldown and no sooner had I reached the little town than I wished I had gone another way.

There were too many people about and, because of my involvement with the Tregarland tragedy, I was an object of interest.

I passed the wool shop. Miss Polgenny was standing at the door.

"Good day to 'ee, Miss Denver. How be you then? 'Tis a nice day."

Her little eyes were alert with curiosity. I could see the thoughts in her mind. I was the sister of "her that went for a swim and was drowned." " 'Twas all part of the curse."

They believed that—most of them. Their lives were governed by superstition.

"Good to see 'ee, Miss." That was one of the fishermen mending his nets. I knew that as soon as I passed, he would be talking to the man beside him. "That was her from Tregarland's. Her sister it were . . ."

There was no escape.

I crossed the bridge and started up the west cliff.

The sea looked docile. There was only the faintest ruffle and little white patches of froth on the tips of the waves as rhythmically they washed the black rocks. Back and forth they went, murmuring soothingly as they did so.

I came to Cliff Cottage and paused to look at the garden. There was the plant I had brought from Tregarland's. It was flourishing, I perceived.

I think she must have seen me from behind the neat lace curtains, for the door opened and she came down the path toward me.

"Hello, Miss Denver," she said.

"Good morning, Mrs. Pardell."

She came out and stood close to the fence. She said, rather anxiously, I thought: "And how are you?"

"I am well, thanks. Are you?"

"Looking at the flowers then?" she said, nodding. "Eee . . . like to come in for a bit? Perhaps a little chat . . . a cup of tea?"

I said eagerly: "I'd like that."

Then I was in the sitting room looking at the picture of Annette, while Mrs. Pardell went into the kitchen to make the tea.

She came in with a tray and when she had poured out the tea she said: "It was a terrible thing . . ."

I knew what she meant and said: "Yes."

"I know how you are feeling. None could know better."

"That's true."

"It was the same, wasn't it? It seemed a bit queer to me."

"It was such a coincidence."

She looked at me steadily. "I don't like it," she said. "It makes you wonder, doesn't it?"

"Wonder . . . ?" I repeated.

She drew her chair closer to mine. "You're staying there now," she said.

"It is because of the child."

"Isn't there a nanny . . . from London or somewhere?"

"Yes. She was my nanny . . . mine and my sister's. My mother arranged for her to come. She trusts her."

"That's good," she said. "I'm glad *she's* here."

I told her: "I promised my sister that if anything happened, I'd look after the baby."

She nodded. "So there you are. These people here . . . they talk about ghosts and things. I've never had much patience with that sort of thing. Ghosts . . . my foot. It wasn't ghosts who got rid of my Annette."

"Got rid of her?"

"You're not kidding me she wouldn't look after herself in the water. And what about your sister?"

"She wasn't by any means a champion swimmer. In fact, I was surprised that she went bathing in the early morning."

"It's clear to me."

"What is clear?"

"Well, a man has two wives. They both die in the same way, and not long after he married them. Doesn't that say something to you?"

"What does it say to you?"

"That it's a funny business, that's what. He marries, then gets tired of them, and then it's goodbye, nice knowing you, but I've had enough and it's time for a change."

"Oh, no," I said.

"What else? They both went the same way. Convenient, wasn't it? There was the sea ready and waiting."

"But how . . . ?"

"Your guess is as good as mine. It worked once. Why not try again?"

"You don't know Dermot Tregarland."

"Don't know my daughter's husband, my own son-in-law, you might say."

"He was that, but you didn't know him."

"I was never asked up there, but I knew of him. In any case, they are now gone. My daughter, your sister. Of course he got rid of them."

"Mrs. Pardell, this is absurd. If he had wanted to get rid of them, he wouldn't have killed the second in the same way as the first. It makes people wonder. It calls attention . . ."

"Look here, Miss Denver, you're too innocent. What about those Brides in the Bath? That man went round murdering women for their money, after he'd married them. He got them in the bath and drowned them. He did several of them that way."

"This is different."

"I don't see how."

"I know Dermot Tregarland well. He couldn't commit one murder . . . let alone two."

"You're too trusting, Miss Denver. If you read any of those detective stories you'd see. It's always the one you'd least suspect."

"It could have been accidental."

She shook her head. "You won't get me believing that. I know how you feel about your sister. Didn't I go through it all? You're living up there, Miss Denver. You've got to keep your eyes open . . . that's what you've got to do. You watch out. I reckon something very funny is going on up at that place. Have another cup of tea."

"No, thanks. I am sure you are misjudging Dermot Tregarland."

"I wish to God my Annette had never married him. I reckon if she hadn't she would have been alive today. I'd have got over her having a baby out of wedlock, but I couldn't get over this. I just want to know . . . if only I knew . . ."

"I understand what you mean," I said. "If one knows, there is nothing to be done, one accepts it."

"That's right." She looked at me shrewdly. "You're a sensible girl, Miss Denver. You keep your eyes open. See if he's got another in mind for number three."

"Oh . . . I'm sure not. He is absolutely devastated with grief."

She looked disbelieving. "Well, he would let you think that, wouldn't he?"

"It's genuine. I know."

"Murderers are clever people. They have to be to get away with it."

"But not two wives, Mrs. Pardell. Not two in the same way."

"How about that Bluebeard?"

In spite of everything, I could not help smiling.

"Look here," she said. "Don't you be too trusting. You watch out. I'm glad you came by. I've been thinking about you. It was good of you to bring that plant. I wouldn't like anything to happen to you."

"To me?"

"Well, when people start trying to find out what people don't want brought to light, they're in danger. It always works that way. You watch out, but don't let him see you're watching."

The picture of Annette smiled at me. She was dead. Her body had been washed up on the beach a few days after she had been drowned. And Dorabella ... perhaps one day ... hers would be found.

I said goodbye to Mrs. Pardell and promised her I would call again.

I made my way back to Tregarland's. Poor Mrs. Pardell! I was thinking. We were all the same. Our grief was so intense that we wanted to blame someone, and she had selected Dermot. Poor, brokenhearted, rather ineffectual Dermot. It was difficult to imagine him in the role of Bluebeard. In fact, it was so absurd that I found myself smiling in a way I had not done for some time.

When I came face-to-face with Dermot I remembered Mrs. Pardell's words and I thought how very mistaken she was.

He was sitting in the garden looking down the slope to where the sea gently lapped the black rocks.

I went and sat beside him and he smiled at me rather feebly.

I said: "Dermot, you must not brood."

"And you?" he asked. "Are you brooding?"

"We both have to stop it."

"I can't get it out of my mind. Why did she do it? And why wasn't I here?"

I laid my hand on his arm.

"We have to try to put it behind us."

"Can you?" he demanded almost angrily.

"No. But we have to try."

"I keep thinking of her. Do you remember how I first saw you, outside that café place? I looked at her and I knew from that moment. I knew she was the one. She was different from anyone I had ever met. She was so full of gaiety and everything seemed a joke. You know what I mean. You laughed at things just because you were happy, I suspect, not because they were particularly funny."

"I know what you mean."

"There was no one like her . . . and she's gone. She's out there somewhere. Do you think we shall ever find her?"

"I just feel that we shall. Poor Dermot, you have been through this . . . twice."

His manner changed slightly. He seemed to draw himself up and his face stiffened.

"That," he said, "was different."

"She was drowned, too."

"It wasn't the same. Dorabella . . . she was everything."

"Annette . . ."

"I don't talk about that much. But this . . . I know you cared about her . . . as I did. She was very close to you, wasn't she? I was afraid, always afraid that I was going to lose her. Oh, not like this. I thought I shouldn't be enough for her. She would find someone else. Sometimes . . ."

"She was your wife, Dermot."

"I know, but . . ."

"I don't understand," I said. He frowned and I went on: "Tell me . . ."

"Well, she was not the sort to go on with something just because she was expected to. She had no respect for conventional behavior. She always wanted to break free from it."

"What do you mean?" I asked.

He was silent and I could see he wished he had not said what he had.

He said: "Annette . . . she was fun. Jolly, good-hearted. But for the child, it would never have been. With Dorabella it was different."

"I understand."

"I can't settle to anything. It all seems blank and not worthwhile. I leave everything to Gordon . . . more than ever."

"Well, you always have, haven't you?"

"Yes. He's so capable. He makes me feel ... inefficient. I was taking more interest when Tristan came. You see, in time, this will all be his ... first mine, of course. But Gordon will always be there. But now this has happened, I just don't care about anything."

"But there is Tristan to think of."

He just sat there, staring out to sea.

"I'm glad you're here, Violetta. I'm glad you're with the baby."

"It was her wish, you know."

"I know. Nanny is good, but she is getting old now. It is better for the baby to have someone young, and you ... you'll be like his own mother. You will stay here, won't you?"

I said: "Everything is so uncertain at the moment. I suppose it would be better really if I went to Caddington, taking Tristan and Nanny Crabtree with me."

"My father is against that."

"I know. He has made it clear. Well, it is all too soon. We'll see how it works out."

I sat with him a little longer and we looked out to sea and thought of Dorabella.

Nanny Crabtree was faintly perturbed.

"Tristan's got a little sniffle. Not much, but I don't like it and I'm keeping him in today."

"I'll come up and see him," I said.

He was lying in his cot, whimpering a little.

I went over and picked him up. That satisfied him for a few minutes. He had an endearing habit of gripping my finger and holding on to it tightly, as though determined not to let me go.

"He looks a little flushed," I said.

"A bit," she replied. "He just wants to be kept warm, that's all."

At midday there was a letter from Richard.

He had written, "Dearest Violetta,"

I am arriving on Thursday. I have discovered there is a hotel in Poldown ... West Poldown. It's a place called Black Rock Hotel. I have booked a room and shall be staying for a few days. I have Tregarland's number and

I'll give you a call as soon as I arrive. There is so much
to talk about.

See you soon.

All my love,

Richard

Thursday, and it was Wednesday today!

My feelings were mixed. I wanted to see him, of course, but
he would try to persuade me to leave Cornwall, and that was
something I could not consider, at least not yet.

Well, I should hear what he had to say and I would make
him understand that I had promised Dorabella to take her
place with her son and that it had been a sacred promise which
I must keep at all costs.

He was reasonable. He would see that.

I thought about him all the afternoon, recalling what a
pleasant time we had had in London, and I was definitely
looking forward to seeing him again.

The first thing I did next morning was to go to the nursery
to see Tristan.

"Still sniffling," said Nanny Crabtree. "So it is another day
indoors for you, my lord."

In the late afternoon there was a call from Richard. He had
just arrived at Black Rock Hotel. He wanted me to have dinner with him that night. Could I come to the hotel or should
he come to me? If I came to the hotel we could be alone together. He had ascertained that he could get a car at the hotel
and come and pick me up.

We arranged that he should do this.

I told Matilda that he was coming. She seemed rather
pleased. She said it would do me good to see him.

She was very friendly when he arrived. Gordon happened to
be there and they were introduced; and after a short time I
went back with him to Black Rock Hotel.

It was a pleasant place with a lounge overlooking the sea.
The black rock, from which the hotel took its name, was very
much in evidence and Richard and I sat in the lounge looking
out on it.

"You will be coming home soon," Richard was saying.

"I don't know what is going to happen. We're just drifting
along at the moment."

"I know. It was such a terrible shock."

"Then there is the baby."

"I understand that he has an excellent nanny."

"Yes, but it is not the same, is it?"

"Isn't it?"

"Oh, no. He has lost his mother . . . and he looks to me, I know."

"Oh, I am sure he is too young to miss her."

"In a way. But somehow . . . I think he needs me."

Richard looked faintly disbelieving.

"Perhaps it is difficult for you to understand," I began.

"Oh, no . . . no," he said. "I understand perfectly how you feel. All this was so sudden, so absolutely shattering. You can't really sort things out at first. I have been talking to your mother."

"What did you say to her?"

"It was she who thought you should leave Cornwall and come home. She thought they might see reason down here and let the baby come with you. She said that would be by far the best for everybody, and she reckons that is what it will come to eventually."

"I don't know."

"It would be the best surely. If you made up your mind . . . about us . . . well, it would only be natural that your mother should take the child."

"He belongs down here, you see. One day he will inherit everything. His grandfather wants him to be brought up here."

"Your mother tells me that the grandfather is rather an odd character, and she wonders if he is resisting in order to be perverse. She says she is sure that at heart he is quite indifferent about the whole matter."

"There is, of course, Tristan's father to be considered."

"He's rather a weak person, according to your mother. He goes where he's put."

"That's not entirely true. But at the moment he is suffering deeply from a terrible shock."

"Of course. But that's enough of these people. What about you? Tell me . . . have you thought any more . . . about us?"

"I haven't been able to think about anything but all this."

"You'll get over it . . . and then . . ."

"Dorabella had been with me all my life until she married.

And now she's gone, I can't believe it. I can't think about anything else."

He looked crestfallen, and I fancied just a little impatient.

"I'm sorry, Richard," I said. "It's just impossible for me to see very far ahead."

"I understand," he said soothingly. "Let me tell you what is happening in London. My mother was hoping you'd come up and stay for a while. There are a lot of things she wants to show you about the house."

"Oh," I said faintly.

"As for Mary Grace, she is already very fond of you."

"Did she do that portrait?"

"Yes, and it was much admired. There are two more people clamoring for her work. You see what you have already done for the family. Oh, Violetta, it can be so good, I know it can. Please, please, do think about it. I am so sure it is the right thing."

But I was not. It was reasonable, of course, for him to think that my mother should care for the baby, but he simply did not understand. I was glad to see him, of course. But somehow it was not quite as it had seemed in London.

He told me he could stay for only two more days. He just had to be back in London by Monday and would have to leave on Sunday. It was a pity it was such a long journey.

"I'll come down again soon," he said. "Give me a ring when you have made up your mind. I shall be waiting for it."

I felt that he was taking too much for granted. He could not understand my uncertainty. He seemed so sure that I was going to marry him.

I wished that I could want to. He did not seem to realize that what had happened had made me unable to make any plans. My mind was still with Dorabella. If she had died naturally, would it have been different? But I could not rid myself of the strange feeling that she was not dead, because I had not *seen* that she was.

It was an unsatisfactory evening and I was not sorry when the time came to drive back to Tregarland's.

The next morning early, Nanny Crabtree came to me in some anxiety.

"I want the doctor to come and look at Tristan," she said. "I don't like that cold of his."

"Why, Nanny, is he worse?"

"He's wheezing. He's past the sniffle stage. And now it seems to be getting onto his chest. I'd just like the doctor to see him."

"We'll send for him right away. I'll give him a ring."

She nodded. "Well, it will set our minds at rest."

I went to see Tristan. He looked pale and lay in his cot with his eyes closed. He was certainly not his usual self, and I wanted to be there when the doctor came.

I telephoned Richard, for I had arranged for him to pick me up at ten o'clock. I was going to take him for a tour of the countryside, lunch out, and return about four, when he would drop me at Tregarland's and collect me to take me back to the hotel for dinner.

I said that after the doctor had been here, I would call him and we would meet later.

The doctor did not arrive until eleven o'clock. He apologized for being so long. One of his patients was about to give birth and he had been delayed with her.

He examined Tristan.

"Rather a nasty chill," he said. "Just keep him away from draughts. He should be all right in a day or so."

Matilda, who was present, said: "Nanny Crabtree will look after him, I know."

"That I will," declared Nanny Crabtree.

"You know how it is with children," said the doctor. "They are up and down. We want to make sure that it doesn't settle on his chest. Wrap him up warm . . . coddle him a bit. He'll be fine in a day or two."

"Well, that's a relief," said Nanny Crabtree.

When the doctor had gone, Matilda said to me: "What about your friend?"

"I postponed our time of meeting. I will ring him now."

"It is nearly lunchtime. Why don't you ask him to have it with us?"

I telephoned Richard and gave him Matilda's invitation. He accepted, but I sensed he was not very pleased. I was learning something about Richard. He hated his plans to be disrupted.

He came. It was quite a pleasant lunch. Dermot was not

present. He could not face meeting people. Gordon was there and he and Richard got on well together.

By the time lunch was over, it was nearly half past two and there would not be much time for us to drive far, so we decided to sit in the gardens.

It was very pleasant there with the house behind us and the sea facing us. Paths wound down to the private beach. I could never look at that beach without imagining Dorabella down there ... taking off her robe and putting it with her shoes at the top of the rock which protruded from the water so that they would not be carried out to sea.

It was not really a very satisfactory day. Richard was certainly a little put out because of the disruption to our plans, which I sensed he felt had not been necessary. The child had a cold and for that reason his brief stay here had been spoiled. He was very charming though and talked of what was going on in London. We spoke of Edward and Gretchen and the plays he had recently seen. I think he was trying to make me see what a rewarding life I should have with him. He spoke of his work and the case he was now working on. His client was accused of fraud and he was beginning to doubt his innocence.

"What happens when you are trying to convince the jury of something you don't altogether believe in yourself?" I asked.

"What I have to think of is the best thing for him if he is found guilty."

"You must learn a great deal about human nature," I said.

"Yes ... perhaps."

We talked of the situation in Europe, which he said was becoming more and more depressing. He did not know where it was going to end. It had been a mistake for England and France to give way over Austria. It would not stop there. There was going to be trouble in Czechoslovakia next. Hitler was instructing Konrad Henlein to agitate there.

"Henlein is the leader of the German minority there, and he is arranging demonstrations by the Sudeten Germans. Of course, Hitler's next plan will be the annexation of Czechoslovakia. There is an uneasy feeling everywhere."

"What do you think will happen?"

"The fact is, there is a growing fear of war. Hitler will take Czechoslovakia. People here say, 'It is a long way off. What is it to do with us?' They can't see any farther than their noses. All they can do is bury their heads in the sand. They call those who see the danger ahead 'war mongers.' We should be arming. Chamberlain knows it. I believe he is abandoning his policy of appeasement. He wants us to arm ourselves as quickly as we can."

"Do you think there will be a war?"

"It's a possibility. And we should be unprepared if it happened now. Even so, there are those who vote against arming ourselves. The Labour Party, the Liberals, and a few Conservatives will vote against it . . . and then . . ."

"You paint a gloomy picture, Richard."

"Yes, I'm sorry. But the way we are going, it does seem grim. They can't really think that Hitler will be satisfied with Austria. He'll soon have Czechoslovakia. Then he will try for Poland, and after that . . . what? It is the people who scream for peace who make the wars."

"Let us hope it never happens."

"None of these catastrophes would happen if people would only show a little foresight."

"Do you think something can be done now?"

"It's getting late. But if we and the French and the rest of the world stood together, that could be the end of Hitler's search for Lebensraum."

I said: "I think of Gretchen."

"Yes, poor girl. I know she is very anxious indeed."

"I am glad she is here with Edward."

"She thinks of her family and her country."

"Isn't it sad to contemplate what can happen to people?"

I was looking down at the beach and in my imagination she was there, throwing off her robe, running into the sea.

No, no, I thought. I cannot believe it of Dorabella. There would be a chill in that sea . . . most people did not bathe until May at least. Dorabella had liked comfort. She was inclined to be lazy. I did not believe it. I could not.

I was aware of Richard beside me. "Don't think I am not interested in what you are saying," I murmured. "It's just that I can't stop thinking of Dorabella."

"You should get away," he told me. "It's the best thing. Get right away from all this." He took my hand and pressed it. "In London . . . it would be different. There's so much to do. You wouldn't have time for brooding."

"Perhaps you are right," I said. "But not yet, Richard. I have to wait. I have to make myself see what I should do."

He nodded patiently and we went on sitting there. Matilda came out to join us.

"I do hope you'll stay to dinner," she said. "It is so nice for Violetta to have her friends down from London."

Richard accepted the invitation.

Before he left he reminded me that he had to get back to London and tomorrow would be his last day.

"We'll do something special," he said.

It was early morning of that Saturday when Nanny Crabtree burst into my room. I had just awakened and was lying in my bed, contemplating getting up. Richard would be coming at ten o'clock. I must be ready. I would try to make up to him for the disappointment of the previous day.

I saw at once that there was something wrong. Nanny Crabtree was pale and her eyes were fierce. She was greatly agitated.

"I want the doctor at once," she said.

I struggled up.

"It's Tristan?" I cried. "He's worse ... I'll telephone the doctor right away."

"Do that. It's on his chest ... having difficulty breathing. Get him quick."

I picked up my dressing gown and ran downstairs, Nanny Crabtree at my heels.

She stood beside me while I telephoned.

The doctor said he would be with us in an hour.

"How bad is he?" I asked Nanny.

"God alone knows. Four o'clock this morning, it was. I thought I heard him cough. It woke me. It's a habit you get when you're with children. I went in and there he was ... all the bedclothes off ... and, could you believe it, that window beside his cot was open ... just enough to let in a draught. I couldn't believe it. I had tucked him in so he couldn't throw anything off. I had that window shut. There's a cold wind blowing in from the sea. It must have been one of them maids, though what she was doing in my nursery I don't know. I'd seen to him and he'd gone off to sleep ..."

"He must have been terribly chilled."

"To the bone. That's what's brought this on. I only hope it's not going to turn to pneumonia. He's too little. If I find out who opened that window, I'll be ready to kill the one who did it."

I went up to see Tristan. He was tucked in with extra blankets and there were hot water bottles on either side of him. His face was flushed and he was shivering every now and then. His eyes had lost their brightness. He opened them for a second or two and then closed them. I felt sick with anxiety. I knew that he was very ill.

"I wish that doctor would come," said Nanny Crabtree. "He's taking his time."

"He said in an hour. It's not fifteen minutes yet. Nanny . . . how is he, really?"

"Not too good. He's had this chill. He was sleeping and warmly tucked in when I left him. I thought he'd be better in the morning. Children throw things off easy. They worry you sick, and then in half an hour they're right as rain. I was a bit anxious about him. You always are . . . you never know what can flare up suddenly. It was four o'clock . . . I just heard that cough and there I was. I felt the draught as I came in. He was lying there . . . uncovered, with that wind blowing in right onto him. Well, I shut the window fast as I could and I got him wrapped up and warm. He was like a little iceberg. But he's taken a chill, no doubt of that. I wish that doctor would come."

I washed and dressed and was ready when the doctor arrived. He went straight to Tristan and I could see by his expression that we had done right to call him immediately.

He said: "We'll have to take care of him. It's not pneumonia . . . yet. Well, we'll do our best. He's a strong little fellow, but he is young, very young. He didn't seem all that bad when I saw him last."

"I found him with the clothes off him," said Nanny. "He was just in his little nightshirt . . ."

"Well, we'll see what we can do."

I could not believe this. Dorabella dead and now the child threatened. There was something evil in this place.

Matilda was deeply concerned.

"Poor little mite," she said. "I thought it was just a cold

and, in fact, when the doctor came yesterday, I didn't think it was really necessary."

"I'm glad he saw him yesterday," I said. "He can see what a big change there has been."

"It's not . . . dangerous?"

"The doctor thinks it could be. It's so sudden. I feel . . ." I turned away and she slipped her arm through mine.

She said: "I know. One thing after another. Life can be like that sometimes. Everything seems to go wrong."

"Nanny went in this morning. She found him frozen. He had thrown off the bedclothes and the window was open—the one by his cot."

"Did Nanny leave it open?"

"Oh, no! She would never do a thing like that. The wind was blowing straight down onto his cot and she wouldn't let him be in a draught. The result might have been disastrous. Thank goodness she woke up when she did."

"I suppose he kicked off his bedclothes. But who opened the window?"

"Nanny says she doesn't understand it. She said she tucked him in so tightly that he couldn't have thrown off the bedclothes. And she certainly didn't leave the window open."

"She must have. I expect she forgot. She is a little old."

"I never thought of her age. She's as efficient as ever. She looks after Tristan as she did after us. Little escapes her."

"But to leave a window open like that."

"I can't believe she did."

Matilda shrugged her shoulders. "Well, it has happened. The thing is to get Tristan well. Dr. Luce is very good. He will do what is best. Do you think I could see Tristan?"

"I don't know what the doctor's orders are. Let's go up and see Nanny."

Nanny Crabtree came to the nursery door.

"I've got to watch him," she said. "If there is a change I'm to call the doctor at once."

Matilda looked startled. "Is it as bad as that then?"

Nanny said: "I don't want him left. Miss Violetta, I want you here."

"Your friend . . ." began Matilda.

I had forgotten Richard. I looked at my watch. It was nine thirty. I had promised to be ready by ten.

"You should go out and have a pleasant day with him," said Matilda.

"I couldn't have a pleasant day. I'd be thinking all the time of what was happening to Tristan."

"You should be here, Miss Violetta," said Nanny Crabtree. "I don't want anyone coming in here and opening windows."

She looked fierce and angry. Matilda exchanged a glance with me.

I said to her: "You see that he is really ill."

She tiptoed to the cot.

"Poor little thing," she said. "He does look poorly."

"I'll pull him through," said Nanny Crabtree. "And then I'll have something to say if I find anyone opening windows in my nursery." She turned to me. "I don't want him throwing off the bedclothes. He's got to be kept warm. The doctor will be back this afternoon to take a look at him."

Matilda said: "If I can be of any help . . ."

"That is kind of you, Mrs. Lewyth," said Nanny. "But we'll be able to manage."

Matilda looked at me helplessly.

I said to Nanny: "I'll be back in a moment," and went out with Matilda.

"You really shouldn't disappoint that nice young man," she said.

"I can't help it."

"I could be up there to help Nanny. You should go off with your friend."

"I couldn't. I must know what is going on. I shall telephone him and explain."

I did. He was amazed and dismayed, and a little indignant. I could understand that. He had made this journey to see me. Yesterday had been a disappointment, and now this.

He said he would call at the house in the afternoon and rang off.

I felt very sorry, but my thoughts were really with Tristan. I knew he was in a precarious state. The doctor had hinted as much, and the fact that he thought it necessary to call again this afternoon confirmed that.

Nanny Crabtree and I sat in the nursery, every now and then glancing toward the cot. If he as much as moved, Nanny

Crabtree was there, murmuring endearments, watching tenderly.

When she talked to me her indignation was apparent.

Someone had come into the room and opened the window. Why? Was it one of those fresh-air people who thought it wasn't healthy unless you were blasted off your feet, and didn't get goose pimples from the cold? If she could find the one who opened that window, she'd see that they didn't show their face in her nursery ever again.

"I mean to say ... to open a window. Why?"

I could not answer that question, and Matilda's hint that Nanny was getting old and could have forgotten to shut it came into my mind. No ... never. Not when she had been wrapping Tristan up and had been told by the doctor to keep him warm.

But who else? One of the maids who came up after Nanny Crabtree had left Tristan for the night? It was ludicrous. But if she had brought something in, thought the room seemed stuffy, might she not have opened the window? No one would have done such a thing. Could it really be that Nanny Crabtree herself had really forgotten to shut the window?

Whatever happened, it was done, and had its dire effect.

All through the morning we were with Tristan. Nanny Crabtree would not allow him to be left alone. If she had to go out of the room for a few minutes, she wanted me to be there.

Richard came in the late afternoon and wanted me to go back with him to the hotel. I said I could not concentrate on anything. I should be thinking of what was happening here.

"Tristan is very ill, indeed," I said. "Nanny Crabtree wants me here."

He said little and Matilda suggested he stay to dinner. He did. I went down to it knowing that Nanny Crabtree would let me know if there was any change. The doctor had been there and had said that at least the child's condition had not worsened.

A pall hung over us all. Dermot joined us. There was a look of haggard misery on his face. Gordon tried to entertain Richard and they talked about the estate, the law, and the situation on the Continent. I was glad when the meal was over.

Richard left soon after. He was a little aloof. He would be

leaving for London early next morning, for he was not sure how the trains ran on Sundays and he must be back in town by Monday.

It had been a disastrous visit; but my thoughts were all with Tristan.

During the night Nanny Crabtree and I took it in turns to sit with Tristan. I had a few hours sleep on her bed while she was on the watch.

In the morning, Tristan seemed to be breathing a little more easily. The doctor came and said he was well pleased. He thought we were going to avoid pneumonia after all.

"Now," said Nanny Crabtree to me, "you are going to get a good night's sleep tonight."

"And what of you?"

"I shall sleep, too. I'll be at hand, though. I think he's over the worst, out of danger now. It never ceases to amaze me how quickly the young recover."

I did sleep. I was exhausted and the first thing I did in the morning was to go to the nursery.

Nanny Crabtree was smiling happily.

"Come and look at him. There he is. Why did you want to give us all that trouble, eh, my lord? You little rogue, you. You had us worried. Now look at you."

I kissed him and he gave a little cluck of pleasure.

I was filled with thankfulness.

I wrote to Richard telling him how sorry I was that his stay had been disrupted. Tristan had almost completely recovered. The doctor had said that in a few days he would be back to normal.

"It was such a pity, Richard," I wrote, "that it should have happened just then. I am so sorry . . ."

I pictured him reading the letter. He had been very disappointed, indeed, and I was sure that he was thinking there had been no need for all the fuss. The child was not ill after all.

I wondered what effect that visit had had on his feelings toward me. I think mine had undergone a change. That was unfair, of course. He had been justly disappointed.

That day Jowan Jermyn telephoned. Would I ride out with him to Brackenleigh, which was on the other side of the moor?

I agreed and we left at ten thirty. We would have lunch, he said, at a place he knew there. He had to call at one of the farms. I might find that interesting.

It was just what I needed.

It was very pleasant. Spring was on the way and the hedgerows were bright with flowers in patriotic colors of red, white, and blue.

He knew that I had had a visitor from London.

I said: "I see the circulation of news is as good as ever."

"It is always to be trusted," he said. "And there was trouble over the little boy?"

"We have had a very anxious time. Tristan is all right now and we are very thankful. But he was really dangerously ill."

"I heard the doctor visited frequently."

"Poor Nanny Crabtree was very distressed."

"You must tell me all about it while we are having lunch. It's single file here. Just follow me."

I did until we came to the moor. We galloped then and came to the King's Head—a pleasant-looking inn. The sign over the door depicted the crowned head of some rather indeterminate monarch who might have been one of the Georges.

Over the table Jowan said, "Tell me about the visitor."

"He was a friend from London. A lawyer."

"And he came down to see you?"

"Yes."

"A great friend?"

"We met in London. He is a friend of Edward's. You know who Edward is?"

He did not, so I gave him a brief summary of Edward's place in the family. He was intrigued by the story.

"My mother regards him as her son," I said.

"You have inherited her talent for looking after motherless infants."

"You mean Tristan. Well, he is my sister's son."

He nodded. "And the lawyer? You were not able to entertain him in the manner which he was expecting."

I could not help smiling. "Why do you need me to tell you anything? You have such an excellent service of your own."

"Nevertheless, tell me. I like to hear it from the horse's mouth."

"Tristan had a cold, a rather bad one. Nanny Crabtree called

the doctor, who said he should stay in bed and be kept warm."
I went on to tell him about the open window and Tristan's kicking off his bedclothes which had brought him close to pneumonia.

"We sat up with him all night ... Nanny Crabtree and I. She didn't want anyone else. She blames someone for coming in and opening the window."

"And taking the clothes off the baby's bed?"

"Oh, no. We thought he threw them off."

"Was he in the habit of doing that?"

"No. He never has before."

"So he only does it when he is in a draught."

I looked at him intently.

"Well," he said. "It was what he did, wasn't it?"

"What are you thinking?"

"Why should he do that?"

"We can't ask Tristan why he kicked off his bedclothes. I suppose he was restless, probably feverish and too hot."

"I wonder why someone should come into the nursery and open the window."

"Mrs. Lewyth thinks that Nanny Crabtree opened it and forgot to shut it."

"I suppose it is a possibility. Is she forgetful?"

"I have never known her be, especially where her charges were concerned."

"And with a child already sick. Doesn't it sound strange to you? I wish you weren't staying there."

"Where else should I stay?"

"I mean it's a pity you can't take the child to your mother. But that is not entirely true, for if you did, what about me?"

"You?"

"Think how desolate I should be if I could not see you."

"Would you be?"

"It is not like you to ask foolish questions when you know the answer."

I did not reply, and nothing was said for a few moments.

I ate a little of the salmon which had been placed before me, and I felt happier than I had for some time. Tristan's quick recovery had lifted my spirits and I always had enjoyed Jowan's company.

He said at length: "Have you made any plans as to what you are going to do?"

I shook my head. "I am still uncertain about everything."

"Something might be decided for us before long," he said.

I looked at him questioningly and he went on: "I mean what is happening abroad."

"Does that involve us?"

"There is a possibility that it will. The way things are going, perhaps I should say a certainty. Do you like the food here?"

"Very much."

"We might come again. I often have to come this way."

He talked to me about the farm at which we should call. There was some question about building another barn.

"It won't take long. I thought you might like to see something of the estate."

It was an interesting afternoon. I chatted to the farmer's wife while Jowan was with her husband, and heard what a good landlord he was to his tenant farmers.

"Couldn't be better," she said. "We're lucky to be on the Jermyn estate. 'Tis not so good over at Tregarland's. Oh, sorry, Miss, I forgot you came from there. It was terrible about your poor sister, and I heard the little one's been poorly."

So it had already spread as far as this.

We rode back the way we had come. I felt better than I had since I lost Dorabella.

When I said goodbye, he took my hand and looked at me intently.

"Take care," he said. "Especial care." An almost imperceptible frown crossed his face as he went on: "Remember, I am not far away."

"Comforting thought," I replied lightly, but I meant it.

Death in the House

Summer was almost with us. Richard wrote now and then, but he did not suggest paying another visit to Cornwall. My mother also wrote. She wondered whether there was any hope of my coming to Caddington. I could travel with the baby and Nanny Crabtree quite easily now, she was sure. She herself was going to London frequently since the birth of Gretchen's baby—a little girl whom they had called Hildegarde.

It was June. I had paid another visit to Mrs. Pardell. She seemed quite pleased to see me. She was obsessed by the belief that Dermot had murdered both his wives and nothing would shift her. She thought he had strangled them, carried them out of the house, and thrown them into the sea.

"There was no sign of strangulation on Annette's body when they found her," I protested. "If there had been, it would have been quickly noticed."

"She had been in the sea all those days, hadn't she?" insisted Mrs. Pardell.

"I think the evidence would still be there."

Nothing would convince her, but she said it was nice to talk to somebody about it. "And you lost your sister, I lost my daughter. It links us . . . if you know what I mean."

I felt faintly depressed after my visit to her.

I was seeing Jowan more frequently. He introduced me to Joe Tregarth who was his manager. He was clearly devoted to Jowan. He told me it was a pity Jowan had not come into the property before and that it was a pleasure to work for someone who knew what he was about.

Whenever I went into the town I was aware of the looks which came my way. True, there was slightly less interest than there had been because the mystery of Dorabella's disappearance was becoming stale news, yet I was still part of one of those old legends which would be revived every now and then.

I found a morbid fascination in the gardens. I used to sit there in the afternoons and look over the beach thinking of Dorabella. I pictured her again and again, going down there that morning, plunging into the cold water and being lost forever. But I could not believe it happened like that.

It was late afternoon. I had been sitting there for about half an hour when I heard footsteps descending and, to my surprise, I saw Gordon Lewyth coming toward me.

"Good afternoon," he said. "You come here often, don't you?"

"Yes," I replied.

"May I sit with you?"

The seat was a stone ledge cut out of the rock. There was room for about four people on it.

He sat down. "It doesn't make you happy, does it, sitting here?" he said. "It brings it all back."

"Yes. I suppose you are right."

"And yet . . . you find it irresistible."

"I cannot understand it at all," I told him. "That my sister should suddenly start bathing in the morning. It would be decidedly chilly, and she was never the Spartan type."

"People have strange fancies."

"I cannot belive that she is dead."

"But she has gone, hasn't she?"

"Her body has never been washed up."

"That does not mean she is alive. Some are never seen again. She could have been washed out to sea . . . or lying on the ocean bed."

I shivered.

He said: "I'm sorry. But I reckon the sooner you face up to the fact that she has gone, the better. You'll start to get over it then. You'd be better away from here."

"Yes, I think so. But I could not go without Tristan."

"I don't think he will be allowed to go."

"I understand that he belongs to this place, but Dermot would not stop his going."

"Dermot is in a mood to be indifferent about everything at the moment."

"It was such a tragedy for him."

"As for you. I think you would be happier with your parents. You're brooding here. You can't escape from it."

"If only I could take Tristan . . ."

"The child has to stay here. His grandfather insists on that."

"And I have promised my sister to look after him if she were not here to do so."

"Did she have a premonition that she might not be?"

"She must have had."

"That's very strange."

"So many strange things have happened."

"It is the interpretation which is put on them. We Cornish are by nature superstitious. I wonder why. Perhaps because we have had a harder life than some. The population is made up of fishermen and miners—both hazardous occupations. When there are fatal accidents at sea or in the mines these legends are born. They will tell you that the knackers who live underground are the ghosts of those who murdered Jesus Christ. There have been many who have said they have seen them. 'The size of a sixpenny doll,' one man told me. I imagine a sixpenny doll in the old days might have been about six inches high—dressed like an old tinner, which is what they call miners in these parts. Miners had to leave what they called a 'didjan,' which was part of their lunch for the knackers, otherwise they could expect trouble. Imagine the hardship for those who found difficulty in providing their own frugal meal."

"You know a great deal about the old legends and customs."

"One picks it up over the years, and I have lived here all my life . . . though not in this house, of course. I am not one of the family."

"I thought there was a distant connection."

He hesitated for a moment, then smiled wryly.

"Oh, there might be. I was telling you about the legends. It is the dangerous occupations. People think of ill luck that could befall them. They talk of black dogs and white hares seen at the mineshafts which are a warning of approaching evil. You must understand that people who are often facing danger look for signs. Now they say that Jermyns and Tregarlands should never have become friendly and, because they have, there will be disaster."

"Do they really think that my sister's death is due to that?"

"I am sure *they* do. They will say that someone brought about this evil."

"Myself!" I cried.

He nodded and looked at me in an odd sort of way.

"They say it is not right that foreigners should come here and meddle with something that has been going on for generations."

"Foreigners!"

"Born the wrong side of the Tamar," he said with a smile.

"That is all ridiculous."

"Of course. But it is what they believe."

"But that feud, it's so absurd. You think so. Everyone with any sense would. Mr. Jermyn does, too."

"But there are many who don't. They love their old superstitions. They don't want them changed. The miners and fishermen don't. They fear the mines and the sea. Look at the sea now. Do you see that ruffling of the waves? There are a number of what we call white horses. It's quite rough down there."

"The wind has sprung up while I have been sitting here."

"It is very treacherous . . . unpredictable." He moved slightly toward me. "It can be smooth, inviting, and then suddenly the wind arises. You haven't seen what a real storm can be like yet. You haven't seen fearsome waves . . . forty- . . . fifty-feet-high waves. They can lash against the rocks. It is like an enraged monster. Oh, yes, you must be very careful of the sea."

I felt his eyes on me as he went on: "There is danger down there. Even in this garden. Just imagine if you should lose your footing—a loose stone, a shifting of the earth. It happens. You could go hurtling down . . . down onto those black rocks."

I felt a sudden fear as I fancied he moved even closer to me. I said: "It didn't occur to me."

"Well, it wouldn't. But you must take care. It looks so peaceful now, but things are not always what they seem. Always remember . . . the dangers of the sea."

"Mr. Lewyth, Mr. Lewyth, are you there?" One of the maids was coming down the slope toward us. It was as though a spell was broken. I gave an involuntary gasp of relief.

"A terrible thing have happened, sir," said the maid. "Mr.

Dermot has had an accident. He have been took to the hospital."

"Accident!" cried Gordon.

"Fell from his horse, sir. Mrs. Lewyth did send me to come and fetch you."

Gordon was already striding up the slope to the house. I followed.

Gordon, Matilda, and I drove to the hospital in Plymouth to which they had taken Dermot. We were not allowed to see him immediately, but we did see the doctor.

"He is badly injured," we were told.

"He's not ... ?" began Matilda.

"He'll recover, but it is going to be a long time and then, perhaps ..."

"Oh, my God," murmured Matilda.

Gordon said: "You mean it is a permanent injury?"

"It is possible. It involves the spine. It was a very bad fall. It could have killed him."

"Do they know how it happened?"

"He was apparently galloping too fast and ... er ... it seems that he was, well, not exactly intoxicated, but ... er ... not entirely sober either."

I said: "He has suffered a great grief recently. He lost his wife."

The doctor nodded.

"You may be able to see him when he comes out of the anesthetic. We had to do an operation—a minor one—but we can see that there is little that can be done."

"Does it mean he must stay here?"

"Oh, no. He'll be out of here in a few days ... if there is nothing further we can do. A little therapy perhaps. But that is for later. We'll have to see."

We were left in a waiting room and told that we should be called when we could see Dermot.

"This is terrible," said Matilda. "What is happening ... ? Things haven't really been right since Annette's death. It all seems so bewildering."

"Life is sometimes like that," said Gordon, glancing at his mother. "This was an accident. No one can be blamed for it."

"I expect the evil forces will be blamed," I said.

Gordon nodded. "He might recover," he said. "Doctors don't always know."

It was some time before a nurse came to us. She told us we could see Dermot now, but must not stay too long.

Dermot was lying in a bed in a ward occupied by several others. The curtains about his bed were drawn back by the nurse.

He looked pale and very ill. He smiled at us faintly.

"I've made a mess of things," he said with a weak smile.

"My dear Dermot," said Matilda, "we are all so concerned for you."

"I'm still here," he said almost regretfully.

"What happened?" asked Gordon.

"I don't know. One moment I was galloping along, and the next I hit the ground. Poor old Sable just went on."

"I know," said Gordon. "She came back to the house."

"I must have been careless," said Dermot.

"Well, rest now," soothed Matilda. "You will be all right. But it will take time."

"Time," he said, and closed his eyes.

A nurse came to us and signaled that we should leave.

We looked at Dermot. His eyes were closed and he seemed unaware of our departure.

As was expected, there was a buzz of speculation. What was happening up at Tregarland's? It was clear enough, wasn't it? Something was wrong. It was one trouble after another. Death for the first Mrs. Tregarland; then the young woman from foreign parts starts meddling, bringing a Jermyn to Tregarland's. It stood to reason that the ghost was not going to stand by and allow that to happen. The trouble with foreigners was that they did not know anything about the spirit world. This would show them.

There were two young women taken by the sea—though the first was before the meddlesome creature arrived and was just a warning that the quarrel was as fierce as it always had been. Then the master fell off his horse and it was reckoned that it would be a long time before he would be in the saddle again. It was a warning. It was saying clear as the nose on your face: Don't meddle with what you don't know.

I felt a great desire to get away from the place. I could, of course, pack and go home tomorrow, but what of Tristan? As Richard would have said, the nanny was quite capable of looking after the child. If only I could take him with me.

There was something else. I should not see Jowan Jermyn, and I should not want that. During this time, my encounters with him had seemed to bring a sort of sanity into my life. He gave the impression that he was concerned for me. He helped me to laugh at the whispering voices; he understood my need to look after Tristan. He took my fears and frustrations and my indecision seriously. He seemed to understand as no one else did.

Dermot came home from the hospital. It was clear that he was badly injured. He walked with great difficulty and he went straight to his bed, for the journey from the hospital had exhausted him.

There was gloom throughout the house. It was the first time old Mr. Tregarland lacked that air of suppressed amusement. He looked really shaken. This was, after all, his only son.

During the days that followed it was brought home to us how incapacitated Dermot was. We had been told that there was little hope that he would regain his full vigor, although the doctors hoped for some improvement. We were warned that it would take a long time.

James Tregarland entered into the discussion as to what was to be done. A wheelchair must be acquired for Dermot and a room on the ground floor prepared. That was easy enough to arrange. Jack, from the stables, was a man to be trusted. He was strong, and if need be they could call in Seth, whose physical strength made up for what he lacked mentally.

The great task would be to keep Dermot cheerful. This following on the death of Dorabella had been too much for him. In fact, the fall was attributed to his grief.

Everyone was eager to do what they could for him. A beautiful ground floor room, its mullioned windows overlooking the sea, was made ready. He had his chair in which he could wheel himself about. He was often in pain and had strong pills to alleviate it. The doctor would come once a week unless called in between times; and everything that could be done would be.

No one could have had more care. There was a constant stream of visitors; we made sure that he was hardly ever alone. Jack was his devoted slave. He liked me to go to see him, and invariably he would talk of Dorabella—how wonderful she had been, how he had loved her from the moment he saw her. And then . . . he had lost her.

I had to keep him from talking too much about her.

He would sit in his chair, freshly shaved and washed, wearing a Paisley dressing gown, and I thought how changed he was from the young man who had sat outside the café with us—so bright, so merry, a young man in love with life and Dorabella. How sad it had turned out to be!

I used to talk to him about Tristan, telling him how he was growing, how bright he was, how he smiled at Nanny Crabtree and me . . . what a blessing he was.

He would nod and smile, but I knew his thoughts were with Dorabella.

The weeks began to pass. There was tension in the air. The great topic of conversation was again what was happening in Europe. There was a sense of uneasiness. People talked of the possibility of war.

Hitler was causing trouble again. Everywhere one went the subject was that of the Sudetenland areas and Czechoslovakia. Would Hitler invade? And if he did, what would England and France do? Would they stand aside again? Would they passively allow him to go in and get on with his demands for Lebensraum for the German nation?

His people were fanatically behind him.

So that uneasy summer began to pass.

I heard from Richard.

He wrote: "I cannot understand why you stay there. Are you never coming home? You seem to have this really rather mad obsession. The child has a perfectly good nurse. Your mother says she is utterly trustworthy. Why do *you* have to stay there?"

I could sense his impatience and veiled criticism. He thought I was foolish—or perhaps had some other reason for wishing to stay.

It was clear that we were breaking away from each other. I was sorry to have hurt him, but I knew now that I had been only momentarily attracted by him and my feelings were not really deep enough for a stronger relationship. Nor, I believed, were his.

I did go to see Mrs. Pardell again. She was quite welcoming in her rather grim way. She took me to her sitting room where I sat looking at the silver-framed picture of Annette.

"And how are things up there?" she asked.

"Sad," I said.

"And there he is ... well, it's just retribution, I reckon. That's what the Bible says. The Lord has seen fit to punish him for his misdeeds."

"Oh, Mrs. Pardell, you must not judge him."

She shook her head. "He killed my girl. I know he did. I've always known it. And your sister. There are men like that. I suppose he has the utmost comfort."

"He is well looked after."

"H'm. Well, serve him right, I say. Goodness knows who'd have been the next. Wife number three, I suppose."

It was no use trying to reason with her. She had made up her mind to that. Dermot had murdered her daughter and my sister, and he had now what she called his "come-uppance." She was not going to let her opinion be shifted.

After I left her, I felt vaguely depressed. Everything was so uncertain. Nobody knew what was going to happen next. There might be war. That was what was in everyone's mind, and I suppose my problems were as nothing compared with the catastrophe that would be.

I often thought of Gretchen with Edward and their little girl. My mother wrote of them from time to time.

We are delighted and Edward is ecstatic. Gretchen is overjoyed about the child in spite of her worries. Alas, she gets more anxious about her parents every day. Your father thinks the situation is rather grim and he is very suspicious of what Hitler will do next if they let him get into Czechoslovakia. What a nuisance that man Hitler is! I wish they could get rid of him.

How are you getting on down there? I do think they are foolish to make all that fuss about Tristan's staying there. After all, it is you and Nanny Crabtree who are looking after him.

I can't see why you couldn't come home ... for a visit, anyway. You must come up for Christmas and bring Tristan and Nanny with you. I'm sure he'd be all right to travel now. He must be getting to be quite a person. I'd love to see him. Come for a long visit. Your father misses you ... as I do.

How is Dermot? It was a terrible thing to happen. You say he gets about in a wheelchair. Well, that's something, and I expect he will eventually improve. Poor boy. Let's hope that one day they can do something for him.

Don't forget, dear, we want you home ... with Tristan. I think they will come round to letting us have him in due course.

I did not think they would, but perhaps in a few months I should be able to take the baby home for a visit.

I often took out the miniature of Dorabella. I would hold it in my hands and look back over the years. It was a foolish habit and could only plunge me into melancholy. Dorabella herself had once said that brooding on what couldn't be changed was like taking your sorrows out to swim instead of drowning them. She had heard that somewhere and liked it.

If only she could come back to me.

Then it occurred to me that she had once said she would always have the miniature of me with her. She kept it in her room, the dressing room in that bedroom she had shared with Dermot.

The room was not occupied now that Dermot had one downstairs. I wanted to see the miniature. The pair should be side by side.

I went up to the room, with its four-poster bed, the large and heavily draped windows.

I had seen the miniature on a little table in the dressing room. It was not there now. I remembered that she had said she would put it away in a drawer because she did not want to be continually reminded of my desertion.

I had once seen her take it from a particular drawer. It would be there now, I guessed, because I had not been in the house when she had gone down to take that fatal bathe.

I opened the drawer. There were a few things in it—some gloves and handkerchiefs and a belt, but no miniature. I took out everything and felt round the inside of the drawer. Nothing.

Where was the miniature, then? Perhaps in another drawer? There were three others. I searched them all, but the miniature was not there.

Puzzled, I looked round the room. I went into the bedroom. In the wardrobe there was a shelf and another drawer. But the picture was not there, either.

I wondered where it could be.

The uneasy weeks were passing quickly. There were long summer days when I met Jowan, perhaps three or four times a week. I met a number of the farmers on his estate; he was always busy and would invite me to accompany him on the calls he was making.

I was getting to know his grandmother. There was a very strong bond between them; she doted on him and I liked his attitude toward her which gave an impression of light-hearted affection, but I sensed it went deep.

Those meetings with him were the highlights of those long summer days. There was an aura of unreality about everything . . . my life . . . the world itself. There were war clouds on the horizon, and I often felt that I was seeing the end of an era. I was drifting along without the ability to exert my will. It was as though everything was being decided for me.

I continued to be baffled by the disappearance of the miniature. I mentioned it to Matilda.

"I've looked in the dressing room and bedroom. That was where she kept it. I can't think of anywhere else she might have put it."

"I expect she put it away somewhere."

"I wonder where? You know I have one of her and they are a pair of frames so would look well together."

"She was very fond of it. It'll turn up one day, no doubt."

Once when I was sitting with Dermot I asked him if he knew where the miniature was.

"It's in the dressing room, I think," he said. "She kept it in a drawer there and took it out when you were there. She didn't want to look at it often when you weren't there. She said you were a beast to stay away and she was hurt by your desertion. She didn't want to think of you. You know what she was like."

"Yes. She said that to me."

"It will be somewhere about."

He was sad and I wished I had not raised the subject because it had set him thinking of her afresh. Not that she was ever far from his thoughts.

"They were beautiful, those miniatures," he mused. "The painter had caught the likeness of you both. It was just like her, wasn't it?"

I said: "Yes, Dermot."

"She had something on her mind . . . at the end. It used to worry me."

"What was that?"

"I didn't know. I just had the feeling that things weren't right somehow."

"What do you mean?"

"Sometimes . . . she was too merry . . . a little . . . well, not spontaneous, but as though she were pretending everything was all right, as though she were planning something. She had some secret. I think she didn't like it much here. It was too dull for her. Sometimes, I used to think . . ."

"What did you think?" I asked sharply.

"I wondered if she were planning . . . to leave me."

"No."

"It was just a fancy."

"That could have been so. She was happy. She had always been the restless sort. She would have told me if anything were wrong."

"Would she?"

"She always did."

"But you weren't here."

"No, but she would have written. She used to talk to me . . . always. I was her confidante from the time we were two years old. If she had a problem she always brought it to me to solve."

"I just had this impression. It worried me."

"No, Dermot, everything was all right."

A tortured look came onto his face and once more I blamed myself for bringing up the subject of the miniature.

"She was everything, Violetta," he said. "You understand."

"Yes, I do."

"Life without her is empty."

"Dermot, do you ever have a feeling that she is not dead?"

"What?"

"They haven't found her body, have they?"

"They wouldn't. She's out there ... lying at the bottom of the sea. I can't bear to think of her. She was so full of life. That's why I felt she wouldn't stay here. She always wanted to have the best in life. She reveled in living. She was able to enjoy it so much ... when she had what she wanted. I was worried about her. I thought she would leave me ... and she did."

"Not of her own free will," I said.

We were doing no good to each other, Dermot and I.

I thought of something else to talk about. The political situation. That was not going to cheer him, though I imagined at that moment he felt as indifferent as I did about the troubles of Europe. I talked about the farm I had visited with Jowan the day before. He pretended to listen, but I knew his thoughts were in the past with Dorabella.

It was September. My mother wrote complaining that she had not seen me for so long. "It is like the old days when you were away at school, but this is even longer than a term. Your father and I are coming down to see you and we are going to try and persuade them to let you and Tristan come to us for Christmas."

They arrived in mid-September. Matilda made them very welcome. It was wonderful to see them. I heard that Hildegarde was the perfect child and that my mother went to London often to see them and they came to Caddington.

"We all miss you so much, Violetta," my mother told me. "It's such a pity that you are shut away down here, particularly as ..."

I knew she meant that they had lost Dorabella, too.

Gordon took my father off to see something of the estate and it was a pleasant visit; but Matilda made it clear to my parents that old Mr. Tregarland was very loath to let Tristan go away just yet.

"He is afraid something might happen to him," she explained. "You see, there has been this terrible accident to Dermot following close on the other tragedy. You understand what I mean. You know that you are welcome here at any time. You must come to us for Christmas."

My mother said they would be delighted to do that.

"We must see Violetta and our little grandson," she added.

Concern about the world situation increased during that September.

I said to Jowan, when he and I were riding together, that I was weary of the names of Adolf Hitler and the Sudetenland.

"That is how we all feel," he replied. "But the situation is grave. War could break out at any time."

"There are many people who think we ought to keep out of trouble."

"You will always have the ostrich types who think that if they bury their heads in the sand and do not look, the trouble will go away."

"Do you think there is going to be war?"

"It is difficult to see how it can be avoided."

This matter was constantly discussed over meals. Gordon and my father could not stop talking about it. James Tregarland listened intently and now and then offered an opinion. He had changed since Dermot's accident. That old, rather cynical amused expression had gone. He seemed older, more serious. He must care for Dermot in his way. He rarely saw Tristan. I supposed babies had little interest for him. He sometimes asked me about him, because I suppose he knew that I, with Nanny Crabtree, was with the baby more than anyone else. He had done this since the time Tristan had come near to having pneumonia.

It was while my parents were at Tregarland's that September that there were significant moves on the Continent.

Germany's recalcitrance over Czechoslovakia was coming to a head and we were on the brink of war. The Prime Minister, Neville Chamberlain, flew to Munich in order to confer with Hitler. And after that there was a certain relief.

Chamberlain and Daladier of France had made a pact with Hitler. He was to have the Sudetenland which he so coveted, and there would be no interference over this. For this concession, peace was to be ensured in our time.

Chamberlain flew back from Munich. There were many pictures of him at the airport. He was surrounded by reporters eager to know the results of the conference.

The Prime Minister was depicted waving a piece of paper in his hands, while quoting the well-known words of Disraeli. He told the waiting reporters that this was "Peace in our Time. Peace with Honour."

There was general rejoicing throughout the country.

My parents went home with promises that they would come down for Christmas.

"And perhaps," my mother said to me on parting, "by that time old Mr. Tregarland will have decided that Tristan is old enough to make a railway journey to see his grandparents."

Jowan was not optimistic about the pact with Hitler.

"I don't trust him," he said. "He wants the whole of Czechoslovakia, not merely the Sudeten territory. And after Czechoslovakia . . . what next?"

"If he tries to take more, what then?"

"I don't know. We have delayed too long already, but there will have to be a halt somewhere. I had heard that as soon as Chamberlain returned he went into conference with the Cabinet and made plans for rearmament."

"That means . . ."

"That he does not trust Hitler."

"Do you think he has made this pact . . . ?"

"To give us time? Maybe. Hitler is armed to the teeth for war. We are far from that. But we shall see. Germany is thriving. She has come a long way from the privation which followed 1918. It may be that they will be content with what they have. I think if they are wise they will settle for that. They have got away with it so far. England and France have stood by, but, of course, they cannot do that indefinitely, and another step might change the picture."

"So much . . . to depend on one man!"

"There is some magic in him. He has bewitched his people. They stand firmly beside him."

"He has done terrible things to the Jews."

"He is a monster, but a monster with a mission."

"I think of Edward's wife, Gretchen. She is beset by anxieties."

"I know, and well she might be."

"How I wish that she had brought her family here!"

"It is what is called the eleventh hour now, I believe. But cheer up. It may not happen. Don't you find that in life something we fear never comes to pass and all our anxiety has been for nothing? When you went away, I thought I would never see you again, and look, here you are, and we have our meetings."

He looked at me earnestly. "That was an unnecessary fear. At least, I hope so."

"I like to think that these meetings will continue," I said.

"You mean that . . . sincerely?"

"But of course. Sometimes I feel they are an escape to sanity."

"I'm glad," he said.

I believed that he understood what was in my mind. He knew that I should never accept the fact that I had lost Dorabella until I had proof that she was dead.

Christmas came and went. I was pleased to see my parents again. I had a letter from Richard. He had ceased to suggest that I return. I think any prospect of a serious relationship between us was fading away. He was disappointed in me and I think I was in him. It had, in a way, been a choice between him and Tristan. I had given my word to Dorabella and I supposed that, even in death, she was closer to me than anyone else.

There were times when I was faintly regretful that I had lost Richard, but others when I felt relieved. If his affection had failed on that issue, it could not have been very firmly implanted. I was beginning to see that we should not have been well suited to each other.

Poor Dermot's condition had not improved and the doctor had hinted that it could be permanent, although naturally Dermot had not been told this. He had changed. The carefree young man had become moody. I could understand that. He was not a man with inner resources. He had enjoyed an active life. He liked to travel, to be with people. I was sorry for him. He was often melancholy during those dark days of winter.

The climate in Cornwall is a little milder than elsewhere in England. Snow was rare but the rainfall was heavy, and sometimes the winds would blow at gale force from the south-west. There were sunny days now and then, and Jack would wheel Dermot out in his chair and take him to the gardens, help him from the chair, and he would sit for a while on one of the seats looking down on the beach. I always thought that was not a good spot to be, where he could see the rocks on which Dorabella's bathrobe had been found.

His father would sometimes sit with him. That showed a change in the old man. I was glad and liked him better because I realized that he really cared for his son.

March had come and the first signs of spring were in the fields and hedgerows. The news suddenly grew more serious. The respite since those days when Neville Chamberlain had returned from Munich brandishing his little piece of paper and declaring there was to be peace in our time was over.

Hitler disregarded his promise and marched into Czechoslovakia.

This was alarming. It confirmed that which many people had thought possible and what must have been in the mind of the Prime Minister when he had returned from Munich and had immediately set about rearmament.

Now even those who had been opposing preparation for war realized the necessity of doing so.

Where would the German dictator turn next? The policy of appeasement was over. There could be no more standing aside. The Prime Minister had a meeting with the French premier and an agreement between the two countries was announced. They would support Poland, Rumania, and Greece if Hitler should attack them.

No longer could people run away from the truth. The storm clouds were gathering fast over Europe. How long would it be before Hitler decided to move into Poland?

He was already stating his claims to that country.

We waited for the news every day and there was a feeling of intense relief when nothing happened.

I rode often with Jowan. We loved to go onto the moors and, if the weather was warm enough, would tether our horses and sit close to an old disused mine while Jowan told me of some of the old legends of Cornwall. He would point out the prehistoric stones, so many of which had a story attached to them.

I arranged to meet him one day and when I went into the stables Seth was there.

He was always interested in me. I think it was because I was Dorabella's sister and he believed she was one of the victims of the ghostly lady of the house of Jermyn.

Only the day before, I had walked down to the beach. I found a certain fascination there. I liked to stand close to the sea and watch the waves advance and recede, while I thought of Dorabella.

Seth had seen me there. I had looked up and there he was in the gardens looking down at me. I lifted my hand in greeting. He had returned the gesture, shaking his head at me. I think he must have meant it as a warning, telling me I should not be there.

I realized that afternoon in the stables that he was referring to this incident when he said: "Shouldn't go down there, Miss. 'Tain't good."

"Do you mean the beach?" I asked. "I always make sure that the tide is not coming in and in any case I could get back into the garden. It was quite different on that day I was caught."

He shook his head. " 'Tain't right. One day 'er'll be after you. You was the one as brought him here."

Knowing the way his mind worked, I realized that he was talking about Jowan and my breaking the feud between the houses of Tregarland and Jermyn.

"I'm all right, Seth," I said.

He shook his head and I thought for a moment that he was going to burst into tears.

" 'Tween't I," he said. "I had naught to do with it. Not really like . . ."

I had lost the train of his thought, but he looked so worried that I wanted to pursue it.

"Didn't do what, Seth?" I asked.

"I didn't 'elp to get 'er in, like. Not really, only . . ."

Something was worrying him very much. This was a different turn to the conversation.

"Who, Seth?" I asked. "Who was the one you did not help?"

He was silent for a moment. Then he murmured: "Not to say. Not to tell. It's a secret."

"Do you mean . . . my sister . . . ?"

"No. Don't know naught about her. T'other."

"The first Mrs. Tregarland?"

He looked at me and half nodded. "Not to say," he went on.

" 'Er was beckoned, 'er was. 'Er had to go in. It was what 'er wanted."

"I don't understand, Seth. Who wanted what?"

"Wasn't what 'er wanted. 'Er had to, didn't 'er? But 'tweren't I, Miss. 'Er 'ad to and 'er went."

Gordon had come into the stable. I wondered how much of this conversation he had heard.

"Oh, hello, Violetta," he said. "Are you going for a ride?"

"Yes."

"It's a good day for it."

I wondered whether he would understand what Seth was trying to say.

I began: "Seth was telling me . . ."

A look of terror came into Seth's face.

"I didn't say nothing," he mumbled. "I didn't know nothing."

"About the first Mrs. Tregarland's accident, I think it was, Seth," I said.

"No. No, I didn't say nothing."

Gordon was watching him intently. Seth lowered his eyes and shuffled away.

Gordon turned to me. He patted Starlight's flank and helped me to mount.

"Poor Seth," he said quietly. "He's worse some days than others. Enjoy your ride."

As I went out I heard him say to Seth: "I want to have a look at Black Eagle. I thought there might be something wrong."

I rode on, thinking of Seth's words. It was a pity he was so incoherent. One could never be sure whether what he said was actual fact or some figment of his addled mind; but I did feel he was trying to say something which was worrying him and for which he must make excuses.

Jowan was waiting for me. As always he looked delighted to see me. We rode onto the moors and, finding a sheltered spot, tethered our horses.

We sat leaning against a stone—one of a little group of six clustered round one of a much larger size. I remarked that they looked like sheep around the shepherd.

I could not forget my conversation with Seth and, as Jowan noticed my preoccupation, I told him about it.

"Poor Seth," said Jowan. "It is sad that he had that accident. He would have been a bright young boy but for that."

"It is sobering to think that one small incident can change our lives. I wish I knew what he was trying to say. It was almost as though he were making excuses."

"For what?"

"Something he had done in connection with the first Mrs. Tregarland."

"Oh . . . what did he say exactly?"

"It's hard to tell what. Something he didn't do. It was almost as though he were making excuses for some action. He kept saying it was the ghost who called her into the water."

"He was excusing himself?"

"Well, it was so muddled, almost as though he were being blamed for something he hadn't done."

"Did he say he was there?"

"He never says anything as straightforward as that."

"Did he *sound* as though he had been there?"

"Well, yes. And he might have gone on but Gordon came into the stables just then and he stopped."

"Did Gordon hear?"

"Some of it, I suppose."

"I wonder what he thought of it."

"Well, no one takes much notice of Seth."

"Sometimes people like that know more than you think they would. It is just possible that he might have some information, something the rest of us don't know."

"You mean about Annette's death?"

"H'm. It always seemed a bit odd to me . . . that the champion swimmer should be drowned. It was not as though there was a gale."

"I thought it might have been cramp."

"Possibly. But why should Seth say it wasn't his fault?"

"He's obsessed by it."

"Why?"

"Because he believes that ancestress of yours who drowned herself wants other young women to do the same . . . if they are connected with Tregarland. It's a sort of revenge on the family."

"I suppose that's so. It mightn't be a bad idea to find out what is in Seth's mind."

"I'll see what I can do. What is happening in the outside world?"

"You mean that part in which we are all extremely interested at the moment?"

"I do indeed."

"Well, things don't get better. They are moving toward some climax. The latest news is that, for the first time in British history, there is to be military conscription in peacetime."

"That sounds as though they are really expecting war."

"If Hitler moves into Poland, there will be. I don't think there is any doubt about his intentions, and now the days of appeasement are over, equally there can be no doubt about ours and those of the French."

"Conscription? Does that mean . . . ?"

"Able-bodied young men will be called up for military service."

I looked at him in dismay.

"I expect they would say I was doing useful work by running the estate. On the other hand, if it came to conflict, I should have to be there."

I continued to look at him. He laughed suddenly and, taking my hand, kissed it.

"It is nice to know you care," he said.

It was a beautiful day. May had come and there was warmth in the air. When I came out of the house I saw Dermot sitting on a seat in the garden. I went over and sat beside him.

"It's a lovely day," I said.

He agreed. He was looking down on the beach with that infinitely sad expression, thinking, I knew, of Dorabella.

"I wonder what's going to happen," I said, trying to turn his thoughts to other things. "Do you think there's going to be war?"

"I suppose so."

"There is such uncertainty everywhere."

He nodded and we fell into silence. I could see it was useless to try to lift him out of his melancholy.

He said suddenly: "The time goes on. They will never find her. She's gone . . . forever."

I put my hand over his and he went on: "You and I—we were the ones who loved her most."

I said: "There are my parents. They loved her dearly, too."

"It is not quite the same."

"My mother hides her grief but it is there. I never found that miniature I gave her."

"She thought a great deal of it. She often told me how she felt about you. She used to laugh about the way in which you helped her out of trouble. She said she was a monster who thought up the wildest adventures and always at the back of her mind was the thought, Violetta will have to get me out of this."

"Yes, it was like that with us."

"She said you were her other self. She called it a cord between you. She said you were the better half."

"Oh, Dermot, I can't bear to think of her."

"Nor I."

After that we were silent. It was no use trying to talk of other things. She was uppermost in our minds and she would keep intruding. She had once said, "Don't ever think you'll be rid of me. I shall always be there."

It was true, of course.

I sat with him until Jack came to take him in.

I watched them. Jack was strong and gentle and helped Dermot into his chair. He lifted his hand to me as Jack wheeled him into the house.

I went down the slope to the beach and stood there watching the waves.

"Dorabella," I said. "Where are you?"

Next morning, when Jack went into Dermot's room, he found that he was dead.

The Ghost on the Cliff

❦

The household was in turmoil. The first I knew of it was when Matilda came to my room while I was preparing to go down to breakfast. She was very pale and obviously trembling.

"Something terrible has happened," she said; and she told me how Jack had gone into Dermot's room to wake him with his early morning cup of tea.

"He said he knocked on the door and when there was no answer he went in. He said good morning and, as there was no response, he went to the bed and saw at once what had happened. The bottle of pills was near the bed and it was empty. Jack knew at once what he had done. There was a glass which had contained whisky. Poor Jack, he is in a terrible state. We all are."

"Oh, poor Dermot," I said. "He was so unhappy."

"He never got over Dorabella's death. I can't believe this has happened. Gordon is taking charge of everything. He has sent for the doctor. Oh, Violetta, this is terrible. What else is going to happen in this house?"

That was a bewildering day: the comings and goings, the whispered conversations, the terrible knowledge that another tragedy had struck us and that there was death in the house.

I kept thinking of our conversation in the garden. I was not surprised in a way. I should have seen it coming. He was in despair. That had been clear. I could understand this. His marriage had been brief and fruitful ... and then she had gone, stupidly, foolishly, because of an impetuous whim she had been taken away.

The entire house was in a state of shock. Matilda's usual

271

calm had deserted her. She was so shaken that the doctor gave her a sedative and advised her to take a rest.

Gordon was calm and essentially practical. The doctor talked to him—obviously relieved to be able to discuss what must be done with someone who was capable of doing it.

It was a nightmare day.

I had a talk with Gordon in the evening.

"There will be an inquest, of course," he said. "The doctor obviously knows what happened. He is not altogether surprised. He said Dermot was very depressed. Before all this started, he could be high spirited at times and right down at others. He was not the sort who could cope with tragedy. When he heard that it was unlikely that he would walk again, the doctor was afraid he might attempt to take his life. He had been about to suggest that the pain-killing pills should only be administered by Jack or someone near at the time he needed them, but that would have had its difficulties. He might have wanted to take them in the night. It was a very sad case but, as the doctor said, not altogether unexpected in the circumstances."

It was a household in mourning.

Matilda was too shaken to leave her bed that day and it was Gordon who had had to break the news to old Mr. Tregarland.

When he came out of the old man's bedroom he was clearly disturbed. I was waiting to hear how the father had received the news of his son's death. He was stricken with grief and horror.

"I thought," said Gordon, "that we were going to have another death in the house. His face turned purple and he opened his mouth to speak but there was no sound. He just stared at me and he was shaking in every limb. I thought he was going to have a stroke. This has been a terrible blow, coming after everything else. He has taken it very badly. We shall have to be very careful with him. The shock has been too much."

Mr. Tregarland stayed in his room for several days. Matilda went about as though in a bad dream. I did not go into the town. I could imagine what people were saying. There was a curse on Tregarland's. It went back a hundred years to when the Tregarlands and the Jermyns were such enemies.

There was no question of the verdict that Dermot had committed suicide while the balance of his mind had been disturbed.

Gloom descended on the house. And not only there. The possibility of war was the constant topic. It was certain that the Germans were preparing to take some action.

Jowan and I met as usual, but I felt uneasy about that. The servants whispered together. Look at what is happening. It was one blow after another for the Tregarlands.

Jowan said: "It is certainly mysterious. I wish you weren't there, and on the other hand I wouldn't want you to go away."

"These disasters are a string of coincidences," I said. "Life is so strange. Dermot's death is explainable. I know how miserable he was. He had lost both of his wives and it is certainly odd that they should both die by drowning. As for Dermot himself, he was so miserable, his horse was out of control, and there was a suggestion that he was not quite sober. There is an explanation for that."

"It's true. I wonder what will happen next. I believe there may well be a war. That will change things for all of us."

"You seem certain . . ."

"It is the way things are going. This alliance . . . what is it they call it? The Pact of Steel, which Hitler is making with Italy. It looks as though he wants to be sure he has a strong ally before he makes some move."

"Surely he will not act against the British and the French?"

"That remains to be seen. There has been too much appeasement in the past. He may think it will continue. Let us hope that he stops in time to prevent our all being plunged into war."

"This is all very depressing and I was looking to you to cheer me up!"

"Oh, dear! I'm sorry. Is it so very bad at Tregarland's?"

"Naturally. Old Mr. Tregarland seems to have changed. He is so overcome with grief at Dermot's death. He stares into space. It is as though he is trying to understand, as though he is searching for some explanation for all these disasters."

"Poor old man! It is a good thing he has Gordon Lewyth to look after everything."

"He is the great bulwark. Matilda, who is usually so calm and practical, seems to be utterly shaken by all this."

"Well, let's look on the bright side, eh? Let's try and forget what has happened. After all, there has to be a turning point somewhere."

We had come to an open space.

"Let's give the horses a bit of fun," he said, and started to gallop across the field. I followed him.

There seemed to be no end to the melancholy.

That night, at dinner, Matilda told us that Mrs. Pengelly's baby had been found dead in her cot.

"The poor woman is prostrate with grief," she said. "The shock was terrible. She had fed the baby, put her in her pram in the garden, and left her. Then she had gone into the house and came out twenty minutes later to find her dead."

"But what happened?" I asked.

"They don't know yet. The child was suffocated in some way. She was blue in the face and not breathing."

"But there must have been some reason," I said.

Gordon said: "It is not the first time this sort of thing has happened. The doctors cannot give an explanation. The child just ceases to breathe . . . and in a few moments is dead."

"But . . ." I began.

"There must be some reason, of course," went on Gordon. "But the doctors don't know what it is. These child deaths are not exactly common, but several babies have died in that way. The medical profession is researching it, and I expect they will find the cause, but so far it is a mystery."

"There was a case over at St. Ives only a few months ago," added Matilda. "Poor Mrs. Pengelly. It's no consolation to her, but at least she knows it is no fault of hers."

"You mean to say that babies can really die like this?" I asked.

"Yes. They die in their cots. They are usually round about three months old, but they can, I believe, die this way up to two or three years. The strange thing is that the doctors don't know what happens to cause it."

"But while they don't know, how can people take precautions against its happening?" said Matilda.

"I have never heard of it before," I added. I was thinking fearfully of Tristan.

As soon as the meal was over I went to the nursery.

"He's asleep," said Nanny. "Come in and have a chat."

"I want first of all to make sure Tristan is all right," I said.

"All right? He's sleeping the sleep of the innocent, bless him."

I looked down on him. He was hugging his teddy bear. He looked angelic, and I was relieved to see he was breathing rhythmically.

"What did you expect?" demanded Nanny Crabtree. "I'm glad he's got that teddy. It's a change from the old blanket he used to suck. My goodness, it was difficult to wean him from that. And what a fuss there was when I washed it. It nearly broke his little heart. But I got him on to this teddy. I'm a bit scared though of those bootbutton eyes. I wonder if they'll come off?"

I sat down and told Nanny about the Pengelly baby.

"I heard about that one in St. Ives," she said. "It makes you wonder."

"I immediately thought of Tristan."

"He'll be all right. I'm going to keep my eyes on him. Why, what's the matter with you?"

"I don't know, Nanny. So many terrible things are happening here . . ."

She came to me and put her arms round me. It was as though I were a child again.

"There," she said. "It's all right. Nothing's going to happen to our baby or to you . . . not now that you've got Nanny Crabtree to look after you."

I just stayed there close to her and I felt like a child again. It would be all right because the all-powerful Nanny Crabtree would make sure of that.

There was a great deal of excitement when Polly Rowe, one of the kitchen maids, came in one afternoon and declared she had seen a ghost.

She was brought to me by the housekeeper, who said: "You'd better hear this, Miss. It sort of concerns you like."

Polly, flushed and very conscious of her newly acquired importance since she had been the one to see this amazing phenomenon, could scarcely speak, so great was her excitement.

"There on the cliff, Miss," she said. "On the west side . . . I was coming back after going to see my mother—over there to Millingarth—and I did see this . . . ghost. Her were coming straight to me. So close we was . . . we passed on that narrow path where it drops down to the sea."

She shivered at the memory.

"Her were wearing something over 'er 'ead . . . so you couldn't see her face like. But I knew her. There weren't no mistake . . . 'twere her all right. Her were looking for something, looking out to sea, 'er was. Her looked like her used to . . . but different . . ."

"Who was it?" I asked.

"It were a ghost, Miss. She were all shadowy like. She looked straight at me. I believe she knew me. Well, I'd seen her now and then, hadn't I? She walked past me, floated as they ghosts do, and then she was gone. I was all shaken up . . . I couldn't move. And then her'd gone."

"But who was it?"

She looked at me fearfully. "It were 'er. It were Mrs. Tregarland, that's who 'twas."

"You mean . . . the first Mrs. Tregarland?"

She shook her head. "Oh, no, Miss, it were the second . . . the second Mrs. Tregarland."

"My sister . . . ?"

She looked at me fearfully . . . nodding.

I put out a hand to steady myself and leaned against a table.

"You all right, Miss?" said the housekeeper.

"Yes, yes, thank you. Where were you when you saw this, Polly?" I asked.

"Out there on the west cliff, Miss . . . not far from Cliff Cottage."

"And you are sure you recognized her?"

"Well, Miss, she had this scarf over her head, hid her face like . . . a bit. But it was her all right. She was quite close. We was almost touching on that narrow bit. There she was, and when I turned round she was gone."

"Gone? Gone where?"

"I don't know, Miss. They ghosts do come and go as they've a mind to. They'll go through walls and cliffs if they want to."

"I think you must have been mistaken, Polly."

Polly shook her head. " 'Twere her all right . . . only in ghost form. That was the only difference."

"What does it mean?" I was talking to myself really, but Polly answered:

"Her can't rest. 'Tis because of Mr. Dermot, sure enough. He's gone, too. Reckon they're looking for each other. They do say it is like that when you get to the other side."

I said: "Thank you for telling me, Polly."

"I thought 'twere due to 'ee, Miss. You being her sister like."

When she had gone I sat down to do battle with my emotions. Dorabella seen on the cliffs. Then I told myself not to be foolish. Polly had seen someone who had borne a resemblance to her and had imagined the rest. The whole household was in a nervous state. It was reasonable to believe that Polly had seen someone like Dorabella on the cliff and that had given rise to her speculations.

In the kitchens they would all be talking of what Polly had seen. She would be reveling in her new importance and no doubt embellishing her story.

I could not sleep that night. I could see Dorabella's mischievous face before me. I remembered an occasion when we were about eleven years old. There was a house in the neighborhood which was reputed to be haunted. Terrified, we often prowled through it, for there was a broken window through which we could climb. Once we had been there when some other children must have decided to do the same. We cowered in one of the rooms, listening to the sound of stealthy, cautious footsteps.

"Let's play ghosts," Dorabella had said. We were wearing light capes and we took them off and covered our faces with them. Then we confronted the other children.

"Go away or we'll get you," chanted Dorabella in hollow tones. "We are ghosts."

The children turned and fled while Dorabella and I collapsed on the floor in helpless laughter.

And now ... Polly had seen *her* ghost on the cliff ... or thought she had.

What a long night it was! It was nonsense, I kept telling myself. There was no substance in the story. It was just typical of the superstitions which were never far from people's thoughts in this place.

It was not until dawn that I slept.

I wanted to talk to someone and the only one I really wanted to see was Jowan. I telephoned his number which took me through to his office quarters.

"Mr. Jermyn is not here," I was told.

I asked if they knew what time he would be back.

"This is Miss Denver speaking," I added.

"Oh, Miss Denver, he's gone to London."

"Oh? When will he be back?"

"I'm not sure. It depends how long his business keeps him there. I'll leave a note to say you called."

I thanked him and rang off.

I felt desolate. He had not mentioned to me that he was going. But then, why should he keep me informed of his business arrangements?

I was deflated, for when I was troubled I had made a point of consulting him.

I could not stop myself brooding. She had been seen on the west cliff. It was nonsense, of course. Just the wild imaginings of a hysterical girl who was now enjoying the notoriety of someone singled out by the powers that be for contact with the supernatural.

If there were such things as ghosts and Dorabella was one of them, surely I was the one she would want to visit?

How I missed Jowan! I wanted so much to talk to him, to listen to his sane views; perhaps I was relying on him too much. I was deeply hurt that he had not told me he was going to London. I wondered if I had let myself believe he was more interested in my affairs than he actually was.

He was amused by the local disapproval of our relationship, of course, and was interested in the old customs and superstitions—and what had been happening at Tregarland's was all part of that. But his main care was the Jermyn estate, and if he had had to go to London urgently, it would not occur to him to tell me.

I wanted so much to talk to someone. I thought of Mrs. Pardell. Her cottage was close by. I would go to see her and ask what she thought about the story of the ghost.

I wondered whether an account of this had reached her already. If it had, it would be interesting to get her views of the subject.

I came to the cottage and paused for a while to look at the neat garden. I opened the gate and, glancing up, I saw a figure behind the lace curtains. She would have heard the faint creaking of the gate. I stood by the door, expecting her to open it. When she did not, I knocked.

Nothing happened.

I lifted the heavy knocker and knocked again. I could hear the sound of it reverberating. Still I waited. Then I thought I heard footsteps, but no one came to the door.

I stood back and looked up at the windows. There was a shadow at one of them ... someone was standing behind the lace curtains. I was sure of it. What could it mean? She knew I was here and did not want to let me in.

I walked down the path and turned back to look. Was it fancy or did I again see that shape behind the curtains? It was there ... and it was gone.

This was strange. I believed Mrs. Pardell had been in the house. Well, I supposed, it must be that she did not want to see me.

A few days passed. The story of Dorabella's ghost was discussed frequently.

"She have come back," people said. "Her be looking for her husband. He'll have gone over, and she be searching for him."

One might have asked why search here if he had "gone over" to join her.

I was expecting to hear that someone else had seen her, but so far no one came forward to say so. When I went into the town people looked at me with interest. I was at the center of the drama, and they did not forget that I had brought myself into this by trying to patch up the quarrel between Tregarland and Jermyn.

More than ever I wished that Jowan was here. I felt lonely without him. I wanted to discuss Dorabella's "ghost" and the unwillingness of Mrs. Pardell to see me. That had surprised and hurt me. I knew that she prided herself on her bluff honesty, which made it all the more strange. She was not the sort to hide behind curtains. Rather I should have expected her to open the door and say, I don't want to see you, and then tell me why.

Her behavior after Jowan's going to London without telling me added to my bewilderment.

Then there was a call from Jowan. My spirits rose at the sound of his voice.

"I'm back," he said, "and I want to talk to you."

"Yes, yes," I said eagerly. "When?"

"Suppose I pick you up in an hour. We'll have lunch at the Stag's Head on the moor. I'll tell you all about it then."

I was excited. The pall of gloom had lifted.

He came on time and greeted me affectionately, but said nothing of significance until we were at the inn. He had chosen a secluded table where we could talk in peace.

I found it hard to contain my impatience, but it was clear to me that he would say nothing until he was ready to do so.

We ordered our food and it was only when it was on the table that he leaned toward me and said: "I've made a discovery. I think it may be significant."

"In London?" I asked.

He nodded. "It was the only place where I could get it. I wanted to keep it to myself in case it came to nothing. It was not easy. I was not sure of dates and could only guess. It would have taken less time if I had had more details."

"You're keeping me in suspense."

"I have unearthed Gordon Lewyth's birth certificate from the records. He is the son of Matilda Lewyth and James Tregarland."

"Oh!" I said.

"I suspected it might be the case, but I wanted to make absolutely sure."

"I understood that his father was dead, and that because Matilda was a distant connection of the family, they came to Tregarland's."

"That was the story. It would have made a big scandal to bring his mistress and illegitimate son to Tregarland's. Not that James Tregarland would care very much about that. He must have had his motives. Do you realize what this could mean?"

"Tell me what is in your mind."

"I have been very uneasy about your staying there. There is something rather sinister about it all. I cannot believe in all these coincidences. Annette Pardell was the first to die."

"I suppose they would say your ancestress was the first."

"She drowned herself and that could have given them the idea."

"Who?"

"Let's see if we can work that out. The significant point is that Annette was going to have a child. After Dermot, that child would inherit Tregarland's. It's a big estate and has become prosperous in the last years."

"Because of Gordon rather than Dermot."

"Exactly. I'm theorizing, of course. But that is all I can do. It is you I am concerned about."

I felt a pleasant glow creep over me and it was not due to the sparkling wine.

"I'd get you out of there quickly," he went on, "but you won't go without the child, Tristan. I can't see how you could kidnap him. Suppose Annette died because she was carrying the child who would be heir to the estate? Now Dermot is dead."

"And Dorabella ... ?"

"That's the part that doesn't fit. Her son was already born. I can't understand that. Why your sister? That is what rather spoils my theory."

"You think that someone murdered Annette because she was going to have a child?"

"Yes. The child would follow Dermot."

"But she went swimming."

"I don't believe she did. She wouldn't have done that. She was warned against it. She was too experienced to be so foolish."

"That is what Mrs. Pardell said. She is convinced that Dermot killed her."

"Dermot would never kill anyone."

"Mrs. Pardell thought he was tired of Annette and that later he was tired of my sister, too, that he was a sort of Bluebeard who married women and then, when he was tired of them, just killed them."

"A likely tale and absolute nonsense!"

I said suddenly, as a terrible fear came to me: "There was that time when Tristan was so ill. Someone must have gone into his room, uncovered him and opened the window, hoping it would kill him, which it might have done if Nanny Crabtree hadn't gone in in time."

"That fits," he said. "Annette's possible heir, then Tristan. And . . . what of Dermot?"

"Are you suggesting that someone in the house murdered Dermot?"

"That would clear the decks a bit, wouldn't it?"

I looked at him in disbelief. "You mean . . . for Gordon?"

He nodded. "Listen. Gordon has been brought up there. He runs the estate . . . excellently. He is devoted to it. He regards it as his. He is Tregarland's son, but because his mother was not married to his father when he was born . . ."

"You think she is now?"

"No. I don't know why James didn't marry her, but it seems he hasn't. But I feel sure that if he had no legitimate heirs everything would go to Gordon."

"You are suggesting that Gordon killed Annette . . . and perhaps Dermot?"

"Who else?"

"But Annette was supposed to have been caught by the tide, by cross-currents or cramp . . ."

"Is that plausible?"

"Not entirely."

"And Dermot?"

"He might have taken those pills himself. On the other hand, he might not. It leaves the way clear, except for . . ."

I was staring at him in horror. "If this is so . . . Tristan is in danger . . . imminent danger."

He nodded.

"Jowan, I'm frightened."

"I knew you would be. The child will have to be watched day and night. If I am right in what I am thinking, there will be an attempt on his life."

"How . . . ?"

"It was attempted before. There is one thing that baffles me. It is your sister's death. She was not in the way. Dermot was the one . . . and now Tristan. Dermot is dead and we cannot be sure how he died. It might have been by his own hand, as the coroner's verdict decided. It would seem that this was a reasonable deduction—apart from one thing. Someone would profit from his death. But there was no reason to be rid of your sister. If there had been a child on the way, yes. But presumably there was not. And that is where the theory falls down."

"I have always felt a little uneasy about Gordon, but it is hard to imagine people one knows as murderers."

"The most unlikely people often are. When I found—as I suspected might be the case—that he was in fact James Tregarland's son, I had a good deal of confidence in my theory. It was only on further consideration that I realized that there were doubts."

"Jowan, what are we going to do?"

"I think try to find proof."

"How?"

He lifted his shoulders. "It is difficult to know. One thing of which I am certain is that you must watch the baby carefully."

I said: "It would be easy for them. There has been that death of a child, an unexplained death which happens to children now and then. It is accepted as something of which the doctors are unsure."

"I have heard of that. Young babies die unexpectedly and inexplicably. It baffles the medical profession, although I have no doubt that in time they will discover what lies behind it."

"Oh, Jowan, I am so glad you are here."

He put his hand across the table and touched mine.

I went on: "And I am glad you went to London when you did."

He released my hand and smiled at me. "You are in the thick of it. How I wish you were not."

"I am glad I am there to watch over the baby. I shall have to take Nanny Crabtree into my confidence. Do you think that is wise?"

He was thoughtful. "It's only a theory," he said.

"Yes, but the child could be in danger."

"You have told me something of her. She was your nurse and you know her well. I suspect she is the sort of woman who would do anything for her charges."

"You could certainly trust her to do that."

"Then take her into your confidence. Tell her your fears and use your discretion as to what you can tell her. I just feel that the child must be watched, for if there is someone in the house who wants to be rid of him, he is in great danger."

"I shall tell her then. I feel relieved that we can take some action. All these things that are happening around me make me wonder what is coming next."

I told him about Polly's seeing Dorabella's ghost.

"What will they think of next?" he asked.

I also mentioned that I had called on Mrs. Pardell, who had not let me in, although I felt certain that she was in the house.

"Some whim, possibly. Though I should have thought she would have come downstairs, opened the door, and told you to your face."

I smiled.

"Oh, I am so glad you are here," I said again.

He replied rather flippantly: "Well, it is nice to be appreciated."

But I felt he was both touched and immensely pleased.

The Watchers in the Night

❧

I went straight to Nanny Crabtree and told her that I wanted to speak to her very seriously.

I began by saying that what I had to tell her was for her ears alone. It might not be true. It was only a theory, but if it were correct, Tristan was in danger.

She was alert and for once listened intently.

"Seems to have some sense in it," she said, and it was characteristic of her that she should immediately think of that occasion when Tristan had been in danger from the open window.

"I never opened that window," she declared. "I do know that. Someone must have. And he wasn't in the habit of throwing his clothes off. And him with that cold on his chest . . . I could murder them as hurts little children."

"We've got to make sure he is not left alone . . . night or day."

She nodded. "And Miss Dorabella . . . ?"

"Well, that is the part that doesn't fit. We can't think why anyone would want her out of the way."

"And we know her. She might have got into her head that she wanted to swim, and if she did, there'd be no holding her back. 'I want this and I'm going to have it.' That was her all over. And Mr. Dermot himself . . ."

"That might have been either way. Oh, Nanny, don't you see how careful we have to be! We must not take chances. There's a lot against what we think may be, but because of Tristan we mustn't dismiss anything."

"I see that all right. No matter if we are barking up the wrong tree, we've got to make sure our boy is safe. I tell you

285

what we'll do ... and this will be just between you and me. You know that divan thing ... in the nursery? I'll sleep on that. Nobody will know. Then I'll be on the alert ... day and night."

"Nanny," I said, "I shan't sleep well in my bed. I'm going to take my turn of watching with you. I am going to sleep in the nursery with him."

"There's no need," said Nanny Crabtree. "I shall be on the watch sleeping in the same room."

"I shouldn't rest in mine," I said. "I'll be wondering what's happening all night."

She looked at me and nodded slowly. "I know you," she said. "Well, all right then. You shall sleep here on the divan and I'll be in my room with the door open."

I was already planning. "I shall come up quietly when the household has retired, and go back to my room before it starts stirring. It is very important that no one else should know of these arrangements ... no one in the house."

"I see that. We mustn't give it away."

"Tonight, then ..."

"Tonight," said Nanny Crabtree.

So that was how it was. I would lie on the divan, and in the starlight I could see the outline of the cot. I slept lightly. The slightest sound from Tristan's cot awakened me and would set me listening.

Sometimes I thought: Can this really be true? Are we dramatizing the situation? Could Gordon possibly have murder in mind? He had been present when his mother had talked of the Pengelly baby. Had I imagined he seemed especially alert? I tried to remember what he had said. It was something the medical profession did not understand. The doctors were researching; they would discover the cause in time. But as yet the deaths were accepted as due to circumstances beyond their knowledge. How easy it would be to snuff out a young life!

My thoughts went back to that day when he had found me caught by the tide. He had gone to great efforts to save my life. But he did not want to be rid of me. I did not stand in his way.

It was hard to believe such a thing of someone one knew. But how well did I know him? He had always been something of an enigma and—I had often felt—a little sinister. Or was I imagining that now?

I had slept on the divan for two nights and this was the third.

There was no moon but the sky was cloudless and the stars bright.

I was looking out of the window at one which was particularly bright—a planet possibly. I remembered Dorabella's saying to me on such a night: "That's God's eye watching us. He saw you take that cake when Cook wasn't looking. You stuffed it into your pocket. He wrote it down in his little book and you'll answer for it one day." And I had retorted: "You ate most of it, so you'll suffer more." "It's not eating it that counts, it's stealing it," was her reply.

Memories of Dorabella would go on like that for ever.

A stair creaked. I was alert. My heart was beating fast as I sat up in bed listening. There it was again. Stealthy steps coming toward the nursery!

I slipped out of bed and stood behind the door. I was there just in time before it was slowly, cautiously, opened.

I could not believe this was happening, although I had been waiting for it. It was like a performance which I had been rehearsing. I saw the pillow first ... the whiteness was clear in the starlight.

Then, like a dream—a nightmare, really—I saw that what we had imagined would happen was taking place in actual fact.

A figure had moved toward the cot, bending over the sleeping child. I ran forward crying, "Nanny, Nanny! Quick ... !"

The figure turned sharply. Not Gordon. Matilda!

Nanny Crabtree was there ... a walking stick in her hand, ready to strike.

Matilda Lewyth turned to face us. Her eyes were wild with what seemed to me like madness.

"What ... what do you think you are doing ... ?" she cried.

"What are *you* doing here?" said Nanny.

"Get out," cried Matilda. "Get out ... both of you."

"It is you who will have to get out of my nursery," said Nanny Crabtree sharply. "How dare you come in here and try to kill my baby?"

"What are you talking about?"

Matilda had dropped the pillow. She fell into a chair and covered her face with her hands.

"Nanny," I said. "Go and wake Mr. Lewyth. I think he is the one who will know what is best to be done about this."

"You watch then and give me that pillow."

Matilda and I were alone and she lowered her hands and looked at me.

I said slowly: "You were going to kill him. You were going to kill Tristan. You thought it would be easy. You were going to pretend that what happened to Mrs. Pengelly's baby happened to him."

She did not answer.

"And the others . . ." I said. "Matilda, what does it mean?"

But I knew what it meant. Jowan's discovery had made it clear. She wanted Tregarland's for her son, hers and James Tregarland's, and she had been ready to remove anyone who stood in his way. She, who had seemed so gentle, so self-effacing, so eager to please, was a murderess.

How thankful I should always be to Jowan. But for his warning Tristan would have died tonight.

I shall never forget Gordon's coming into that room. He took one look at his mother. I knew that Nanny had told him what had happened. And what I saw in his face, although it was acute horror, was not surprise.

He was clearly deeply shocked. He went to her and put an arm round her.

"Mother," he murmured. "Mother . . . oh, what have you done?"

She began to sob tempestuously. He comforted her and turned to us.

"I'll take her to her room. I'll give her something to make her sleep. She'll go mad if I don't. Oh, my God, this is terrible. Please, let me take her away. I'll come back. There are things I can tell you. I want you please to try and understand."

Nanny Crabtree said: "My baby could have been killed!"

Matilda was shaking. I thought she would have some sort of fit. She began to tear at her clothes and her hair in a frenzy of madness. She threw herself at Gordon.

"It was for you," she said. "For you . . . my boy. It was your right . . ."

He tried to soothe her. I had never witnessed such a harrowing scene.

His arm around his mother, Gordon led her away.

Nanny and I went over to Tristan's cot. He had slept through it all.

"You were right then," said Nanny. "Thank God you were here. She's mad, that woman. I know madness when I see it, and I've seen it tonight. Her of all people. You look shaken, dear. And no wonder. You did well. To think of what might have been. He's shook up, too. Seemed to me as if he knew what she might be up to. Do you think we ought to wake someone else . . . in case he comes back and kills us?"

"There's only Mr. James Tregarland. We don't want any of the servants in this. He could have attacked us already if he were going to. As a matter of fact, I think he is a very worried man. I have misjudged him. She has been the one . . . and there *is* madness there . . ."

Nanny was looking down on Tristan.

"And the little mite slept through it all."

It seemed a long time before Gordon joined us. He looked pale and anxious. Nanny Crabtree brought a chair for him. He sat down and looked from one to the other of us almost pleadingly.

I thought: He loves his mother and he is afraid for her.

"I must make you understand," he said. "I must tell you everything from the beginning in the hope that you will. Of course, there is no excuse. She has attempted to do this terrible thing. For some time she has had one aim in life. She is determined to see me master of Tregarland's. It has become an obsession with her.

"James Tregarland is my father. He and my mother met long ago. There has been a relationship of long standing. My mother came from a poor but respectable family. She worked in one of the hotels in Plymouth as a chambermaid. My father stayed there now and then and that was how they met. He was attracted by her. He was married, of course, and when my mother was about to have me her parents were deeply shocked. She had disgraced them and they disowned her. My father set her up in a house where I was born. He continued to visit her. I remember the days when he came. He was interested in me. He used to watch me with an amused look in his eyes, as though he found our situation amusing.

"It was not amusing to my mother. She had been brought up very strictly and was always uneasy about the situation. When my father's wife died, she thought he might marry her. He did not do so. But it was arranged that she and I should come to Tregarland's. I know my mother thought this was a beginning, a step in the right direction, and that eventually she would be mistress of the house. Before she had died, my father's wife had given birth to Dermot.

"I remember the day my mother told me we were going to live in the big house. There was some story about my mother's being a distant connection of the Tregarland family, in reduced circumstances, which was said to be the reason why she came to keep house. She did this very successfully. But she wanted two things: marriage for herself . . . and the estate for me. That became the aim of her life. My father knew this. The idea amused him. He liked to keep her on tenterhooks. Would he? Wouldn't he? He used to tease my mother. I think he may have hinted that I should have had the estate if there had been no legitimate heirs. Well, of course, there was Dermot. Who would have thought that would happen to him? He was young and strong. True, he was not very interested in the place, but it went well enough with my management.

"That was the role my father had decided for me. It irked my mother. I was her son . . . and my father's eldest. I had brought prosperity to the estate. Dermot would never have been able to do that, yet it was to be his because I was not legitimate. He could have married her but he would not. I don't know why he was adamant about that. He was fond of her. I think he liked to keep her guessing. He liked to see how she would act—how we all acted. He was very conscious, too, of the family honor. Perhaps he did not think it would be fitting to marry an ex-chambermaid.

"Please understand. She has lived with this for years. Her hopes would be allowed to rise . . . and then be dashed. As I said, it had become an obsession. Perhaps if she had talked of it more—not tried to hide it—it might have helped. But she kept it shut away within herself. I alone knew the depth of her feeling, her suppressed bitterness. She would talk vehemently about my rights, but only to me. I have for some time feared for her."

"You did not think she would attempt ... murder," I said.

He hesitated. Then he said: "Lately ... I feared."

"What of the first Mrs. Tregarland?"

"I know nothing of that. She went for a swim which was foolish in her condition."

"And Dermot?"

He hesitated again. "I ... I did not speak to her of that. I think I preferred to assure myself that he died by his own hand. He was very depressed and guessed he would never be able to walk properly again. There seemed reason for him to take his life."

"And now ... ?"

"There is only the child left now ..."

Nanny Crabtree listened without speaking.

"What will happen now?" I asked.

"I don't know," said Gordon helplessly. "We shall have to wait. I will call the doctor to her first thing in the morning."

"You will have to tell him what happened?"

"Yes, I think he will have to be told everything."

"What do you think will happen to her?"

"They give people some sort of treatment. There have been lots of advances in dealing with it. I think she desperately needs psychiatric treatment."

"So we must wait until the morning. I am so sorry for you, Gordon."

He smiled at me mournfully. "It had to come. I was not altogether unprepared. I knew she would have to go away sooner or later. After tonight, I feel she will have to have some sort of care."

The clock in Nanny's room chimed two.

Nanny Crabtree said: "I think we ought to try and get some sleep. Miss Violetta, you go to that divan, and as for you ..." She looked at Gordon as though he were one of her children. "You should try and get some sleep, too. You're going to have a lot to do tomorrow."

He gave us both a pathetic smile, but there was a certain gratitude in it.

"I know," he said, "that you will both do all you can to help."

He left us then.

Nanny said: "Poor man. I liked him better tonight. He's very fond of his mother, I will say that for him. A man who's fond of his mother can't be all that bad. Now, I think I'll make us a nice cup of tea and then we'll see if we can get a bit of sleep. I was right when I said there'd be a lot to do tomorrow . . . or today, rather."

I sat there thoughtfully. There was no hurry. I knew neither of us would sleep.

We took one last look at Tristan. The teddy bear had slipped from his grasp, but he was smiling in his sleep.

The next two days were indeed chaotic. Two doctors came to see Matilda.

She had awakened on that first morning in a bemused state. Gordon was with her at the time. He had sat by her bedside all through the rest of the night, to be sure to be there when she awoke.

She only half realized what had happened on the previous night. She wept bitterly and was in a state of complete mental disorder.

The family doctor came first. He said she needed immediate attention. Then he called another doctor, as was, I believed, usual in such cases; and at the end of the second day, she was taken away. They had to sedate her because she had shown a tendency to violence. Gordon was very sad, indeed, and I was touched because he turned to me for comfort.

He confided in me a good deal and told me that he had been very concerned for her for a long time. He had tried to make her understand that he accepted his position and, because he realized that it was unlikely that he would ever inherit the estate, he had come to terms with that fact.

He loved it and indeed he had complete control of it; and it would be years before Tristan could take it over. He would work with the boy, teach him what had to be taught. He had been content with that.

But it had not been good enough for his mother. She had set her heart on his being recognized as a Tregarland and master of the family home.

"Obsession," he said. "It can ruin a life . . . as it has hers."

"You will see her often," I said.

"Yes. She will be at Bodmin. I shall go at least once a week. It may be that they will be able to help her. They have all sorts of wonderful treatment these days."

"I do hope so, Gordon."

"I shall always be grateful to you," he replied. "If you had not been there she would have killed the child. I feel it would be something she would never have got over."

I was thinking then of Annette, for I could not believe that she had deliberately chosen to go into the sea that morning.

I wondered whether there was at least one murder on Matilda's mind, and whether that had helped her to go completely mad.

James Tregarland was very upset by what had happened. He stayed in his room, and after they had taken Matilda away he sent one of the servants to ask if I would come to his room as he would like to talk to me.

I went to him at once and there I found him like a different person. He seemed old and shrunken.

"Oh, Violetta," he said. "You have come into a strange household. What are you thinking of us, eh? There has been nothing but trouble. It is strange, is it not? For years we went on peacefully—uneventfully—and then everything erupted like a volcano that has been inactive for years and once it starts cannot stop."

"A great deal has certainly happened," I said. "I think one thing has grown out of another."

He nodded. "My poor Matty. I was fond of her, you know. She was always an interesting girl. That calm exterior hiding her explosive passions. I treated her badly. I have discovered I have a conscience. Not a pleasant discovery at my time of life, when it is too late to do anything about it. She wanted me to marry her. Why didn't I? It would have given her peace of mind. Those parents of hers—it was the way they had brought her up. Poor Matty. Conventionality was their way of life, and hell fire was awaiting those who strayed. It was implanted in her and nothing could change that. I teased her, though I'm ashamed to say I enjoyed that. Well, I made a will . . . everything for my legitimate heirs, and if they were unable to inherit, it went to my natural son, Gordon Lewyth. That was when it started . . . once she had got that out of me. I enjoyed watching it, you see. I knew Matty pretty well. So prim she had been at first, and then not so prim. I didn't think it would last very long when it started ... I thought I'd give her something and say goodbye. But it did not work that way. It went on. There was the boy, you see. I liked him and he was damned useful on the estate when he grew up. He was a worker, different from some of the Tregarlands who'd gone before. I'm to blame for a lot of this, Violetta."

"You had no idea how far she would go."

"I should have had. And she tried to murder my grandson! Thank God you were sleeping in the room."

"Yes. I found out that Gordon was your son. I misjudged him. I thought he might attempt to murder Tristan. There was talk about babies who died mysteriously and it had been mentioned in my hearing. Then Nanny Crabtree and I worked out what we would do."

"I'm grateful to you both. He's a bright little fellow, our Tristan. To think he might have been snuffed out like a candle. I'm grateful to you."

"And to Nanny Crabtree."

"Yes, indeed. She's an old stalwart, she is. A real dragon, a battleaxe. I like that. I can't see anyone getting the better of her."

His chin started to wag and for a few seconds he looked like his old self.

"She loves those she calls her children dearly," I said. "I am so pleased my mother arranged for her to come and look after Tristan."

"Oh, yes, we have to be thankful for that. And most of all we are thankful to you, my dear. I like to feel my grandson is in your hands. And what will happen to my poor Matty?"

"Gordon thinks they may be able to help her."

"Just now she won't be aware of where she is and what she has done. It will be better for her to remain in ignorance of that."

"And what she may already have done."

"You are thinking of Dermot's first wife ..."

"Yes, Annette."

"That was a strange affair. I was glad when Dermot brought your sister here. And then ..."

"Do you have any idea what happened?"

He shook his head. "I wondered. The first wife was drowned when she was carrying an unborn child. The thought came to me later as to whether Matty had a hand in it. Though naturally it didn't occur to me at the time."

"Do you think she could have killed Annette?"

"I don't know."

"And Dermot?"

"It would have been easy for her to slip his pills to him, perhaps. I wonder . . . would she have gone as far as that?"

"He stood in Gordon's way, just as Tristan did. And it would have been so easy with him . . . as it would have been with Tristan. But . . . Annette . . . and my sister . . ."

"My dear, you have suffered with us all. Your stay here has been marked by tragedy. Too many tragedies."

"Too many to be natural," I repeated. "And now that we see there was a motive . . ."

He nodded slowly. "I want you to know how grateful I am to you. This household needs you particularly now. Will you promise me you will not leave us?"

"I cannot say what the future will bring. For a time I shall be here. Tristan means a lot to me."

"I will be satisfied with that. My poor Matty! How I wish this had not happened to her. She has gone, hasn't she? There will be no coming back. So calmly efficient outwardly, and a raging furnace of resentments within. Does it not show how complex human beings are? It has always been a sort of hobby with me . . . to observe them."

"They are, indeed, complex, and I will leave you now, if you will excuse me. I have promised Nanny Crabtree that I will be in the nursery this morning."

He nodded. "We need you here," he said. "I . . . Gordon . . . Tristan. Yes, we do. I would not feel happy about the child if you left us."

I said: "I shall stay for a while."

That satisfied him. He nodded again and closed his eyes. He looked very tired and infinitely sad.

Seth had changed. It was strange to see a big strong man looking like a helpless child. Oddly enough, he seemed to turn to me. I knew that he had regarded Matilda with a kind of awe, coupled with a great admiration and trust. I thought sometimes that he had looked at her as though she were some sort of deity.

She had been kind to him. How strange that she, who had contemplated killing one child, could be so considerate to a poor creature like Seth.

And now she had gone, Seth seemed lost and bewildered. Poor, uncertain Seth, whose life had been blighted when he was ten years old, and he had never really developed after that.

I often found him close to me, and suddenly it dawned on me that I was a substitute for Matilda. He would hurry to me if I were carrying something. He would take it from me, and clearly showed what gratification it gave him to help me.

That was how I came to talk to him and to learn what I had always wanted to know.

I would chat about horses and the work he did in the garden. One day I saw him working there and I went down to the seat which was close by and said: "Hello, Seth. How are you this morning?"

His face creased with pleasure, as it always did when I spoke to him.

"I be well, Miss Violetta." He slurred my name. He had always had difficulty with it.

"The sea is a little rough today," I went on. "Is that how it was the morning the first Mrs. Tregarland went in to bathe?"

He had lost that look of anxiety he had always had before when I mentioned that occasion.

"He said: "Oh, 'tweren't morning . . . 'twere night . . . weren't it?"

I was startled. This was a new angle on the case.

"Night?" I said.

"Sea be different by night," he said, scratching his head. "Don't know what it be, but it be different."

"Where were you then, Seth?"

He looked puzzled and I saw the shut-in look come into his face.

"You could tell me, Seth," I said.

He looked at me steadily and I saw the look I had often in the past seen him bestow on Matilda. Now it was given to me. He looked relieved.

" 'Twere night," he said. " 'Er were there with 'un."

"Mrs. Lewyth was there . . . with the first Mrs. Tregarland?"

He nodded and, turning toward the house, pointed to the glass door which opened onto the terrace from which four steps led down to the garden.

"In the drawing room they were."

"They were doing something?" I prompted.

"Just the two of them . . . talking. It was about the baby that was to be."

"Why did you think that?"

"I dunno. Just did. They was always talking about the baby."

"And what happened?"

"She come out. 'Er was rolling . . . unsteady like. I watched 'un." He started to giggle. " 'Er be drunk, I thought. Mrs. be drunk."

"What happened to her then?"

"Mrs. Lewyth . . . she took her arm. They was coming to the garden."

"Did they see you?"

"Not then . . . I watched 'un. Mrs. Lewyth was bringing her down. 'Tweren't easy on the slope. Her was drunk like. They got to the beach. Then 'er fell over."

"Who?"

"T'other."

"The first Mrs. Tregarland?"

"That's 'er. I watched. Proper drunk, 'er were."

"And then what happened?"

"Mrs. Lewyth took off her clothes and put on her bathing things. Then she pulled her down to the sea. 'Er couldn't manage. Awful heavy, she were. So I went and helped her."

"Seth! And what did Mrs. Lewyth say?"

" 'Er didn't seem to like it much. She was a bit cross with me . . . at first. She was nice after. She told me the ghost of the long-dead lady wanted to have a talk with the first Mrs. Tregarland and she had to get her out to sea . . . 'cos she'd been told to. We had to get her down. She said, 'You can see her beckoning.' "

"Did you?"

"Mrs. Lewyth said I did, so must be. I helped drag her in . . . and I pushed her out to sea. 'She just wants to have a word with her,' Mrs. Lewyth said. 'Just friendly like.' She took her clothes away and later on came down with her bathrobe, so's it would be there for her when she come back. She didn't. Reckon the ghost wanted her to stay."

"Seth," I said. "You knew this all the time and you didn't tell anyone."

"Her said not to, didn't 'er? 'Er said she reckoned they got on so well—one didn't want to lose t'other. Her would stop haunting because 'er was so pleased to have the first Mrs. Tregarland with her."

I sat there, staring out to sea. And I thought, so now I know. But what of Dorabella?

I said: "Seth, the second Mrs. Tregarland. Do you know what happened to her?"

"I don't know nothing about her. I never seed that 'un."

"She did go down to the sea," I said.

"May 'ave. I didn't see 'er."

"Are you sure, Seth?"

"Certain sure. It were only t'other."

"Thank you, Seth," I said. "You have been a great help."

A slow smile of satisfaction spread over his face. I could see that he now looked on me as his friend and protector.

So now I knew that Matilda was indeed a murderess and had been one when I first met her. Hers was indeed a devious mind. It was hard to believe that she had preserved that quiet, almost benevolent exterior with such guilt on her conscience.

I could piece together what had happened. She had obviously drugged Annette, got her to the beach, and thrown her into the sea.

I was, indeed, relieved that she was now put away where she could do no more harm.

It was some little time since I had seen Jowan. He would, of course, have heard of the drama at Tregarland's, for the matter would be discussed throughout the neighborhood. He would be anxious, I knew.

He came to the house this time, and we sat in the garden while I told him the story.

He was deeply shocked.

"We have to be grateful to you, Jowan," I said. "Your discovery about the relationship between James Tregarland and Gordon made it all fall into shape."

"It was you and Nanny Crabtree who saved the child."

"Yes, but you put us on the alert, and I remembered then that Matilda and Gordon had spoken of the children's deaths."

I described those moments when Matilda had come into the nursery with the pillow in her hand.

"Poor Gordon," I said. "He is a very sad man. She is safely away now. She can do no more harm. Jowan, what should we do about this? I now know that Annette's death was murder. We are not sure of Dermot's, but I suppose it is likely. I wonder about Dorabella."

"There was no reason to kill Dorabella. Matilda Lewyth was consistent. She did not murder without reason. Annette was going to have a child who would inherit the estate after his father. So she got rid of both Annette and the child. She might have waited until it was born, but perhaps she hadn't heard of the cot deaths then. Besides, Annette could have more children. She rid herself of that possibility at one stroke."

"Might she not have felt that it was a good idea to be rid of Dorabella? She had succeeded with the first wife, why not with the second?"

"No. She would not murder for such a flimsy reason. There was already a child. And it wasn't easy. She had been seen by Seth. He must have been an anxiety to her. I suppose she might have turned on him."

"That wouldn't be easy. She had had trouble with Annette. Seth is big and very strong. No. She trusted him not to betray her and he did not until she was gone and I was there, as he saw it, in her place. He regards me as a substitute for her. He talked to me as he would not to anyone else. But what should be done about this?"

"Probably nothing. What would happen if the police were informed? Would Seth's testimony be trusted? What good would it do? It might mean trouble for him. Suppose there was a trial? Mrs. Lewyth, not being of sound mind, could not take part in it. And the result? Guilty of murder while the balance of her mind was disturbed. She would spend the rest of her life in a mental home which she will probably do in any case. There is nothing that can be done. It would just be the satisfaction of making known the facts."

"There is Mrs. Pardell. She has accused Dermot of murdering both Annette and Dorabella."

He was silent. "She might want the matter brought to light," he said after a pause.

"She's a strange woman. After what happened last time I called on her, I feel I don't understand her."

"Well, at least we have learned something."

"You believe Seth, do you?"

"Yes. It fits. Matilda Lewyth had committed one murder and was going to commit another because she had not been found out. This obsession had taken possession of her. She had convinced herself that her son must have what she considered was due to him, and she would stop at nothing to bring it about."

"So . . . we do nothing."

"At the moment I think it might be best."

"Jowan, I am so relieved to have you around."

"Thank you," he said. "I feel the same about having you around. You won't go away, will you?"

"I've had a talk with James Tregarland. He was very pleasant and . . . revealing. He has made me promise to stay awhile."

"I'm not surprised. You and the stalwart Nanny Crabtree saved his grandson's life."

"They are talking about all this in the town, I suppose."

"They are saying that Mrs. Lewyth has gone out of her mind due to all that has been happening at Tregarland lately. Soon, however, they will have something else to talk about."

"What?"

"It is almost certain that there is going to be war."

Dorabella

✺

The departure of Matilda had made a great deal of difference to the household. Then Mrs. Yeo, the cook, took charge and everything seemed to run more smoothly after that.

One morning a letter arrived for me. It was from Mrs. Pardell. She wrote that it was a long time since she had seen me, and she would be glad if I would call that afternoon at three o'clock.

I was astonished. I felt there was something very mysterious afoot, for I was certain she had been in the house that day when I had called, and for some reason she did not want to see me. However, she did now.

At three o'clock I was at the cottage. I looked up at the windows. There was the shadow of what must be a figure behind the curtains, as there had been on that other occasion. I knocked on the door. It was opened almost immediately.

I stared. I felt the blood rush into my face. Then I started to tremble. A hand stretched out and I was pulled into the cottage. I was overcome by shock and disbelief.

She was laughing and crying all at once.

"Violetta! Violetta . . . I couldn't bear to be away from you. That old cord was pulling me all the time. I've come back."

I stammered: "Is this . . . real . . . ? Is it really you, Dorabella?"

She drew back a little and looked intently at me. She was beautiful . . . tearful and wildly happy . . . contented because we were together.

"Dorabella," I murmured.

"Yes, yes it really is. I'm back with you again—the prodigal's returned. Oh, Vee, dearest sister, my darling twin. You will have to help me out of this one."

I started to question. "When . . . ? Why . . . ? How . . . ?"

"It's wonderful to be back with you. I should never have left. I never will again."

"Dorabella!" I cried. "What is this all about? What have you done? Where have you been?"

She looked at me searchingly. "You look strange, sister. I'm really here. Do you think I'm a ghost?"

"Tell me, please, what this is all about."

"First of all, I'm here. I'm back. I'm really here and we've got to talk . . . quickly."

"Yes, we have to talk. What are you doing here . . . in Mrs. Pardell's house?"

"Come into the sitting room. You look as if you are going to pass out at any moment."

"Dorabella, I can't believe this."

"I know you can't." She pouted slightly in a gesture I remembered so well. "I thought you'd be glad to see me."

"Oh, Dorabella, it's what I wanted more than anything."

"Well then, be glad. Show me you're glad."

"Of course I am. But I'm bewildered."

"Well, prepare yourself."

"I am prepared. Tell me."

"There are two versions." She was rapidly becoming her old self. She grinned slightly. "One for public consumption, the other for your ears alone. Then you can advise me and tell me what I ought to do."

"Well, get on with it."

"We're one person, aren't we? No matter what happens. We have to stand together, help each other."

"Please tell me."

"Your version first."

"I want the true one."

"Very well. But you are going to be rather shocked. Perhaps you'd better have the other one first. It's more respectable."

"I want the true one."

"Then it will have to be your version."

"For Heaven's sake, stop prevaricating!"

"Well, it was like this. I couldn't stand it here. I had had enough. I knew it was a mistake . . . Dermot and me. He seemed so different once he was here. In Germany he was such fun, so gallant. You remember how he brought us out of the forest mist? Then at Tregarland's it was all different. The old man always watching. Matilda so prim . . . and Gordon . . . I never understood him. Then there was the sea. I'd hear it at night. It was as though people were whispering, taunting. Anyway, I knew I'd made a mistake. I wanted to get away. Then I met this man . . ."

"What man?"

"Wait . . . and hear it in good time. He was painting on the cliff. You did meet him once . . . that Christmas at the Jermyn place. He and the German were there. He was the French one, Jacques Dubois, an artist, and I went on meeting him. He wanted me to go to Paris with him. I said, How could I? And he said it was possible. We started to make plans . . . half in fun at first. But I just had to get away from that place . . . all that spookiness going back hundreds of years." She paused and looked pleadingly at me. "I can see you are very shocked with me. Shall I go on?"

"Don't be silly. Of course you'll go on."

"All right, then. Prepare for the worst. I had to get away. I thought it would be fun to go to Paris—*la vie bohème*. Mimi and Rudolfo. Your tiny hand is frozen—all that. It sounded so romantic. We wondered how I could do it easily . . . without causing too much bother. So we worked it out. There was all that talk about the Jermyn girl who, a long time ago, walked into the sea and cursed the House of Tregarland for ever. Then there was Dermot's first wife who died at sea, and you know how they all thought this was part of the curse. So I thought . . . if I could do it that way, they'd all think I was another victim of the Jermyn ghost and it wouldn't hurt Dermot so much. So I started that bathing in the morning plan. I smuggled a few things out before. Jacques would have the car waiting nearby to take them. So when I actually went I could slip away easily."

"You took my miniature with you."

"I had to take that. It was like taking part of you. I couldn't do without it. Though I did think it might be missed. But I couldn't leave that. Jacques said I could buy what I wanted in Paris. We thought a lot about how to make it look authentic. Then we waited for the night when Dermot was away. I put my bathrobe and shoes on a rock. It was nearly midnight. The household was asleep and Jacques was waiting for me. We drove down to Portsmouth to the ferry. By the time the household was awake we were crossing the Channel."

I stared at her in disbelief.

"You could do that! You could leave Tristan."

"I knew you would look after him . . . and you'd do it better than I could. You'd promised. And Dermot . . . well, he would find someone else probably."

"Dorabella! How could you!"

"I knew you'd say that. You've said it a hundred times in the past. You ought to have learned by now that I do things like that. You'll always be saying it, I suppose. Well, I've done it again."

"And what are you doing here?"

"As I told you, it didn't work. I soon saw that. I was bored with all those painters. Paris was wonderful for a while. I bought some clothes and that was exciting. But I kept thinking of you and the parents and what I'd done to you all. I wanted Tristan. I just knew I'd made a big mistake."

"And what about this . . . Jacques?"

"To him it was just a light-hearted affair, fun for a while. It wasn't the life for me. Then there was this talk about war. There were some English people in Paris. They were always saying we ought to go home. And I was homesick. I didn't want to go back to Tregarland's and all that that meant. I wanted to see you, Daddy and Mummy, and Tristan. How is Tristan?"

"He's well. Nanny Crabtree and I see to that."

"I knew you would. That's been my comfort. So I came back. I've been here for two weeks. When I got back I didn't know what to do. I couldn't just turn up. I was in London for a while. Then I was afraid I'd run into Edward. Most of all I wanted to see you . . . and Tristan. I knew you'd work out for me what I could do and we'd decide between us."

"I can't believe this . . . even of you. And why are you here in Mrs. Pardell's cottage?"

"I wanted to be near. You know what gossip there is here. I thought of getting in touch with you. I remembered Mrs. Pardell. She's always hated them up at Tregarland's, hasn't she? She hated Dermot particularly because of her daughter

Annette. I knew that you had had some contact with Mrs. Pardell and she had been quite friendly to you. She wasn't one to mix with people, and her cottage was fairly isolated. I decided I could see what I could do through her. I waited until it was darkish and I went to her cottage."

"Good Heavens! You must have given her a shock!"

"She wasn't so shocked as some might have been. She doesn't believe in ghosts. I stood at her door and I said, 'Mrs. Pardell, you know my sister. I am Dorabella Tregarland. They think I'm dead, but I am here and alive and I am hoping you'll help me.' She turned rather pale and I could see the old Northern common sense and rejection of ghosts and such daft things battling away there and triumphing.

"She said, 'Come in, then.' And so I went in and I told her the tale I had prepared, for I guessed that if she had known I had eloped with a French artist, I should not have been allowed to darken her doors. Hence the story I had concocted. I could not be happy at Tregarland's, I told her. There was something that frightened me about the place. I constantly thought of the first Mrs. Tregarland, her daughter, who had met her death in a strange way. In other words, I was afraid. I could see that went down well. I took to early morning bathing, I told her. It was not something I would have done normally, but when people are in the mood I was in, they do strange things. On that morning I went into the sea. I think my head struck a rock. In any case I was only half conscious and I was carried out to sea. By a very extraordinary stroke of fortune a fishing boat was nearby. I was picked up unconscious. They took me back with them to the North of England somewhere. A place near Grimsby. I was in a hospital there. I could not remember exactly where it was. They kept me there. I could not remember my name. Then gradually memory came back and I remembered that I wanted to get back to my sister. But I was afraid to go back to Tregarland's. There was something mysterious there which I could not understand. I could not bring myself to go back ... nor did I know what to do. Mrs. Pardell was sympathetic when I told her about Tregarland's. She thought I shouldn't go back to that place. She had a spare room, and I could use that till I made up my mind. She said, 'You ought to find some way of letting your sister know, because she's been real cut up about this.' I said I wanted time to think . . . I couldn't go back to that house yet . . . and you were there. She told me Dermot had died and how. Believe me, Violetta, I was very, very sad about that. I felt responsible. I suppose I was in a way. Mrs. Pardell understood that I wanted to wait awhile, particularly when I stressed there was something about the house which frightened me."

"Did she believe this fantastic story?"

"Yes, why shouldn't she?"

"Because it is so implausible. You struck your head on a rock enough to make you lose your memory, then you float gracefully out to sea and are picked up by a fishing boat? What is a fishing boat from Grimsby doing fishing off the Cornish coast? Even suppose the story about hitting your head was true, the boat which picked you up would have belonged to one of the fishermen from Poldown. He'd have said at once, 'Here be that Mrs. Tregarland . . . her that went swimming in the early morning.' And you would have been taken to West Poldown hospital and the family would have been informed without delay."

"It was a good story. Don't pick holes."

"It is an impossible story. Go on, though!"

"Mrs. Pardell believed it. I told it so well. I am just giving you a brief synopsis. I gloss over the difficult parts and look vague if they ask difficult questions. Remember, I did lose my memory."

"One of the maids saw you on the cliffs."

"I know. But she thought I was a ghost, of course."

"She did."

"Well, that's what I did. So what am I going to do now?"

"The first thing we shall do is telephone the parents. Can you imagine what they have been through, what I've been through?"

"I know. It was awful of me. But you see, I meant to write to you and you could all have come to Paris to see me . . . if I had stayed there."

"You'll come back to us. The sooner the better."

"I can't tell people I ran away . . . just like that . . . staged my disappearance. I won't do it."

"It will be difficult. I don't know what the authorities will say. They made a search, you know. All along the coast. They won't be pleased with all the trouble you've caused. You'll be reprimanded rather severely, I imagine. I don't like the true version at all. You left your husband and child of a few months to go off to Paris with an artist you scarcely knew."

"Put like that it does seem thoughtless."

"Thoughtless! People would call it wanton. You'd never live it down. It would be remembered for ever. Tristan would know when he grew old enough to understand. People will remember, if you don't."

"You haven't changed, Violetta. Still the old crusader for the right. What shall I do?"

"We'll have to work out a better story than yours."

"Yes. Go on."

"We'll have to keep to the swimming idea . . . otherwise we shall be in trouble. I don't think you should have hit your head on a rock. The sea was cold. You were exhausted. You had swum too far out. You were on the point of drowning. You were picked up by a yacht. The owner came from the North of England and had been to Spain. He was on his way home. Your experience had been such a shock that you temporarily lost your memory. You were taken to Grimsby, or wherever it was."

"I only thought of that place because it's biggish on the map and it was a long way off."

"We shall have to be vague about all this."

"But if I lost my memory . . ."

"There were pictures in the papers. The yacht people who were going home would have soon discovered. Then . . . you were in your swimming costume, so you couldn't have come from anywhere but Cornwall. It all sounds so very implausible. The only one you told your fantastic story to was Mrs. Pardell."

"Yes."

"And she did not question it."

"No. She was too interested in the Tregarlands and the way I felt about that."

"You'll have to tell our parents the truth, of course."

"Do I have to?"

"Of course. Daddy will find a way of getting round all this. The sooner they know the better. They have been terribly unhappy."

"Bless them, Violetta, you'll tell them, won't you?"

"I will do that at once. Then they'll come down and we can talk to them and work something out."

"I knew you'd work it out."

"You're such a devious schemer. I should have thought you could have thought up a better story than that one."

"Well, I had to lose my memory, didn't I? I had to do the swimming. It was really all due to that legend. I wanted them to think I was just another victim of the Jermyn ghost."

"That part was ingenious, but it is no use planning an elaborate story if you haven't worked out a suitable ending. It was you who was here that day when I called. You peeped through the curtains."

"Yes. I wanted so much to speak to you, but I wasn't ready. I told myself I was a fool to let you go, but I could not see you just then. Mrs. Pardell understood. I must say, she has been a great help to me. Who would have thought it?"

"You know what has happened at Tregarland's?"

"I know that Dermot died and that Matilda has gone mad."

I decided that this was not the moment to tell her that Tristan would have died but for the vigilance of Nanny Crabtree and myself.

Moreover, I was filled with joy because she was back. I forgot all the grief and anxiety she had caused. She was back again and that was the most wonderful thing that could have happened.

I now applied myself to the task of extricating her in the best possible way from the net she had woven about herself.

I wanted to laugh—with happiness rather than amusement—at the manner in which she gazed at me; she was completely confident that we should work this out together and, because I was there, I would get her through, as I had been doing all our lives.

The first thing I did when I returned to Tregarland's was to telephone my parents. I was glad my mother answered.

"You must prepare yourself for wonderful news," I said. "Dorabella is safe."

I heard the gasp and the words which came tumbling out.

"She is well," I went on. "I have seen her. I can't tell you on the telephone. Both of you, get the first train. That will be quickest. I'll tell you all about it when I see you. Don't worry. She's well. We're longing to see you. I'm so happy."

I could picture her. She would rush to my father. They would cling together, laughing and crying. Just at first they would not care how it had come about. All that would matter would be that she was alive.

They would catch the first train and would probably arrive at midnight or later.

Then I went and told Nanny Crabtree. She stared at me in amazement. Then the tears started to run down her cheeks and we fell into each other's arms.

"I've seen her! I've seen her! Oh Nanny, it's wonderful."

There were the inevitable questions. I pushed them aside. It was not so difficult because all that really mattered was that she was back.

I told Gordon and James Tregarland that she was here. She had been rescued and had lost her memory. I could not go into details because I did not know what they would be told. The news was spreading through the household and that meant it would soon be through the neighborhood.

Then I went to Cliff Cottage and brought her to Tregarland's.

There was an emotional scene between her and Nanny Crabtree. Then she went to Tristan. He gazed at her in bewilderment. Then he turned to me and held out his arms.

"He'll get to know you in time," I said.

I was amazed that the story which we finally put together when my parents arrived was accepted. This was due, I believe, to the fact that weightier matters arose at that time; and the strange disappearance and reappearance of the second Mrs. Tregarland slipped into insignificance beside them.

During that August Hitler made a non-aggression pact with the Soviet Union and that, with the Pact of Steel with Italy, showed clearly that he was preparing to march into Poland.

"Will it be war?" was the question asked everywhere, not "What about that Mrs. Tregarland losing her memory like that?"

And on the first day of September the news came: Hitler had invaded Poland, in spite of the ultimatum from Britain and

France that if he did he would be at war with those two countries.

And on the third day of that September we heard the voice of Neville Chamberlain coming to us over the wireless, telling us that we were at war with Germany.

Everything had changed. There were rumors everywhere. People could talk of nothing but war.

I did not see Jowan Jermyn for some days. I was wondering how much I could tell him of Dorabella's escapade. I thought it must be the truth. I could trust him, of course.

When he did come to the house I knew something had happened. We sat in the garden together.

He said: "I've come to tell you I've joined the Army."

I stared at him in dismay.

"Well," he said. "The country's at war. What else can I do?"

I was filled with desolation. I had been elated since Dorabella's return. The whole world had seemed different. My parents were overjoyed. We could not think very much of what Hitler was doing. The fact that Dorabella was back overshadowed everything else.

And now it was all brought home to me—the uncertainty of the future, the fears for those we loved, all the heartbreak that war could bring.

I could not bear the thought of his going into danger, and I knew then how important he had become to me. I knew that I loved him.

I stammered: "What of the estate?"

"It will be left in good hands. It won't be for long. They are saying it will be over by Christmas."

I could not control my features. My lips were trembling.

He saw that and, coming close to me, put his arms around me.

"I shall be back soon," he said. "You will wait for me, Violetta?"

"Yes," I said. "I shall wait."